This book belongs to Alyce Ray —
The authoress was [...]
Laon — when we lived there [...] we
knew Marilyn & Col. Tate, her husband
The Characters had a counter part —
but the names were changed.

ONE

KISS

FOR

FRANCE

Marilyn F. Tate

ONE
KISS
FOR
FRANCE

DOUBLEDAY & COMPANY, INC.

GARDEN CITY, NEW YORK, 1963

ALL OF THE CHARACTERS IN THIS BOOK ARE FICTITIOUS, AND ANY RESEMBLANCE TO ACTUAL PERSONS, LIVING OR DEAD, IS PURELY COINCIDENTAL.

Library of Congress Catalog Card Number 61-12589
Copyright © 1963 by Marilyn F. Tate
All Rights Reserved
Printed in the United States of America
First Edition

TO ANNA BERRYHILL VANCE,

who knows why . . .

ONE KISS FOR FRANCE

BOOK ONE

1

On its fourth pass the transatlantic plane touched down at Le Bourget. A drizzle—thicker than fog, lighter than rain, and a degree or two above freezing—filtered down upon purple-cheeked workmen, who wheeled rusting luggage carts. The motors of the great plane wheezed and coughed as they died.

Laurel emerged from the plane with a baby in her arms and a small boy at her side. "I hope I can manage the train connection by myself," she thought. Her glance went down to the foot of the ramp where, on either side, idling workers sent grins into the concave shadow of her hem. Turning away from them, she said more to herself than to three-year-old Brick, "Come along."

They went to the end of a serpentine queue of fifty passengers, the more worldly of whom tapped their feet or frowned, because nowhere in sight was there a customs agent, or even a passport inspector. Such indolence was typical of the French, they said, but Laurel was not to be drawn into petty conversation. The solace of being on firm ground had fled, leaving panicky depression. A sense of isolation permeated her blood as icily as the weather. She dared not look beyond the barrier, so certain was she that embraces and smiles, or at least greetings, awaited each of the other passengers, and she refused to feel sorry for herself, though it was undeniable that at the present rate of progress she could not reach the Gare du Nord for the ten A.M. train. Why hadn't Zero thought to write how often trains ran north? Where and how did a woman spend six or eight or twelve hours before the next train with two little boys in unknown Paris?

Laurel began to fume inwardly. Sometimes I can't help wondering how it would be—married to a man not utterly dedicated to the Air Force. Almost any other squadron commander would have asked to leave the gunnery range a day or two early if his wife was coming—his wife and children—after four long months. But that's probably why he's been a lieutenant colonel for six years. Always bragging he'll be a general because he's such a natural. What is a natural? Bright, fearless, and busy, they mean. A thumbnail description of twenty thousand officers.

He's all of that, thought Laurel. But he'll be a general because he chauffeured Laikenhauf all over the ETO during those years before the President made Laikenhauf the Chief. Before death felled the most stalwart and idolized of U.S. flyers. How strange that his clique continued to hang together—those older men, pervading the foundations of Air Force from Washington, to a dozen star-studded chairs flung about the globe, and the younger ones, such as her husband, who were tomorrow's generals.

Too bad, she thought glumly, that Laikenhauf's essential selflessness had not reached back from the mysterious beyond, as had his strength and brilliance and loyalty: It was his lack of pettiness, that disinterest in self-seeking that drew men to him, qualities now lost except in effigy. Laurel dismissed the subject at this point. She disliked thinking about politics in uniform.

The continuance of military existence into her peacetime world could be likened roughly to having had a visitor—a distant relative, perhaps—arrive for sustaining through a critical period, who, grown comfortable and accustomed, no longer speaks of the hoped-for leaving. At marriage, tremulous Laurel had not questioned the future: Zero would come back when peace returned and take charge of "Paradis," her Louisiana home and her inheritance. He would help her restore the sprawling old house, and the fields—long empty of corn, cotton, and cane—and meanwhile, people the scene with children, six or eight. Peace came and the months dragged by and he did not mention the matter of discharge. He made no move to discuss their way of life as civilians. She waited out the winter.

Near the end of spring, Laurel could wait no longer. Because she had waited so long, her approach must have been faulty, she thought, for his reaction was simply amazement. Later in the dark bed, he said, "I thought you understood, Laurel. The day they tell me I can't fly, I'm dead!"

"But I'm afraid of airplanes, afraid of—the military."

"Why?"

"Not for you. For me."

"Why?"

"I had an awful dream night before last . . . about my brother. Peter was shot in the back and I was running from the same gun—I don't know whose—but it shot me here—where my spine would make a right angle with the line of my arms if I held them out. And it felt so real—so deadening—no pain—just that certainty that life was ending."

"Peter may turn up in prison camp. For Christ's sake, Laurel, try to hope. I wish I'd known him before so I could feel something about it. But I didn't, and I can't help it—oh, God! Laurel, I'm sorry."

Sometimes Laurel wept. It was four or five years and several barrels of bourbon before Zero got rid of the nightmares in which he screamed and choked, waiting for some German pilot to get out of a wounded fighter before he came in to finish it off, or cursed in the vilest words at some American newcomer who had violated the tacit rules of the deadly game, played at ten to thirty-five thousand feet above earth with the Luftwaffe.

Laurel, learning patience and tolerance in the last of her formative years, had grown calluses in unsuspected places. She had learned to live with the military—the arriving and the departing, the quick intimacies soon over, the finality of farewell. She had learned to live with airplanes and nightmares.

Laurel reflected now on the first time she had seen Zero, the morning at Baton Rouge Air Base she looked up from her papers to find him standing before her desk—his eyes riveted on her, measuring, weighing, almost undressing her, while behind her own lips three words of French wandered up as nonchalantly as truant children, Quel bel étranger.

At this memory, she ached to glance at the Le Bourget waiting room to pretend even for a second that she had spotted Zero. But she was proud. The impulse was futile. Thus, she cheated herself, for a silvery blond head jutted above the crowd.

Standing six feet five inches tall, Zeno Richfield Compton (called Zero because of his fantastic targeting during four years of war) shivered and swore at the growing length of his wait to surprise his beauteous Laurel.

2

Compton had a square, slightly flared jaw, a determined arc in his neck, and broad-set eyes skilled in penetration. From long habit, he stood slightly bent. Grace in motion and faultless tailoring minimized his shortage of ten or fifteen pounds and besides, he regarded leanness as a badge of pride for a middle-aged man. God! It hurt to be thirty-five!

At the moment, albeit, his thoughts were not of age or obesity but of an overcoat which hung in a metal locker at Beaumonde Air Base, his station a hundred kilometers to the north. Zero had arrived in Paris the previous midnight, direct from North Africa where he had spent six sandy, grinding weeks on temporary duty, polishing his own mechanized marksmanship and that of his Squadron.

Sluggish from travel and loss of sleep, he arose from his hotel bed at six A.M. and went to meet Dr. Abach, a childhood friend of his wife's from Baton Rouge, now stationed at the American Hospital in Paris. The two were detained an hour on Avenue MacDonald by a traffic accident, and it was ten minutes after Laurel was scheduled to arrive that the pair of lieutenant colonels dashed into the French terminal where Samuel F. Abach, fluent in French, ascertained that the plane then abandoning its first pass at the fog-shrouded runway was Laurel's flight.

To Zero, the next forty minutes seemed longer than the four

months he had been in and out of France. With eight thousand hours of pilot time, he trusted at the controls no one as completely as himself; moreover, it mattered sorely to him that his wife acquire no valid reason to fear flying.

Now, crisis past, he jingled his keys against the worn goodluck silver dollar carried through combat, and eyed the trio beyond the barrier. He had no intention of calling out to her, for he was already enjoying the impact his unexpected presence would have on Laurel. Learning from somewhere that Compton's wife and children were landing the next day in Paris, his Group Commander had ordered him with an understanding smile to be off Corliss Air Base and out of Africa within the hour. On extremely short notice Zero obtained reservations via Air France to Paris. His idea of telephoning Abach was a spontaneous try to avoid coping with some French-speaking cab driver before dawn the next morning; besides, he knew that Laurel would be pleased to see her old friend. The two had grown up outside Baton Rouge on neighboring plantations. In fact, Abach's father had delivered Laurel, and Abach had delivered Laurel's first son.

Zero was grateful, though his gratitude took the form of complete respect. To him, Abach looked the way a doctor ought to look. He talked, walked, and even grinned with the unegotistical self-assurance befitting a dedicated physician. He was dependable but aloof, he was affectionate but impersonal, and, most impressive to Zero, he was skillful.

However, on this twentieth day of December, Zero stood beside Abach and in his impatience thought of none of these things. It nettled him to suffer viciously from the cold. A man must be getting both soft and old to feel such misery for want of a few layers of wool, he lamented to himself. But, God damn the French anyway! You couldn't hurry the bastards except to bed or table!

Abach glanced away from Zero's jaw-flexing endurance, "She doesn't realize people are staring."

"People aren't. Just men."

"Serves you right for snaring a beauty!" There was an empty little pause before the doctor went on; "Look at her! The way she's bent down there with that hair swinging really takes me back! You know, Zero, when we were kids, she couldn't pass a mangy flea hound without giving it a pat as she went by."

"Why didn't you learn to bark and scratch?" grinned the flyer.

"Go to Hell!" said Abach.

He switched his attention to the infant in Laurel's arm, the child which had been born several weeks after the doctor's arrival in France. "How long did the birth require?" he demanded.

"Two hours."

"Well, it happens that way more often than the other."

Compton offered a cigarette but Abach declined. After lighting his, the tall man stared straight ahead at his wife and children, saying finally, "I told her that was because you weren't around to shower her with another week of professional sympathy." Zero meant to add a dry laugh until he saw that the doctor wore a frown.

"Well, placenta previa doesn't occur twice to one woman. In fact, Zero, it numbers something like one in a thousand, but that's no excuse for the two days I let her suffer." Zero sighed and spat his cigarette to the ground. Both men turned back to Laurel and her children.

Simultaneously, their gazes halted on the hem of rich fur now dipping in the shallow puddle. "Stand up!" ordered Compton instinctively, but she could not hear. Abach's hand fell across his forearm in restraint.

"You wouldn't scold her before you've had a chance to kiss her! Good God, Zero! She doesn't even know you're here!"

Compton jerked his arm free, not looking. "There isn't a drop of surface water in France that isn't half urine."

"It's a coat, Zero. A coat. It will clean." But Zero did not favor him with a glance.

"Laurel!" The mist was heavy; normal acoustics were defied. Abach could abide the prospective scene no longer. He dug into his pocket and came up with a zipped key case. He peeled back layers of cuff, making a show of scanning his watch. He said that he had to be in surgery in fifty-five minutes.

"Here. The keys. You'll take the car?"

"Where?" Zero eyed him quizzically.

"To Beaumonde, or Monceau, or wherever you're going today." He glanced down at the glistening toes of his black shoes. "But you'll be afoot. . . ."

"Your car won't be arriving for six or eight weeks." Abach took a step back, his arm half up to wave. "Good-bye, Zero!"

Compton scowled in new dismay, "What'll I tell her?"

Shrugging in a manner decidedly French, Abach lifted his blue garrison cap at the front and let two fingers smooth his ruff of thinning, maize-colored curls. He grinned abruptly: "Oh, tell her Arf! Arf!"

As he disappeared, Zero stalked back toward the barrier, disconcerted by Abach's unexpected departure. He decided not to mention the doctor's presence to Laurel. It would save time, for she would never accept a casual explanation of his disappearance.

Zero Compton pondered his nagging dilemma. He knew how to tell her that the only house he had been able to rent had no dining room, a tenant landlady, cold water kitchen, coal and wood to heat and cook with; that the dismal region around the American Air Base was populated with childlike, impoverished peasants whose distrust of each other was exceeded only by their contempt for strangers.

He could tell Laurel without pulling punches that vandals shared with Communists in villainous tire-slashing, rock-throwing, and the nocturnal heckling of wives when the squadrons departed for Africa—that such things happened in any village where Americans lived, and that, unfortunately, they were to be the only American family yet in Monceau. But Christ-a-mighty! He couldn't tell her he was in trouble because of a woman!

Maybe he'd been wrong to accept a squadron, he thought, remembering how little it had bothered him to learn upon his arrival in late August that he was to assume command of the sagging 104th, tail-end Charlie of Beaumonde Air Base's three flying squadrons.

From old experience, Zero knew the ground rules for pulling a bastard squadron together. You singled out the odd balls, the morning drinkers, the overbold and the congenitally fearful, and the weaklings who lied to superiors with carbon-copy yeses. You posted flying schedules the men couldn't possibly meet. You rode maintenance's ass night and day to keep the planes in commission. And you prayed for at least a five-hundred-foot ceiling by morning. You kept track of your best pilot and flew ten hours and three missions a month to outdo him, because the commander of a squadron either led it or didn't. You had to exceed the best score on the bomb range and at gunnery. You had to be the pace-setter because when the chips were up or down, the real leader in any flying squadron was the hottest pilot.

There was no other recipe. As the contagion of example seeped down the line, the graph of hours and missions flown, the score at gunnery, even the morale of the enlisted men would begin to rise and soon trophies and certificates of award and commendation would evidence superiority.

Indeed, there was no other pattern, but there was another ingredient. A squadron commander was no stronger than his men's devotion to him. Zero had spent nearly a decade understudying older men, not catering to subordinates. Immediately, however, he set a policy of being at the bar daily at five P.M. to drink with his pilots. He drank apace of the thirstiest and showed it the least. He kept a straight face and a rapt eye, while they boasted of narrow escapes, weird encounters, aerial phenomena, and some broad in Paris. Fourteen of the 104th pilots were under twenty-five! And more often than not, whatever they told was merely to uphold a private contention that each had the world by the yang-yang on a downhill pull—but Zero accepted his listening obligation and soon began to reflect that commanding a squadron was a little like revisiting his youth.

It was beside the bar of the makeshift Officers' Club that he first observed the malaise of the American women. Painted, décolleté, they gathered each afternoon at the unlovely bar. They drank too fast. They laughed too loudly. They talked too much. And they stayed and stayed and stayed, even those whose husbands were off on practice missions or at distant points on temporary duty.

He listened patiently as wives bragged of outbidding other Americans for desirable French housing. He longed for Laurel's cool handling of conversational runaways as they plied him with tatters of domesticity—the price of coal, the charm of French public school, and the wisdom of proselyting the first decent maid one chanced upon. But the most painful of the stages for Zero arrived around six-thirty or seven each evening when the crowd got oiled up.

Women without husbands—seldom less than ten, sometimes twice that many—moved from officer to officer. They reminded Zero of a congress of friendly bitches in heat, particularly when one rammed her feeling hand up the back of his blouse and shot him rhythmically with his own suspenders. Sure, you were walking a tightrope! If you ignored them, they'd call you rank-happy. If you brushed one's ear with your lips and whispered, Don't act like a slut! she'd start a rumor you were queer—the most deadly rumor for an officer.

Christ! Women were a mystery, and in lots of ways, a mess. But a man was lucky these days if he could call his wife good—and a good screw, too. Two things usually didn't come together. Edney, a Major, former Commander and now Deputy Commander of the 104th, agreed with Zero on this. He said so with a mere nod, but a nod from him was worth four yeses from other men, Zero sensed from the beginning.

Zero sought Edney's advice before he approved the Squadron Adjutant's request in October to attend a ten-day school in Germany. About halfway through the ten days Zero told Edney what had happened the night before. The Adjutant's wife, Karen Philipps, had telephoned Zero at the BOQ around ten P.M. to say that her furnace was broken, and that she only lived four miles away in La Barmontère.

Louis Edney said tactfully, "I live in Nouilly, two miles from La Barmontère. She should have phoned me."

"Hell, you're living with a wife!"

"You make that sound like a felony," mumbled Edney. Both men laughed, Zero loudly, but he was thinking with mild satisfaction that he had finally connected Edney's resonant, encouraging bass to the voice it resembled—Abach's.

"Well, Christ! Aren't you gonna ask me whether I got the furnace fixed?" The handsome blond face wore a splendid scowl, evoking Edney's shy grin.

"You didn't go," he said flatly.

He was right. Zero had advised the young woman to wrap herself and her babes well until morning when he would dispatch a French-speaking sergeant to negotiate the needed repairs, if her French maid could not cope as was usual. But hers was merely the first in a series of calls, including an invitation for Zero to become a fourth at bridge with three 104th "widows." They had heard, glowed the vivacious voice, that he always won the penny-a-point games in the BOQ: "Is that right?—a long, tall drink o' water like *you*, Colonel Compton?"

Zero did accept legitimate invitations. He arrived that October night by staff car at the village where Captain Arnold and his wife lived. Arnold was his Squadron Supply Officer but Zero believed he had not met his wife. He hoped to God the woman was a decent cook. A decade on the brink of ulcers plus Laurel's capable and imaginative way with food had ill-fitted Zero for what he called the abortions performed on helpless customers by the Officers' Mess. He had already told the Club-Mess Officer that Laurel would find him a chef as soon as she came, so he could fire the glorified dishwasher who was there because he spoke English, or claimed he did.

Waiting at the Arnold's door after the staff car had driven away, Zero worried a bit. He was thinking of the services he had volunteered of Laurel. The Protestant Chapel had no organist. Several wives desired bridge lessons, and a class in French—beginners' French. His thoughts were interrupted by the opening of the door. I know her, puzzled Zero, long afflicted with a bad memory of names. Maybe the shapely brunette was a random guest, or maybe she was Arnold's wife. Zero knew her face from the bar.

Well, he shrugged behind an engaging smile as he slipped out of his overcoat, I don't hear anybody talking in the other rooms. *Must* be Mrs. Arnold. . . .

She had hung his coat, linked her arm into his as they turned into the next room—dimly lighted and wretchedly furnished with the castoffs of a French landlord—before she said in a blithe tone, "We'll be two at table. I decided not to go all out."

"Where's Arnold?"

"I supposed *you* of *all* people knew."

"Where is he?"

"Why, he left for Vienna four days ago, the day before I called you about coming to dinner."

When he was seated, Dorothy Arnold crossed the room to bring from the window sill, the outside, a fruit jar of martinis. No refrigerator, thought Zero dully, warding off assessment of his own stupidity.

Arnold was a damned fine supply man. He was also Edney's wingman when they flew low-level missions. But Christ! There were thirty-eight first and second pilots in the 104th that month —and two more due in from the States any day. How the Hell could he know where everybody was all the time without memorizing the morning report? God damn it, the staff car wouldn't return until a half hour before midnight.

Worse, Zero perceived a dubious secret in the bottom of his fourth martini. The bitch could say a hundred things about having the C.O. at her house all evening and no doubt she intended to do just that. It was what she *wouldn't* say, though, which would cinch her success. But women like her, thought Zero, were occasionally capable of gratitude. Yes, the only hope of discretion from such a female lay in horizontal concession. For days afterward he felt so contemptuous of himself that he arranged secretly with the bartender to mix only grenadine syrup in dry soda. Then he thought of having Captain Arnold transferred to the detachment in Germany.

Now, freezing, exhausted, and saturated with impatience, Zero Compton grasped the top rail of the passenger barrier with his ungloved hands, not knowing why he felt perversely consoled by the biting, frigid metal. Not wanting to, he recalled the greedy, passionate, foul-mouthed Arnold woman, and reflected that such a woman could prostitute her husband through one—maybe two —promotions with the right sucker for a commanding officer.

Dynamite! I wouldn't tolerate a wife like that for thirty seconds, swore Zero, but it was strange, when you thought about it, the different kinds of women officers married. Take Laurel— whimsical, moody, headstrong, independent as a hog on ice. Most beautiful woman he'd ever seen. Cool, firm body like a shaded spring where a man could drink forever without settling his thirst.

3

Swaying from the long flight and the car ride, Laurel fought off a sensation that the mammoth checkerboard tiles of black and white on the salon floor were rising. Half the square room was taken by dining furniture, a round table, matching buffet, and monstrous china cabinet, all veneered in bird's eye maple and freckled with wormholes. A ghastly square piano loomed Germanic in size and angularity, the ivory of its keys as broken and discolored as the teeth of a hag.

In contrast, a miniature loveseat with twin armchairs hinted at some earlier bliss, perhaps in the sitting area of a demoiselle's boudoir. Lacking cushions and springs, the skirted, upholstered trio nevertheless had demure charm and pleased Laurel until she tried to envision Zero lounging on any of the three pieces.

She had seen but the entrance foyer and the salon when Zero said, "I don't think much of the house, either. This room hasn't got a God damned window except there on the south wall!"

"It's nice they're on the south," answered Laurel, eyeing the fresh, unpatterned wallpaper. The vista was almost spacious. "Our things always pick up a room. They'll be arriving before you know it!"

"Laurel, our things will have to go to storage. We can't even unpack them here."

"Why?"

"This room. A kitchen there behind that foyer. Two bedrooms. No closets, Laurel."

"I'll find a larger place. Next week."

"Laurel, there aren't any."

"You don't speak French."

"I had an interpreter with me every time."

"That's bad. French people don't trust secondhand impressions."

"Laurel, there aren't any other houses. If there hadn't been a paint bucket and a ladder in this yard, and if I hadn't happened to drive by the day after the renovation was completed. . . ."

Suddenly, she beamed, "What does the house matter? We're together!"

For two days, Laurel coasted on the impetus of reunion. Then she began to rationalize. The house, four rooms or not, had possibilities; adjustment to a new scene required time; with a car and a telephone, there was no such thing as isolation; discomfort required repeated improvisations; and as for being bored, she had never had time. But she had not reckoned with the special odds against sane daily existence in northern and rural France.

Daylight—always gray—lasted from about eight-thirty of a morning until four in the afternoon. The salon needed electric light night and day. Neither of the Comptons knew that rural electric current was undergoing conversion to 220-volt in their area. They only saw that electricity in France disappeared with the caprice of a gazelle—for as long as four hours in daytime—and that, regardless of its steadfastness after dark, the constant flickering through forty-watt drops was about as effective, proposed Laurel, as upside down candles in a cathedral.

Then there was the matter of water. Laurel, Brick, and even the seven-month-old baby were replete with immunizations against typhoid, cholera, and other dread diseases, but Zero refused adamantly to have them even brush their teeth with tap water in the French house. He made a ritual of dissolving Halazone tablets in measured containers. When Laurel decried the antiseptic taste, he admonished her to boil reserves of water. Hearing this too affected the taste, he produced from the dirt-floored cellar a case of mineral water purchased as a stopgap. After Laurel read on the label that it was therapeutic for gout, diabetes, rheumatism, and nephritis, she warned Brick discreetly not to drink it.

The Monceau village pump broke down for as long as twenty-four hours at a time. Between these spells, laundry was hurriedly done (by hand, in the bathtub) only to freeze where it hung in the attic, or, by midafternoon, to form round puddles which circled the new paper of the salon ceiling. In critical stages of dampness, washed diapers were strung head-high in rows of white banners which jungled both bedrooms and beneath which Zero sidled with his body at a right angle.

The worst obstacle, however, was the kitchen coal range, from which foods emerged after Laurel's efforts either burned or semiraw, to the gloating sneer of a laggard, sullen, and unclean fifteen-year-old whom the landlady described as "your maid." She, like a ton of coal and a cord of wood, had simply come with the house. In the first three days, eight-hour-a-day Blanche brought three requests from Maman: Loaves of American bread to make breakfast toast for eleven children. "It makes better toast than French bread." A night's loan of the Sears Roebuck catalog. "My fiancé's sister works as a maid in Nouilly and the Americans she works for order things for her whole family." And third, "all the infant and children's clothes which your sons have outgrown."

Laurel glanced swiftly to and away from the girl's apron pocket and said, "Tell Maman we will speak of privileges when you no longer come to work with paper novelettes to read while you supposedly iron."

The imposition of this lazy French child upon her house was insignificant, in that Laurel regarded it as temporary. She was scarcely as philosophic toward an event on their fourth night in the house, one that was to spread despair over layers of disappointment like raw frosting on a fallen cake. Save for its temperature, the cold wave (ice-rain and ice-particled fog) seemed made in Hell.

The unheated toilet froze first, and by morning, no water ran at the kitchen sink or the tub and bidet between the two bedrooms or either handbasin in the bedrooms. Zero mobilized the household candles, ordering Laurel to send the maid twice to the village store for reinforcements, which he kept lighted beneath various pipes. By late afternoon, order seemed restored. But the temperature dropped still lower the second night. Wood, coal, and oil heaters expired sometime after midnight.

Madame-the-landlady peregrinated back and forth between her two rooms and the American apartment, seeking Laurel's commiseration on the prospect of broken pipes once the temperature rose, but Laurel was too cold to care. The stone and mortar walls were over a foot thick, simpered Madame. It would have required a solid year of sunshine to warm the house in milder weather, for it was only the previous winter that the windowless north wall had been built in the renovation, had been backsided into the black hill. Perhaps, rued Madame, it would never dry.

Laurel smiled at her limply and spoke as briefly as possible in hope Madame would depart, for regardless of her ignorance of English, no woman on earth could have been deceived by Zero's mutterings, his asides to Laurel while the landlady, unbidden to sit down, lingered in the door.

"Tell her by God for a hundred and fifty a month rent, it wouldn't hurt her to put in central heating. Tell her I said we could be staying in the Écu Hotel in Beaumonde for what we're paying here. Tell the old bitch. . . ."

"Zero! She's a schoolteacher!"

"Well, Christ! Tell her to go on to school and get outta here. It makes me sick to look at her with both my kids in bed because the floor's too cold for 'em to play on and my . . . I'm sore from Brick tromping my lap."

Laurel turned to the questioning French face. "My husband suspects you made a mistake not to have installed central heating."

A broad grin lighted the whole door. "Tell him it is not my fault if American men are too vain to wear proper winter underwear!"

Laurel turned back to Zero. "She says where's your winter undies?"

His eyes darted in disgust toward the fiftyish matron and returned to his wife. "Tell her I had to leave them in the BOQ because there isn't enough room in this cowshed to store 'em. Tell her! And put in a by God!"

17

Laurel regarded him a moment in hasty thought. "There's no way to say that exactly in French," she lied.

Madame spoke up in a voice liquid with satisfaction, almost pleasure. "Madame Compton," she sighed, "votre mari, quand il fâche, il est magnifique! Splendid!"

As she bowed backwards and away from the door, chuckling approvingly, Zero grumbled to Laurel, "Well, is she thinking about buying us a bigger heater?"

"No, you've had it, Zero! She says when you're angry, you're splendid."

4

Except for the whole measure of each spring, Laurel's favorite time of year was the last week of December. But she would look back on this one in years to come and remember feeling like a collision victim. She was stunned a day or two before Christmas by the onslaught of cold, did not revive entirely until the morning of New Year's Eve with the shrill first ring of their telephone.

As Zero spoke with a person he kept calling "Philipps," Laurel reflected on the passage of days. Like a piece of driftwood in the tide, she had let herself be propelled with the current. Mealtime. Bedtime. Mealtime. Bedtime. Mealtime. Bedtime. The diversions were heating bottles of formula, or peering through the shutters to see whether it was day or night. That system by which days had names appeared to have vanished forever. Laurel had not admitted to herself yet that she had some vague sensation of being walked backwards off a plank, downhill toward the ocean, not until her pulse leapt at the mere sound of the telephone ringing.

What's wrong with me? she demanded of herself. We're all well. We're alive. The food cache is holding out wonderfully. We have all the canned and dried stuff available. But if I had a head of lettuce, I wouldn't even wait to salt it! Oh, well, I'll find a real maid when Zero goes back to work. Even in the States, he's always restless during this holiday period. Of course, I'm exhausted from the trip. And I'm learning to live with a man again. After all, he was away at school those months I waited for Chris's birth at Paradis. He was home six weeks before he came here and then, four months apart. I hadn't thought of it that way, but we've lived together a month and a half the past year—for all practical purposes. No wonder I'd forgotten how much he curses.

As Zero entered the salon after his telephone conversation, Laurel remeasured his height, his careless grace. What a shame, she thought, that wives allow the humdrum burden of everyday life to blind them to the qualities which captured them initially. How pleasing to the eye was Zero's sleekly shaven jaw, the dormant strength implied in the breadth of his shoulders, and the swirl of dark platinum hair, combed so perfectly as to appear unreal.

Zero explained that Philipps, his Adjutant, had reminded him of the New Year's Eve party at the Officers' Club. "The Club is horrible, Laurel. A converted mess hall. Cement floor." She picked up her knitting. "Besides," he added, "the roads will be glazed by midnight."

"Don't apologize, Zero," she answered earnestly. "New Year's Eve is just another night at our age. Besides, we ought not leave Brick yet. He's terribly uprooted by this move and the change. Don't you agree?"

She glanced up from her handwork just in time to catch the wry, doubtful lift of his brows. Laurel squared her shoulders. The honeymoon was truly over after each reunion when Zero began to scold her for being an overanxious mother. But he only nodded. Then, he squatted with slow ease before the end of the buffet where he kept his bar supplies. He swung up with a polished glass and a bottle of bonded bourbon.

"Laurel," he began, not turning around, "we ought to go, but

I want them to be sober when they meet you. New Year's Eve is the wrong beginning for what we have to do."

His implication was lost in her concern. This was the fourth morning in a row Zero had started drinking before noon. She watched the amber liquid gurgle from the bottle and slosh into the glass—two, maybe two and a half ounces. Zero replaced the bottle, slammed the buffet door with his bent knee, and swallowed his whiskey in a few gulps. Laurel glanced down at her knitting and heard the glass jar against the marble top of the buffet.

For a time, he sat on the wide ledge before the south windows, regarding the hoar-frosted yard. Then he came behind her chair and bent down to unbotton both cashmere cardigans beneath which she wore, according to his wish, nothing. He bent further and buried his face in the warmth between her breasts. Hastily, she swept from her lap the dangerously fine needles lodged in the half-done sock. A semi-sweet cloud of fresh bourbon assaulted her nostrils. She heard herself saying, if he had to drink before noon, why didn't he drink straight from the bottle? (It would not have occurred to her to say what she really meant: Zero, by God, no husband of mine can be a morning drinker! She did not even know she thought it.)

She felt the twinge of stiffening in his hands, but whatever he might have replied was intercepted by the heraldic click of his German cuckoo clock. Zero raised up, his hands gripping the back of the chair, while he observed the mechanical exhibition of a poorly carved bright blue inch-high bird shooting to the end of the tiny runway and, seemingly paralyzed in fear, enduring the strafing from hidden bellows for ten raucous toots.

As the miniature door locked the bird away, Zero exclaimed, "Those Krauts have the know-how!" Still admiring his clock, he let his hands reach down again; Laurel had moved to the opposite chair, not in rejection of him but to turn her back on the clock.

Zero drew a deep breath and pocketed his hands. "You really don't like it, do you?"

"It's as if everytime that bluebird shoots out, all the faults of France are assembled for head count!" Her choked laugh chided herself, not her husband. "However," she said, "the symbolism doesn't hold water. Cuckoos are German, not French."

"Yeah, I guess they're all German." Zero wandered aimlessly about the salon. "Reminds me of the first one I ever saw. Southeast edge of Kansas City, hanging over a beaded lampshade."

She laughed, "Sounds like a whorehouse!"

"It was, by Jesus!"

"Zero!" Her smile had wilted.

"Oh, where's your sense of humor? I'll bet I'm the only stepson in the world who got fifty cents worth of ass for his sixteenth birthday! You know. . . ." He halted. "I'm sorry, Laurel."

"I don't care if we're married a thousand years. . . . I don't care if you slept with a. . . ."

"I said I'm sorry."

She bent nimbly to pick up the sock she had been knitting. Her fingers flew in a pace accelerated by anger, although the rich alto voice neither quavered nor lashed as she said, "It only bears out my theory that every child has to grow up with . . . I mean—suffers if he doesn't grow up with his father. His *own* father."

Laurel was thinking, as she seldom did anymore, of Mrs. Compton who, with Zero's stepfather, had been killed in a head-on collision about a week after the younger Comptons' fifth anniversary. The first husband, father of Zero's three half-sisters, had been shot by a prowler, killed in his own kitchen, and her second husband, Zero's father, had been killed two months before his son's birth while attempting to rescue an itinerant Mexican from the intake of a threshing machine. But the redoubtable matron married, in Zero's third winter, a boarder who stayed past harvest into Christmas, and who—Zero could not say why—had adopted him but not the three girls. Laurel could not grasp why Zero never spoke of Ambrose without a softening of eye.

Her resentment of the older man, a resentment vigorous enough to have survived his death, was centered in an event which took place on the Compton farm. Zero had postponed her meeting with his parents until the most direct route between his old and new station led them across midcountry and within three hundred miles of the Comptons. There was simply no alibi left for Zero.

Up to that time, Laurel felt certain Zero's reluctance to go home, his postponement of the meeting between herself and the older Comptons, was a result of his lack of sentimentality, for none of the Comptons even wrote letters unless there was a wedding, birth, or funeral to be announced.

Zero's mother was then fifty-one years old and some forty pounds overweight, but she bore traces of earlier and blonde beauty. She laughed, patted people when she talked to them, chain-smoked, and took a bottle of Coors beer on the hour starting at nine or ten in the morning. Zero scolded her for this, and, privately, Laurel scolded him for scolding his mother.

Ambrose Compton walked with the vigor of a man far younger than his sixty-three years. Laurel knew that her mere presence had somehow evoked a situation in which it was imperative for him to assert patriarchy in his realm. With a determination she did not bother to understand, she joined their nickel limit pitch game and by concentration and lucky cards, managed to win about eleven dollars, some eight of it from Ambrose.

"Downright indecent for a woman to win that much. I'd rather have your luck, Daughter, than a permit to steal!"

Humor went awry in his very tone, though. Zero howled at his stepfather's consternation. His mother neither played nor laughed nor spoke that evening. She merely watched, and next morning, when the two men had gone to check the pump at the stock water vat, Zero's mother brought forth her son's Distinguished Flying Cross and his Air Medal, and the framed citations and letters of commendation and his high-school diploma, and three Dutch Havana boxes of souvenirs, including a sterling replica of male genitals with spread wings from Pompeii.

These presentations were her only thanks to Laurel, who understood and who, with some confusion, examined the honor she had been paid, but what happened that afternoon convinced Laurel she would never see Zero's mother again while Ambrose Compton lived. Mother and son had no more than departed for the five-mile drive to a Richfield grocery store than doughty

Ambrose put his daughter-in-law to what she knew he would have labeled "the supreme test."

When Zero asked him where he got the bright red scratch which extended from his cheekbone's apex to the lobe of his ear, he replied that a man was getting too old to farm when he couldn't patch a strand of "bobwire" without getting caught in his own fence. Listening, Laurel studied the loose stone on her right finger—a two-and-one-half carat rosecut emerald with one Tiffany prong wedged straight where it should have hugged the stone. For four or five years, she had meant to have it fixed.

Laurel stared at the emerald now, bitterly, almost defensively, and said, "I don't see how your mother could have married Ambrose."

Zero went to the buffet and poured himself a drink. He came back to the fireplace area to sit down as he replied, "He taught me the things a man needs to know." She said nothing. "Laurel, he didn't go batting around three or four continents with some broad."

Suddenly she was aware of the moving chill which issued from the earth-backed hall, a long corridor leading to the two bedrooms. She buttoned her sweaters and glanced up then at Zero, who was staring, as if seeing her for the first time. Laurel asked what he was thinking.

The crow's-feet at the corners of his eyes wrinkled until they blended into his temples. His grin broke, "What was I thinking? How stupid I am to ever say an unkind word to you. Laurel, I love you."

"What were you thinking?"

"That it was the best day of my life, the day I married you."

Her smile grew, helpless before his lowered tone and admiring eyes. With a lilt in her voice, she demanded, "What were you really thinking?"

"That you have the prettiest breasts I ever . . . that God ever put on a woman."

5

That night Zero broached the subject of his Squadron difficulties. The trouble, he said, was Louis Edney, former Commander of the Squadron, now 104th's Deputy Commander. The first thing against him was that he went through the war in Infantry, having wedged himself through flying school after VJ Day.

"To these kids, Laurel, he's an old man who doesn't know a God damned thing about tactics—except what they can read in a textbook, too. Then Edney's got this thing about education. These last ten years, he's gotten himself a degree in philosophy. And now, whatdya suppose? He goes to night classes twice a week at the Base. He's studying French IV. Good God!

"Blake, the Group Commander, told me before I met him that Edney's too weak to goad or discipline. That's not so. He's too damned sentimental about his men. Makes for softness. The same slobs who wrecked him, though, have a father complex about him now. I get lip service and filled flying commitments, but he's their Scoutmaster-confessor. Other day, I walked in on him and Stone, who's youngest lieutenant in the 104th—the rawest, too. He was badgering ole Edney into going to bat with me. Stone wants leave to marry some French babe. Christ, he's a brat. I'll lay you fifty to one he doesn't shave every day yet. I told the son of a bitch he could get married on a Saturday night, long as he's six missions behind the low man in my Squadron."

"Did Stone get his leave?" interrupted Laurel.

"Why, yes. Edney gave it to him the next month, while I was in Germany. He gave him a three-day pass."

"The girl was pregnant?"

"That's what all the commotion was about. Some mayor's niece in a town near Reims. Edney said we *had* to—noblesse oblige. But Christ-a-mighty, Laurel! I'm not running a home for unlucky studs! I'm running a flying squadron which is supposed to be combat-ready twenty-four hours a day. Try to understand my job—which is to keep these kids sharp enough to get to the target and back in case war breaks out, to do the ultimate damage with their weapons in minimum time, and to take care of themselves in the air well enough to fight their way back so we have a pilot and a plane for the next mission. That's the way it is, Laurel, until planes don't need pilots."

A sylph in black leotard and sleeveless tunic of ocelot fur, she sat with her legs wound beneath her body for warmth, the same reason her waist-length red hair swung loose. Beside her, Zero lounged uncomfortably on the little loveseat. Both of them stared into the fire, Zero cuddling an empty brandy glass. Above their heads, the four unfrosted bulbs in the spindly fixture glimmered in their peculiar brand of brightness. Two candles on the mantelpiece flickered, spilling wax on Tuborg beer bottles. From the window ledge, Zero's portable radio spewed its French, "Buy Psschitt! Zestful, refreshing, healthy! Everybody drinks Psssschitttt! Buy it in the litre, demi-litre, quarter-litre, as you wish! Psschitt! Pssssschitttt! Psssssschittttttt!"

"Sounds like a dirty word," said Zero.

"It's French 7up," she replied.

Then, only three or four bars into the renewed music, the electricity in the room went off. Zero and Laurel were alone with the fire and the candle flames and somebody named Louis Edney.

The soles of Zero's shoes grated back and forth on the cold tile as he shifted his position. He said flatly, "Laurel, I'm in Dutch with my Squadron. I've got to have your help to pull the people together. All the help you can give me."

She sighed. The plea was familiar. In other years Laurel had taught music appreciation, bridge, knitting, and French to groups of Air Force people, not only officers and their wives but also airmen and civilians. She had taught Sunday School, kindergarten, swimming to handicapped children, and charcoal sketching. She had played organ music for both Catholic and Protestant services, sewed three dozen pairs of drapes and six couch covers for an enlisted lounge. She had planned a bachelor wing commander's gala official reception for a visiting shah.

She prided herself, however, on keeping in mind her motivation; Laurel believed she did such things only because it pleased her—the same reason that, domestic help available or not in the States, she entertained frequently, sometimes lavishly. She felt that in her present domestic circumstances any teaching or entertaining would be utterly impossible. And she felt that Zero was being selfish and unreasonable.

Well, she thought, if the day comes Zero can't sustain himself in his own career, that suits me fine. We can head back to Louisiana and start planting those nine hundred acres. If we could reclaim that tract in the marsh, that would be another three hundred . . .

"Laurel? Laurel, are you listening?" She turned around to face him. "Laurel, what are you thinking?"

She blinked as the lights came back on and looked half wistfully at Zero before she answered. "I was thinking about reclaiming those marsh tracts. You know, where it was leveed until the flood of 'twenty-seven. Abach reclaimed two tracts north of there. The work was finished last summer."

"Abach?" Zero's tone implied, Oh, him again! It was the first time his name had been mentioned between them since the drive from the airport, when Zero had explained glibly and falsely that he had the doctor's car because a temporary duty assignment would keep Abach at Ankara through January. Now, Laurel felt guilty for having mentioned Abach's name, as Zero inquired, "Where'd he get that kind of money?"

"He had help. Flood control. State. Federal government, too."

"And what did you have to do with it?"

"I referred Evelyn McClade to him as a patient, three or four years ago," said Laurel. "You don't know her. She had triplets. Abach delivered them. Isn't that something? Then, the year after that, well, her husband—he is a lawyer—won his race for senator. That's all."

Zero crossed his foot over a bent knee in imitation calm, but

Laurel caught his alertness and the loaded silence. His eyes were cold, his tone relentless, "What kind of a wife have I got who'll help a kike with a crooked senator but won't. . . ."

"Shut up!" wailed Laurel, not only in dismayed rejection of his slur against Abach but at the audacity of his ingratitude to the doctor.

Maybe I was wrong, she mused, not to have told him what it was like those three days after Brick came, with Abach sitting there, his face like a red light on a buoy in that gray sea, when all I wanted to do was sink. But it's too late. What would it mean to Zero if I said now that I didn't get a blood pressure good enough to count until the day Abach handed me back the will to live?

"Laurel, why should you help him and refuse me? I'm your husband."

She steeled herself, squaring her shoulders, and taking a deep breath to shift the subject. "Zero, if Edney's your trouble, why didn't you—why don't you transfer him out?"

At this instant, there came a sudden rapping against the window glass. Laurel turned in time to glimpse a brightly lipsticked, laughing mouth and pallid ivory face waft back into the night. Zero, chuckling, was already halfway across the salon.

6

"Well!" huffed the plump woman, "You're too smashing for me!"

"You're English!" shrieked Laurel in delight.

"I'm British!" argued Regina Edney. The two women burst into laughter while their husbands exchanged hopeless shrugs.

Regina was pretty with her cameo pallor, blue eyes, and fine black hair. Laurel's first impression of Louis Edney was multi-faceted; he seemed quiet, self-possessed, massive, and virile. Drawn to him, Laurel tried not to stare at the black eyes and blue-black hair which were explained by Regina's comment that he was "mostly" Choctaw Indian.

The Britisher spoke of herself, her marrying after the Battle of Britain, her birthing four sons in six years, her experiences in America.

"I like hot dogs and Cary Grant and ball games, but I saw in the first week that I could never be a proper flag-waving American. I kept hoisting that bloody Union Jack!"

Laurel watched Regina's eyes flick devilishly at Edney upon completion of her remark. But Zero was already on his feet, suggesting to Edney that they go out to the kitchen and ice down some champagne for midnight toasts.

"Aren't you going to the Officers' Club?" Laurel asked Regina in surprise.

The Britisher regarded the men's exit with a patient smile. Then she leaned closer, although the two sat side by side on the loveseat. "Louis thought we ought to come and pay our respects to you two." Her tone implied resignation.

"You waited ten days. A few more wouldn't have mattered," Laurel replied in flat monotone, having decided to employ candor and be done with the barrier which through no fault of either woman had been established between them months earlier, the day Zero Compton replaced Louis Edney at the head of the Squadron.

"I say!" sputtered Regina, crimsoning. "With the holidays and the cold wave and all. . . ."

Laurel interrupted, her tilted smile amused, "You didn't go to the Club because you aren't very popular with Americans—women, that is?"

Regina leaned still closer, forgetting to register indignity, "They're a bitchy lot here—bridge-playing gossips, outbragging each other, black marketing cigarettes, taking maids to the Officers' Club for Sunday dinner!" She paused long enough to check Laurel's bland, unchanging expression. "There are two we *have* to be nice to, Smokey Fritsch and Kilian Blake." Laurel remarked idly that it sounded as if Runyon had named them, but Regina lumbered on.

Smokey was the wife of the Wing Commander, and unlike her husband, a democratic person. They had three children, but Smokey planned to divorce Fritsch when they returned to the States in early summer.

Laurel stretched her legs from under her and said, "She found something better over here?"

"Oh, a Frenchman couldn't touch her with an *eleven* foot pole!" chortled Regina. Having waited in vain for Laurel's laugh, the Britisher giggled rather desperately and spurted on to the effect that there was nothing wrong with the Fritsch marriage which couldn't be solved if Fritsch had the guts to rape his wife about once a night. "He's weak. Raised by two old maid aunts. You know the type?"

"I'm old fashioned, Regina. Nobody's bedroom interests me except my own."

Their eyes met in understanding, Regina's searching and Laurel's affirming. Suddenly, Regina leaned away from her and relaxed in an enormous sigh.

"I say, Laurel! You and Zero will be making the conventional New Year's Day calls on our bosses tomorrow?"

"Why?"

Regina sputtered, "Why, it's tradi . . . why, old Fritsch is a West Point officer. He goes for all the trimmings."

"When that New Year's Day call on the commander was the most rigid social rule in the military—in those days, Regina, the Army had all kinds of graces. A unit commander assigned an officer and his wife to stock your kitchen before you arrived, to greet you, dine you, take you to town the first time, and see that you weren't lonely."

"What's the matter, Laurel?"

"That was Army, not Air Force." She eyed Regina contemplatively before she went on, "Why the Hell should I play the game when both Zero's bosses have cut the first act? Blake, the Group Commander, knows I'm here. He sent Zero out of Corliss in time to meet me. Do you suppose he forgot to tell his wife?"

Regina shrugged, "We've all known what day you were due

since the first of December. Everybody's been waiting to see what kind of woman a man like Zero would have married. But, Laurel, Kilian Blake's house is thirty miles from here."

"Does she drive?" Laurel asked. Regina nodded. Laurel asked then whether Mrs. Blake spoke French.

"No." The leonine head tossed vigorously. "You may as well know—everybody else does—how she deceived Blake into keeping Louis here. She told her husband Louis and I are the only link between the village French and the Air Base people."

"Is it true?"

"You don't expect me to answer that, I say!"

"Then what's the truth?"

"Kilian uses me when she needs a French interpreter, or when she wants to go antique hunting. I bargain for prices, too, you see."

"Where do you usually go for antiques?"

"Oh, there's a precious little secondhand store in the edge of Soissons."

"Oh? You go sixty miles just for antiques?"

"Sure!" extolled Regina. "Why we were there only two days ago."

Laurel's lips curled in a half smile. "But Kilian Blake hasn't time to come here and say a simple welcome to a squadron commander's wife—and Zero only one rank removed from Blake?"

Regina crimsoned, slowly and long. "Regina, I didn't mean to take a fling at you. I'm just . . . well, I'm probably hunting alibis not to get involved with an American life over here. You'd do me a big favor by passing the word around tomorrow that Zero and I don't expect Squadron couples to drive clear out here. Tell the wives I've got a mild case of infectious hepatitis."

Regina said, "All I have to tell them is that you've chosen me for a friend."

There was a pause while Laurel did not respond to the witticism. Regina went on, "I say, Laurel! We'll have a good time while the men are gone! I may call you Laurel, mayn't I?"

Laurel did not answer because she had not heard beyond "while the men are gone."

Regina saw that Laurel did not know. "Zero should have told you. The 104th is leaving Monday morning. For the States. Two or three weeks—bringing back the new twin jets. Didn't Zero tell you this Base is converting from these old twin-engine Maurauders to Cougars? B-87's?"

Two or three weeks? Laurel envisioned a span of hourless days, begun and ended with buckets of anthracite, chunks of tree, elephant-nosed yellow cans of kerosene—frozen plumbing, trapped children. No husband for two or three weeks in this archaic outpost of civilization.

She stretched her arms and legs now in what appeared to be casual, feline grace, but what was no more than concealment of a crazy urge to run from the house—run, run, keep running. "Regina," she heard herself saying, "I've wanted to go home from about the third day in this house." The sound of footsteps coming from the kitchen interrupted her.

The pair turned around to watch their husbands enter the room. Louis Edney's curious glance darted from one feminine face to the other. Zero's quick perusal of his wife's expression ended on a relieved sigh. You never could be certain how much a woman like Regina Edney would talk—but you could be God damned certain she *knew*.

Zero cared little for champagne and so, as the evening wore on, he became quite sober. He realized he had handled the Squadron impasse badly. Laurel had damned near trapped him about Louis Edney. Hence, through the evening, he had reversed his plans. He meant to restore respect at least on the return trip from the States. Louis Edney had given him a sound idea. If he filed the clearance for thirty to thirty-five thousand feet on the stretch from Goosebay to Keflavik, he might crack the jet record for the run. Secretly, Zero had already improved on the idea. He meant to file for that altitude, and then fly ten thousand higher to be damned sure. Oh, God! All this mess of jet stream and prevailing winds and North Atlantic air masses. Flying used to be fun in the old days when all you had to worry about was pulling the wings off in a tight turn because you kept your P-38 mercuried up more than the manufacturer said you oughta.

But Laurel. Regina could serve as a buffer to keep some nosy bitch from haranguing Laurel with hints. Of course, he reflected as they lay in bed, Regina was scarcely Laurel's type; he'd better make sure the tie didn't abort before it got off the ground, "Laurel," he said in the dark, "if I were you, I'd avoid Regina."

"Why?"

"She's vulgar."

"She's been with vulgar people."

"There's more than that. The wives consider her unscrupulous. Vicious enemy."

"Is there any other kind of enemy?"

"I don't think you can handle her, Laurel."

7

Laurel kept no formal diary but since the age of fourteen she had been scribbling random comments in loose-leaf notebooks. In the second half of January, she entered Regina Edney's name for the first time: "—the sort of European who never arrives without a handful of goodwill—daffodils, a packet of dried lavendar, fresh sage, a mince pie, or what have you? The first maid she brought lasted a week. Although more ambitious than languid Blanche, the girl could resist neither my toothbrush nor the boys' combs and brushes. I have not told Regina that the present hopeful is carrying home canned goods, and feasting here on dried fruit, tuna, zwieback, butter, etc. I shall wait until I can go to the Beaumonde employment agency and find my own.

"Beaumonde, twelve miles from Monceau, has fifteen thousand people and is built on a lovely hill three or four hundred feet high. It rises out of the black Picardy plains like a firm breast.

Regina tells me there are fifteen or twenty American names on waiting lists for the few rent houses—steam heat, city gas, and real electricity! Twice she has taken me to the Wednesday open market (an adventure in this freezing weather!) and she admits quite frankly that her ties with Beaumonde are limited to shopping. The professors, successful merchants, and civil service officials who constitute the town's elite are beyond her social realm because they have summered across the Channel too often. 'They can tell I'm not even tradespeople!' She looked so pathetic. I'd hate to be British below Crown level! Worse, she suffers an actual martyr complex about being married to an American while in France, because of 'these bacchanalian Yankees' sent to represent my country in France.

"Regina is a bluffer and a windbag, but she's as full of charming swatches as a bundle of quilt scraps. During a three-hour visit at her house, I saw her doctor two French children for ringworm, lend an old man three mille francs, write down the name of an American lieutenant whose widow-landlady claimed to have received no payment in two months. These were people who knocked at her door during my visit, which concluded, by the way, with our drive to the Beaumonde hospital, where Regina took an old lady for her regular X-ray treatment.

"Between these 'assaults,' she spent her time plying me with tidbits about uppercrust Beaumonders, as she calls them. It became obvious that she has delectable visions of my crashing Beaumonde 'society'—her vicarious success.

"She took infinite care to describe Zero's secretary, Yvette Hachère. Her father owns the Citroën agency of Beaumonde. Before my arrival, Yvette extended Zero an invitation to play bridge with the family, but he refused. As soon as Regina told me that neither Mama nor Papa Hachère speaks a word of English, I knew why Zero refused. He foresaw a disagreeable game mucked up with translations. When I explained this, Regina had a quick rebuttal: Madame Hachère, Mama, had reached the semi-finals in the Paris bridge tournament the previous year. Wouldn't that make Zero's tolerance worthwhile? I told her we'd see, and the next afternoon, I drove back to Beaumonde by myself and played an old European trick—newcomer with calling cards left at the Hachère door in midafternoon, which, apparently, is as safe an hour in Beaumonde as it once was in Louisiana.

"I felt rather pleased up to that point, but when I emerged from the employment agency, some miscreant had painted all four of Abach's car windows with lipstick—'U.S. Go Home!'— 'Americans in Amérique'—'Yankee Chien'—and on the fourth, that famous four-letter English word found in no dictionary. No wonder Regina believes in driving a small Continental car over here! I stood there like an idiot, trying to decide whether to drive twelve miles home with red mottoes or ruin my gloves and handkerchief erasing the big letters, and suddenly, I realized a crowd of ten or twelve curious onlookers had gathered, so I got in and drove away—six or seven blocks to the first filling station— and of course, the attendant tried to swallow his grin, but you knew the first thing he'd say—and he did—'Someone wrote on your car, Madame?' I smiled as widely as possible and said, 'You know, I thought surely you were going to ask me whether I was American!' He had been taking in my speed with his language and the accent, I guess, for he said as confidently as a language professor: 'Oh, no! I can tell by your accent. You're Canadian, Madame. My youngest sister lives there, married to a Canadian, and she wrote me how they speak. Here! I just happen to be carrying a picture—a colored picture, Madame—of her three children—my two nephews and my niece. My youngest sister, you see, Madame. My own children are grown. . . .' He handed me not his wallet but a laminated plastic album from its center, pausing to raise his head above the car and shout at five youths who stared at the car windows from the sidewalk. 'Go on! Get away! Only the car is American.' And when they began to giggle, without moving away, he called them sales bêtes and threatened to telephone the police. They left. And as soon as I could, so did I, without ever telling him I was American because by that point, we were such 'old friends' it seemed cruel to disillusion him.

"At any rate, Zero returned in unexplainably high spirits yesterday about noon and is now in his eighteenth hour of sleep, recovering from the exhaustion of his over-water flight and, I suppose, the change in hours. Before he went to bed, however, I read him Madame Hachère's invitation to play bridge which came three days after I left my card at her house. He assumed a look of cautious consent and said, 'Why, Hell, yes'!"

8

The Hachère dwelling lay in that section of Beaumonde considered truly elite because many of the structures atop the flat L-shaped pinnacle contained portions of rock walls laid in the sixteenth century or earlier.

Zero and Laurel did not speak of this, however, after he had pushed the boxed buzzer appliquéd to a giant door no more than a foot from the cobblestone street. During a wait of two or three minutes, they continued to rehearse for Zero's benefit the conventional bridge bids in French.

Suddenly, the door swung open, squeaking regally from all four hinges. A genial man with heavy black and white hair extended his hands to greet them. In lavish French, Monsieur Hachère apologized for his role of doorman—"We lost another maid today!"—while leading them into a small den or salon, a room oddly warmed by a mixture of worn leather armchairs, an Arabic coffee table, and many flamboyant throw rugs.

Here waited Yvette Hachère, a poised young woman about twenty-five years old whose blonde drabness, thought Laurel, was relieved by a scrubbed sheen. Like Laurel, she wore no make-up. Her manner was both reserved and gracious as she sat down with her employer.

At the other end of the room, Hachère questioned Laurel courteously, his eyes glistening. Did France please her? Did she like Beaumonde? Oh—Monceau? How dismal! Too bad his house in Beaumonde was long leased to Americans!

Where had she learned to speak literary French, he inquired, and with such a charming accent? Was her exquisite coloring peculiar to beauties of her region of America? He commented on the depth of the emerald she wore on her right hand, afterwards noting that he was the only Citroën agent north of Paris. He had on consignment, he murmured, a certain number of Jaguars, one in palest green, and would she honor him by permitting him to drive her through the great Monceau forest, a landmark of national pride!

Beneath the flow of English in the opposite end of the room, Papa's voice droned on in intimate chatter. It's all irrelevant, thought Laurel, if only he'd have the grace to stop staring. But as she glanced high above his head at an oil painting of sunburst roses, he exclaimed in a whisper, "You like flowers, Madame?"

"Yes, Monsieur," she breathed tonelessly, "roses most of all." Laurel glanced down at his hand, which sensuously pummeled his own thigh. She was edging away gradually, when Madame Hachère's entry saved her.

A well-corseted blonde, Mama had dancing blue eyes, a solicitous smile, and skin less lined than her daughter's. She radiated a blend of self-assurance and vivacity. The youthful woman was trailed by three robust sons.

After the complicated introductions, Paul the eldest came to sit by Laurel. Madame smilingly arranged herself near Zero, requesting Yvette to bring the paper-thin gold-monogrammed coffee service to the table at her side. Meanwhile, Paul's expert handling of English dealt out his father and teen-age brothers. He spoke to Laurel of the Americans he had known, the water sports he adored each summer at Cannes, and the sports car races which he entered each August.

As he spoke, his glance tumbled from soft peak to ripe curve beneath Laurel's artfully simple purple wool dress. He confided glumly his parents' vexation because he was thirty-one years old and not *about* to be married!

"I'll be thirty-two pretty soon," Laurel chirped, "and I'm very married!" His gay laugh tossed off her rebuke. Without meaning to, she giggled. Paul was so overdone, like a high-school senior playing the proverbial Frenchman, limp of wrist, oozing with charm, self-assured, and unintentionally comical.

As Yvette reappeared with a tray of brandy glasses and a decanter, Laurel noted about twenty glasses. Coping with a demitasse, a brandy snifter, a lighted cigarette, Papa's leer, and—for Heaven's sake!—Paul's right knee, she tensed further as the first group of French guests burst gaily into the salon without having bothered to ring at the outside door. But when all the guests had arrived, some spark was still missing.

Zero was quickly engrossed by the spirited, almost fierce bridge system played by the expert crowd. Near midnight when Madame Hachère gaily rapped on the cobalt base of a Sèvres mantel urn to silence the crowd, Laurel was stunned to hear her own name read first, for she had suffered a run of bad cards, and had been distracted by the intimacies directed her way, as soon as male guests understood the language situation in the Compton family.

However, Madame Hachère was reading every score, having started with the lowest. She reached the last one and said, "Our American Colonel is the champion!"

"My mother insisted on doing everything the American way tonight," laughed Paul. He went on to explain that while they normally played neither for money nor prizes, his mother had sent him that day to buy a high and low prize. "They're ashtrays," he confided to Laurel, "and when you get home, you must force the Colonel to trade with you."

Laurel did, not because of Paul's suggestion, but because the inexpensive white pottery disc was gilded with the motto: "Le mariage est une loterie mais où sont les gagnants?" Marriage is a gamble but where are the winners?

Before the month was out, there had been six more bridge parties given by members of the Hachère circle. Zero seemed satisfied with the brilliant bridge these people played, but Laurel longed for a way out. Their card tables were replete with second-grade blanched almonds, bought pastries, half-price champagne, and illegally gotten American cigarettes from which hostesses did not even bother to remove the telltale blue stamp.

In the safety of his family and associates, old Hachère continued to badger her, while Paul tiptoed between overattention to Laurel and fraternal intimacy toward Zero.

The houses were cruelly cold, often stale-smelling. The matrons' black dresses generally needed cleaning. Talk was banal. Neither men nor women discussed music, art, politics, literature, or local history. "We finished all that in school, dear Madame Compton!"

Of all the thirty or forty Beaumonde citizens they had met there was only one to whom Laurel was instantly drawn. Monsieur Vervins apologized to her at the outset because he neither spoke English nor played bridge. "I am the king of dullards, Madame Compton, but the Risseaus were kind enough to invite me here tonight because there seemed no other way for me to meet you and your husband."

He was immaculate. He had about him an odor of good cigars. His French was devoid of the hackneyed colloquialisms which grated on Laurel's ear. But as the play commenced, he disappeared, and the next time, he did not come, nor the next.

Having learned that he lived but ten miles from Monceau, she proposed to Zero one Saturday afternoon that they pay the old man a formal call. Clearly, the prospect chilled Zero.

"Why don't you drop by his farm and leave your own card?" he asked.

"His servants would be pleased, anyway."

"How come?" asked Zero.

"Vervins has no wife."

Then Zero revealed that he had attended the bridge parties for just one reason. Since Laurel apparently wanted nothing to do with the Air Base social life, he thought she needed some diversion outside the tiresome house. "Laurel, if you only knew the Hell it plays with my nerves to hear every sentence secondhand, and those God damned flowery people!"

"But I never cared about going after the first night!" she retorted.

When Zero proposed that they were too deeply involved to back out, she answered, "Oh, no! We've only to have the next party, repay our obligations, and make excuses afterwards if we're asked again."

With their things in storage, Zero wanted to know where the Hell Laurel could get enough tables to give a party? Regina could manage that, Laurel said. "We'll ask her tonight."

"Tonight?" Yes, she reminded him, the Edneys were coming for dinner. "Good! I need to talk to Edney anyway."

In a demure voice Laurel murmured, "Squadron troubles?"

"Oh, Christ, no! The 104th is second now in hours flown and bombing score. Another ninety days we'll be on top."

Displeased that he evaded her question, Laurel said, "No morale problems anymore?"

His smile was frank. "Nope. Not since I cut six minutes off the twin-jet record from Goosebay to Iceland." His eyes held her in an extra moment of scrutiny. "Funny damned thing to think a wind was all it took to restore standing."

That night, the four lingered at the round dining table in the wake of Laurel's concoctions: a pâté en croûte of brains and mushrooms, rare tenderloin of beef, souffléed potatoes, salad of white endive, and a pecan pie, Zero's favorite dessert. Emerging from the lethargy of well-being, Laurel arose from the table to prepare the coffee tray. When she returned from the kitchen, Zero was saying, "God damn it to Hell! I don't care what I fly, but right now, I wish I'd never seen inside a C-47."

Laurel's gaze darted to Edney, whose head swayed in sympathy with Zero. He said, "I don't blame you. It's hard enough to run a jet squadron without having an additional flying job. But you'll never get a waiver from this passenger-carrying duty, not with fifteen hundred hours C-47 time before you came here."

Zero's handsome brows knitted in a mean frown. "It's exactly like being a taxi driver. If the weather is too foul for Fritsch or Blake to fly a jet to Headquarters in Germany or anywhere else, I have to drop whatever I'm doing and take them in a C-47. When a woman goes into labor—the general hospital is at Weisbaden. And the baseball and basketball teams have to be delivered and returned. Laurel, you can prepare yourself not to see much of me between this mess and the Squadron."

Then Zero turned to Louis Edney and said, "You're the one I'm worried about. You'll have my work and yours about half the time, and not a God damned bit more credit."

Edney's response was a slow, closed-mouth smile.

"Aw, Christ!" exploded Zero, "let me get you transferred to Germany. I can get by without you now. You need a bailiwick of your own, while you've still got a year or so in Europe. I know Blythe up at Headquarters. Personnel type. Fact, he owes me a favor."

Before Edney could answer, Regina broke her longest silence. "Oh, Zero! Don't you know by now he has to stay here and sacrifice his ego on the Squadron altar? He doesn't care if he never gets a promotion. His family's position, his future, he doesn't care. . . ."

"Laurel, how about a cup of coffee?" broke in Edney.

Zero with unwonted tact turned to Regina and asked whether she could find five card tables to lend them for the coming Wednesday night.

"We have to pay off the Hachères and their friends," said Laurel in a half-supplicating tone.

Regina was delighted to help, though she did not play bridge and in any case could not be invited to the party.

9

The bite of Zero's additional job as passenger-carrying pilot was not felt until a few hours before the planned bridge party. He was called to the Base to fly Colonel Fritsch on a three-day trip to Germany.

From the outset of the party, however, the strain of Zero's absence was lessened by Paul Hachère, who usurped the host's place, steadfastly and capably. The affair went routinely. Laurel thanked Paul for this afterwards, dismissing him and the others from her mind. Around two-thirty next afternoon, she heard Paul's voice emerging from the foyer. Instantly, she glanced at her housecoat of bright green corduroy and regretted that she had not bothered to dress.

"Hello, Paul!" she called over her shoulder without getting up. He came swiftly, gracefully across the room. His eyes swept her admiringly before he released her hand from a healthy squeeze.

"Ah, but you are stunning!"

"You only say that because it's true," she chided, hoping such a reply would perplex him for he was so cocksure with his English.

"My family was much impressed with your hospitality," he said smoothly.

"There is no one I should like better to please!" Paul shrugged and dropped down on the loveseat beside her. Whatever he had come for, surmised Laurel, the opening was giving him trouble. Why not tell him briefly and firmly that. . . .

"Laurel. . . ."

"Paul, I must tell you that you shouldn't visit an American ménage during American duty hours."

"Zero won't mind," Paul snorted. "We're friends, he and I."

"Be that as it may, I imagine his reaction to your presence here in midafternoon will depend on your reason for coming."

"But you won't tell him," smiled Paul, "because I come for secret advice. You must not betray me! My parents would be furious."

"Advice?" she queried thoughtfully. "What do I know that you do not?"

"You're an American. You're a woman."

Her smile surfaced. "Your stand seems indisputable so far!"

"Laurel, there's an American girl in love with me. . . ."

"I adore the way you put it. . . ."

"Please! Please! I have a terrible decision to make. Her family has already taken her back to the States. Anyway, we can't marry until she's eighteen. I promised to go to America in two years and become a citizen. Then we'll marry."

Laurel watched the contortions of his eyes and mouth as he

attempted to fit his thoughts precisely into speech. Abruptly, she felt ashamed. Paul indeed had a problem. Marriage, emigration, rehabilitation in a strange country. Ideas piled on top of each other faster than she could examine them.

"You've already applied to get your name on the quota?" asked Laurel. "And you'll need a letter of credit and a sponsor's deposition. Why, of course, Paul! I think it's entirely possible that Zero and I can help you, if you furnish proper references for credit and all that."

"No! No!" He tossed his hands up. "I can handle all that. It's too early. I've lots and lots of connections when the time comes. But, Laurel, the problem I need to discuss with you is immediate."

"You're not going to ask whether I think a sixteen-year-old will wait that long?"

"Give me a chance! She'll wait. She promised. My question is whether I am a fool to. . . ." Again, he halted. Laurel murmured in confusion that anything worthwhile was worth waiting for, but saying this made her feel extremely platitudinous.

"Am I a fool to wait . . . er . . . uh . . . fidèle? How do you say—faithful? Will an American girl expect that of a normal, healthy male, Laurel?"

Apprehension walled up in her throat, demanding only the wrong flick of his eyelid, or a careless gesture of his hand to trigger her indignation. Then the horrid little cuckoo shot out of his cage and piped three clarion toots. Paul laughed in nervous surprise at the intrusion. He stood up, walked to the fireplace and rammed his hands in his trouser pockets. He doubled his fists so that the unpleated slacks were strained across his athletically flat belly.

He said: "Well, Laurel?"

"I have one bit of advice. You came to the wrong Compton. That is a question for Zero."

"I know what he'd say. I wanted an American woman's point of view."

She thought I'd like to tell him to go straight to Hell—through the front door. But Zero would tell me I only imagined Paul made a pass at me, and that, if he did, I brought it on.

She glanced down at her watch. "I wonder what's made Regina Edney late?" she murmured. The effect on Paul was magical. "I hope the maid hasn't started coffee?" He was moving toward the salon door.

"No, why?" asked Laurel, getting up to follow him.

He had forgotten, he said, an appointment at the Air Base. "I'll see you another day, Laurel."

When his departure had been accomplished with decorum, she dressed in heavy clothing and struck out afoot in the sub-freezing air. At the village bakery, she bought a small golden baguette of bread and departed, munching broken morsels the way villagers did.

She turned uphill, past the village school, the general store, and down the road which was walled on either side by hovels. As her mind turned over Paul's words, her subconscious noted the scene about her—the anemic tower of coal smoke spewing lazily from the chimney of each dwelling; the hunger-frayed cat or dog reigning on each set of decayed steps; the missing portions of front fences.

Smarting from what she now regarded as Paul's vulgar insinuation, she turned down a sloped path which split the sprawling hillside cemetery. Arriving at the opposite gate of the cemetery, Laurel flung down the remaining portion of bread and turned into the denuded forest of Monceau, where she walked until the first blue cast of twilight settled. Then she made her way home.

She slipped out of her boots and stepped to the threshold, but scarcely had she closed the door when she saw a black Homburg, black overcoat, and ebony-handled umbrella on the big coat rack. Directly across from her, the door between foyer and kitchen swung open a crack and the bovine face of the maid inched into view. Laurel slipped into the kitchen and closed the door. An older man with wonderful black and white hair, tittered the maid, had been waiting over an hour. Laurel braced her hands against the kitchen table and sneezed.

"Go tell him I have caught cold from walking in the wet forest. Tell him I am indisposed." The cow-face fell. "Go! Quickly!"

As the sound of the motor zoomed away, Laurel trudged into her foyer. The day was simply too much. With self-deception of which she was unaware, she began to undermine her certainty. Paul, she now proposed, did not realize what his question implied. And Papa? He had a clientele which exceeded the city limits of Beaumonde. It was entirely possible, it was probable that he had chosen the back route from Redan at this late afternoon traffic hour. It was reasonable that the unexpected sight of the country cottage piqued his curiosity and thus tempted him to pause and say hello, to witness whether by daylight the house was as quaint as it had appeared the previous, flickering evening.

She entered the salon determined not to give another thought to the Hachère men. But her gaze landed at once on a ribbon-bound florist box. In earthy sprays of fern and pink and garnet carnations, she found Hachère Senior's formal calling card, with the message "Hélas, there were no roses, but I enclose my heart."

10

Because Zero had earlier stated his dislike for the bridge evenings, Laurel felt doubly justified in declining invitations to the next three soirées. She blithely pretended her problem with the Hachères was solved, never guessing that already the groundwork had been laid for a new liaison between her husband and Hachère Senior.

Hunting and shooting were Zero's favorite sports. He had been philosophical about missing a whole season, the first since their marriage, but Laurel rued his deprivation. She felt he needed to get out-of-doors. Hence, she was scarcely less jubilant than he one Friday evening in late February when he explained, as he polished his twenty-gauge shotgun, that a French official in Base liaison offices had invited him to shoot in a trap contest the next afternoon at a private club in Redan.

Near seven P.M. Zero returned wreathed in champagne fumes and with his pockets stuffed with paper franc notes. His victory was repeated on two consecutive Saturdays, which was enough of an event to be noted in a boxed item on the front page of the Beaumonde paper.

This brought from Hachère a bid for Zero to shoot at the Beaumonde Club on the third Saturday of March when live pigeons were to be used in lieu of the usual clay discs. Zero made no attempt to conceal his excitement before his wife. He had shot live pigeons only three times. It would be exacting and unpredictable for, regardless of aptitude or experience, no marksman could guess whether live birds would soar right or left when released from the buried traps, nor at what height from the ground target would veer, rambled Zero. The sharpest eye, the steadiest hand, the surest gun, and—to a great degree—the luckiest shooter would win.

Laurel remained quiet during the next few evenings, while Zero paced the floor as he talked. He had limited himself to a drink a night to sharpen his aim. She had never seen him so intent on winning, and she regretted that she would not view the process, could not. On the eve of the contest, however, he remarked that Hachère expected her to be among the spectators.

Too patiently, she replied that neither betting nor the spirited competition interested her. "Of course, you'll go!" he replied, as if she had been teasing.

"I can't." Laurel's voice remained level, but she feared he knew her well enough to catch the overcontrol which signified the edge of panic.

Zero walked over and caught her shoulders firmly. "You've refused to go hunting with me many a time and that's normal, I suppose, but tell me, Laurel, does my contest shooting all of a sudden bore you?"

"No, but I'd like to avoid Hachère. He makes me fidgety. So does Paul."

Zero's snort was hale, contemptuous. "Now, Laurel! I'll tell you about these French men. They're trained from the time they go to dancing school to make a fuss over women. You might as well get used to it. Anyway, Paul, he knows I'd wipe the earth up with him if he so much as winks at you when I'm not around. It's all a big show. Like a parlor game. They feel safe with husbands standing by. Laurel, in your lingo, it's a very sophisticated courtesy over here. Now, why don't you grow up?"

She surged against him, burying her face in the wool of his sweater rather than chance his reading her mind. Then, to her dismay, she began to cry.

Zero's arms tightened in confused surprise. "Why? Laurel, for Christ's sake?"

She did not reply. Zero gave her his handkerchief and turned away. Laurel wiped her eyes and blew her nose, watching his grace of movement as he sauntered to the fireplace and leaned against the mantel with his back to her.

"Hachère said he wouldn't let you get bored. He said he'll be a spectator too because his eyesight is too dull to sight live birds. He isn't fooling me for a minute. The old bastard knows he couldn't win if he shot a fifty-millimeter cannon, and he's too tight to shoot pigeons at a dollar a bird."

He flopped onto the little loveseat and stretched his legs toward the hearth. Aloud, he computed: Two sets of three rounds each, ten birds per round. Sixty birds. And three—no—four hundred dollars' worth of francs for the betting. It would depend how his luck held in the first set, said Zero.

Laurel, seated in the little armchair to the left of the hearth, said without emotion, "That's half a month's salary, almost."

"Well, what the Hell? It won't harelip the firm if we have to dig a little in your ten thousand per annum while we're over here."

"It's never been that much until this past year. After all, Zero, the bottom could drop out of sugar anytime. I never want us to get used to living off that. We went seven good years without an inheritance. I still feel queer about getting a windfall from an old lady I can't even remember having seen."

"That's a nice way to talk about your father's mother!" He laughed wryly. "Doesn't seem to bother you when you put on her sable coat."

"That's different! If I hadn't taken it, some housemaid would have."

Zero frowned contemplatively: "Someday, you're going to have to make up your mind to sell her town house in New Orleans. The idea, Laurel—letting those DAR's use it for an office!"

"They're not DAR's! It's a society for the restoration of period houses."

"How much do you think it's worth?"

"Not much. She kept it for sentimental reasons. Went there as a bride, and lived there until Grandfather Deschamps sort of reclaimed the family status—financially."

"I know why you don't want to sell the other house."

"Why?"

"You gotta thing about being born there."

"Maybe."

"You realize, Laurel, if you liquidated both those houses and that thousand acres Paradis is on, we'd have a quarter of a million dollars?"

"And do you realize, Zero, by the time Brick and Chris are grown up, a quarter of a million dollars might not be much. Zero, land may decrease in value but it never shrinks."

"That scarcely applies to houses."

"You're right."

"But what?"

"Your hair's too blond. You've got the wrong complexion to go with cirrhosis of the liver."

"You bitch," he said lovingly.

11

Laurel was dressed and ready to leave the house when Zero said, "You look like a French peasant in that God damned trench coat. Laurel, the Mayor of Beaumonde, or the Governor of Gregny may be there today. Let's not go native yet!"

Annoyed, she returned to the bedroom and changed into a mauve-toned herringbone suit with its matching topcoat lined in gray caracul. In gray suède boots and gloves, and a tiny black velvet cap billed in black grosgrain, she was a picture of careful, restrained but whimsical elegance. She knew that Zero would be pleased but that the beige-poplined French matrons would gradually move away and leave her to the mercy of Hachères. She stared carefully at her mirrored reflection and said to herself, "In the scheme of things eternal, does it really matter?"

Shortly thereafter she stood gazing out of the spectator shed across winter sod to the concrete stands from which the contestants shot. Beside her, Mama Hachère boasted fiercely, "Oui, Monsieur Vervins is a very rich man. He was a gifted marksman and a magnificent sportsman. You should have seen him a few years ago at his prime. Voyez! He is seventy-one years old! And what courage! Oh, the tragedies he has survived!"

Zero had won the first set and was now halfway toward victory in the second and final contest. After his turn came Vervins who, out-of-doors and with spurts of cloud breath steaming from his nostrils, resembled some spry giant of middle age.

At the close of the contest, he paused beside the car where Laurel waited in relief from the biting mist. As she rolled down the window, he said, "But you are coming to my house with the others? There is already champagne chilled for the vin d'honneur!"

"No one told me."

Vervins' brows leapt up in dramatic surprise and his arms soared skyward. The old fellow was nearly as tall as Zero and a third again as broad.

"After all," he bellowed, "how can we drink the day's toasts without the champion?" He halted, breaking into a smile and cocking his head forward, adding, "And his beautiful wife!"

Vervins strode away, his face still wreathed in a smile, as Zero got into the car and settled his gun into its case. Laurel repeated with gestures the old fellow's performance, sighing afterwards, "He's the dearest person I've met in France. The only gentle man."

Zero did not catch her meaning. He snorted, "He's a farmer, Laurel. A rich farmer and a damned swell egg. But he's no gentleman."

She forced a rebuttal to die on her lips, for what more stupid argument was there than that of gentle heart against pedigree?

They were the last to reach Vervins' sprawling farm, where they joined a jovial mass of people who clung about a table of empty glasses. After the host wrenched the cork from a moisture-beaded bottle, he handed the first filled glass to Laurel.

Vervins offered a convivial salute to the winner, and to his beautiful wife, and to the "eternity of friendship between our countries." Laurel squared her shoulders to offset a piquant stab of emotion. She glanced toward Zero, who did not notice her, for he was encircled by a cordon of admirers.

Zero hoisted his glass in a gesture which evoked sudden quiet, "I drink to the kindness of France," he declared huskily, "and to the warmth you have shown me." His eyes found Laurel now. "I drink to my second country!"

The guests mingled noisily, but Laurel, French-blooded or not, admitted that she had never felt more of an outsider in her life. The French matrons, about a dozen in all, behaved as if the crowd consisted entirely of men. This no longer disconcerted Laurel after the bridge evenings where, except for lavish, fluttery greetings and good-byes, women simply ignored each other's presence. Even so, she felt obliged to admit that this was an improvement over the American military party system by which wives gossiped around the coffee table while their husbands told military secrets and dirty jokes in the kitchen.

Suddenly, a man lifted his glass and delivered a risqué toast that brought howling laughter. Laurel missed the joke but she recognized the speaker. She had not met him, but had noticed him hovering at Zero's elbow when neither was firing. Laurel remembered, watching him across Vervins' dining room, his concern with the angle at which his broken .210 Browning teetered over his forearm between rounds as if he had been a male model posing for a photograph.

She laughed to herself, watching him hold his audience with a regular machine-gun flow of words to which she paid no heed, for she was absorbed with his staging. As he stepped up on the hearth, he grew about three inches higher. Laurel moved to one side and had a clear view of him which included his low slung paunch. Textbook plate of a Norman, she thought; Grandfather Aimes used to say they were all born talking.

When Zero edged nearby, he whispered, "Remember his jokes!"

"Who is he?"

"His name is. . . . I don't know. I have his calling card in my pocket."

"His calling card?" she asked softly. "What does he sell?"

"We'll talk later. Remember the jokes!"

Laurel dutifully turned away toward the speaker, who was saying, "And so I said to the man, 'No, I have no idea what they call people who practice the rhythm system of birth control. Do tell me!'" He stared at the floor in an effective pause, afterwards closing his joke with a whispered word: *"Parents!"*

The crowd guffawed, with the exception of Zero, who smiled wistfully, and Vervins, who was making his way slowly toward Laurel. "Chère Madame!" he cried, as he bent down, "You are neglected!"

"Oh, no, Monsieur! Your house has its own special air of welcome!"

With a dubious smile, the oldster peered into his champagne

glass. "For you to be lost in this miserable section of France is worse than losing a pearl in an oyster!" Laurel laughed at his figure of speech. At once, he objected: "Do not laugh, Madame! It saddens me to realize that thirty years ago, I should have been able to show you the beauties of Vichy, Cannes, Deauville, Biarritz, the high spots of France."

She twinkled, unwilling to retort that thirty years ago, she had been a year and ten months old. Instead she asked, "What would we do with my husband?"

Vervins' shrug was pleased. "We would take him, if he insisted!" But as their laughter ran down, he showed sadness in his face. "Two wars. Today, I own little more than what you have seen driving here."

Laurel replied that war had taken its toll on landowners in America. "I was born in New Orleans, but the house in which I grew up—near Baton Rouge—once centered a ten-thousand acre grant. Today, it has less than a tenth of that, and the house is crumbling." A shadow crossed her face. "Since the last war, you see, it costs more in America to repair such a house than the house is worth. Monsieur, no American today would buy a house that size except a politician or a gangster. Anyway, it is difficult to put a price on two hundred years of tradition and heritage."

She took a cigarette from the pocket of her mauve suit and Vervins' arm swung up with a flame from a wooden match which he had ignited by a jerk across the seat of his trousers.

"I have not seen a man who could light a match that way since the day my Grandfather Aimes went to bed for good, Monsieur!"

"Ah!" he cried with a new found laugh, "If I am granted one prayer, it will be to die standing up!" He shook his head in emphasis.

He lumbered away, dropping pleased chuckles in his wake, and leaving behind him a solemn, eavesdropping Hachère. "It is a long time, Madame Compton, since I have had the pleasure of seeing you."

His grieved tone disconcerted Laurel. For a moment, she was tempted to thank him for the flowers, but common sense forbade this. Instead she replied, "I hear your name very often in my house. You are exceedingly considerate of my husband." Then she saw her solution; why hadn't she realized it before? "Monsieur," she added softly, "I feel it my duty to confide to you that in coming to Monceau that day, you avoided your son by little more than an hour."

Laurel turned into the hall before he could register his shock or chagrin. He wouldn't come again, for she had left open the question of whether Paul was welcome. Now, she had only to hint to Paul of Papa's coming, and he too would avoid her house except by invitation. She had her arms half into her coat when Zero caught it by the collar and swept it on. Why was she smiling? Too much champagne, answered Laurel. They went through protracted farewells.

As Zero started the motor, the joke teller popped his head into the car window on Laurel's side. "Oh," he cried to Zero, "I feared I had lost you!" Laurel's gaze fell to his delicate fingers gripping the rim of the car window. He had a round hand, tapering and rather plump, each knuckle signposted with a flag of dimple.

"We don't need introducing," he addressed Laurel. "Your husband told me of your interest in art."

She stared at him, thinking, If you're not a queer, I'm a chimpanzee's mustache and that's not likely.

"I have a small château not far from here with a few fair paintings." She said nothing. He shifted back to Zero. "I was wondering, would you two have tea with me on Saturday?"

Abruptly, Laurel inclined her face to signal a discreet negative to Zero, but it was too late. The two men immediately began discussing the route to his château.

Laurel laughed when they were safely out of the drive. Defensively, Zero said, "There's your gentleman. The only one in the Redan-Beaumonde radius."

"But you're out of character, Zero. I never thought I'd see the day you'd accept *anybody's* bid to tea."

"We're in France," he retorted sharply, digging into his green suède coat to hand over a Continental-sized calling card of fine quality and engraving. Laurel read "Le Marquis de Berteaux." I don't care, she said to herself as she tossed the card onto the dashboard, he still looks like a fairy.

A mile of silence went by, and another. Zero said softly, "A penny?"

"Bel Ami."

"Who's he?"

"A character from de Maupassant."

"So?"

"He died in a duel."

"So?"

"Trying to buy a title."

Their eyes met and held the length of time Zero dared ignore the narrow black-topped road at seventy-five miles an hour. "You're going to tea."

"You don't want him for a friend."

"He's got five thousand acres of land in one tract, all planted with pheasant, deer, and partridge."

"He's got limp wrists."

"By God, I wouldn't mind having a friend I wouldn't have to worry about when I'm out of town overnight."

Anger rose in Laurel until, from the corner of her eye, she caught his mischievous look. Calmly, she said, "That narrows the field to Edney, Abach, and Vervins."

"How so?"

"I like all three of them." Zero did not laugh, as she expected, so she took a different tack. "I suppose at my age, most wives would be flattered. But I know you, Zero. You're as certain of me as you are of sunrise. You don't know how to worry."

"I have nothing to worry about. You're irreproachable. You haven't got the guts to break a Commandment. Anyway, I have a piece of paper that says you're mine, and you know, much as I love you, I wouldn't hesitate five minutes to take the children if you ever start bitching around."

Laurel dealt forcefully with herself in a struggle for the calm necessary to ward off this unprecedented, undeserved blast. Then, unwillingly, a tiny candle flame of suspicion was allowed to brighten. "Zero," she began, "I should have known there was some reason you sent Abach's car to Paris by an airman."

His knuckles were white on the wheel. "God damn it, the son

of a bitch ought to know better than to write letters addressed to you as if I didn't exist."

"What did he say?" murmured Laurel, her eye on the speedometer needle now at eighty-two miles an hour.

"He said if you couldn't persuade me to get away for a weekend in Paris that he'd like for you and the children to come. He had two bedrooms in his apartment."

Oh, God! I know them both too well. Complete security is always just out of Zero's reach and Abach's so pure-hearted. Oh, my God! It's the end—the end. There's nothing I can say to mend it . . . oh, my God. . . .

12

Laurel's hostility toward the Marquis was kept alive during the week by two telephone calls. He wanted to make sure both times that directions to his estate were clear. She begged Zero to go alone, but he refused and seemed to take delight in her aversion.

Twenty minutes after they left Monceau, the Comptons were speeding by a head-high brick fence recognizable from the description provided by its owner, except that he had neglected to mention a weathered sign reading, "U.S. Go Home!" Laurel was prepared for an ornate country house, but not for the three-storied Georgian mansion of silver-flecked white granite. The shrubbery was freshly groomed. The grounds were spacious; the drives and walks asymmetrically spaced. Massive oaks centering either side of the lawn were regal in a spread of five or six hundred years.

Berteaux sprang to the side of the car from the grande porte across the veranda, and bounced onto the drive. Stepping back and forth, he chattered gaily, while Zero parked the car.

Zero frowned at Laurel when she asked the Marquis why he had left the anti-American slogan on his fence. "Why, to tell the complete truth, I have been rather pleased with the way that one is fading." He turned to Zero. "These naughty French would only paint a new one beside it. Surely, *you* understand?"

As he spoke animatedly to Zero, her gaze roamed the vast foyer—its floor of snowy marble, its wall plastered and painted in stark white, the Gothic double doors of oak at front and back, and, off to the right, a spiral stairway railed in black wrought iron. Mentally, Laurel placed Persian rugs, leather couches, lion-footed ebony tables, and mammoth water-color-tinted lithographs of hunting scenes in groupings about the hall.

Discreetly over her tea cup, she studied Michel Berteaux for a sign of aristocracy in façade or manner, but there was only his elegant, flexible English. He had a British accent which reminded Laurel of a Jamaican Negro who had been the first butler she could remember at Paradis.

She was aghast at the three floors of paintings he invited them to view. The plumbing fixtures, flooring, and the door fastenings throughout the house proved it to be of twenties vintage. Rebuilt, said Berteaux, after 'eighteen. Laurel saw that the paintings appeared three and four hundred years old. After Berteaux had shown them some of his own work—unframed water colors, charcoals, and pastels of commendable style—she had a nagging, if unlikely, suspicion about the authenticity of the massive paintings on his walls. Copying would have required interminable hours, but Berteaux' own small pieces showed astounding skill!

Then he showed the Americans two rooms of ruined furniture, a veritable graveyard of once regal pieces. He explained that since he had no family to house, no entertaining to be done, he found it feasible to send the furniture for repair only as reparations payments afforded. The Germans had vandalized every item in the house, he insisted, while Laurel's gaze narrowed on a standing portrait of a lady in Empire costume, a painting which covered half the wall.

As if he might have been reading her mind, Berteaux said, "Feel the nail holes there in the paneled frame? They are left from false walls which hid these pictures from those Germans."

Yes, thought Laurel, he certainly bought himself a bargain!

Back on the first floor, he fondled the wall thermostat, and spoke then of the injustice done him by an American couple from the Air Base, to whom he had offered shelter—on the condition that they board him and pay the fuel bill. No rent. No other utilities. But it had been over a year since they came to see the house. They had promised to return for him the following week and settle the details over a meal in the Officers' Mess, but they had stood him up.

Laurel longed to retort that Americans couldn't live in a house with a thermostat kept at fifty degrees, or in one without furniture. As she regarded his mended sweater she wondered if he had sunk his wad in the house and paintings, expecting to recover with revenue from tenant Americans.

It did not matter, for she had no intention of seeing him again, and she hoped that Zero had had enough of his magpie chatter. But when her husband proposed to end the two-hour visit, Berteaux exhibited such regret that Zero insisted he accompany them home.

His answer was to scurry about barring windows and locking doors. He drove behind them to Monceau where, determined to insult him permanently, Laurel gave the new maid, a veritable jewel she had located two weeks earlier through the employment agency, unexpected time off. Afterwards, with the children bundled into the car, they drove to the Air Base, to a boarded tent called the snack bar. Zero and Michel went inside and stood in a line of airmen for a sack of hamburgers and soggy French-fries.

Zero returned to the car complaining. Michel Berteaux's excitement, however, was similar to that of an American tourist leaving his first Left Bank "cave." In fact, he was so excited that when he attempted to hand Laurel a poorly capped carton, her leather-lined purse was suddenly full of milkshake. The baby began to cry, and Brick said without whispering, "Laurel, why'd that man do that? I *like* milkshake."

She snapped the purse shut on a half pint of liquid, as she felt more of it seeping into her shoe. Michel Berteaux was so abject, so distraught, that Laurel tried to belittle chaos. Apparently she succeeded, for he remained long after Zero exited apologetically for his bed. Berteaux stayed until six o'clock Sunday morning, whereafter Laurel hated him in earnest. There was no sense in her going to bed at that hour with no maid.

Next day, Zero took off for a four-day conference in Germany with Fritsch, and a week later, Laurel kissed him goodbye before his ten-day trip to Vienna. That night Brick went to bed with a mild fever. Next morning, a dispensary doctor informed her the child had measles, the twenty-first case he had seen in the current cycle. This encounter was undramatic until Laurel mentioned that she had an infant of nearly ten months.

"If he were mine, I wouldn't go to bed tonight without finding some gamma globulin for him. Measles are dangerous at his age." He explained to Laurel that a fifty-bed field hospital was not allowed to store "gg," but that there was a French pediatrician in Beaumonde who could order a full series from Paris.

Unnerved by the physician's rather detailed account of measles meningitis, and other terrifying possibilities, Laurel sped home with Brick. She took Chris to Beaumonde where, in an alley darkened by three-story structures on either side, she located the miniature gold-lettered plaque of a Dr. Necchi.

Seated across from him, cuddling her baby and outlining her mission, she saw that the balding man was amenable enough. He remarked to her that in the two years since the Base came, she was his first American client. When Laurel sought his commitment about the gamma globulin, he switched to questions about her infant's diet, development pattern, and general regime: then he scolded her sharply against too much milk drinking. "Wine, Madame! A little water with it, but it is time for wine! Milk is bad for the liver, once bones have a proper start."

She longed to say, Drop dead twice! Time was closing in. Chris was in potential danger, perhaps grave danger. Rather desperately, she rephrased her request.

"Madame! Madame!" he spattered air through pursed lips. "I once saw a man fall on the curb and break his skull, but it has never discouraged me from walking! Let your baby have measles if he must. Sooner or later, they all get them!"

She fled from his office without paying, without thanking him, or even saying good day. Back at Monceau, her spirits fell further. Brick was glassy-eyed with a sharply rising temperature. Aspirin, cold enemas, alcohol rubs, and her night-long vigil notwithstanding, the fever held at 105 until next morning around ten when, mottled and heavy-lidded, the boy fell asleep. She settled Brick in his own bed and hurried from the room, attention now turned to Chris.

In her desperation Laurel found a solution. Abach could get his hands on gamma globulin in five minutes, and he could put it on a train. But she did not want to talk to him, not after Zero's reaction to his letter.

Laurel went into the kitchen. "Olande!" she said softly, "you must place a telephone call for me to the American Hospital in Paris, and ask for Dr. Abach." She spelled the name in French letter-sounds, and carefully explained the entire message. The maid got the call through in good time and spoke intelligently.

Laurel fell into a half-sleep on the loveseat. Shortly before three o'clock Olande rushed in to whisper excitedly that a car with an American license was being parked in the courtyard. Laurel sat up, blinked at expectant Olande, and said, "He doesn't know where Monceau is, or the house. . . ." But a tidal wave of relief swept through her drained body. She bounded from the salon into the foyer where Abach was closing the outside door. Three or four feet from him, she froze, remembering Zero. Neither she nor Abach extended a hand.

His eyes were measuring the pale violet circles and drawn cheeks as he sat his black bag on the umbrella stand and pocketed his gray gloves. Clinical scrutiny from Abach filled her with dread. She could not speak as he opened the ominous kit. From a small bottle, he shook out a vermilion capsule, and from another, a white pill.

A sigh caught in Laurel's throat. "See the children quickly and I'll have Olande dream up some sort of dinner for us. We can sit up and talk all night. I've a million things to ask you, and about two thousand to tell you." A dry sob, unexpected and unnatural, interrupted her speech. "Oh, Abach! I've been so lonely!"

He palmed the medicine and slung his cap at a hook. Then he ducked past her into the kitchen and she heard the sound of gushing water. Laurel spun around and followed him. Abach held a coffee mug filled with Monceau water. Fighting down tears, she managed a pleading smile.

She murmured in mock obedience: "All right! I surrender, but would it be asking too much just to hear the sound of your voice, or has the cat got your tongue?"

"I have two things to say to you, Laurel. Welcome to France, and open your mouth!"

In fleet motion, her hand swiped his and came away with both pills. "Good-bye, cruel world!" she sighed in exhausted farce. Then she reached for the water.

13

In midafternoon, Laurel sauntered into the yard for the dozenth time that day, marveling at the warmth and buoyancy of sundrenched air. Beside a tree-shaped holly bush, she regarded the mat of glossy green spiked leaves which knew no seasonal death. Of course, she reflected, spring's return always brought renewed hope. Suddenly, a pleat of color caught her eye and she dropped beside the holly tree to gaze at a pink crocus.

In the distance a dove mourned, a French dove, but she imagined she was in Louisiana and heard the cry of a small boy who ran behind, furious at being unable to catch his sister. Brick interrupted her reverie by shouting, "Laurel! Laurel! What is it? A worm?"

She swallowed a throat full of hot tears and said in a choked voice, "I'm sorry, Brick, it's only a flower."

Later when they took Chris into the garden to see the progress of the pink crocus, they found another one burst through the soil and three promises in nearby cracks. While the three were bent down, she heard the plane in the distance. It was headed directly toward Monceau. Zero soon zoomed about three hundred feet above the chimney. Both children squealed in joy. Laurel's eyes danced at the prospect of being with Zero and hearing about Rome, where he had been for the past few days. She reflected upon their recent state of rapport: Zero had been understanding about and thankful for Abach's visit.

However, Zero entered his house complaining of bone-gnawing fatigue. He had four drinks in the hour before dinner, and afterwards, when the children were settled for the night, he stretched out across the springless loveseat, which, as ever, did not fit him.

Through five or six silent minutes, Laurel tried to think of something to say which would interest him. During dinner they had discussed Chris's new tooth and his walking, a recently acquired skill. Brick had given his father an encyclopedic account of the afternoon's adventures in flora and fauna. With a sigh, Laurel took up her handwork, adding to the sounds of burning wood the click of aluminum knitting needles in the quiet room.

Tensed by the duration of silence, she thought half wistfully of the soothing brandy, but it would never do to have Zero suspect she could condone drinking on the grounds of boredom. She glanced up at him, finding his eyes on her. He arose as if her scrutiny released him, crossed the little space, and kissed her good night. At the door to the hall, he tossed back an apologetic grin.

Scarcely had he closed the door when the cuckoo shot out of his den for seven counts. Rage consumed Laurel. A husband for ninety minutes! With exploding fury, she flung her bundled knitting at the clock, but missed it by a foot or more. Irked even with herself now, she strode over to pick up the ball of yarn, a futile little smile twisting her lips as she watched the half-finished sock jerk closer like a bass plug on dry sand.

Too restive to sit still, she walked to the windows, a split second before the blinding, white flash enveloped her. A vicious crack of thunder jarred the whole house. A deluge broke against the slate roof, wind slapped the panes wetly and shrieked its siren atop the chimney. She heard above the cacophony of the storm a sound like knocking. A loose shutter somewhere, she reasoned, but the sound grew urgent, almost impatient. Probably some American lost on the road, or a Frenchman wanting to know the way to the Reims highway, or a neighbor needing to telephone a doctor.

Laurel crossed the foyer and opened the door, scarcely prepared for the burst of gale which threatened to jerk the knob from her hand. Occupied with halting the heavy arc before the door slammed against the wall, she heard Berteaux's voice before she saw him.

"What took you so long? I'm *drowning!*"

"What a night to be out!" she exclaimed with distinctly loaded meaning as they shook hands. Then she caught the expectant, almost tense expression, that of a small boy who expects his new haircut, his birthday tie, or even the grass snake in his pocket to be noticed. Laurel glanced beyond him into the murky blackness but found only the silver lace of after-image.

Suddenly, her hand tightened on the door; the outline merged into being, a pair of eyes in a misted oval. The face had that keenly chiseled perfection highly prized of stage and screen. He had a widow's peak above the classic brow and a cleft in his chin.

"Well!" chortled Michel Berteaux. "What's happened to you two? No use, she's married!" Then, he added in afterthought, "To a champion sharpshooter!"

"You must forgive my rude friend!" It was not the resonance which surprised her, but the intimacy of his voice, as if only the two of them in all the world understood how really rude Berteaux was.

"Yes, he might at least have introduced you!"

For Laurel, handshaking in France had become so habitual as to be reflexive, and Guy de Brières took her hand, but he paused part of a second to scan her face once more, not as if something were passing between them, but rather as if already they shared some unknown bond.

Smiling faintly, he turned away to remove and hang his coat. Laurel's eyes were downcast, seemingly riveted on Michel's tapping toe. His silence was sinister in its very length, she realized before their gazes met, his leering insinuation. Then a movement at the salon door drew all three pairs of eyes.

Zero stood framed in the door. Because Laurel and Michel were watching him, they both missed the flat spark of recognition which for an instant kindled Guy's eyes. Laurel felt relief that Zero had not stalked out of the bedroom in his drawers.

"Zero!" exulted Michel, rushing toward him, his hand out, "I have brought my oldest, closest friend for you to meet. This is the Count of Brières."

As the night wore on, Laurel felt less and less a part of the foursome. Guy's moth-balled English disconcerted her to such an extent that her own English began to stumble. "And you like Michel have no wife, alas?"

Zero snickered indiscreetly, but the tall Frenchman rushed a covering retort, "Alas is right!"

She glanced from one bachelor to the other and asked what was wrong with modern France's young manhood. Berteaux sprang up and crossed the salon to snuff out a half-finished cigarette in a clean ashtray, saying, "I chose freedom!"

Brières gave him a patient, tolerant look. "Truthfully, we are sickened by our mothers' planting eligible girls at luncheon tables. We must choose our own."

They began then to talk of the war, but when Zero expressed a wish to hear about Brières' experiences after the fall of France, Michel jumped up and demanded that Guy play the piano. His modest exhibition proved that he also sang, but to Laurel his tunes were on the melancholy side. Perhaps he was depressed that night, for, when she returned to the room after a brief absence to look at the children, he was leaning against the piano, saying that France was finished.

"It is done, Michel. We will never be again. . . ."

Having no idea that eulogizing his country's mondial demise

could be consoling to a devout Frenchman, Laurel said brightly, "Then why not migrate to America?"

Michel stood up and asked Zero to come with him to the kitchen; he needed a fresh drink. Arm in arm, the pair left the salon. Laurel heard the door snap on their companionable chatter.

They were alone, Guy and Laurel, and her unfortunate question lingered between them.

"France is my home, Laurel. My *home*, no matter how finished she may be."

Yes. Yes, of course. But how beautiful my name sounds upon his lips. Helpless to avoid his eyes, she looked up slowly into his waiting face. "But, Guy, what do you bequeath your children by staying in a country you admit to be finished?"

His laugh chimed emptily, "What children?"

"You make it sound as if children are a cardinal sin!"

"My dear Laurel," he said, "children are a cardinal blessing. As Romans, you and I. . . ."

She interrupted, "I am not Roman."

"Well, you are *something*?" Guy's eyes darted now from her face to the trim lines of her toreador pants. "I am sorry, Laurel, to touch a point of sensitivity."

Perplexed, she asked, "What are you saying?"

"My poor choice of repartee. For various reasons, I never expect to be blessed with children, but it becomes obvious that I have been too little in the world of women or I should have noticed."

Her gaze flew instantly to her abdomen, as if in these minutes she might have suddenly sprouted evidence of a pregnancy not known to herself. She glanced up at Guy, her mouth ajar.

"Yes, Laurel, it should have been evident to me that with your child's body, no man would hazard your life with . . . no doctor would countenance. . . ."

Her lips curled in a smile, her eyes widened merrily as she understood. Laurel reached for his hand and led him down the hall to the first bedroom where, by the faint nightlight which burned continually from sunset until dawn, they bent above the sleeping children, and where, with a warning finger across her lips, Laurel pointed out the source of snoring in one corner, the unsuspecting Olande.

They regained the salon seconds before Zero and Michel emerged with fresh drinks. "Laurel," said Zero, "I'm getting the dry heaves from all this Scotch. How about some sausage and eggs—and maybe hot biscuits?"

She glanced up at the cuckoo clock: a quarter before two. The four went to the kitchen, where Laurel began to knead biscuit dough. Michel complained of an old back injury and the straight chair. He and Zero departed for the salon. When the room was silent, deathly silent, Laurel turned from the sinkboard to see if Guy was still there.

"I supposed you'd gone with the men," smiled Laurel.

"I should have," he said flatly.

"But what?" She concentrated on scraping glutenous dough to the end of each finger.

"But I should enjoy very much to hear about this house."

Surprised, she regarded him, but he was not joking. So she pulled no punches. Guy listened thoughtfully, getting up from time to time to add two or three lumps of coal to the fire box of the coal range.

By the time he went to the salon to summon the others to come and eat, Guy de Brières knew a great deal more than Zero Compton about the history of his household in the Monceau dwelling. Laurel saw no oddity in this; Zero would have been upset, while Guy listened in the manner of a deeply concerned but unemotional friend.

Yes, Guy had all the qualities of a cherished, long-time friend. That was exactly the sum total, thought Laurel, at the door where the four exchanged their dawn good nights. Michel spent a final burst. He and Guy were going to take Zero hunting all the way from Germany to Spain in the coming two winters. For Laurel, he added, there would be couturier openings, opera, museums, sight-seeing, and everything!

"We're going to show you Paris!" he extolled.

Guy's arm swung up. He laughed softly as he placed a restraining hand on Michel's arm. "No, we're going to show Paris Laurel!"

Behind a shielding hand, she gave birth to a yawn but she laughed agreeably. Tentacled in Zero's arms and legs some seven hours later, she awoke clawing his chest in her urgency to have him awake. "Zero!" She shook him until his eyes opened. Instantly, she whispered: "We can't go!"

"Where?"

"With them."

"Who?"

"Last night."

"Oh?"

"Paris."

Awake now, Zero loosened her grip and raised himself on an elbow, trying to appear serious. Why? he asked with a quick grin. They're queers, replied Laurel, guileless. Zero collapsed against his pillow. His laughter boomed in the huskiness of too much smoking, too much drinking, and of waking at an unusual hour.

"Oh, God!" he cried. "Every man in the world needs a wife like you. You're an unpredictable bitch, Laurel, but nobody will ever accuse you of being dull!"

In the succeeding weeks of May, narcissus, daffodils, tulips, and gladioli lifted Monceau's face. Forsythia and japonica merged their yellow and vermilion tours. Higher up, green-gold jeweled twigs and branches. Earth was the loveliest of goddesses, rising from cold sleep and Laurel was a placid worshiper caught and carried in heady procession toward the altar of pastoral beauty.

Finding the landlady in the foyer a few mornings after Guy's visit, Laurel was pleased to see that spring had made Madame almost good humored. After restraining herself through conventional exchanges, Laurel said, "We have met a very interesting French person in the region, a Monsieur Berteaux who lives between Monceau and Redan. You have heard of the Château de Noël?"

The landlady frowned skeptically, and gave her slow negative nod. Was Madame Compton certain it was a château? Had she been there? Why? In the onslaught of questions, Laurel smilingly changed the subject and thought no more of investigating Michel Berteaux until next day, when she entered her kitchen as Olande was putting to soak a fine armload of violet-tipped white asparagus. The girl explained that the gift came from Mademoiselle Lily, the old maid who lived four houses down the road. "You know, Madame, the one whose fiancé was killed in the war of 1914, and afterwards, Mademoiselle vowed never to be courted, or to marry."

The first time Laurel had approached her, Mlle Lily had insisted that she be seated in the pristine "Company" house—six rooms of provincial furnishings which few of the villagers had seen because Lily existed in two rooms adjacent to the barn. While her farming acreage was vast and she was regarded as Monceau's "rich woman," she tolerated no servant. She supervised her fields and spent the remainder of her time polishing the virgin cottage in which no one lived.

The asparagus prompted Laurel to pay another call on Lily. This time she was asked to take tea. Afterwards she waited until she was outside the rusted black iron gate and had pushed it shut before asking Lily, as if in afterthought, whether she knew a Monsieur Berteaux. Lily wagged a careful no.

"He lives near Redan," said Laurel with a casual sigh. "You were raised in this vicinity, weren't you?" Lily nodded. Laurel shrugged and pursed her lips in unconscious mimicry of the older woman. She leaned close to the gate and whispered: "You disappoint me not to have some gossip of the only Marquis in the region!" Laurel carefully lifted one brow: "He is single."

"Ah!" cried Lily on an intake of breath. "A *marquis?*" Laurel shrugged. "He said *that?*" screeched the spinster as her brows lifted wrinkles into her hairline. "No, petite Américaine, no real marquis stops in Monceau unless his car goes en panne." But Lily wedged her face between a pair of grills to whisper: "Was he good looking?" (Est il beau?)

"Ah, oui!" cried Laurel with unbounded verve. "His teeth are the color of café au lait, and his face looks as if it were originally painted on an egg. It is the reason I believed him authentic—for we read in books that nobility is now inbred and often grotesque!" But Lily could not reply, could not even wag her head in accord. Bent double, she wept in her mirth.

Laurel's question remained unanswered. On the following Wednesday morning, she found another person to ask—Regina Edney.

"The Marquis de Berteaux? I don't know. Some Gilbert and Sullivan fob? By Jove, Laurel! You're trying to trick me!"

After Laurel explained that he was a bachelor whom Zero had met at the Beaumonde Shooting Club, and that he claimed a title, Regina exploded: "Well, let him!"

"You don't understand. You'd have to see him—"

"I'm terribly sorry," replied the gregarious Britisher with extra layers of accent, "I've more in my own ménage than I can handle."

"More what?"

"More sex! That's what! And, I say! Why should you be rousting up spares when you're married to the original Swedish stallion!"

"*Regina!*"

"Oh, all right! What's bothering you about this phony Marquis?"

"I've only seen him two or three times, but they were extremely long times," she faltered. "I need his background—"

"Why?"

"To protect Zero."

Regina's murmured oath was inaudible. "Is that the whole story?"

"Last week, the Marquis brought a friend who claims to be a Count. The latter lives at Reims—I mean he lives in a Paris apartment by himself. His mother lives at Reims. He was raised there."

Regina's eyes were too contemplative, too smug on Laurel. "Which one is it you really want to know about?"

"Berteaux doesn't live far from us."

"Where?"

"Near Redan. He calls his château 'Noël'."

"I never fool around north of Beaumonde. That area's too full of steel mills and hotheads. Louis had a chance to get us a good deal on a big house up there. The house is white granite, must be twenty-five rooms. The owner wanted us to pay the oil bill and board him, and bring our own furniture. It would have been a good deal for us—and for him, too."

"Why didn't you take it?" asked Laurel quietly, recalling in full Michel's account of the American couple who had stood him up.

Regina shrugged, "I wanted to. We were still in the Écu Hotel in Beaumonde, and it was breaking us. But Louis can't be budged when he makes up his mind, Laurel. He and this Mike Besse met the next morning without me. When Louis came back to the hotel that afternoon, he told me to forget the whole thing."

"Mike Besse?" murmured Laurel thoughtfully.

It was two weeks after Laurel had met Guy that Michel returned. Near four o'clock on a Friday afternoon, he burst through the open door in a breathless flurry. "I've just time for a spot of tea with you while I deliver my messages. Guy and I are both free the first week end in June. It's Pentecost, Laurel, and everybody who's anybody will be out of Paris, but the four of us can make our own fun."

"All right, Mike Besse."

His smile was more self-conscious than amazed. "It's a nickname I use with provincial Americans," he said.

"That's me."

"You're pastoral," he protested.

"And of course, you'd like to paint me?" Her grin was enigmatic.

"How did you know?"

"Conversation opener. Early American."

"You're flip!"

Laurel said, "Your family's name is Besse?"

"Éluard-Besse of Rouen," he murmured with a sort of negligent pride—the way an American might have said Dupont of Dover or Washington of Virginia.

When tea was over he said nothing at all about leaving. In fact, he remained quite naturally, and without being invited, through dinner and until ten o'clock that evening. Laurel found the house almost pleasant when emptied of his incessant chatter, his nervous pacing.

Next day at noon when Zero returned from a flight to Berlin, she told him of Michel's visit. He seemed amused, almost delighted. "He's a real character, Laurel. You keep him on the string and I'll be bringing home the boar-bacon next winter! And the same thing goes for Guy! Christ, yes!—we'll go with them to Paris."

Perhaps Laurel told Zero of Michel's stay out of a fair assurance that the Frenchman would have mentioned it to her husband sooner or later. She did not ask herself why she failed to tell him of Guy's midmorning arrival a week later. He looked for all the world like a Saturday-morning American—open shirt, cashmere sweater, and infectious grin. The scene took a Gallic turn as he brandished from behind his back a mass of cherry and white peonies. Neither of them spoke. Laurel buried her face in the fragrant flowers, and an electric silence pursued them through the foyer and into the salon.

Her cheeks felt hot; her hands were cold. Guy's opening line had the wrongness of a very bad play. "Where is he?"

Laurel breathed too deeply. "He drove to Liège this morning."

"I've found a house—eight kilometers this side of Reims. My mother found it. I have the key, Laurel. . . ." He chuckled in futility. ". . . and I hoped by coming on Saturday to take both of you to see it. . . ."

"That's extremely kind."

"And I took the liberty of saying to my mother that I might bring you both to lunch if we were in the vicinity."

She eyed him thoughtfully. "How far is your mother's place from the vacant house?"

"Ten minutes. Maybe twelve. She's west of Reims."

"Guy, there's no use. It would mean a thirty mile drive each way for Zero—daily."

"I see."

"You shouldn't have gone to such trouble."

"Not at all!" He stood up from the loveseat and came near the window ledge where she sat. Laurel tensed. "Then if the house is out of the question, let us go for lunch?"

"Why does it seem improper," began Laurel, avoiding his eyes, "to meet your mother without my husband?"

Guy took one of her hands. "You are a bit too civilized, Laurel. How did you guess she knows no Americans?"

She stared out the window, afraid to withdraw her hand and afraid to leave it in his. Olande and the children would be returning from the bakery any moment.

"Laurel, let's go to Arcel's."

"Where is that?"

"A country hostelry—twenty minutes or so. . . ." He spoke lightly of the food and atmosphere but she only half heard. In her mind the scene took life—the fun, the revelry of a tête-à-tête lunch with an intelligent, attractive Frenchman. No.

Her eyes met his, her pupils dilated with suppressed panic. She knew that he had felt the faint trembling in her hand.

He said, "You will have me believe Zero beats you!" His tone was teasing, more explicit, more complicit than if he had used a hundred words to say he understood, he had erred, he was sorry.

Her eyes began to feel wet. "Why did you come? We'll all be together next week end in Paris."

Guy dropped her hand and walked away to the mantel. "I came about the house."

"You could have telephoned," replied Laurel, almost accusingly.

"Laurel, do you know what Michel said to me in Paris when he wanted to bring me here that night?" She shook her head vigorously, waiting with a smile. "He said—twenty-five times, at least—'I've found two Americans who are not cowboys.'"

Their laughter collided before Laurel said, "He's so comical!"

Guy's brows lifted. "He's a snob. And you know, Laurel, after we got here that night, he kept signaling for confirmation. I ignored him. When we left, he questioned me even before we got into the car. I can tell you, Laurel, the only thing I enjoyed more than the visit here was refusing to answer him."

In one liquid motion too fleet for her eyes to follow, Guy's hands darted beneath her armpits and lifted her from the floor. He swung her at arm's length; the room made several complete circles. Laurel heard her voice drowned in squeals: Let me down!

Let me down! The loveseat gently met her back. Guy was laughing. She flung a forearm across her face to stop him and the mantel from twirling by again and again.

"Laurel! Who is he? Can I play that game too?" She opened her eyes. Guy was across the room, bent down, talking to Brick and pulling a flat, thin leather-bound book from his pocket. He laid the book on the floor.

Brick sat down and began to leaf through it. "I can't read yet."

"That is why I chose to bring you this dictionary instead of a story book. . . ."

Laurel watched the pair, listened to their easy rapport in French, as Brick asked a natural question. "What shall I call you? Monsieur?" No, his name was Guy. "But Laurel won't let me call you that." Laurel lets you call her Laurel. Brick replied in four-year-old logic, "That's her name." Then what would Laurel permit him to be called? "You know women. She will tell me to call you Uncle."

She picked up her knitting, fingers flying between stitches. On and on their voices mingled. When the cuckoo clock sounded eleven, she laid her work aside and glanced over her shoulder at man and boy stretched side by side, their stomachs on the unyielding tile. She went down the hall to her bedroom and closed the door. At the window, she braced her hands on the ledge and leaned forward until her head was well outdoors, anesthetized in budding lilac fragrance. Involuntarily, it seemed, she leapt over the sill and landed lightly on grass no more than three feet below, and began to walk toward the forest across a meadow of calf-high grass.

The verdant growth recalled a line of poetry—"where we still lie, strewn on the grass." Like one ghost reviving another, it found a second line: "Come back from that marriage that we did not foresee, return not into life, but into magic, where we have never died, into the enchanted wood, where we still lie, strewn on the grass." No, it was not a poem. Thomas Wolfe.

When she returned to the house in midafternoon, Guy was gone and Brick was napping.

Zero returned at two A.M. on Sunday. Later that morning Brick said, "Daddy, a tall man named Uncle Guy came to see me yesterday."

"What'd he come for, Laurel? Is the trip to Paris postponed?"

"Apparently, he came to bring Brick a book."

"Where were you?"

"I went for a walk in the woods yesterday."

"God damn it, can't you just stay at home like your mother or my mother did? Would it kill you just to sit still one whole day? Would it?"

She tried to feel angry, but a south breeze had invaded the room, trailing blends of lilac, peony, and honeysuckle; a rich, intoxicating fragrance which spoke to her of all the springs which had ever been. She watched Brick's lips moved gently. His confused frown was eased the moment he caught her smiling wink.

"Show your father the book."

The boy swooped up his treasure and sniffed it as he bounded toward Zero. "Daddy, you know what? He taught me how to tell if leather is real. Do you know how? Do you know that? Do you?"

14

Michel insisted that the Comptons be lodged with him at his family's flat near the Arc, but since his mother and brother were already in summer residence, Zero agreed with Laurel that they ought to stay at a hotel. For dinner the first night, Guy drove them to a miniature restaurant that had no more than a dozen and a half places.

It was the way a segment of Paris would be displayed in an

American movie, thought Laurel, before the elderly zither player wandered to their table, bowed low and asked her in French, "And what do you wish, dear Marquise?"

"Ah, Michel!" roared Guy, "Frederich must have told him you are married!"

"Yes, I've stayed away too long, Laurel. But what shall they play?"

Quickly, she said that it would be nice to hear the last number replayed, although she had no idea of its title.

The next day, they met before lunch, afterwards hurrying from high spot to high spot of daytime Paris. Exhausted by the chase, they stopped at tea time in a Champs café. Zero and Michel had beer, Guy and Laurel, café filtre. It was then that Michel began to badger Guy into telephoning "girls for tonight." Guy's answer was a thoughtful silent smile.

"Why not? Up to now, Zero and Laurel have a perfect right to suppose you and I go steady with each other!"

Zero chuckled toward Laurel, but she kept her eyes on her coffee, listening to Guy's protest that any girl either he or Michel knew was probably out of town for the holiday week end.

"What about Félicité Moreau?" Guy did not reply. "All right!" shouted Michel, "I'll telephone her myself if you won't!" He turned to Zero and Laurel. "She never leaves town except when Guy does."

Laurel's gaze narrowed on Guy, waiting for some change in his expression. Impetuously, she said, "I think you ought to telephone her." Beneath the table, Zero gripped her knee in a silencing gesture.

Michel stood up, his hands on his hips, "Well, Guy? Who shall it be—you or I?"

Guy's glance hung on Laurel a fraction of a second before he arose and disappeared inside the café. Five hours later Laurel was waiting with her husband and Michel in a car before a dignified brownstone apartment building, which silent Guy had entered.

He emerged with a doe-eyed beauty in her late twenties who wore a sullen pout. Her eyes were blue. She had a voluptuous, overpainted mouth and a figure so statuesque that it was incongruous with her notched, ragged gamin coiffure. Laurel felt offended without knowing why; she could have abided petulance in an eighteen-year-old, but Félicité Moreau wore hardness in her eyes.

In their tour of Pigalle, the quintet made a stop at one of the more luxurious clubs. When a waiter began to move before them mushroom-sized tables, Michel whispered, "Félicité has dared him to dine us all in this place. It will cost two hundred dollars, I think!" And when the champagne arrived, he leaned again to Laurel. "This is Chimmery. Did you notice? Guy's mother *is* Chimmery. Has he taken you through the Chimmery caves yet?"

Laurel did not reply.

"You realize champagne is the principal industry of Reims?"

"Oh?" she said in wry farce. "I thought it was the home of a Cathedral."

Later Michel said, "Who's for dancing?" Before anyone could respond, he turned to Laurel and added, "I never learnt, you know."

"I know how," groaned Zero, "but I hate it. Thank God, it's one punishment Laurel spares me!"

Beside him, Félicité lifted a neat ankle across her knee to show a sprain she claimed to have incurred the previous day at tennis.

"Well, mon vieux!" said Michel to Guy. "It appears your work is cut out for the night!"

Laurel and Guy danced together like reeds caught in the same wind. Until five o'clock Sunday morning and through a galaxy of night spots, however, Guy had not spoken a single word to her on any dance floor. She did not understand his strategy. She saw him not as a weakling against Michel's mischief, but unfeeling in his stoical acceptance. Obviously, she fumed to herself, he had not once considered her role as pawn in the musical chess game. And what of Zero? God damn him anyway! He had the crust; he could have called Michel's hand—no matter how discreetly! Was this to be the future balance in the entente? Was she the clay pigeon?

Zero's snoring in the hotel bed had been regular a long time, but Laurel sat in an armchair facing the double doors to a sixth floor balcony scarcely larger than a bathmat. Her feet throbbed from the unaccustomed exercise and ten or twelve hours of high heels, but she kept her eyes fastened to a rhinestone star studding the dark turquoise of Sunday's morning sky. No longer was she thinking of the night's complications or her own disappointment in Paris. She had never before been away from her children overnight. From the moment she had entered the hotel room to go to bed, anxiety had roosted on her shoulder, a nagging vulture.

At seven-thirty, she placed a collect call to the Monceau house. Olande seemed unnerved by her calling, but said the children were all right. Still Laurel could not lie in bed. At eight o'clock she ordered coffee, and at ten she awoke Zero.

"Why?" he grumbled, ruffling his hair in agitation.

"To get dressed for lunch."

"Lunch? Christ, Laurel! We're not meeting them until twelve o'clock!"

As he resumed his snoring, she left the room and took the elevator to the street floor. Couples, whole families, ambled along Avenue Friedland in their Sunday finery. Laurel bought a newspaper and a handful of miniature yellow roses which matched the simple linen suit she wore. To pass the time, she took a chair in the hotel lobby and tried to read the paper, but she could not for the life of her concentrate on what was happening in Algeria. She wanted to care, but a mother with two small children—five thousand miles from home—dared not dwell on war.

She went upstairs and found Zero in the shower. Laurel unfastened her chignon and carefully braided a single plait which she wound into a turbanlike coil a bit to the left of her crown. One at a time, she carefully tucked a miniature rose into each arc of the braid. Zero, emerging from the bath-dressing room, paused with a slight widening of his dark and bloodshot eyes.

"My God! You're better'n aspirin!"

Laurel laughed a little because the thickness of his tongue could not lie. Zero was still a little tight. She had seen it happen before. As soon as his first cup of coffee took effect, there would be the briefest interim of sobriety before a monstrous hangover began in earnest.

They took a cab to the Bois de Boulogne, to a lovely old

restaurant in the edge of the woods. As Zero settled the fare, Michel ran to meet Laurel from his vantage point near the steps. He looked harassed, and his eyes were much like Zero's this morning.

"Listen! Listen! Before Zero comes—you've got to help me!"

"Help you?"

"I drank too much, Laurel. I must have been out of my mind."

Then he was remorseful for the way he had treated Guy and herself. She stammered a bit in acceptance. "It's all—it doesn't matter. After all, it was a celebration."

Michel glanced nervously around her to be sure Zero was still occupied. "You don't understand! When I got home, I telephoned that Moreau girl."

Oh, God! So what? Laurel decided to say it, "So what?"

"She's going back with us. That's what!"

She started to walk past him toward the steps, but he stepped across her path.

She looked at him in contempt. "Happy landing!"

"But you don't understand! I can't receive her at my house. There's no chaperone."

She longed to laugh at his distress, but she said flatly, "There's a shortage of bedrooms at our house, Michel. We have two and they're full of married people, maids, and children. You know that!"

"Hey, Mike!" exclaimed Zero.

They shook hands. Michel's expression was that of an invalid determined temporarily to convalesce. His spirits brightened further as they joined Guy on the outdoor terrace, and soon they were sipping coffee, which Zero took almost thick with sugar and cream. Laurel knew that he was going to be ill. Before long he was obliged to ask Michel to direct him to the needed area. Michel, paling himself, led his American friend away.

After they left, she turned to Guy, noting for the first time the hollows in his cheeks and beneath his sober eyes. He said without looking at her, "Do you understand French very well?"

"I'm learning more each day."

"Do you hear the people at tables around us asking waiters to ask the maître d'hôtel who is the woman with yellow roses in her red hair?"

"Be quiet!"

"You're too dazzling to regard this morning—like the sunrays bouncing against this white cloth. I feel hypnotized—no, mesmerized."

"My, what big English words you wear this morning, cried Le Petit Chaperon Rouge!"

Guy tossed back his head and gave her a laughing glance. "But naturally! cried the big bad wolf. I study English three hours a day now, the better to hear you!"

Then, without warning, solemnity fell between them. Guy offered to pour her another cup of coffee. Laurel nodded. He lighted her cigarette. For the first time since entering the terrace, she regarded the scene about her. Guy too gazed here and there, so silent, so pensive that Laurel was startled when he spoke. "I may not see you and Zero again this summer."

At first, she had a sinking sensation, as if Guy had just revealed that he had some fatal ailment. On second thought, she felt justified in protest. "Why should you say such a thing—when it's only the first week in June?" she queried.

"You've ruined my whole defense, Laurel," he said without spirit. "I was going to tell you . . . well, never mind what lies I planned. I shall be going to Switzerland for August, and during two weeks in July, I am obliged to meet my sister and her children at Majorca. Those are not lies. But last night is a very serious lesson to me. Michel will not allow us to be friends—you and Zero and I."

"You were angry—beneath that fine mask?"

Guy lifted one sure, quick brow: "Oh, no! I was, in point of fact, taking extreme and very stealthy advantage of his mischief. . . ."

"Guy!"

"It is true, Laurel, and in such a move, I dishonored you."

"I had not thought of it that way."

"But it is true, and, Laurel, you must help me."

"How?"

"Well, first of all, he will probably insist that I return to Noël with him for a few days. That way, he could prolong this party at your house and his. I would be his excuse, a guest, you see. He is idle, Laurel, except when he paints, and during hunting season."

"But how can I help?"

Guy's tone was almost cryptic though his smile was kind. "When he comes forth with the invitation to me, don't jump in and push me over the cliff the way you did yesterday when he decided I should telephone Félicité."

"I'm sorry, Guy," she replied sincerely. Suddenly, the implication of Guy's act was clear to her. Obviously he was about to leave Michel to his own devices since Michel had invited Félicité as a houseguest.

But Guy was saying, "Don't give it a thought. Félicité is an old friend of mine, and a very complex individual. She's hostile to women, Laurel, thinks they're all banal and trite. But I'm sure you'll never see her again!"

Then he didn't know of Michel's invitation? Damn Michel Berteaux! She leaned toward Guy's chair and beckoned him to bend closer. "Guy, there's something I must. . . ."

But he leaned back; Laurel followed his gaze toward the terrace entrance. Zero, a little pale but hopeful, appeared, carrying in his hand a beaded glass of beer as if he were traversing a Long Island beer garden. Michel, chuckling nervously, glancing from side to side, carried a full brown bottle and an empty glass.

The meal, six courses, went on like a dream. What happened between the crayfish and the fresh raspberries in thick cream was vague to Laurel. She felt a vast need for sleep. She said, "I wish we could go home."

Zero made a festive display of relief. Guy admitted he was tired. Then Zero and Guy made a simultaneous effort to get the check. Overcoming the language barrier with the waiter, Zero succeeded in paying.

In the meantime, Michel arose and backed a little distance from his chair, his eyes never leaving Guy. He said, "You're coming to Noël today. I need you to help me walk off the measurements for the hunt stands. We can't wait until the day before the season opens."

Guy retorted pleasantly that they had approximately six months in which to finish the chore. Zero, who had been dealing with the tip, asked, "What's the trouble?"

Michel's green eyes glittered. His mouth had an ugly downward cast. He did not look away from Guy. "We'll go first and get Félicité. While you and Laurel danced all night, I felt sorry enough for her that I invited her to accompany us north today."

Zero blossomed into back-slapping camaraderie and said, "Well, well! Old Michel! You won't hardly need all of us!"

Laurel remained a spectator, indifferent to the outcome, for Guy had said he was not going and she did not care in the least what Michel and Félicité did, or where, or why. But she had not heard the finish.

"I need every damned one of you!" cried Michel. "I've got the whole plan worked out. I've already explained to Félicité that she'll be perfectly comfortable in an American house for three nights. You'll give her your bedroom, Laurel. Yours and Zero's. He'll come to Noël and sleep with Guy and me."

Laurel glared at him, incredulous. "But Zero has to go to work at eight o'clock every morning!"

"I can take the alarm clock," replied Zero as exultantly as if he had solved the final problem.

Laurel fought to suppress her fury, finding it possible only from a fatigue now supreme. "What do you need Guy for?" she said acidly to Michel.

He did not waste a second in replying, "To keep you off Zero's back."

Zero's laughter reverberated over the terrace. He did not see Guy push back his chair and rise. Laurel's suppressed rage died in the cold finality of Guy's voice. "Michel, in the name of God!" he said.

Michel answered him in French, "Shut your mouth! Don't be an ass! *They* know I'm teasing. What's the matter with *you?*"

Guy started to circle behind Laurel's chair toward him, but she timed her movement perfectly, knowing that he would be interrupted by the reflex of drawing back her chair. Zero and Michel were descending the terrace steps before Guy had replaced the empty chair beneath the table. Laurel accepted his arm without glancing at his face.

"You're going to Noël, then?"

"I can scarcely desert you now."

"I'm not afraid."

"You don't understand. Michel doesn't know."

"Doesn't know what?"

"What he's doing, Laurel. It's bad. It's wrong. And somehow, it's all my fault. But Laurel, remember, whatever Félicité says or does, it's not because you're American. It's because—because wars never end. Not really. Oh, Laurel!" He sighed deeply and whispered a few paces from Michel's car, "I'm sorry."

15

Michel said, "Drive three cars? Don't be silly! I'll bring you back to Reims or Paris the day you're ready to return, Guy."

Then he turned to Zero. "I'm a bit lightheaded. Liver flare-up from the drinking, I suppose. I wonder, would you find it gross of me if I asked you to drive my car?"

Zero nodded affably, while Laurel sought his eye in vain. It would be far more reasonable for Guy to drive Michel's car, she thought, but I'll only be playing into Michel's hands if I create a scene. He'll somehow make it seem that I'm too jealous to have Zero ride a hundred miles with an unmarried French girl. When she glanced at Guy, he wore the previous night's impenetrable mask.

At Zero's suggestion, Guy led the two-car convoy through the maze of Paris to the sprawling north highway. Once in the open country, he held the Buick station wagon to a steady sixty-five miles an hour. In a flurry of honking and waving, the trio in Michel's Simca sped past them, and past two other cars. Zero pulled back into his lane seconds before an oncoming car came even with the Simca. Laurel's fright evaporated in an audible sigh. Guy relaxed his grip on the wheel. She broke their half-hour silence. "He ought not take such chances!"

Guy shrugged. "We probably don't understand that with his kind of co-ordination, it's not really taking a chance as it would be for us."

"I don't care!" she replied, frowning. "He has no right to widow me by showing off in a car."

Without an instant's hesitation, Guy said in a quiet tone, "How much psychology did you study?"

"As little as the law allowed," she chuckled. "Why do you ask?"

He spared one affectionate glance from his driving. "Loss of sleep must be affecting my brain. For a moment, I saw your remark about being widowed as a—a death wish."

She replied rather thoughtfully, "I wouldn't know. Pilots' wives get accustomed to putting extra zing in every good-bye, because they live with that potential flight-without-a-landing. But I have a fear about my children being deprived of their father."

"I see," he replied. "What *did* you study at college, Laurel?"

"The English language. But I didn't get far. I—oh, you wouldn't understand."

"Tell me anyway."

"I quit in the middle of my third semester, mostly because of the sorority system. That's a peculiarly American institution. I really can't explain. Anyhow, it's a dull story."

"Did you go home?"

"Not right away. I had a job in New Orleans. I returned to Paradis the week after Pearl Harbor."

"Why?"

"I don't know. Sense of obligation, I suppose. The government began to build an air base near Baton Rouge, and my mother suggested I ought to do something toward the war effort. I became secretary to the Chief of Engineers, the outfit constructing the base, and when he left, I found my new boss was the Wing Commander."

"How long did you do that?"

"All in all? Nearly four years. Until Zero came on the scene."

"You knew each other a long time?"

"Eight days," she laughed.

"There must have been someone else before that."

"Yes, Sam. I was in love with him. He used to tell me that I would write because my affair with life was strictly observatory."

Laurel stopped and laughed, lost momentarily in her own reminiscence. "He was trying to say I was neurotic, that no woman could hide forever from reality by reliance on the intangibles. . . ."

"For instance?"

"Well, the humanities. Mainly, beauty—beauty of art, beauty of nature, beauty of music, literature—you know. He asked me then to define reality. I said truth, beauty, sorrow, and the love of God for man."

"How did he answer that?"

"Well, as I recall, he proposed an object lesson in the love of man for woman. Three years of college had equipped him in several fields. I was finding it harder and harder to cope with either his hands or his intellect. I told him I'd been to college too and I'd had enough of learned professors who insisted Genesis couldn't possibly have happened the way it said, and of learned seniors who insisted virginity was as unsightly as a birthmark and ought to be removed as clinically. Oh, God! It hurts me to return to all that—even now—but we settled the proposition once and for all."

"How?"

"I began to cry and he asked me what was wrong. Well, as I often do, I said the first thing which came to my mind, probably to see if it sounded as effective in words as in thought.

"I said, 'How would you feel if a burst of genes in prenatal darkness doomed you forever to the role of pursued instead of pursuer?'"

"What did he say?"

"Nothing. For three whole years. I only saw him once again

—at dinner—tête-à-tête. Everything was changed. He was suave, calm, kind, almost superior. He ordered dinner without consulting me. He controlled the conversation without trying, and when dinner was over, we had three hours before his train left for an overseas port. Looking back, it seems to me that night represents the last major act I can assign to free will. I could not cope with his restraint. I asked him—no, I begged him to marry me. Then and now. That hour. Before he left. Ah, there's no refusal as heartbreaking as a silent smile! I threw myself at him, but his shell was impenetrable."

"Why do you say shell?"

"He wrote me en route to England, but the letter did not reach me until some three months after we'd said good-bye. He said in the letter that I'd farewelled him with the most difficult hours of his life because it was only through having deprived himself of my love three years that he came to understand its true worth. He said he lived only for the day we could take up our destinies together, but he would not take a chance on dragging me through life if he came back from the war without an eye or an arm or a leg or even a hand. No compromise, Guy. It was going to be perfect or not at all."

"Where was he killed? Normandy?"

"Oh, no. He got a bit of shrapnel. Nothing irreparable."

"Why, Laurel? In God's name, why?"

"I had been married about six weeks when the letter reached me. I'll never forget that day. We'd been settled a couple of weeks at Zero's first Stateside assignment, and he came in at five o'clock one afternoon with a huge stack of mail. He handed me a letter with Sam's APO return. I read it. I read the letter and dropped it in the fireplace. I had no thought further than the necessity to keep it from Zero's knowledge, but as I watched the flames swallow it, I had the crazy notion that I'd bought the ticket to the right place, but I was on the wrong bus!"

"Then I couldn't turn back, because Zero handed me a sheaf of papers which had been sent him from a medical board in Italy. A board of psychiatrists. You see, he'd been in flying combat almost four years, and it was nearly that long before some

Group Surgeon picked up the fact in the records. As you probably know, by then, Americans were cracking up like kindling—men who'd flown only one or two tours and couldn't take chaos any longer. Anyway, Zero had been ordered before this psychiatric board. His orders read rest camp at Capri. I read his own summation of why he'd stayed so long without outward effects—he was able to sleep as long as eighteen hours in a stretch; he liked to fly; he liked living a sort of nonscheduled debacle between missions. When this doctor asked him whether it was true that he had a wire staked from the squadron bar tent to his tent door, he answered, 'Christ, yes! You don't think I'm going to have some second-john helping me to the bunk if I can't walk!' And the doctor asked next, 'Compton, you don't see anything erratic in the kind of example you're setting before these younger men, these kids on their first or eighth or twentieth mission?' Zero answered that he hadn't signed on as a chaplain. The doctor said no man could fly forever with a perpetual hangover. Zero said, 'How I preserve my sanity isn't a God damned bit of your business!' The doctor told him then that the board dissented on the state of his nerves; two out of five considered him on the verge of a major crack-up. Ah, Guy! You can imagine what that must have done to him. He told the doctor his nerves might be going, but his spine hadn't started changing color, and he dared the doctor to ride piggy-back in his P-38. He asked the doctor where he'd been the day of Dieppe while he flew five missions in as many hours. Then, the doctor caught him. He asked Zero how long it had been since Dieppe. Zero said maybe six months; he'd lost track."

"That's understandable, Laurel. Time loses its essence after so much war."

"Ah, yes. But you see, Guy, Dieppe had long passed. Zero had been in North Africa and Italy for almost two years when this interview took place.

"Anyway, through some unbelievable fluke, these papers had been forwarded from Italy to Zero by mistake. They were supposed to have gone to Washington. But Zero had them. He thought it was the joke of the century. Of course, if he hadn't come home when he did—he left when his best friend was killed —he'd probably have been sent home to a hospital."

"But he sought treatment, Laurel. Surely?"

"No. Any time I mentioned it, he got royally drunk, and he'd get this fixation about proving how steady his nerves were. One night—no, I won't tell that—there's no use to talk about the wildness of youth. Suffice it to say, I took the papers and showed them to my family doctor. He was old, Guy—maybe eighty. He tore up the papers. Just tore them up. And he said, 'Love, Laurel. *Love.* No other medicine heals the sickness a man's soul gets in war.'"

She faced Guy with a forced smile. He watched the road, as she said, "Now, turn about's fair play. What happened to you between 1938 and yesterday?"

Slowly, he shook his head. "Another time. Some other time, Laurel."

"No!"

"My heart is too full."

Of what? thought Laurel, examining his toneless words. A textbook illustration of the sensitive, compassionate Gaul?

Slowly she drew her knees up and her feet beneath her body. She switched her weight to one side and leaned against the car seat, almost huddled in a ball. She watched him, her eyes soulful and compelling, as if she were willing him to speak, and after some twenty miles he did. His words evoked their first quarrel.

"Laurel," said Guy, "turn away."

"With pleasure!" She did, straightening and smoothing her dress. "And if you must speak French, you might spare me that intimate tense, please."

She had spoken a clear, concise, perfectly cadenced sentence to him in his own language. His foot lifted the briefest instant from the accelerator as if the possibility of pulling off the road had been examined and declined in one breath. When she stole a glance, he was opening his eyes in the manner of a person released from a stab of pain.

Guy de Brières was indeed staggered by the succession of miseries love had brought him. He knew he was in love; he had known from the first because he had not been accustomed in his lifetime to deceiving himself. Now, he had heard the answer for which he had longed since meeting Laurel: How had a man like Zero Compton won and kept her?

16

Before seven next morning, Zero arrived to change into his uniform and drink four cups of coffee with Laurel. As he kissed her good-bye at the door, he gave his advice. Michel and Guy were planning to drive "Felix" about the countryside. "Maybe you ought not go. It might look like a double date, you know."

She smiled. "I don't want to go. Tell me, Zero. Why do you call her Felix?"

He laughed as if the answer were self-evident. "I can't say her real name without stopping to practice it. You know me and French."

"You're lazy in the brain. That's all!" Her rebuke was affectionate, good-natured.

"Well, don't worry! You won't be stuck forever. Guy gave Michel Hell last night."

"What about?"

"It was French Hell. I got left out." His shrug was wry. "But this morning, Michel said she'll be going back to Paris on the train tomorrow. He says Guy's furious about the imposition on us."

"What do you think?"

"Oh, Christ! You know me, Laurel. I play it all by ear. That girl won't make a dime off you!" Then he remembered to tell her they were all dining at Noël that night.

"Dining" was a loose term for cold cuts, cheese, and fruit. Laurel was starving, and she found it annoying, too, that Michel chose her to share waiter's duties with him. After they left the vast, undraped dining room and settled in a huddle of chairs ringing the fireless hearth, he brought her a tray of coffee cups and saucers, a pot of boiling water, and a tin of Nescafé.

"Laurel, you don't mind serving coffee?"

She was tired, still hungry, and chilled. Zero's eyes followed the French girl as she paced here and there about the room, flipping through a magazine and tossing it aside, or turning suddenly to look at the nightful of stars framed in the open door. She had an insolence which permeated the whole room, while the opulence of her figure made Laurel feel like an adolescent shadow.

Guy was glum, tired, almost old looking, and Laurel had not forgiven him the last silent hour in the car on the way home. Today, she had from him only three handkisses and two half-hearted smiles.

"Laurel? I say! Do you mind serving coffee?"

She glanced up at Michel, longing to say, I certainly don't, if you'll bring me some, but not this damned powdered ink! Instead, she reached for the utensils and quickly performed the chore. Félicité did not sit down to drink her coffee. She stood by the door.

Silence immobilized them for a while. Then Zero arose, complaining of lethargy, and began to arrange the coffee service on the tray. He departed toward the kitchen with his load.

Félicité sighed deeply and peered again into the dark, "It is a gorgeous night, but there is no moon. The stars are magnificent!" When Zero emerged from the dining room, she cried, "Zero! Come! Take me to see these stars! I am afraid of the dark alone."

Surely, surely, Zero could worm his way out of her bold approach, thought Laurel. But after a neat recovery from his blank expression, he glanced toward the trio across the hall and said with a grin, "Anyone for stargazing?"

No one answered. The pair sauntered through the door and disappeared into the night. No, thought Laurel numbly. No. God damn it, no! Michel sat poised with that greedy expectancy through which he had spoken to Laurel of a two-hundred-dollar dinner in Paris. Transfixed, he waited, his eyes devoid of pretense.

"Guy," began Laurel, unable to guess what she would say but determined to thwart Michel, "Guy, there's something I've meant to ask you all week end."

He bent his knuckles until they yielded three or four muffled cracks. After a deep sigh, he met her eyes.

"Guy, I'm worried over the turn of events in Algeria. What does the new crisis mean?"

Dramatically, Michel winced and fell against his chair. His arms sprawled in drama-class inanity, but his play acting was ignored by both Guy and Laurel. Guy answered her question gravely. They sustained conversation during the hour Zero was absent. Laurel's self-assurance was restored by what she recognized in Guy's eyes.

Without him, she was desolate, unable to speak to Félicité Moreau as they departed from Noël around eleven and Laurel drove the few miles home. They retired with civil, cool good nights. Three times before morning, Laurel left her bed to retch violently.

Prone and white, she remained in bed despite knowledge that the two Frenchmen were to call for her houseguest before eight-thirty. When she heard through the closed door their sounds of arrival and departure, she gasped in relief.

About an hour later she was awakened by the aroma of coffee. Her stomach revolted. She remained inert until the new wave of nausea subsided.

"Bonjour, Madame! I have been so alarmed. Can you not take some coffee?"

"Not yet, thank you, Olande."

"Madame, excuse me, but may I not call Dr. Abach? Surely, he would come."

"I shall be up and about by noon."

"Oh, no, Madame!"

"Excuse me, Olande, but I am very tired." Laurel felt a new wave of nausea in the offing as the coffee scent again wafted toward her nose.

"But what shall I tell *him*?"

"Him who?" She feared the girl mumbled in answer Monsieur le Comte. She flung into a sitting position so rapidly that the room spun about her for a moment as she shouted, "Monsieur le qui?"

"Monsieur le Marquis will return for him at noon."

"Why did he remain?"

Olande averted her gaze. "Monsieur de Brières was gravely angry to hear that Madame had been ill the entire night."

Laurel's eyes glinted, sick as she was. "And I suppose a little bird told him Madame was ill."

"Oh, Madame! Madame! *Madame!*" The service of coffee rattled, almost danced against the silver tray.

Oh, God, thought Laurel, how pitiful to be that afraid of another human being! I wish she could watch Zero tonight when I tell him he's either going to cut off every tie with this French trio or I'm going home. And I will, by God! This is it! I've had it. It's one thing to break out in a cold sweat when something flips my lid, but having to get out of bed to vomit all night. . . . No! Life's too short to tolerate this kind of— I wonder what they could have done outside for a whole hour when they've nothing in common, and Felix speaks broken English and Zero hardly a phrase in French. What could they talk about? What could they see with the yard and fields and garden as black as God's pocket? And Zero walking back in like a little boy. And of all the ten million remarks he could have made. "Man, it's sure a night out there!"

"Get out, Olande!" No please. No merciful inflection. But the girl had not even reached the door when Laurel demanded, "Where is he now?"

The maid turned back and stared at her employer. "Walking in the woods with Brick, Madame. I beg forgiveness."

"I should fire you."

"Oui, Madame," she whispered on indrawn breath, but still she did not exit. Laurel drew the covers to her chin as she collapsed against the pillows.

"Say that I am indisposed by the long week end. I cannot see anyone." She turned over on her stomach and closed her eyes to court sleep. Sleep. Blessed, sightless sleep. A dream. Guy waiting beside a bed, ordering her to wake up, his voice devastatingly real.

"I've something for you! Dépêche-toi!"

With her face hidden in the pillow and beneath her spread hair, she blinked several times before raising on her elbows. She peeked sideways through the red tresses and glimpsed vertical slivers of herringbone, and higher, the ribbed waistband of his white sweater. Still suspended above the pillows, she glanced to the throat of his open shirt, and finally into his alert face.

"Dépêche!" he ordered. The cup rattled mildly against the saucer as he squatted beside the bed. Their faces were level. "I've sent Olande all the way to the Tabac, and she must know already I don't smoke. Besides, the trip takes little time. Here!" Laurel did not budge. "Brick and I walked an hour in the woods to find this root. Drink it, Laurel, and I swear you shall survive Michel's cruel joke. Here, will you not try it?"

She edged slowly over, still on her stomach, far enough to glance into the amber-pink liquid. Steamy sassafras met her nose. She said, "We have that in Louisiana."

With infantile solemnity, she took the cup and drained it, afterwards sinking back into the pillow and sliding her arms far underneath.

"How did you learn to do everything, Guy?"

He exhaled a long sigh, apparently in relief. "I knew someday," he replied, "that I would meet a woman with the courage to sleep in red pajamas, and so I must try to become extremely clever."

"You're laughing at me," accused Laurel as she rolled onto her back.

"On the contrary, I've never seen anything more charming in my life."

"All you English-speaking Frenchmen overwork the word charming."

Guy pocketed his hands and grinned. "Nevertheless, how many women can be sick and beautiful at one time?" He turned to the window and sat down on the wide ledge. "Besides, Laurel,

I've a notion by now you're an English-speaking Frenchman yourself. What's the story?"

"You sound like Michel—what's the story?"

"What is the story?"

"Zero wants me to be American while we're over here."

"You know, I own by inheritance a very small tract in upper Louisiana. Many Frenchmen do."

"But you have to go and claim it?" He nodded without glancing back at her.

She remembered his reference to Michel's bad joke. "Why am I sick, Guy?"

"You don't know?" he faced her, unsmiling. She shook her head. "Michel confessed to me in your foyer, when the maid spoke of your illness during the night. He tells me he persuaded you to taste that yellow fat which came around a tin of foie gras he opened in his kitchen before dinner last night. It's not to eat, Laurel. It protects the meat from the flavor of the tin."

"My God! I was starving. He persuaded me to *taste* it? I must have eaten half a can while he played with a fruit arrangement for the centerpiece."

Then she saw the scene in its comical aspect. "But I'm so relieved! Guy, I thought all this vomiting was my pride's defense mechanism."

They fell silent now, each alone with secret thoughts. Briefly, she forgot he was there. Rediscovering him, his scrutiny of the yard, she felt a smile seep into her eyes. "You're sitting in my bedroom," she said.

Guy leaned against the window facing and did not look back at her. "Far worse, I am enjoying it."

"Go into the salon and wait for me, Guy."

She swung her feet off the side of the bed, oblivious to his turning around, or to the intensity with which his eyes guarded her uncertain movements. She covered her eyes with both hands and waited for the room to settle. She began to get up, but her weakness was startling. Guy was only a step or two away as he suggested gently that she lie down for a while longer.

"I can't. I don't want the children to see me like this."

"I've nothing to do the whole morning but keep them busy and out of here."

"You're kind, Guy. Open that armoire and hand me the first robe you feel."

He pulled out a woolly garment and she stood to put it on and then eased down on the side of the bed. "Guy, what are you doing with my hair brush?"

"Stand up, and I'll show you!"

She laughed helplessly and stood up. Guy, Count of Brières towered above and behind her, brushing her hair, brushing inexpertly, too gently. Laurel smiled the most feminine of smiles. Guy-Count-of-Brières had always longed to brush a woman's hair. The brush was tossed into the middle of the bed. His fingers sped deftly to make a neat, single plait of the red mane, which he tossed as he had the brush. It landed with a silent thud on her breast.

"Voilà, Madame! Trois mille francs!" He came before her.

"And the tip?" Laurel's laugh died half-born. Her knees began to give way; she had stood too long. Alarm flitted across Guy's countenance as his arms came beneath her knees and her shoulder at one instant. He took a step toward her bed. Laurel's fist landed one time on the hard shoulder. "No! Not bed!"

His frown melted as he wagged his head in imitation hopelessness and turned toward the salon.

"I feel a perfect idiot!" she said, as he deposited her efficiently on the loveseat.

"You'll be kinder to your liver from now on, Madame. It's an old French tradition," he said while he refurbished the dying fire.

"How did you know I feel cold?"

"I could say because I'm psychic, but in point of fact I felt from your body a sizable fever, and, moreover, there won't be two days this summer you can do without a fire in this room because that wall which sweats is on the north and there is earth behind it."

"You feel fever very fast, Doctor Day-bri-airs!"

"Oh, Laurel! You poor foreign angel! Your eyes are too bright this morning—like the globes on the Christmas tree. Christmas eyes." His gaze narrowed. "Laurel, my Christmas-eyed angel. . . ."

"You're a poet, Guy. A poet." She half-raised herself from the loveseat but sank back. "You write. You write!"

"No, Laurel. I do not write."

"But what?"

"Worse. I live among writers. Do you know the French definition of an editor? An author who cannot write."

"What do you edit?"

"Nothing terribly impressive. Shall we speak of it another day?"

"Why not now?"

"Because there is a standard joke—a cliché—no, I don't know the word in English—but people who hear what field I am limited to always make the same joke and I could not bear to have you say that to me today. My heart is heavy today, Laurel. We must say good-bye—for a while. . . ."

"Don't be morbid, Guy! I've worked the whole thing out in my mind. I shall tell Zero tonight—I shouldn't show you my claws, but there is only one thing I can tell him. If he doesn't give up his association with Michel, I shall be forced to take the children and go home. Not leave him, you understand, but go home and wait until he is done here."

Guy's face was shadowed. "Be realistic, Laurel! Zero and Michel are fond of each other."

She felt strong enough to say, "Guy, only one thing would ever permit me to question *your* motives."

"I know what you mean. I tolerate Michel because in both our families, first sons in five generations have gone to one boarding school. By tradition, they are friends. I suppose it is honest to say that my father and his had more in common than he and I. In their way, they belonged to one unit. They married women who were fourth cousins. But at any rate, such ties as I first mentioned are equal to blood in France, except for inheritance."

Suddenly she felt deserted, lonely, uncertain. She thought, if I were in love with a man like Guy, I could live forever without touching him, satisfied to see the feeling returned in his eyes.

93

"Laurel," whispered Guy, "I would trade my interest in Hell to know what idea curls your lips in such a fashion."

"Your words are well chosen," she said, "for it was a thought born of the Devil."

He stood up to go, insisting that she not rise from her place. "When Michel comes, say to him that I decided to walk to Noël."

"But, Guy! That's twelve miles!"

"By the forest, it is no more than nine or ten kilometers."

He wore a smile and the wistfulness of parting which, to Laurel, had become his trademark. "Laurel, I should like to kiss you good-bye."

Her pulse raged in her wrists, temples, throat, and against her eardrums. She closed her eyes and sensed infinity. But his lips were cool and firm and kind as he bent to plant a traditional buss on either of her cheeks, and a small, swift bonus atop her brow.

Zero had committed himself to drive to Normandy and spend three days at the Berteaux family castle near Deauville, with Michel's mother, the dowager Marquise of Berteaux.

"We can't go, Zero. You don't understand! Propriety over here *demands* her personal invitation. We cannot!" This was a week before the scheduled visit. But Zero was unimpressed by her argument.

"That's their problem, Laurel. Personally, I think it's damned white of Michel to go to all this trouble."

She fumed, knowing it useless to bore him with lectures on manners. And that very night, Michel made his third uninvited dinnertime descent in ten days. He had adapted himself well, in Laurel's opinion, to the early dinner hour and to the presence of a four-year-old at the table. (She had included Brick each time, knowing well enough that French people of Michel's status were unaccustomed to such a deviation.)

During the evening, Michel referred often to the coming trip. Finally, he bared his "heart." "You're the first Americans I've dared subject to my mother's scrutiny. She finds it unthinkable, the way you feed me dinner or lunch or tea, Laurel, whenever I pop in. Such a thing is unknown in France, but on the other hand, she finds you must be kind because you tolerate me."

Guy's gone. I'll never see him again, she raged to herself. Why should my life be wrecked by this ingrate Michel! No! No!

At bedtime Laurel said to Zero, "I can't go. I won't. I'm too old to stand inspection. I'll develop a little female trouble or something. I'll go to bed for a week before I'll go to Normandy and let his mother pick our bones!"

Zero replied that he had never thought of her as ungrateful: "Laurel, he must have spent four hundred dollars on us that week end in Paris. Why, that dinner in the night club cost half that much!"

"Guy paid for that." Laurel ripped off her handmade slip of ivory satin.

How did she know? asked Zero.

"If you'd take the trouble to study French, you could have heard for yourself. Félicité badgered Guy into paying for that dinner." Her eyes sparkled warily in the full lamp light.

"Felix wouldn't do that. She's a good sport."

Laurel's hands flew to her naked hips. "She's a *sport!* I'll buy that! But F-E-L-I-C-I-T-E accent aigu doesn't spell Felix!" Trembling with indignation, she turned her back on Zero and jerked the two tortoise-shell pins from her hair. She waited, almost prayerfully, for him to say something—anything—which would destroy her unrest about his relationship with the French girl, but the light went off in the room.

Laurel beat her fists against Zero's chest in denial, but he laughed in the excitement of chase and swept her off the floor, and each time she tried to speak as they lay in the bed, his lips smothered her words.

Two nights later, when Zero returned from a brief trip, she paced the salon floor. Zero was sipping his third bourbon and water before dinner, and Laurel did not mind for once. Perhaps it would soften his resistance.

"Even if I'd liked him, which I never did, I'd have been finished with him the first time he said we weren't cowboys like other Americans. Zero, you can't have him and me, too."

"Why?"

"He's fatuous. He's pigheaded. He's narrow-minded. He's ostentatious. He's a megalomaniac and, in my opinion, a masochist."

"Laurel Unabridged Compton."

"Go to Hell!"

"We're not going to Hell. We're going to see his mother. I'm going. And I'm going to take Olande and the kids." His tone had grown impatient. "Be my guest!"

In the taut, overstrained silence, Laurel sidled to the mantel and stared at a hideous pottery vase decorated with faded Egyptian scrolls. She took it in her hands, her back to Zero, reflecting that the world would not greatly miss it. But she missed Zero by a foot or two, and before the last shattered fragment thudded against the floor, he had pinned her to the loveseat, and soon stifled all evidence of struggle except fiery sparks shooting from her green eyes.

"Zero! The children—they're not *tied* in the kitchen!"

He laughed like a glorious conqueror. "You should have thought of that when you assaulted me with that vase!" His kiss fell across her mouth again. He mumbled against her lips. "I like a wench with spirit!"

Laurel began to sob in blind, violent gusts as she ran toward the bedroom, her senses numbed with fury. She gave up when the pale gray envelope was delivered next morning by Monceau's postman.

"I extend to you and your husband warmest regards ahead of our meeting. Life here at L'Alouette will surely bore you, but we shall do our best to make you comfortable, despite our 'broken' English. I pray you, do not leave your children at home. Bring them, for I am anxious to try what Michel says is called 'baby sitting' in America! Best regards. Véronique de Berteaux."

Laurel laid the letter aside with a fixed certainty that the author could not be a mean woman.

Michel was there at teatime the same day, holding her hand, twiddling the emerald ring, and inquiring shyly, Had Laurel received a letter from his mother that day?

"How did you know?" she asked, handing him the letter.

"Oh, we're American about long-distance telephoning. We're American in lots of ways."

A day before the scheduled departure, he again set fire to Laurel's apprehension. He merely looked at the handsome green ring this time as he said, "You'd do me a great favor to leave that thing at home. My mother doesn't understand this costume jewelry you Americans have such a flair for."

As they left a Rouen restaurant after lunch and took to the road again, Michel turned from the front seat and said to her, "I hope I haven't frightened you about my mother. She's quite happy that I spend my time with married people. She hopes it is a contagious state. You know, Laurel, she grieves for grandchildren."

"Laurel," piped Brick's voice from between Zero and Michel, "does that mean she likes Chris and me before she sees us?"

Jubilant Michel leaned down and hugged the boy. Laurel found it enough of an answer, nor did she reply to Olande's "Madame, mon dieu!" as Zero braked the long car to a halt before the incredible castle.

Michel smiled in total approval of the girl's shock. "Oui, Olande, L'Alouette has sixty-two bedrooms. They are numbered above each door from the old days when sixty-two breakfasts had to be delivered at sixty-two doors before a hunt. Now, three of those diagonal wings are closed off."

"Ah, Monsieur!" whispered Olande in near suffocation. "And has it a ghost?"

Michel glanced down at Brick's upturned, waiting face and winked at the boy as he replied, "No. Only a witch."

He turned back to Laurel and said immediately: "She has fought with me since I can remember. She is determined to run my life. But don't worry. She'll be completely charming to you. She loves all that is beautiful."

17

Michel explained, "Yes, the Germans used it as a headquarters in the First World War, and a hospital this time—before General Craig's tanks got rolling. Zero, can you imagine how I felt, riding toward my mother's house in an American tank?"

Zero shook his head slowly, while his eyes roved the maze of windowed wings jutting off diagonally in four directions from the main structure.

"And you know," Michel went on, "I was pretty proud of the old girl. She refused to leave the premises. Kept a three-room apartment on the second floor, even when every other bedroom in the house was full of sick or wounded Krauts. She kept a sender and a receiver both," Michel chuckled, "in the guts of a grand piano!"

Zero's voice might have belonged to the son of a stoned suffragette. "Yeah, it's a shame they never give medals to the women!"

Domineering. Critical. Awesome. And now valiant. This was Laurel's picture of the woman she had not yet seen, but who in the vaporous confines of imagination loomed as slightly taller than Michel, heavy-voiced and as fat as Regina Edney. Oh, God! To get it over with—to get it behind. . . .

Michel gave her elbow an impatient but alerting push. From the grand entrance a graceful, smiling lady descended the great steps. Her gray hair was smartly coifed, her tweeds immaculate over a figure which Laurel guessed to be no more than an American size seven.

Without waiting for introductions, Madame Berteaux took

Laurel's hands. "You have made our lives happy by taking time to come here. Philippe and I welcome you and your family!"

For an instant, Laurel could think of nothing except Michel's unfairness. The two women gazed at one another. Laurel recognized the origin of Michel's clear, large eyes, and saw in his mother's face but two kinds of lines, those of laughter and of suffering.

"Thank you, Madame!"

"Madame?" Protest was born more in outspread hands than in eyes or voice. "Must we call each other Madame these days under one roof? Ah, my dear Laurel! I should feel ten years younger if you call me Véronique."

Laurel tried not to let relief run away with her as Véronique Berteaux bent to Brick and said in French, "And what have you to say for yourself, Brick?"

The boy's facial expression was as French as the ground on which he stood, and the words he replied. "I would have come sooner had they left it up to me."

The burst of merriment caused by the four-year-old got the group inside the great house—the five travelers, plus the awed maid; the hostess; and Philippe de Berteaux, Michel's twenty-five-year-old brother, whose blue eyes seemed telescoped in reverse, so thick were the lenses of his black-rimmed glasses.

Laurel discarded the last vestige of her reservations against Michel's mother and at the same time grew more resentful than ever at Michel's deceit. She followed Véronique through a series of halls, up flights of stairs, and past innumerable closed doors to the third-floor suite prepared for the boys and the maid. Then they descended to the second-floor bedrooms marked for the American couple. Laurel saw Zero's room, a manly looking chamber with a heavy commode and recessed three-quarter bed, and turned to her own room, a showplace of Louis XIV furnishings in antique white with small bouquets of fresh pink roses here and there accenting the printed fabric which was used over the walls, in draperies and on the tufted headboard of the bed.

"I am pleased," said Véronique, "to believe that you admire this room."

99

"We have troubled you greatly."

"On the contrary! You have befriended my lonely son. Now, you bring to this tired house a sparkle, the joy of children." Her brows drew into a quizzical frown. "Are you sure nine o'clock isn't too early for your breakfast trays?" Laurel smiled and shook her head.

The days at L'Alouette were rich in tranquil, rewarding moments which fell in sequence as pearls slip down a strand of filament. However, Laurel felt a vague misgiving when, some twenty-four hours before their scheduled departure, Zero consented to telephone for a three-day extension of leave, which literally would double the length of their stay. Of course, Zero wanted time to visit Mont St Michel, the Deauville Casino, Bagniole, and the Allied beaches, or so he agreed with Michel.

On the fourth morning of the visit when Laurel awoke from a servant's knock, Zero had left the room. Disdaining for the first time the delicious ivory-colored bread, sweet cream butter and marmalade, she downed her coffee as she dressed and sped downstairs and out the door. She arrived in time to see Brick struggling inexpertly with a pair of fishing rods. He walked between Zero and Michel, who carried shotguns over their shoulders. A rowboat, thought Laurel, alarm freezing her. That's all there is at the landing, a rowboat the color and texture of driftwood. I saw it yesterday. And that murky stream. Not really a stream. Just stagnant water. Brick can't swim. They're going to shoot out of a rowboat. Shoot! With a child who can't swim? No. No! Not Brick. Nothing but a grappling hook could find anything in that water!

"Zero! Zero!" Laurel sprinted as fast as her feet could move. Zero glanced back and halted, his face showing surprise and a bit of smirk.

Brick yelled, "Hey, Laurel!"

Undiluted contempt lined each pore and crevice of Michel's face. Zero listened politely, almost coldly to Laurel's protests, but he said nothing in reply, even when Michel's voice crackled in the morning air, "Zero, my God! You could at least send her back to the house!"

She whirled with hot tears racing down her face, and halfway to the second floor, she collided with Véronique who cried, "Child! What on earth?"

Laurel's reply was in telegraphic prose. The older woman sped down the stairs well before those few words were finished. It was perhaps an hour and a half before the French woman entered the sunny lounge, where Laurel sat knitting in a cane rocker. Brick extended to his mother a basket of fresh raspberries which he vowed he had picked alone.

"They're for you, Laurel," he said, "even if we are mad. Uncle Michel said you wanted to keep me a baby and I think he's right. But I'm not as mad as I was. . . ." He glanced up at Madame Berteaux and spoke as emphatically, "And now, Madame, I will see your horses."

Laurel opened her mouth to scold him for his unbecoming lordliness, but Véronique signaled her into silence as she dispatched the boy to the kitchen. Then she said hastily to Laurel, "We'll be in for a deal of lashing from Michel, you know. But I want you to promise me, Laurel. When he goads you, say nothing. He can hurt you less that way."

There was no reply to be made, or at least, Laurel could not find one.

"My dear, it seems unfair to involve you in family tragedies, but Michel's contrariness is my own fault. You see, after the First War, after certain injuries, my husband had but a short time to live. Like a candle burning out. All depended on how rapidly he spent his strength. Gassed. You know. And don't weep, my dear. Brick will fly back in here any moment. He has seen enough today. But let me finish. My dear husband had known a victorious and vigorous life. Perhaps you saw in the trophy room, Laurel, those ancient cups won at polo and tennis and marksmanship, and yet, by the time he had a son to train for the same life—Michel was born three years after 1918 Armistice—well, by that time, you can see what the situation came to. My husband had such pride. He, well, I could not hurt him by having the child aware of the truth, and so Michel was allowed to believe it was my concern with his being injured or made ill. Ah, Laurel! Had I but been born in your generation of all that psychological aid!"

Laurel eyed her gravely. "The psychology books? Véronique, for a layman, they are merely—I speak of motherhood, you understand?—they are scarcely more beneficial than mileposts along a railroad track, telling you the destination and how much further."

Brick entered the room at this moment, and the older woman beamed upon him, as she said, "My, Brick! Your mother speaks matchless wisdom this morning."

His expression was agreeable if bored. "My Daddy calls it diarrhea of the mouth, but he—Laurel, he didn't mean. . . ." The boy's face was worried suddenly. "He didn't mean I can't tell *you*, did he?"

"Oh, I believe you can tell him or me anything, Brick," she replied without a muscle twitching to reveal her inner feelings. Would Zero never realize how much a child of four could repeat? Would Zero continue to speak and act without restraint before his sons when they were eight and ten and twelve and sixteen and twenty? Which was the child, Brick or Zero? Then Laurel called upon the old array of excuses: Ambrose Compton, four years of war, and Zero's present gristmill of duties. Zero Compton was upright. Decent. Albeit, unrepressed and sometimes crude—under pressure. But he was a good man. A *good* man. He was Brick's and Chris's father.

Laurel was obliged to parade some of these tenets across her discouraged heart through the dinner hour, the first time she had seen Zero since early morning. He did not look at her throughout the meal. Neither did Michel whose venom spilled over at the outset of the coffee period in L'Alouette's drawing room.

"Well, Laurel! I hope you're satisfied with the pall you've laid over the outing." She crimsoned, shocked almost to numbness, not so much for her own feelings as the position his accusation created for Véronique. Michel turned to Zero and said as glibly as if he were discussing politics or weather, "The incident this morning proves a point I've made for some time. American wives are not properly trained."

Véronique retorted quickly, "You make me ashamed that you

are my son, to speak in such a manner of our guests!" She turned to Laurel. "You've known him a few months now. There is nothing I can explain away, but take my advice, dear Laurel: pay no attention!"

No one seemed to have noticed Philippe until he spoke in a shaky voice, "Since my brother chose what he calls freedom, on what basis shall he judge any wife, French or American?"

18

Laurel rode away from the château looking back and waving, until Véronique and Philippe were out of sight. The first half-hour of the drive back to Beaumonde, she rode placidly, resavoring aspects of the stay which had been so pleasing—the healthy irreverence for clocks, unhurried talk, aimless walks through the forest, rides to the village, and, often, unembarrassed silence.

At noon, Zero halted the car near the same excellent restaurant in Rouen where they had lunched a week earlier. During the meal, Michel's manner was breezy, self-satisfied, as if the over-all conduct of the visit was a personal success. As they returned to the road, however, he began to speak to Laurel of different remarks she had made to his mother in his presence, not in a condemnatory air, but a sort of how-could-you-have-said-that attitude. She smiled tolerantly through all of this, determined not to become angry in such a confined space and before the children and maid.

Michel eyed the fringed brim of her natural-colored cart-wheel hat and the sheath of black linen, both of which she had worn upon her arrival at the château. In a voice as silky as the straw, he said, "Why did you wear a beach hat to meet my mother?" Hostility washed her anew, but still, she managed a smile.

Later, she was obliged to listen to a vaguely clinical comparison of French and American houses of ill repute. The conversation was going on in the front seat where Brick was asleep. Laurel lay with her head on the back of the rear seat, the big hat shielding her face from the sun.

In midafternoon, when Michel began to teach Brick the words of a naughty French song, she kept herself in check. The child was reasonable. She could explain to him when they were alone why he must forget it. But in late afternoon, only three or four miles from Monceau, Michel achieved what he had apparently been aiming for—the unforgivable.

Of all French habits to which Laurel refused to adjust, public urination was far and away the leader. Three, maybe three and a half miles from home, Michel asked Zero to stop the car. No tree. No hedge. A flat span of road splicing two endless fields of soybeans. Laurel had thought her humiliation complete—until Zero joined him.

For the remainder of the way home, she kept her face turned to the window. Desperately she searched for ways and means to sever Zero's ties with the loathsome Norman. *I won't put it off. I won't have to. As soon as Michel leaves and Olande starts feeding the children, I'll tell Zero, and this time, I'll say—I'll speak in his language. I'll say, by God, it's him or me. Michel or I. No more double harness.* And if Zero said no, it would be clear that he no longer loved her because you couldn't love somebody and not give a damn what you made somebody suffer!

The children went to bed early. So did Olande. Zero intended to but was briefly delayed. When Laurel had finished enumerating the list of reasons why she could not tolerate Michel Berteaux another day, Zero's silence endured a full minute. He scowled pensively and bit his lower lip. At first, she believed success was assured by his failure to react with anger, but the silence grew too long, too uncertain. She felt undermined, half lost, before he began to explain.

"Laurel, I don't know how to say this, but I've felt like an ass ever since I let your birthday pass in April without doing a thing. Surprises are always difficult, but I had planned a little dinner tomorrow night. . . ."

"Where?" she demanded harshly.

"At the Officers' Club, of course. There's a costume dance. A hobo dance." His gaze was unyielding, his voice firm.

"But Michel?"

"I've already invited him."

"Then I'm not going."

"Laurel! My God!"

"All right! I'll go to keep you from being embarrassed, on one condition. Zero?" He glanced away from her. "If you promise me never, never to let him come here again or make me go where he is. You can hunt with him from now until doomsday. I don't care. But promise me! Promise me!"

"It's not quite that simple."

"Zero," she sobbed, "you really, really don't love me anymore. . . ."

"Oh, for Christ's sake, Laurel. Michel's done something important for us. I wanted this to be a surprise, too. But you won't let me do anything my way, will you? Laurel, we'll be moving to Beaumonde in a week or two."

Under any circumstances except a quarrel involving Michel, her heart would have leapt for joy at the prospect of a house in Beaumonde. When her eyes met Zero's, he was trying hard not to grin: "Michel has found a house—fourteen rooms—steam heat—servants' apartment—all for a hundred a month. It's in the bag. He did it for you. And you want me to think he despises you."

She leaned forward, hands on hips and said through clenched teeth, "I won't take it! I won't, not even if it has all that, not even if I like it!"

"For God's sake, when will you grow up? You've got to take it. I already committed myself."

Bitter tears pushed at her eyes. She no longer knew for certain what she felt, but she had lost. She arose and tripped over Zero's feet in a hasty retreat to the bedroom. The cuckoo struck eight times.

Laurel entertained Brick through most of the day, allowing him to help her sew tufts of red yarn inside the circumference of a billed cap, a makeshift wig for her Raggedy Andy costume. Hair hidden, her face dotted with penciled freckles, Laurel, petite in knee pants and a checked shirt, was almost unrecognizable until she spoke. However unlikely, the truth of the matter was that she became homely.

This reversal had its effect even upon Michel. He was, to Laurel's annoyance, almost solicitous. At the party he wore baggy black breeches, a chimney sweep's hat, and a very dirty sheepskin bolero over naked chest and shoulders. Sometimes his navel winked at the whole room.

As for Zero, he was not too much with them. Wigged, painted, clutching a rented fur piece, swinging his beaded purse, and wearing teacups in the bosom of a flowered silk dress unearthed by Michel, he created sensation beside the bar, in the men's room, and at whatever table he visited during the evening.

Laurel saw that he was exhilarated to be in American revelry again. Cordially, he went about spreading goodwill among pilots of the 104th Squadron, leaving Laurel and Michel at a table which had included the Edneys, Blakes, and the other two Squadron Commanders, whose wives were on a Scandinavian tour that week.

The pair of officers departed the table for the bar when dinner was finished. The Edneys danced as long as any song lasted, and while Edney's exchange with Berteaux had been stoically casual, the air was strained between Regina and "Mike Besse." As for the Blakes, it was their farewell appearance at the Club. Colonel Blake was being moved to Turkey and his angry wife was returning to the States. She was scarcely civil to Regina Edney and virtually ignored Laurel, whom she had not met before. When others were dancing, Laurel and Michel were isolated in the crowded room.

Meanwhile he chatted amiably and endlessly of rich Americans he had met at the Jockey Club, of General Craig, U.S. Army, who "took a shine to me" in England. He gazed at Laurel with all the intensity of a paramour, or so a passer-by might have assumed. They watched the toga-garbed Caesar, whose gilt olive wreath sat askance, as he dragged his flailing cave woman the length of the dance floor by her hair. The crowd had not stopped laughing at this exhibition when a heavy thud from the bar area jarred the floor. Michel and Laurel turned to see a uniformed captain who had slipped backwards off his bar stool and whose arms and legs held their angled positions as if he were yet seated. Laurel gasped in amazement as two laughing comrades paused to set him back on his stool and one replaced his drink between arched, rigid, and suppliant hands which clutched the glass as needfully as those of a baby on the day's first bottle.

"But he'll certainly ruin his liver!" lamented Michel.

The orchestra began an extremely loud selection. Laurel shouted, "I can't hear you." Michel leaned close but before he could repeat his words, Zero's voice boomed behind them.

"Well, by God! They've signed the Magna Charter, I mean the peace treaty." Mirthful response echoed from surrounding tables and even from the edge of the bar area. He roared like a tickled lion: "That's spelt p-e-a-c-e, like peace of mind, not p-i-e-c-e like a piece of—piece of—of my mind."

Laurel eased from her chair, excusing herself, determined not to show by the slightest frown that Zero's intoxication was making her ill. On light, quick steps she entered the women's restroom. It contained two booths behind pressed board painted robin's egg blue, a wastebasket, two sinks, and two dime-store mirrors. An uncurtained window painted the same sickly blue, even the glass, was marked with coal soot pointing up where winter had come through.

She saw a pair of neatly clad feet in either booth. She stood, soundless, back against the door, wondering whether it would seem gauche to clear her throat in announcement, but the time for decision vanished.

"Susan, you still there?"

"Sure."

"Thought I heard somebody come in. Or maybe you went out."

"I can't. Oh brother! If I ever mix champagne again on top of martinis. I'm not drunk. Not even tight. Just sick."

"I haven't had a thing. I can't drink when I'm pregnant. Can't stand the smell of alcohol. Say, did you get a gander at the famous sable out in the cloakroom?"

"Sable?"

"Yeah. It's sable all right!"

"Whose is it?"

"Compton. You know. The 104 C.O. The one Arnold's wife took a fix on."

"Who's Arnold?"

"I keep forgetting you only been here two months. Compton, well, he shafted Arnold off to Germany right after the hayroll."

"Arnold know why?"

"You must be some shook besides sick. We got some bastards in the Squadron but none that big."

"Compton's wife find out yet?"

"Don't know. Kilian Blake claims she's gone native with the French, but everybody knows there's nothing but beetpickers and cheating landlords in these parts. Personally, I'm beginning to suspect she knows all about him, and feels too hangdog to come out except behind a mess like that costume. She's Andy. Raggedy Andy. Tennis shoes! My God!"

Laurel regained the table and sat down with grace and a little smile at Michel. He excused himself and she was left alone to stare at her hands in her lap and retrace the overheard conversation, though in her heart, she knew there was no possibility of misconstrual. She remembered what Zero had said New Year's Eve. "I'm in Dutch with my Squadron already." Murderous rage filled Laurel. Damn his adulterous soul! Damn him—damn him—damn. . . . she looked up to see Regina seating herself across the table.

"Who is Arnold? Who's his wife?" Laurel demanded tersely.

"The biggest tramp who ever set foot on this Base. Psychopathic liar, congenital nymphomaniac. In fact, I think she's a double feature. Had a nude photograph taken of herself with another gal to see who had the best figure. A pig, Laurel. A regular pig."

Laurel said, "Zero would." Her tone implied it might have been the ten thousandth time.

"Don't blame him," said Regina. "I watched every kind of female in this motley crowd make every kind of pass, before you came, and he wouldn't give 'em a tumble. I'll bet she got him trapped *and* drunk. I don't know how."

Silence grew between them. Regina stared steadily at Laurel's veiled eyes.

"You'd better forget what's past, Laurel, and consider the present. You've *got* to shake this Berteaux. He's practically crawling in your lap!"

"I'm well over twenty-one, Regina."

"All right, I'll say what I mean. It's not you I'm especially worried about. Zero Compton is a beautiful hunk of man even to men. Suppose Berteaux is clever enough to be coming at him through you?"

"You really hate him, don't you?"

"I'll tell you how much. Tomorrow, let's each give your maid a hundred dollars in greenbacks to hold for the winner 'til Christmas."

"What winner?"

"The winner of my wager that Michel Berteaux is in bed with one of the Comptons before then." Laurel eyed her in a vaguely catatonic haze. "What say, Laurel? Tomorrow, let's put up the stakes!"

"I can't do anything tomorrow. I'm going to Paris."

"To Paris?" Regina's brows lifted in surprise.

"To Paris."

"I'll drive you."

Laurel studied the hopeful, almost conspiratorial certainty in Regina's tone.

"No," said Laurel. "I'm going on the train, the way I dreamed of a year ago when Zero first told me how near we'd be to Paris."

"I'm going with you, Laurel."

"No, you're not."

"We'll separate at the Gare du Nord and meet before time to come home."

"Why, Regina?"

"I don't know, Laurel. It has something to do with the way you look when you're dressed up—and the size of Paris—or maybe even thwarting Zero's suspicions."

Laurel studied her astutely and saw in Regina's eyes only concern and affection.

The pair rode in silence during the two-hour trip to Paris. "I'll be at the Lafayette or Printemps all day," said Regina, her hand already braced on the handle of a cab door.

Laurel smiled firmly. "I'll see you here. Track 23. A quarter 'til four. You were kind to come with me, Regina."

And thus they separated, Regina to meander through the gigantic wells of merchandise and Laurel to locate the big American Hospital which she had never seen, but where she was certain to find Abach.

During the thirty-minute taxi ride she tried to plan her strategy. It would be necessary to tell Abach the exact story of what Zero had done. Otherwise, how could she justify to him the imperativeness of testing her for syphilis?

Of course, she reflected, Abach would say no to her second demand. He would say no and mean it. She would then be obliged to recount in the barest of outlines the story of Michel and Guy. Just enough to force Abach to arrive by himself at the realization that if he did not open the door of adultery to her, he left her no choice but to hunt elsewhere. After all, everybody knew men didn't have to be emotionally involved to do a thing like that.

Submerged except for her head in a full tub of hot water made murky by a half-bottle of lavender shaving lotion, she closed her eyes and tried to convince herself she was in a man's apartment. Then Abach was standing in the door. She opened her eyes and smiled at him, unable to do otherwise for he looked incredibly young without his glasses.

She glanced away from the light brown fur which carpeted his breast and abdomen in the shape of a cross. "Go get some clothes on. You look like a bear rug standing up."

"I want to ask you something first. You had any backaches lately?"

"Not in fifteen minutes."

"Be serious, Laurel. No pain at all?"

She shook her head slowly. "Only a small volcanic disturbance somewhat below the left clavicle," she avowed.

"No, I'm serious, Laurel."

In no mood for a clinical harangue, she sank below the water line, unmindful of the train ride less than two hours off, or of her hair which would be wet in the rainy day. She remained under water until his grip closed on her shoulders without a trace of playfulness.

As Abach dragged her up, she was swiping at her eyes. She spat and snorted water from her nose. "That lavender lotion has alcohol in it!" Spiritedly, she rubbed her smarting eyes.

"I wanted to tell you your womb is tilted," said Abach.

Something in Laurel died. She studied his frown. "Guy would never have said a thing like that!"

"How dare you play coy vixen with me, Laurel?"

"Damn you! Would the sky fall if you stopped playing dedicated doctor for five minutes?"

He lifted one brow, "Why should you wish to hurt me with words?"

"Because—because no woman wants to be lectured on anatomy faults when she has come to give her—her. . . ."

He interrupted her muddled sentence. "You came here to give, Laurel? No. You came to take. And, as long as we're on the subject of sex, if this was a fair example of what Zero has put up with. . . ." Her eyes narrowed with incredulity. *My God! Is he on Zero's side?* "Laurel, it's difficult just now for me to tell you, but I feel obligated. . . ." *He's going to challenge me to soar back to the nest.* "Responsiveness, you see, is requisite to marital. . . ."

She edged forward gradually until her hand reached the cold-water tap. Idly, she opened it and regarded the stream of water as Abach went calmly on.

And I thought he knew me! Laurel throbbed with resentment. She studied him through a little smile, apparently enthralled by what he said—until her thumb caught the outlet and stoppered a fierce spray which peppered the doctor's neck and shoulder. The icy shock cut his words, as Laurel had hoped, but she had scarcely forseen the next sequence. In fact, rage in Abach was untenable, unbearable, and so, like a child whose mischief has boomeranged with devastating force, Laurel put off admitting that he slapped her.

BOOK TWO

1

The July morning had a frisky softness, like the somersault of a kitten. Laurel patiently purchased fresh tuna, Gruyère cheese, and a dozen Talisman roses, but it was no day for marketing.

Alone, she drove from the market square beneath the overpass to Reims, and proceeded halfway up the hill of Beaumonde to a neat little park, a spread of formal gardens centered by a concrete statue. She turned right and eased down the interesting street. There was a new stucco apartment house of eight stories, a wine bottler's "cave," a yarn shop, and a dry cleaner on the left side of this block, and across, hugged close as if bracing each other from slipping backward down the hill, were five houses—dark, dignified, and as French as a trimmed truffle.

Before the middle house, 14 rue Père Marquette, Laurel drove the two right wheels of her station wagon onto the sand-filled curb and turned off the motor. She regarded the little courtyard, no larger than the inside of a bus, but jeweled with peonies, pansies, carnations, and roses. The fence, of spiked iron rods set in waist-high brick, was hardly visible beneath its burden of red ramblers.

Laurel gripped two of the gate bars and leaned her forehead against them to study the house. It was prim in its clean lines, almost square-fronted with three floors, mansard roof, and miniature balcony jutting over the street entrance. Built of red brick long rusted to a burgundy shade, the structure wore, inches below the faint eaves, a strip of bright gingerbread—a band of coral, white, and sky-blue tiles in careful geometric design.

The maid who let her into the hall wore black slacks and

pin curls. One jaw was inflated with food she continued to chew amongst indifferent replies, as she walked ahead of Laurel, leading her to her American mistress who sat in the kitchen nursing a baby no more than a month old.

Packing crates and cartons littered the kitchen, a lovely big room wainscoted with imitation Delft tiles and ceilinged in pearl gray. Laurel's gaze darted at once through the massive window to the lengthy garden which descended the slope to the next block, to the marshalling yards beyond, and in the distance, the twin orange silos of Monsieur Vervins' farm.

Then she glanced at the slacks-clad servant who now resumed her chair opposite Mrs. Frakes, a petite woman in her early twenties.

"Should I leave and come back later?" asked Laurel.

"Oh, no," replied the American tenant, "I wanted to talk with you before we move out. You see, we'll be leaving a week earlier than the landlord's been told. He's got it coming!"

Laurel dropped down on a wooden crate, wishing she had waited until later in the day. Zero had not told her the Frakes had a new baby. He had told her only that Monsieur Risseau with whom they had played bridge in the late winter, and who was a Beaumonde attorney, had obliged Michel Berteaux by persuading the owners of 14 rue Père Marquette to skip the fourteen American families on a waiting list and rent the house to the Marquis's friends. As for the Frakes, Laurel knew only that the young Captain was being transferred to Turkey.

"Mrs. Compton, do you speak French?" Laurel nodded. "Then would you ask the maid to go on upstairs and put the baby in the crib, to get the diapers down from the attic and fold them. . . ." Her smile was appreciative. "It would save us some time."

Laurel glanced swiftly over the tired face, the doelike brown eyes, and gaunt cheeks, and the hungry baby emptying her breast. The smell of excelsior, that aromatic and arid sentinel of transiency, seemed everywhere.

"Do you mind, Mrs. Compton?" Laurel shook her head slowly, unable yet to turn away from this bedraggled little compatriot who looked for all the world like a once-lovely animal caught in a helpless trap. How long in France? wondered Laurel. A year? A year and a half? And she has to ask a stranger to command her maid in French? What's the matter with the people they send to France? Why should this woman be here if she doesn't want to be? Or why did they let her come?

Not anger but futile frustration washed Laurel as she spoke sharply to the maid, "Get your seat off that chair and go comb your hair! Get upstairs and change into a skirt!"

Impudence oozed from the languid eyes, the sullen mouth. She leaned back in the chair until the two front posts were off the tile floor, her arm slouched over the back of the rungs. In lucid implication, she said, "The Captain speaks French."

Laurel said, "Stand up." When the servant made no effort to get to her feet, Laurel fixed her mouth in amused smile and continued, "You learned your manners from the invaders?"

The girl not only stood up but also swept unnecessarily close, and directly before Laurel to leave the room. Laurel waited until she neared the door. "You did not return to the beet fields this summer. You must be very loyal to Madame to sacrifice such a wage!"

The servant whirled on her, eyes blazing, "I do not have to be insulted. The Captain will force your apology!" Her eyes veiled and then widened. "The Captain slept here each night—the whole month she was in Germany to have that baby!"

Laurel chuckled with aplomb scarcely felt. "Did you please him?" The pair regarded each other in that reckoning candor which decries separate nationalities. When Laurel's gaze did not alter, the maid dropped hers.

Laurel finished quickly, "It is a tired story among the Americans. That Captain and you. Madame knows everything. The cigarettes. The nylons." Laurel lowered her voice, saying the girl had been a fool to confide in her friends—that now, even the landlord and neighbors knew the story. "You were stupid not to have foreseen their jealousy, weren't you?"

Seemingly divided between defiance and horror, the maid nodded yes, and then changed to no.

"Alors, I take the liberty of warning you. Madame Frakes is seriously considering going to your mother. Were I you, I should try extremely hard to please her this last week. It is a terrible thing you have done, and you know, it is entirely possible that at your age your mother can arrange detention—not to mention what the Douane will have to say if he hears of the nylons."

Laurel turned questioningly to Mrs. Frakes. "The diapers. The beds. The dishes. The furnace. And the morning marketing. Anything else?"

The American shook her head.

Without looking back at the maid, Laurel said pointedly, "Good day, *Mademoiselle*."

As the hurried footsteps padded to nothingness overhead, silent, smiling Laurel reached for the sleeping baby. She carried her the next quarter-hour as they toured the interior of the house.

They began in the four-roomed basement and proceeded to the ground floor. There were marble-fronted fireplaces in salon, dining room, and library, and each room had a radiator. In addition there was another radiator in the L end of the hall where basement and second floor stairs went their separate directions.

The flight of stairs was adequately carpeted. The four bedrooms on the second floor also had fireplaces, as did the two unfurnished bedrooms on the third. The remainder of the top floor, about half the space, was in its original attic state, although a large, finished cubicle with a locked door in this area was described by Mrs. Frakes as the landlady's closet.

"They keep that locked. And that tool shed down in the garden."

"What's in the closet?" asked Laurel idly.

"Nothing, if you ask me. I think Madame Hachère keeps it to have a pretense to come through the house on inspection, but she'll never come while you're at home. She checks with the maid first on the telephone."

Madame Hachère. Laurel's gaze swept about the cluttered attic. Madame Hachère. Of course. We met Risseau at their party. He's their attorney, I remember. But Michel got us the house. Zero doesn't know and I'm not going to tell him. He can find out by chance the way I did!

As they descended to the street floor, Mrs. Frakes rambled endlessly. The Hachères were rotten landlords. The worst. They had failed during six months to replace the hot-water heater, which was as old as the house. It exploded each time she or her husband attempted to light it, and so, complained Mrs. Frakes, she had bathed at a friend's house twelve blocks away.

Yes, thought Laurel, she's truly overwrought. "For six months?" she repeated placatingly.

"That's right. And you know, really, Mrs. Compton, they're not good people. That old man tries to court American women. He came here to see me before I was so big with the baby, before he knew. And everybody knows about Madame. She likes them young, old, or medium—especially Americans. I say everybody—I mean French people. I have a friend, you see. Madame Tricot. She got me my maid, by the way. You'll have to get to know her. She's the leader of Beaumonde's society. And you speak French. She'll probably even take you to Paris!"

The doe eyes were wistful, as Laurel began her adieux. At the door Nora Frakes exclaimed, as Laurel handed her the baby, "Oh, I almost forgot the most important part. I started to tell you before why we're leaving the house a week earlier. Oh, Mrs. Compton! I know you're an older woman, but you're so—so pretty and so understanding. I'm going to tell you the exact truth. My husband accidentally set one of their mattresses on fire. A cigarette rolled off an ashtray in the middle of the bed, while he was on the telephone. This was when I was in Germany. And I set a hot casserole on their black dining table; it left an awful ring. But you see, Mrs. Compton, the minute my husband tried to pressure them into buying the promised hot-water heater so we could bathe here, they got their lawyer on us to make us have the tiles relaid in the front walk, and I swear to you, the walk was that way the first time we came to look at the house. Anyway, Harold, my husband, that is, thinks they'll get Colonel Fritsch—you know, the Wing Commander—no, he's gone home, hasn't he?—well, anyway, Harold thinks they'll attach his salary or write the American Embassy or something. And we feel like things are pretty even."

She may be right about the family morals, surmised Laurel, but the Hachères couldn't be miserly. They just couldn't. This woman's sweet, and rather pitiful, but she's incompetent. "What is the legal French rent on the place?"

"Forty-three dollars—in francs," she answered gravely, "but we were perfectly willing to play along with their price and no legal receipt."

Laurel did not reply to Nora Frakes that it was a lot of house for a hundred dollars a month in any country. Running water. Hot water! City electricity. And a radiator and a fireplace in every room! Ah, Laurel had had a winter too dire to have been dulled in memory by these few weeks of neo-summer!

"Well, thank you, Mrs. Frakes, and good luck in Turkey!"

"Oh, we'll love it," cooed the small woman. "Just think! To be warm, really warm again without any of these crazy French laws and taxes and—and customs."

If Captain Frakes had had a choice of remaining in France, he was making a dreadful mistake to hoist his month-old baby to such a climate as that of the NATO base in Turkey. Laurel was overcome with a desire to say this to his wife, but it was too late.

By Alouette's measurements, Hachère's rent house was minuscule and compared to Paradis or Noël, it was hardly spacious, but when Laurel reviewed the miserable four rooms at Monceau, 14 rue Père Marquette already loomed as her special made-to-order French haven.

She tried to evaluate all the things the Frakes woman had contended, but even if every word of her complaint were true, little mattered now to Laurel except the prospect of warmth and comfort.

She remembered for no reason the only bedroom among the six which was absolutely devoid of furniture, the third floor bedroom directly over that she had chosen on sight for Brick. Both bedrooms had the same view as the kitchen of the downhill slope, rail yards, and distant farms. But she recalled now what it was in the empty room she had seen fleetingly: a pale gold marble fireplace carved in a Roman manner. A motto chiseled in one neat line two or three inches below the mantelpiece read SEMEL INSANIVIMUS OMNES.

Who but a Frenchman would have the whimsy to mount such a platitude in a bedroom? WE HAVE ALL BEEN MAD ONCE.

2

Of course, Zero Compton knew whose house he was renting. "I would have sworn I told you that, Laurel!" he said.

He had just informed her, an hour ahead of the fact, that they were making a six P.M. call at the Hachères' home in Beaumonde to clarify the "verbal contract" in the presence of Hachères and their attorney. Laurel objected vociferously, "Where's *our* lawyer, if they're going to elevate the agreement into legalities? Zero, you're making a mistake!"

But he laughed her out of further objections, and soon she was gazing above a champagne glass at Lawyer Risseau, soft-mannered, glib in English, and bearer of a false limb from the left forearm down. A hard black leather glove concluded his coat sleeve.

Risseau was suave. His favorite opening line to any American in the region concerned his year in Harvard Law School—1923 —and Laurel had suspected from the first that his attitude toward American wives (slightly cocked head, bent waist, and a superfluous but charming French accent) suggested he had spent a night course in Charles Boyer movies. No remark in English could be uttered so fast he missed it; Americans tagged him with such words as sympathetic, sharp, and witty. In the lingo of Beaumonde Air Base that year, "old Risseau can hack it."

Hachère popped to his feet with the crowning toast: "To the

champion of the shoot, the champion of the air, the champion of the war, the champion of the bridge, and, sans doute, a champion of the women!"

Laurel found this in extremely poor taste, but Risseau translated literally and Zero guffawed. Hachère twinkled—at Zero, not Laurel. Madame Hachère beamed glowing approval upon the lengthy American.

Then, as the discussion became serious, certain agreements were reached. The hundred dollars a month rental was to be paid in cash only on the first day of each month, and without a legal receipt. "To save all parties trouble," supplemented Risseau needlessly. On the following day, Risseau's plumber son-in-law would install a new hot-water heater in the house. If Colonel Compton furnished the price of the paint, all areas on the first floor except the kitchen were to be painted sage green. For this concession, the Hachères now requested that Laurel agree to leave behind whatever draperies she installed in the redone rooms. Surprised but amicable, she conceded this point.

As if there was nothing else to be discussed, Papa Hachère took up a second bottle of champagne and opened it. Risseau, having dropped his professional manner, began to translate something Madame Hachère wished to have said to Compton. The moment he finished this task, Laurel regained his attention.

"I want the garden," she said.

His chuckle held dismissal. "The Americans have not found it interesting."

Laurel and Zero exchanged a glance, after which he bent closer to Madame Hachère and began to twirl his glass of champagne and stare into it while charming the French woman with his helpless French phrases. Laurel said to Risseau, "Tell Monsieur Hachère I will have it."

His expression firming, the lawyer replied, "We discussed it earlier. The Hachères put in the garden. It is theirs. The previous tenant relinquished all rights."

She beamed her finest smile upon him and lied, "But I despise to have market vegetables in my house. It is one reason I have accepted the house." She bit her lip in deep-seeming quandary. "Tell Monsieur Hachère I will pay him for one-half the labor already put in the plot, one-half the seed and plant investment, and use, for the remainder of this season, only those vegetables needed for our table."

After a disapproving grimace, Risseau crossed over to Hachère's chair and bent beside him, whispering in such mumbled, rapid sounds that Laurel could not hear what was being reported. Still squatted by the chair, Risseau said, "Seventy dollars—in francs."

Laurel extinguished her quick flame of anger; after all, she scolded herself, it was only a bargain to be driven. But seventy dollars! Outrageous! Laurel called Zero's name, and explained to him rapidly the current state of the garden question.

He scowled energetically and said, "God damn!" Then he looked up at Risseau with mild contempt. "Half of seventy dollars will buy a helluva lot of potatoes!" The lawyer met his gaze unwaveringly. Zero changed his tactics to an engaging grin. "Tell Hachère what I said—about the potatoes!"

Laurel listened as Risseau said to Hachère, "It appears you will be obliged to surrender the garden, but only at the end of this growing season, say, the first of November. Not before. And they can clean it for the winter that way."

Laurel's eyes blazed, although she held her close-lipped smile. Hachère's expression, of course, had not changed from one of solemn contemplation. He appeared neither pleased nor displeased. For an instant, she longed to give sway to impulse and tell Hachère what Zero had said, for Hachère's sense of humor was unfailing, but after all, she reminded herself, we've all got two years to live in this town together. The madder I make Risseau, the greater our disadvantage.

Zero spoke up again, glancing from Hachère's face to Risseau. "Tell him what I said."

"I did."

"Well, tell him it's a joke."

"I did," he said, losing patience, spreading his palms, and opening every crevice in his face, "but it's your joke, and my client doesn't buy it."

Laurel fixed a whimsical but intent gaze on Risseau and said loudly enough for both Hachères to hear her rapid sentence, "I fear then we shall have to postpone the household inventory a day, until I can obtain my own lawyer."

Madame Hachère seemed to fly out of her chair, lips rounded in solicitous no. She caught both Laurel's hands and bent down to her.

"Ah, my poor Madame Compton! What have these naughty men denied you to necessitate that?" She turned to Risseau with a pout. "You see? I told you friends of the Marquis ought not be subjected to useless, boring routines like ordinary tenants!"

Hachère gave his wife a bemused glance and said nothing. She turned back to Laurel and said, "Whatever is wrong, you and I shall work it out without this pair of villains!"

Her exaggerated gesturing and her excessive feminity combined to silence Laurel, who believed anyway that women were able to compromise with far less clumsiness than men were. She smiled at Madame Hachère, thinking how delightful it would be to have artichokes cut from the rear garden the first night dinner was served at 14 rue Père Marquette. . . .

Later, when she narrated the entire account to Zero, he halfscolded her, "We don't give a damn about their old vegetables, Laurel. And as for our getting a lawyer, it looks as if we don't trust the Hachères. It's getting off on the wrong foot."

The inventory began at four P.M. next day with Papa Hachère, nervous, alert, and wisecracking, tacitly in charge. Laurel wondered whether the older married couple had not counseled each other in the interim as had she and Zero, for Risseau today was only the figurehead who held the list of furnishings as they ambled through the house.

Hachère, however, lost a good deal of his effervescent sparkle when he understood that the items Madame Compton rejected with a wave of her hand were to spend the next two years in the attic. As tactfully as possible, Laurel explained that the boys might damage the thirty-inch-high bronze statue, a monstrosity of Cupid, a collie dog, and a clock. This provoked Hachère into a little farce as he demonstrated from various angles his inability to budge his treasure. How could small lads upset it? he demanded.

But Laurel waded on through her vetoes: a circular table with a marble top lost in its frame of chipped enamel; a caned piano bench once painted gold; a Victorian chair with a torn needlepoint scene obscured by grime. And in the dining room, there was a cheap black modernistic dining table.

Watching Laurel's face closely, Madame Hachère said, "See that ring on my lovely new table! Ah, Madame Frakes has treated us badly. We were friends, I thought, when her husband came so often to dinner, while she was in Germany having her baby. But suddenly, poof! They did not like us." She sighed through pursed lips. "Of course, we are not very entertaining, Madame Compton, but I hope it will never be different for us, you and I. Do not worry about that garden."

Ah, thought Laurel with a sigh of relief and pleasure, she's going to tell me right now, while her husband isn't listening, to take what I need from that big garden. But Madame Hachère did not say that. She said, "Do not fret! I will give you cabbage and leeks and potatoes and onions from time to time. We shall understand each other perfectly."

Laurel and Zero had been in bed a half-hour that night before her mind clicked on what had been missing in the Beaumonde house: no sign of a plumber installing the new heater. But Zero rebuked her sleepily, "You don't trust anybody in the world except yourself, do you, Laurel? So they're a day late? Have faith. They said they'd do it, didn't they?"

A week later with a key of her own, Laurel entered the premises alone for the first time and was able to ramble over the empty rooms a half-hour or so before the truck was due to arrive with her household shipment, which had not been unpacked in nearly two years.

Olande had been left to care for the children at Monceau, but Francis Soleil, her fiancé, had volunteered a day of his vacation to help the Americans unpack. Hence, with his help and that of three movers, every object of furniture was in its rightful room before five o'clock. When Laurel returned next morning, Soleil was waiting at the gate.

By noon, he had unpacked twelve crates of kitchenware and placed it on lined cupboard shelves. He then set up the traverse rods and hung the green velvet draperies in the salon and dining room. He hung the six paintings in either room, and when Laurel came down from making beds, she found that he had cleaned the entire first floor of excelsior.

During the next three days while she performed finishing touches a room at a time, Soleil worked in the basement, papering and painting what was to be a bedroom-sitting room. Thus, a week before the scheduled wedding of Francis and Olande, their two-room apartment was pristine and colorful. Laurel bought a dozen pots of red geraniums and divided them between Olande's kitchen and bedroom. She dug out a bright red chenille spread for their bed. From M. Hachère's attic supply came a small desk, a mahogany gooseneck rocker, and a Victorian loveseat. Laurel stood in the door for one last survey. The scene was complete, charming and full of promise for contentment. How delighted Olande should be. She had not been in the house and Laurel did not wish her to come until after her wedding.

Some wordless esteem had sprung up between the American and stoical Francis Soleil, perhaps a tie born of mutual admiration for industry. (Soleil had appeared ready to faint upon discovering Laurel standing atop an eight-rung stepladder polishing the prisms of the salon chandelier.) At no time had she asked him to do a specific task, nor had he inquired. In truth, they had seldom spoken to each other in these days of work. Now, with the house completely ready for entrance, there was nothing left to do except pack electrical appliances and clothing and groceries at Monceau. Laurel felt an enormous pressure of emotion that afternoon as she locked the front door after her own and Soleil's exist. She gestured to him to follow her to the car, where she tossed him the keys and got into the second seat. Soleil stuck his head through the window and said, "But Madame, I have no license to drive an American car."

Laurel replied, "We are not in America. Let's go up to the clothing store atop the Hill. You can help me find what I wish to give Olande."

When the lovely, ballerina-length white gown of silk organza had been selected and paid for, Laurel directed Soleil to the lace shop a few doors away where he agreed, with classless male confusion in such matters, that the slender tiara encrusted with seed pearls would indeed become Olande, and also the waist-length veil.

They proceeded to the florist shop across from the railroad station, where the fascinated laborer watched the American woman design for the owner of the shop—she drew on paper—an arrangement of stephanotis, forget-me-nots, and six white roses (unopened, Monsieur!), a nosegay to fill two hands. "And no paper ribbon, Monsieur. I will pay for satin!"

Laurel changed from her place to the driver's seat while Francis Soleil unlocked the Beaumonde house and carried the tiara and the boxed dress down to the basement bedroom. When he returned, Laurel beckoned him to the car. First she handed him a litre of Calvados from beneath the front seat of the car.

"Put it quickly in that box on your motorcycle. If I am caught smuggling it from Normandy, Francis, I hear that one is fined equal to the value of one's car—on the French market!"

She laughed, but Soleil's eyes were awed. "Madame! No! Monsieur will not. . . ."

"Monsieur does not know. I brought it back specifically for the reception after Olande's wedding." She blinked, surprised by a sudden misting of her eyes. Marriage is only a biological booby trap, she scolded herself inwardly. What makes women weep at the mere idea of a wedding?

She took the last large franc note from her billfold and handed it to Soleil. Ten thousand francs. About thirty dollars. Olande's salary for one month. "This is for your help, Francis."

He glanced down, not reaching for the money. "I helped in gratitude for a place to live. And a nice place."

"I understand. But you must buy Olande something. A strand of pearls, or a pair of white gloves. A bit long, Francis. One is not often a bride."

He accepted the bill. "You spent nine times this much on Olande today."

"Not quite."

"Then I shall be obliged to buy better champagne for the reception—in honor of your and your husband's presence."

She glanced away from him. "I have not told Olande. We cannot attend the wedding."

Soleil made no attempt to conceal his disapproval. "Madame, in France, it is the custom to. . . ."

Laurel cut in, "for a girl's employer to help celebrate the wedding." She decided not to tell him that she was obliged to be in Paris the Saturday of his wedding, that her husband was being entered in an international shooting exhibition, or that. . . .

"Ah, Madame!" he said, shaking his head in a way that determined her absence would not have offended him at all, save for his bride's feelings. Then Soleil extended the ten-mille note toward her. Laurel glanced down at it, shocked.

Eyes kindling, she declared, "You must not confuse kindness with weakness. You shall live under my roof exactly as long as you honor the difference."

Soleil continued to hold the ten-mille paper between them with a passive detachment which made Laurel long to shake him—so immovable, so untouchable he seemed. He eyed her coldly as she drove away.

On the thirtieth day of July, the Comptons quit the Monceau house and moved to Beaumonde. On the morning of August first, when Madame Hachère arrived at eight-thirty A.M. to collect her thirty-five mille rent, Zero beamed his broadest smile upon the French woman while instructing his wife to say no rent would be paid until he could bathe in his own house. Madame Hachère mustered a fixed smile, uncertain apologies, and backed out of the door, unpaid and unbelieving.

3

The Compton children were deposited in gay expectation— a whole week end with the four Edney boys! The first week end in August.

After dining at a country inn between Villers-Cotteret and Soissons, Michel, Zero, and Laurel reached Paris around eleven P.M. on Friday evening and drove directly to the Berteaux flat, which had been closed since Easter.

Laurel was ill at ease passing room after room of furnishings secreted beneath beige-muslin dust covers, although she had assured Véronique Berteaux during the Normandy visit that she would use the family flat on her next overnight stay in Paris. As she and Zero were getting into bed, she joked that they ought to pull the sheets over their heads so they blended with the prevailing atmosphere in the ghostlike flat.

The next morning brought a vigorous knock on the bedroom door. "May I come in?" Michel chirped.

Half awake and totally amenable, Zero sang out, "Certainly!" He dashed for his robe. Laurel gathered the covers higher, as the host bounded in and dropped into a covered object near the bedside which was, after all, a chair. He arranged himself comfortably and offered Zero a cigarette, a French cigarette.

Neither man alluded to her presence as Zero sat on the side of the bed and smoked and talked with Michel. She regarded her husband's disheveled hair, his pleased tone of voice, and thought—for no reason—of the countless times in the States when he had caught her eye across a roomful of people to signal that her skirt had edged a centimeter beyond propriety, or that she was gripping some man's arm in an effort to carry across her point.

She heard Zero say, "Excuse me," and felt the bed return level as he quit the side. She knew he was going to the bathroom and so she did not open her eyes, for it was easier to endure the heavy smell of French tobacco without looking at Michel.

He said, "Guy's joining us for lunch."

"You're a liar! He's in Switzerland."

Michel laughed maliciously, "You're a fool! You don't really believe he'd leave Paris when he knows you're coming? Laurel, he's spending August in the city for the first time in eight years."

Her heart hammered in her throat and temples. She was grateful when Zero came back into the room, asking another question about some rule of the international shooting match in which Michel was sponsoring him.

Guy was waiting at a veranda table as Laurel walked between Michel and Zero along a gravel path ribboned between two rows of tulips, past the gatekeeper, and onto the green terrace. The white-timbered clubhouse was not impressive in size, but with the forest for a backdrop, its naked white brilliance in young August sun reminded Laurel of a baguette diamond nestled in emerald velvet.

The grass, trees, and flowers had none of the withered taint associated with late summer in America. Zero mentioned this.

Guy said, "In my mind, America is green ten months of every year."

Zero retorted that Kansas, on the contrary, was brown about that much of any year. Michel asked Laurel whether this was true of Louisiana, and there ensued between the Comptons a friendly argument about the vegetation near Baton Rouge at the time of their late August marriage.

Michel queried, "Then your wedding anniversary is near?"

"Look out!" interceded Guy. "My esteemed friend is about to invite himself to the party!"

Laurel gazed confidently at Zero who, during eight anniversaries, held that such a party would be crowded with more than the two people concerned. But his smile was broad. "We're having two dozen guests for cocktails and dinner, a combination housewarming and ninth anniversary party. I'm surprised Laurel didn't beat me to telling you."

She glanced at her hands, which were folded in her lap and said, "Of course! You're both expected!" For some reason, she could not look at Guy just now.

"You better come, by God!" added Zero, "because two days after the party, I'll be heading back to Africa for another five or six weeks at the gunnery range with the Squadron."

There was a taut little silence before Michel said to Guy, "You've never seen the kind of parties Americans have. Guy, you'll have the time of your life. They're champions at having fun!"

After lunch Michel and Zero went off to make arrangements for Zero's entry in the shooting, abandoning Laurel and Guy. For a long moment, the pair regarded each other in a kind of wistful admiration illicit only by virtue of their isolation. Laurel admitted a sharp stab of ecstatic pain given her in rare moments of perception.

"Laurel, that day when I drove your car back from Paris, you spoke a great deal. . . ."

"An old affliction," she interrupted, remembering well enough her overintimate account. "Too much wine that day, Guy. No sleep. You know. . . ."

Her eyes implored acceptance but Guy said, "Speak to me of childhood."

"No. I should have to begin with birth, and alas! I do not remember that." Immediately, he pressured her with a specific question. What was Paradis like? Pale pink, faded, Doric-columned, she answered, with a path of trees leading to an old boat landing. A land grant. 1734.

Guy narrowed his next question to her fondest memory as a child. She replied flatly: a groaning table. He called her a beautiful cynic, evoking in her a mixed feeling of shyness and guilt.

"All right! A black horse. He was called Old Nig. A pre-integration steed, I suppose."

"I can't move with you in English idiom. I'm not Michel."

Thank God, thought Laurel. "I used to catch the horse with a bucket of oats. I led him into the stable and while he lapped up his grain, I climbed on something high enough to get on him. No saddle. No bridle. I wasn't tall enough to put them on. And anyway, I liked racing him over the fields and pretending I could ride like a Cajun. There were fields, Guy. . . ." Her voice trailed off. What would a Frenchman care about the way June wheat waved like a sea of green water? She picked up her wine glass and drained the last acrid sip.

"What are you thinking of now, Laurel?"

"The fragrance of a clean barn. The way hot wind feels. The way a horse smells when you've really run him."

His burst of laughter was unexpected, "Ah, Laurel! The thousand French women who would pay to have that chair at this exhibition, to be inside these grounds, and probably the two or three of them who know how horse sweat smells would be afraid to admit it, much less speak of it voluntarily."

"But Guy, you must take a turn at this game. Of your own childhood, what do you like best to remember?"

"A cave, Laurel. A secret place with an ancient grapevine growing across the entrance. I gathered stones, sticks, even frogs and hid them there, pretending to be extremely rich because I owned a different kind of cave than did my father."

She recognized tender nostalgia in his voice. "It is strange. I have been unable to speak of that since. . . ."

"Since what, Guy?" The air was shimmering, undependable. She held her breath.

"My brother, Arnaud. He was four years younger than I. And the day he became six, I kept a promise to take him to my cave. He often spoke of that in the weeks before—well, in the war."

Intuition dizzied her now. She longed to reach over and still his words with her lips, for she could not bear to hear that this was the bond she had sensed in the early seconds of their meeting. Not death—no. No!

"We were guarding a pass. Eighteen-hour tours. I was a blind fool, thinking him safer beside me. We only went two at a time. A pass. A mountain pass. The Germans had sent an armored vehicle in that morning. The first time. The route was useless unless a grenade could be discharged inside the vehicle. And I made the mistake of saying this to Arnaud. Oh, Laurel! A baby! Fourteen years and seven months of life. I should have forced him to stay at boarding school, where my father believed he was."

She could not speak, could not look at him. Her heart seemed frozen as he resumed his tale—his ignorance of the machine-gun nest installed by the Germans during the night on the opposite flank of the pass. "With that wretched valor peculiar to children, Arnaud struck out uncovered to hurl his grenade. No one could have made it. Besides, it was too far. But when I dragged him back, there came the worst part. Laurel. . . ." He reached out and touched her chin with a gesture which brought them face to face, and she longed to take his hand, to reach from between the bars of her prison, to touch him. Merely touch him. "Laurel, do you know how futile is physical strength? The mute plea as

Arnaud lay in my arms. Dying. And the enormity of my crime. And no priest. And my father to be told."

A constriction intruded upon his voice, almost a sob before he went on. "For a long time, I consoled myself by saying I was not made for war, but one arrives at that philosophy which reveals no man is made for war. My father had always symbolized to me the kind of strength and courage war requires of men. Of course, with his past training and experience in the other War, he was one of the first to—well, you see, he was taken prisoner in the Maginot days. And we believed he was alive until after Liberation."

Guy bit his lip in a sudden silence, trying gravely to control his overwrought emotions. Laurel said in a comforting tone, "My father was killed at sea in 1944. A Japanese torpedo." But you couldn't say to a man like Guy that your father had been too old for the Navy, that he compromised by the Merchant Marine, or that you hadn't seen him since you were four years old, and that hearing he was dead was like reading about some stranger's gallant demise.

"Laurel," he whispered, "were we ever children?"

He leaned forward to put a hand on her shoulder, and she knew the moment he touched her the sob building in her throat would claim its wet destiny, but Michel was running toward them, running and shouting that a half-hour intermission had been declared. Then he saw their faces. "What's the matter?" he demanded. "You both seem ready to cry!"

Guy rose to his feet. "Laurel weeps from boredom with my life story, and I weep, naturally, because she is married."

Michel complained of the heat as he got out his handkerchief and wiped his neck and face with the boldness of a man wielding a bath towel. Laurel saw Zero several yards away depositing his gun in a rack. He took out his handkerchief, unfolded it, and neatly dried his palms. As she anticipated, he refolded the linen square with precision and ambled toward the table, not yet looking up.

During the rest of the afternoon, Laurel and Guy pursued a tacit aim of avoiding mutual tragedies. They spoke of philosophy,

American Indians, two-party political systems, Algeria, modern art, and at times they sat in placid silence.

Zero tied an Egyptian marksman for first place, which left Michel disconcerted. After arranging for the pair to shoot off the match (unofficially) next morning, he insisted that they dine early in some quiet place to enhance Zero's physical prowess for the informal finish Sunday morning.

Near the close of the meal in the staid Jockey Club, however, Michel espied the party of Egyptians and their sponsors lolling in the bar area. Nervously he insisted Zero join him in a friendly overture and so, once again, Laurel and Guy were relegated to each other.

When Michel was out of hearing range, she said, "He'll probably hire the bartender to fix the Egyptian's drinks!"

Guy replied flatly, "He shouldn't have overextended himself in the betting."

To cover her surprise, she said quickly, "What about you?"

Guy shrugged indifferently. "I have no money to play with. Or let me say, whatever cash I have goes down one well."

In the strange Berteaux bed with its stiff mattress Zero soon snored with regularity while Laurel coped with wakeful night. Restlessness akin to panic drove her from bed shortly after midnight. In the dark, she felt her way to the dressing table, her handbag, a cigarette and lighter, but the smoke tasted disagreeable. It made the stuffy room smell foul. She crushed out the cigarette on the glass-covered vanity table and felt her way back to bed where she edged the length of her body against Zero's back to warm. With a jerk, he turned over, flailing an elbow into her breast and pinning her briefly into the mattress. She freed herself and moved away as he rolled his head in the throes of some difficult dream.

In his sleep, he said, "Helluva place to start from. Get that French tower operator. Tell the bastard I'm holding at twenty-three thousand. No! Call CoCoHoTel and tell 'em I've got twelve minutes' fuel. And order me a double dry martini."

Staring blindly at the ceiling, Laurel repeated to herself, "Twenty-three thousand altitude, twelve minutes' fuel, and a double martini! God in Heaven, must each of us live in our own little handmade Hell?" On this thought, she sighed deeply, somehow hopelessly, and turned on her side. Then, as a light turned off leaves no afterglow, so her mind surrendered wakefulness.

Zero roused her early and said, "Let's get dressed, Laurel, and slip out for some coffee before Michel wakes up. I can't stand another French cigarette this morning before coffee." She arose and dressed hastily, her mind blurred with fatigue, but, a few hours later, she felt grateful for mental exhaustion. It seemed to take the edge from apprehension toward what Guy might say when Michel and Zero once again deserted them on the shooting club terrace.

She examined the clarity of morning's sounds—the raucous shotgun blasts which echoed behind them, the indistinct mumble of spectators here and there, and, far away in the woods, a mourning dove's poignant cry. She glanced up at a fragment of lost cloud passing before the sun.

When Guy spoke, his voice emerged in peculiar volume. "You did not sleep?" She averted her gaze to the tile terrace between their chairs. "Laurel, your eyes wear circles."

Her snort was delicate but precise. "So does my brain this morning. I feel remote, as if I were viewing all this scene through binoculars, hearing your voice from a recording."

"That's not fatigue, Laurel," he said softly. "It's the heart's need to flee reality now and then."

She said flatly, "Not the heart, the mind." Guy shrugged mildly, indicating not concession but indifference to argument. She heard her own words with surprise. "Guy, what is reality to you?"

His eyes narrowed as he planned his reply. "Awareness of impurity."

"That's nebulous, almost vaporous."

"All right. Separation from God."

"You're not excommunicate?"

He laughed in quick rebuttal. "No, Laurel. But after Liberation, I belonged nowhere. I couldn't go back to school and finish my education. Let us say, my legs had grown too long for a desk. I tried for a year to fill the place expected of me—at the head of my father's—my mother's interests." He paused in reflection. "I went through all the motions of religion. But no inner peace came as it once did."

She said, "And so you compromised with service to literature?"

"Well, not exactly. I . . . it seemed to me the field of children's books had been neglected in France always."

"Juveniles?" she said in a disappointed voice.

"So I began in a very small way—with my own funds."

"I see." Never, never had she supposed anything he could say might bore her, but as he spoke further of his endeavor, she fell to remembering the book he had brought Brick, the kind of elegant book which might attest to a doting aunt's or a pleased godfather's unselfish affluence. Certainly, she reflected, the person who planned such a book was no more dedicated than commercial!

"What brings your sad expression, Laurel?"

She chuckled too quickly. "I was thinking how cruel the world of children's fantasy is—how I wept because I knew no matter what the writer said that Pinocchio was really wooden—and how I brooded over the pathetic little girl with only three matches and no place to get warm."

Guy laughed and shook his head in mock hopelessness. "Laurel, there's no woman on this earth like you. Only your body and your mind grew. I suspect your heart is still ten years old."

Her eyes danced as she said, "Well, I'm glad you found something to laugh about even if it had to be me."

"Nominative," he said quickly. " 'If it had to be *I*'."

"Go to Hell!" she retorted gaily.

"I will, if you go with me." His eyes upon her were luminous, depthless. A wave of weakness swept from her heart, out and over her body and limbs: Why haven't I known? Guy knows. Oh, God! How could I have been such a fool?

She had a faint sensation that the whole scene—Guy, the table, the terrace, even the sky—was moving away from her—growing smaller—less real—less dangerous.

"Laurel!" he shouted in controlled anxiety. "Are you ill? You're suddenly pale."

When she opened her eyes, distortion had righted. "I don't know what's the matter. I have a sort of chill. . . ."

He stood up. "I'll tell Zero we're going to the car."

"No!" she cried. "You'll embarrass him before these foreigners. I feel better already. Perhaps you'll order us some coffee," she proposed, clasping her hands in her lap and leaning forward so Guy would not perceive their trembling.

He arose at once and strode in swift steps toward the interior of the Club. Laurel too arose and sped past the gatekeeper, down the gravel path between the drooping red tulips and beyond the station wagon into the leafy forest.

I love him, cried her heart in heavy dirge. I've never loved anyone else. I never will. Oh, God! God! God! And if I reach out to him, I'll destroy him, and if I don't. . . . She walked as rapidly as the tundralike growth and her high heels allowed, staring at the verdant bushes and vines along the path as if solace would soon bud beside the leaves and be hers for the plucking.

A little distance from the path, Laurel stumbled onto a pair of lovers in an unsunned patch of grass surrounded by brambles. Her hurried departure was interrupted by a sprawled bicycle, unnoticed until now, but she freed her foot and darted off so fast that the ball-bearing whir of the spinning wheel seemed to follow her.

Her face flamed, her heart pounded until—a safe distance—she slowed to catch her breath. Suddenly, she perceived the weighty stillness in the forest and glanced overhead to find nature's lace—thick, green leaves lined in cloud taffeta of purple gray. Birds no longer flitted from limb to limb, but twittered close to ashen trunks with their morose little heads sunk into their chests, feathers plumped against the oncoming fury.

Acutely, Laurel listened. Leaves brushing each other in passive, farewell kiss. Another sound—a strange muffled thud, like long-legged fleet running steps. And the distant sound of shooting—ugly even from this distance.

The forest floor glimmered in weird light pink. Laurel glanced about her, immovable, unafraid, as if she were seeing lightning for the first time in her life. Then it repeated, and thunder rolled as if the king of elephants had stumped his toe and fractured earth's crust. Laurel, who had said no real prayer since that uttered at Le Bourget airport in gratitude for safe voyage, looked toward Heaven. I promise never to see him again—after the anniversary party. I promise!

The lightning repeated—again and again. Laurel remained rooted beneath the giant trees, staring through their umbrella branches.

4

Seven o'clock, ten o'clock, midnight passed—with no sign of Guy at the anniversary party, and no explanation. When the last guest departed, except Michel, who was remaining the night, Laurel busied herself collecting glasses and wiping ashtrays while Zero and his friend relaxed with three A.M. "nightcaps" at opposite posts on the Victorian sofa.

"I shall never speak to him again," roared the tipsy Marquis. "He has violated our friendship, the gentleman's code, and France's honor!"

Why don't you slap him with a glove? thought Laurel.

Michel continued, "You haven't said a word all night about the most eligible bachelor in Paris insulting your hospitality!"

She had no desire for a discussion at that hour. She picked up the last full ashtray and tossed its debris into the embers on the hearth. It's over, she thought. The only sensible thing. A clean, quick, uncomplicated cut. But he could have told me.

Laurel delved then into self-promises. She had been abominably selfish, confining herself to the French. She would turn now to American interests and live up to her obligation in this foreign country. Yes, she mused darkly, I've only to alienate Michel Berteaux—permanently. And I will, by God, even if I have to do it by physical means. A frontal attack? How funny! He'd die before he'd have any woman aware of his impotency.

The next morning, however, it appeared that Michel might accidentally write *himself* off with his host. When he renewed the subject of Guy, Zero showed disgust and said, "Save your breath, Michel! Maybe Guy had a flat tire. Maybe he found a girl!"

Michel then took up another irritating subject, one he had been hammering at for the past three weeks. He was still stunned, he averred, by Zero's refusal of the Paris club's bid to sponsor him in shooting matches the coming spring. "You beat that Brazilian, that Italian, and the Swiss champion, and finally, that damned Egyptian!"

"And you won three hundred thousand francs. Whatdya want? An egg in your wine?"

Michel shrugged impatiently and got to his feet to begin the inevitable pacing. "You don't understand. . . ."

"Why don't you try to understand? I'm an Air Force officer on active duty. I'm part of a defense line to help save you and your God damned lazy countrymen. If you titled noblemen—" (Zero put a vicious inflection in both words) "—weren't so all-fired worried about the next ball or hunt, maybe France wouldn't be in the shape it's in. Ever think about that?"

Michel paled. He seemed frozen. His lower lip gaped as he stared in disbelief at his American friend, who, insult upon insult, grinned challengingly. "Mike, I haven't got time to go in training three or four hours a day. I'm not in condition. And there isn't a single officer above me who gives a pot shot about sport shooting."

"Then it's up to you to convince them."

"*Can* it!"

"I won't can it! I'll have my say! One outstanding American such as you can raise USA stock in France higher than all the lend lease dollars. Why don't Americans figure that out for themselves?" Intuitively, Laurel opened her mouth, for she was accustomed by now to wedge herself between her husband's wrath and its victims. But Michel hurried on. "Zero, is *every*

American your country sends over here too stupid to comprehend *that?*"

She waited, breathless, as Zero's angled brows formed their signal of contempt. She felt unfairness in the match, unbalance in the whole scene, for Michel was no more than a mouse, already wounded, running from the cat.

She stood up and said blithely, "I think it's time we had a new pot of coffee." Before either man had a chance to reply, the door bell rang. As Laurel entered the hall, Madame Hachère came through the entrance, smiling, affable, dewy as morning. Bonjour, Madame! Bonjour, Madame Compton! Then, casting aside further preliminaries, the French woman spoke of the rent.

"It is a month already," whispered Madame with sweetness.

"I have no francs," breathed Laurel politely.

"Borrow from your maid." Madame leaned closer.

"She is not so well paid."

"Si! Si!" exclaimed the French matron prudently. "I borrow often from servants. They always have a hidden cache!"

Zero slipped into the hall and closed the door neatly behind himself, still gripping the knob. "If she's here about the rent, tell her Hell no! Not until we have a hot water heater."

Laurel smiled at him glowingly, "I won't tell her a damned thing until you say good morning to her."

"For Christ's sake!"

"Say it! Or do you want her peddling tales of our incivilities through the Beaumonde storekeepers? *Say it!*"

Zero half nodded and begrudged a smile. Then he glanced in annoyance at his hand as the knob turned and Michel tugged the door open. As Laurel expected, he was fully apprised of the entire situation, which he now embarked upon describing to Madame Hachère in terms of wretched politeness. It was embarrassing to him, having obtained—no, having *recommended*—the house to his friends, and he would appreciate a satisfactory conclusion of the verbal agreement.

Throughout his little speech, Madame Hachère never quite managed to maintain a composed mouth. Her good day was a mixture of bow and nod as she backed out of the house. Shortly after lunch, 14 rue Père Marquette vibrated and resounded with the noise of hammered pipes and welding torches and that night, Zero had an honest bath in his own house.

Next morning, September first, Laurel called Olande to her desk and gave her a pair of unsealed envelopes each containing a month's rent—seventy thousand francs in all. "And if Madame Hachère says anything to you which indicates her displeasure that I have sent the money by a servant; if she declares that the envelopes are unsealed, or implies that you have opened them, you must confide in her, Olande, that I am a difficult woman. You will say to her, if at all possible, that it displeases me to have her come here for the rent, and hint that, if she stops coming here to collect money, I shall start bringing it myself. You see, Olande, things are not as agreeable as I had hoped. I saw by your shoes waiting to be cleaned in the basement—twice this month—she has sent you to the garden to select her vegetables when it rains. I do not doubt that she telephoned you to say what to have ready, and that she went through my attic, and that you quite happily offered to let her see your apartment in the basement."

Laurel watched amazement touch the girl's face and knew that she had struck several hits. "I do not blame you, Olande, but now it is different. Did she offer you leeks or a cabbage?" The maid shook her head, eyes round and sad. "No potatoes or lettuce?"

"No, Madame. She gave Brick the last six strawberries, but they were too old. I was afraid to let him have them."

"Olande, did she go through all of my house?"

"Every room, Madame."

"Damn you!" said Laurel, her eyes aflame.

"What could I do?" the maid nearly shouted. "She's French. I'm French. She lets me live under her roof. She told me that!"

Laurel pushed the swivel chair away from the roll-top desk and swept to her feet. "Olande, I need your loyalty, but I will not stoop to beg it."

Olande's eyes were downcast in familiar contrition. "I am sorry, Madame. It is only that—that. . . ."

"That she implied she can withdraw her generosity at any time and oust you from your apartment?" Olande nodded. Laurel hunted frantically for something positive to say, anything that would impress the confused maid as tangible. "Olande, I shall obtain a waiver—in writing—from the Hachères' lawyer, permitting your and Francis' residence here until the day Colonel Compton and I leave the house for good."

The servant's eyes were doubtful even as she nodded in gratitude. And suddenly, Laurel heard herself recalling a story which she had not consciously thought about since it happened. The American refrigerator which the Frakes had deposited in the basement. Zero's shrugging reply to Laurel that it was probably Air Base property and would soon be picked up. The account in the Beaumonde newspaper of the Risseau daughter's wedding. And the piece of gossip brought into Laurel's house by Olande herself. Risseau's gift of an American refrigerator to the bride and groom was a sensation at various echelons of Beaumonde society.

"You know what kind of fine the government of France would impose on him for buying that refrigerator minus customs?" Olande nodded, her pupils dilated in excitement. "Well, you were here when the two Frenchmen came after it in a truck. I wasn't."

"Ah, oui, Madame! The truck had no Air Base license!"

Laurel turned in a gesture of dismissal. "Don't be a fool and go telling that story about the neighborhood. Save it until it is needed, and I predict that won't be long. Vengeance is one quality which has no nationality . . ." Laurel paused in reflection before she went on. ". . . but neither has *right*."

"Do you mean neither *is* right, Madame?"

"No, Olande, I mean that right has no nationality, either. What is moral in France is moral in America."

5

"Laurel, I won't bother writing . . . since we'll be able to talk each Sunday afternoon over the MARS radio hook up. You know where to go on the Base—that shack two doors from Operations?"

She nodded, puzzled by Zero's nonchalant air as he stood in the door of 14 rue Père Marquette at a quarter of four that afternoon. She felt he was wrong in refusing to wake the children from their naps to kiss him good-bye. After all, it would be an absence of six or seven weeks.

Her own cool kiss in farewell was a blend of relief and rationalization. Zero had been unfaithful physically; she said to herself with no hint of emotion. She did not remind herself that with Abach she had overstepped the bond. In Laurel's analysis, this no longer counted. Her sin against her marriage was one of love for Guy. She could not minimize its meaning, nor will love not to exist. However, she had come to terms with the futility of such an affair. Affair was the right word, come to think of it, for that was exactly what she had no intention of having.

She slept soundly that night and woke with an inner peace grounded on acceptance of fact. The entire morning, she roamed about the house searching for improvements in plaster, plumbing, or weather stripping which needed attention before frost time. She lunched with both boys. When they began their naps, she sat at her desk with a stack of note paper, a calendar, and a roster of Beaumonde Air Base officers.

Laurel's first luncheon was for eight wives whose husbands were also in Africa. Within the month of September, she held two more luncheons, a tea, and six bridge foursomes.

Because 14 rue Père Marquette was on the "route to everywhere" from small villages where many of the families lived, Laurel had instructed Olande to perfection in one English sentence. Except to Regina Edney, the maid was obliged to say to any drop-in callers; "Madame Compton will return before five." Laurel did this because she anticipated how agreeable it would seem to other American women to return to the convenient location and sit a while in American atmosphere to drink coffee or sip sherry. She had no intention of allowing her house to become the kind of day-long hostelry it had seemed now and then in the States.

The most interesting incident in September came at the halfway point of the month with arrival of the new Commander of Beaumonde Air Base, Colonel Willard Echardt Parker. Laurel knew that he had visited the Squadrons in North Africa, direct from the States, and that he had come to Beaumonde for two or three days en route to Headquarters in Germany to be briefed by his superiors before returning again to North Africa.

She had, however, no thought of inviting him to dinner in this brief interim until a moment or two after she received a telephone call from her mother's oldest friend, Mrs. Hungerford, who declared she had allowed one night from her Paris tour to pay Laurel and her children a visit.

By a telephone call to Parker's office, Laurel obtained an immediate acceptance. Then, spurred by some impish idea of unique table conversation, she decided to invite the only French Marquis in the region, who ought to give both the new Wing Commander and the touring American a bit of certified French flavor!

Michel had dropped in the second, fourth, sixth, and tenth nights of Zero's absence, had dropped in before dinner and remained well after. He had been on his best behavior and Laurel at her most tolerant. But across from Parker, Michel became despicable. Laurel had informed him earlier that Parker spoke no French, that he had spent two years in Nazi prison, that his wife refused to come to Europe, that he was a stellar member of something called the Laikenhauf team, of which Zero was also a part. "Michel, it's something like a fraternity with unwritten bylaws. I can only tell you it's terribly important to Zero that you treat this man with kid gloves. And don't, for God's sake, taunt him about his Achilles' heel!"

"What do you mean?" Bland, false innocence!

"Well, you can imagine how sensitive he's going to be—Commander of a French Air Base and unable to say much more than Bonjour!"

Perhaps, she reflected later, it was Parker's fault for having bragged so blatantly of his finesse at German. After Michel sniggered at this, Laurel longed to shout at him, "But you speak it and read it! I saw you translate a paper for Zero, a gun brochure from Munich!" She had said nothing, and neither had stricken Mrs. Hungerford. The Colonel blundered on. He had never cared for France, he avowed. He disliked hunting, wine, lethargy, chauvinism, weak-sister politics, apathy, and above all, the God damned language.

"Did you . . . were you forced to accept the command?" asked Michel.

Parker shrugged without affectation, "It's a God damned good way to get a star and I don't mind telling you, I'm a bit overdue for my first."

Laurel glanced at Mrs. Hungerford and then down at her own hands, which lay in her lap. She heard Michel utter Hmmmm! in a voice absurdly civil. But her relief was premature. He then said in a quiet tone, "I don't believe Cameron Laikenhauf would have sent you to a base in a country with which America has guarded its ties since the days of Lafayette. Laikenhauf was a patriot."

Parker's surprise was evident. "You knew him?"

Laurel stared at the Colonel's diamond-set West Point class ring. She heard Michel say, "I dined with him on one occasion, I am proud to say. I was eleven or twelve years old when Laikenhauf was sent to France to award my father a medal, something because of his participation in the First World War. Laikenhauf was a captain then, as my father had been at the end of that War, and my father said he was very young to be a captain, but that someday he would lead the whole United States military force because it was already a flying age and Laikenhauf had wings in his heart."

Laurel was stunned to find her eyes moist as she glanced at Parker who studied his dinner plate. She sighed inwardly, thinking the crisis truly past now, if she could only begin a new conversation.

But Michel was not done. "Yes, disappointment in himself ate up Laikenhauf's life. You can call it cancer . . ." He glared at Parker who now studied him unwaveringly. ". . . but there are among us French certain ones who call your country's misfortunes for what we see in them. What kind of men did Laikenhauf leave his legacy to? Well, Parker?"

Parker said swiftly, "This is none of your God damned business." He turned to beam an unexpected smile upon Laurel. "Is your hair naturally that color?"

She laughed: "No, it's Roux fourteen!"

Michel made a purse of his lips. Parker guffawed. And at the table across from Laurel, a feminine voice intruded; "Why, that child's hair has been that color since the day she was born! Her father wrote so in her babybook!"

The others turned en masse toward Mrs. Hungerford, as if her presence surprised them. "You had a father?" assailed Michel gleefully. "It's strange, Laurel—I always imagined you as being hatched on a stump."

Laurel straightened in her chair, imbued now with the total loss of propriety which had overtaken the dinner scene. "I believe Mrs. Hungerford will have a perfect right to go back and tell her friends that people over here act as if they're *all* hatched on a stump."

The morning after the dinner party, Parker's after-image seemed to surround Laurel. She had an idea he was like Zero, that the two were cursed with the same instinctive authority, the same ponderous disdain for self which is nearly tantamount to self-absorption. Who could miss Parker's air of being immune to effrontery from a subordinate?

She mentioned this to Regina later in the day, but Regina was interested in something else. "Laurel," she leaned forward, "are you all over your affair with that—with Berteaux's friend?"

She longed to say the right thing. "If you had just recovered from a nervous breakdown, I wouldn't ask you to hold out your hand and let me see whether it shook." Consternation on the plump face upset Laurel. "It was all too complicated, Regina. I loved him."

Cried Regina, "Is that news?"

"You don't understand," said Laurel quietly. "He loved me."

"Its a regular fairy tale," murmured Regina in facetious anticlimax. "A story."

"Yeah. A short short."

"I say, this is life, Laurel. It wouldn't hurt if you gathered a few memories for your old age. There's no better place than France to do it."

Laurel was bored now. "What are you proving or trying to prove?"

"I started out to suggest that you have a perfect right to sleep with this man, considering that Zero—I mean. . . ." She glanced at Laurel for help, but Laurel merely waited. "You said you love him."

"That's no license to steal."

"You said he looks like the man in the steamship ad, the one holding up the rail with his tux."

"You fool!" laughed Laurel.

"Why not?" demanded Regina.

"Because when two people are in love, and have no right to consummate it with marriage, who's to call the breaks? I mean —disaster is practically guaranteed—if there are others to consider."

"Then who *did* you see in Paris?"

Laurel yawned now and stretched her arms wide. "An old friend. A doctor whom I've known a long time."

"Laurel, damn! How could you be in love with one man and go voluntarily pop in bed with another man just because you found out your husband has an oiled zipper?"

"You're congenitally vulgar, Regina Edney!"

"I may be but I'm not playing leapfrog through life with my own integrity."

"You don't know what integrity is. It's—I mean—well, it's like brains. Everybody gets a certain measure. What you do with it is up to you!"

"I don't like your inference!" said Regina grimly.

"Neither do I. But I know you take a cut from French landlords when you get an American a house. I know these French maids you place successfully bring you a week's salary."

"You wouldn't tell Louis?"

"Of course not! Why would I want to hurt him?" When Regina lifted her face, Laurel was appalled. Tears streaming, no sobbing —just tears, unhurried and unwanted. "Stop blubbering!" she commanded. "You're going to ride the white horse roughshod over these American women who snub you. They had no right to use you and cast you aside, these ex-waitresses and car hops. You're as good as they are!"

Regina's tears stopped immediately. "Ruth MacDonald is a school teacher."

"And the only one in the bunch I've met who isn't a snob." Thought controlled Laurel's eyes a fraction of a minute. "But she doesn't need me, Regina. You do. . . ."

"But what?"

"But the ride won't be free, Regina."

Silence grew between the pair as Regina mustered her guard, but she was too avidly curious to outlast Laurel. "What must I do?"

"Promise me to stop taking a cut—stop making a profit on anything you do with or for or to the French, even padding the magazine subscriptions."

Laurel waited, brows lifted toward Regina's answer, but the wary Britisher asked: "What else?"

"Never advise me about my love life. Never question me about Paris."

"That's easy enough, that last part," sighed Regina in aplomb. "But . . ." She lifted her chin defiantly, almost proudly. "I don't believe you're aware of Louis's financial. . . ."

"I'm not aware of—and I don't care. I have one goal, Regina, from here on. To leave a modicum of red, white, and blue goodwill in our American trail over here—and don't start lecturing me about your citizenship. You're part of us, whether you like it or not."

"Why, Laurel?"

"Why what?"

"Why this sudden frenzy of flag waving?"

Before answering, Laurel sauntered leisurely to the Louis XIV marble-topped commode and poured two glasses of sherry from a decanter of ruby-coated crystal. She held her goblet toward Regina's and said: "I could say I love my country that much—which by-God I do—or I could say, more apropos of this moment, I've got to fill my life with something. Regina, I'm not going to play Orpheus to the departure of personal happiness."

"What does that mean?"

"Never mind!" Laurel extended her glass an inch further. "Well? Yes or no—and don't make me a false promise."

Regina eyed her a second in exaggerated admiration. "I can't say no."

"Say something!"

Regina swerved her glass until the two clinked lightly. "All right! I'll try!"

6

Toward the end of September Laurel received a letter postmarked from Paris. She recognized Abach's handwriting at once.

Dear Laurel,

Believe it or not, I was enjoying my first leave from this bone factory (my first leave in Europe) and pleased by both the temperature of the sand and the Bikini air of Nice when one of those Beaumonde AB gooney birds stopped off to hie me to Corliss because the bacteriologist from AmHop had been felled by the criminal he was tracking down at Corliss.

How boring all that is so far, but I must tell you your new Wing Commander Parker was on the same plane and we were thrown together often in the next two days. I had a fantastic piece of luck in isolating the germ-lode in a grease trough above the Corliss Officers' Club kitchen range. But of course, Parker claimed it was a feat of brilliance, and he had no idea I had already heard Wiesbaden General's diagnosis of his present Hospital Commander's ailment (leukemia, poor devil).

You're way ahead of me. Parker has asked me to assume command of his hospital there at Beaumonde. I find on returning here that I cannot be released before November 1. And, Laurel, I had intended for a time to seek your approval before I answered Parker, but then I arrived at a point of wanting too much to say yes and so I did. By the way, I saw Zero often in those two days, being usually pestered by both him and Parker in their urgency to have the scourge deterred. I take the liberty of saying to you that he was extremely cordial. He made a clean breast of that note I addressed to you early this year—at Monceau or his office or wherever it was sent. And he seemed enthusiastic toward Parker's discussion of my coming to Beaumonde Air Base. Parker is obviously picking his people and I propose he has his eye on your husband. Since they're both Laikenhauf men, I'll predict that ole Zero is about to lose his Squadron and be 'kicked upstairs' as the saying goes. As a Colonel, Parker can't have an aide, but it will be interesting to see what job he creates for him.

Enough of my prattling, except to tender a plea that I can leave Mr. Candle at your house until I locate a place for him to live. Perhaps you'll ask for me whether there's a kennel in the Beaumonde area. At any rate, I can't leave a dog this big in the BOQ all day while I'm at work. As I told you in June, Paris has been all kennel life for him except a few week ends—and I did take him along to Nice—and to Corliss and what a hit! But next time you give me a dog, don't make it a Weimaraner. The sight of him paralyzes even the Paris traffic cops. One day, we snarled the entire noon rush circling the Arc!

Good night, give my boys two bear hugs—and remember to throw away all the apples before November First. . . .

S.F.A.

Laurel's face was radiant as she approached her desk and took pen and paper to reply by return post:

Dear, dear Abach:
What could be more gratifying than to be told in one letter that it is well between you and Zero, that Parker had the intelligence to choose you (I held a low opinion of him before your letter!), and that Mr. Candle might be allowed to live with us a while. Having kept him his first nine months, I expect him to remember me and Brick will be fascinated to know 'someone' his own age—ha! By the way, this house has six bedrooms, only three being occupied and perhaps you will stay with us until you are settled. Certainly, you will enjoy a command, and how relieved all the pregnant women will be to hear of your reputation —and perhaps some of those who would like to become pregnant. But what a retort that statement would bring from you, were I not safely distanced by French mail. Bless you anyway!

Love,
Laurel

P.S. Abach, there's no way to say it delicately, but I feel things will go on a great deal better if we minimize the length of our acquaintance before Zero's followers. This seems particularly wise in view of a couple named Edney, whom you will be meeting, and before a French bachelor named Michel Berteaux— strictly Zero's friend. But you will come to understand all and quickly.

LDC

7

"But, darling! You really are stunning!"

Laurel had opened the door herself, Abach's letter in her hand. Now, she laughed into Paul Hachère's face while snugging more closely together the double-breasted lapels of her white fleece coachman's robe. "You've been reading American movie magazines!" she accused.

"Why do you say that?"

"It's unrefined to call everybody 'darling,' Paul! Regardless of what anybody tells you!"

He minimized her rebuke with a delighted shrug. Then he opened the salon door and waited until she passed through. She dropped into the Gainsborough chair beside the black gold marble hearth, but Paul remained standing as his gaze flew to the Sèvres urn on a corner of the lyre-legged grand piano. He found the Degas painting above the Louis commode, and the Royal Copenhagen jardiniere, which stood a half-meter tall. Noticing that Laurel held an unlighted cigarette, he swept over and presented a flame from his own lighter. Then he flopped down on the sofa and let his eyes rove the room once more.

"Zero married an heiress."

Laurel tried to suppress her grin. "It's the wrong thing to say—French or American."

"You're angry with me, Laurel? I've neglected you terribly since you moved to my mother's house—but, tiens! You've done magic." He breathed deeply, acquiring steam to haul on. He spoke of trophies he had won in water contests at Cannes, of auto races he had attended, and a tennis cup he had acquired at Lille. While she gave him the attention of her gaze and a few nods, she reflected on the number of times his name arose among groups of American wives, who talked of his skill at dancing, his savoir-faire, his Franco goodwill.

When Olande brought the coffee Laurel had ordered, Paul's speech ran out. As soon as the girl left the room, Laurel said, "Paul, I'm glad you came. There's something I've wanted to ask you. Mrs. Frakes, the former tenant, told me that Madame Tricot takes care of whoever lives in this house. . . ."

She let the statement hang, not quite a question, and Paul seemed troubled in preparing his answer. "Oh, Laurel, she tries to run all our lives—that Belle Tricot! She means well, but she keeps my parents on my neck half the time." She handed him a Why? with his cup of coffee. "Because I'm thirty-two and still not married. Why else?"

Miffed inwardly at his detour, Laurel tried anew. "Why haven't I ever seen her? She plays bridge, but she was absent from every party we attended last winter."

"Perhaps she was in Paris for the winter opera season just then. I don't really know."

"She's your mother's best friend?"

"Laurel, what are you asking?" He was obviously annoyed.

She took a deep breath and spoke candidly: "Whenever I think about her, I get a feeling she's avoiding me. I've met several American wives who boast of her parties—I don't know what it is I feel—perhaps as if they all know why I'm not eligible. What is it, Paul?"

"You've wounded her sorely."

"That's a lie!"

Paul snorted. "You've apparently captured the only Frenchman she can't get an introduction to . . ." In his little pause, Laurel had an immediate vision of Guy before her mind, but Paul said, ". . . Michel, Marquis de Berteaux."

"Oh, God!" she cried with helpless laughter. Paul watched her from the corner of his eyes, saying that Belle Tricot had waited eight years to meet him and all of a sudden, some American-come-lately grabbed him off. Laurel still couldn't accept the explanation. "But what would any woman want with—with. . . ."

"With him?" supplied Paul dryly. "You're not French enough, Laurel, and apparently, you lack ambition. She doesn't give a damn about his personality. She's just never had a Marquis at her table, and she's run out of things to brag about since she got tired of talking about her diamond necklace. A beautiful woman ten years ago, Laurel. Now she's fat. And rich. And no children. There's the tragedy. But watch out! She's vicious."

"Oh, you men!" sneered Laurel in good humor. "Women's foibles frighten you to death! Don't you understand the way we talk so scathingly about each other? I bet if I met Belle Tricot this afternoon, butter wouldn't melt in our mouths. We'd greet each other charmingly."

She drank two cups of coffee before he finished his first, and, having received an answer to her question, she felt an urge to have him leave. Happily, she watched him stand up and place his cup on the table. She was tensing to arise when he sat back down, one foot folded beneath himself and his left arm rimming the back of the Victorian sofa.

"Come over here by me, Laurel. I want to tell you something."

"I hear you very well from here," she demurred. But Paul beckoned rigidly with his head, and warned her that she was careless of her maid.

"She's bound to be picking up some English, and you'll be wondering soon how certain tales get out of the house." Laurel shrugged and came to the opposite end of the couch. Paul began to speak of his time at Cannes. "I met a swimmer in the finals, a magnificent girl named Moreau. She calls herself Felix. . . ." He drew a soft sigh.

"Yes," said Laurel, "she stayed with us at Monceau. We met her first in Paris."

"Oh?" exclaimed Paul in honest surprise. "She did not say—that is, I had the idea she only knew Zero. . . ."

Laurel decided to aid him. "I had the same idea at the time."

"She told me only that she and her fiancé were slumming in Pigalle when Zero and another American joined their table at a place called Aunt Lizzie's. . . ."

Fiancé? Fiancé! Laurel's heart cried in rage—but she dared not mention Guy's name before Paul, or give any clue to the situation. She glanced down at the cup and saucer in her hands, surprised at the steadiness. Paul rambled on. Felix plainly implied that meeting Zero caused her to end her engagement. "But, Laurel, I don't care about all that. I'm not one of those antiquated, melancholy Gauls. I intend to live life!" When she faced him, he exuded mellow intensity. "Set that cup down and give me your hands. I want to ask you something."

Her thoughts swerved wildly. Why had she obeyed?

"My brother is in Switzerland for the next four months. There wouldn't even be the bother of a hotel. His apartment is empty." His lips began to spew precise whispers. "I'm wild, Laurel! I can't face another winter watching you deal cards or pour drinks or play piano while I ache to know your body!"

She laughed weakly, then madly. Paul began to anger; "A polite no would have been enough."

"I said no last spring at Monceau."

"What is it with you, Laurel?" His frown was wounded but it was contemptuous, too. "Does a man *have* to have a title?"

"Paul, I once felt sorry for you because you're the only Frenchman I know who wants to be an American. You despise the gray label of middle class—the restrictions—and you're not idealistic enough to be satisfied by glancing down the ladder and seeing your numerical European advantage. You want to be at the top, don't you? But, Paul, you've made a terrible mistake. You came here to disclose Zero's irregularity only to persuade me into an alliance which is revolting to me. I resent it, and if some idiot told you all officers' wives are on the make, you're an ass to believe it. Now, get out!"

He was standing near the door, smoothing his hair with one hand. Apparently determined to part without negating the future, he simpered; "You're in a foul mood today. Let's forget the whole thing. Well, au revoir, Laurel!"

"No, Paul. Adieu!—or à bas! Take your choice!"

Laurel sat very still for nearly an hour, considering alternately the bizarre idea of Félicité Moreau claiming to have been Guy's fiancée, and the superiority of hindsight to foresight. If only I'd had the common sense not to have run to Abach in Paris. I debased him and myself because—because it made no sense. The

Lord's probably sending him back to this base just so I'll have to wince each time I look at him and think of what I forced him to do.

What I should have done was set a trap for Zero. God, I can just see him lounging in Aunt Lizzie's—wherever that is—and watching Felix and her watching him in the safe dimness of the floor show, her developing some pretext on which to get Guy to the American's table, her persuading Guy into some kind of entente cordiale, and her departing early to call Zero at his hotel. Hmmmm. He sent me and the boys a postcard each—five or six or seven week ends from Paris: "This is a wonderful city to do Christmas shopping in." And somewhere in the same time, Dorothy Arnold.

How many since we've married? How tall is the mean average? What color is her hair? Were they educated or intelligent? How many of them were favored with return calls? Who was first? Who was last? Yes, instead of shooting off to Abach, I should have figured out some way to intercept Zero in the act; then it would have been real to me—I'd have been angry enough to force him into reform. But that's a king-sized challenge when your husband's a pilot and when the airport is Europe and the Mediterranean. . . .

Tears. Hopeless, blinding, scalding. And finally vented. Curled into a ball within her husband's chair, Laurel hid her face in the crook of her arm and, waiting for the snuffing to depart completely, felt ashamed to engorge her lonely sphere with the vision of Guy's face—as if the mere summoning of his likeness might debase him too.

8

Willard Echardt Parker, on his first trip to the North African base, had remained less than six hours—time enough to drive to the desert gunnery range and meander through the tents and talk to a few officers and technicians not then on duty—while an engine was pulled on the C-54 which was carrying him from Savannah, Georgia, to Beaumonde, France.

Zero Compton was flying the afternoon this happened and therefore had not seen Parker, but the next week when Parker returned, all flying was halted so that the two hundred men could muster on the blistering sand immediately after the C-47 pilot carrying Parker radioed the Commander's insistence that they land in the desert instead of on the airstrip at Corliss.

Zero had read the manifest and knew that Abach was aboard. A virulent strain of dysentery had reduced a majority of the Beaumonde personnel from five to twenty pounds each. Although Zero had escaped the disease entirely, he was pleased at the thought of Abach's presence and hadn't a doubt in the world that he would find the source of the dysentery and apply an effective remedy. Abach was just that way. Hence, Zero strode forward to meet the doctor, while the other two Squadron Commanders and the Group Commander busied themselves with greeting Parker.

Zero and Abach had time to exchange only a few words when the new Commander of Beaumonde Air Base climbed to the hood of a jeep and faced the assemblage.

"I'm Willard Parker, lately of Hunter Field and proud to be here. There'll be some changes. I don't know what they'll be, but I give you my word: if you mechanics keep the planes off the ground and you rated men keep them over the target, I'll keep your wives happy!" A great roar of laughter went up from the sweating, gaunt-cheeked men. When they were quiet, Parker said: "We all know the mission. Not defense. Ours is the strike-back team if the balloon goes up. Remember that! Now, I ask you these things: get goosebumps when you salute your flag; spit in every Red track you find, leave your French landlords to me. I can lick the God-damn French singlehanded if you stay oiled up against The Bear. That's all, men!"

As the crowd broke up and wandered away, Zero stood alone for a few moments, thinking of Parker's fourteen German kills and two years in Nazi prison. He had their respect before he came, and now, he's got more than that. I might have known—if Laikenhauf chose him—but God damn! He should have had a star six or seven years ago.

That night, Parker's staff car took Worthington, the new Group Commander, MacDonald, Stevens, and Compton ten miles across the desert to Corliss Officers' Club, where it was monthly stag night. Zero had scarcely gotten over his renewed pleasure in the white tablecloth, real dishes, and nickelodeon music when someone declared that the floor show was a "corker."

The five Beaumonde officers moved to a better location, a table adjacent to the small dance floor, just as music from an electric organ began to set a frivolous mood. Small spotlights illuminated the center of the empty floor as eight young girls in nose veils and Egyptianlike headdresses moved one at a time into the blue white disc to pivot their bodies about dimpled rib cages and bare navels. Zero studied the bodies of the dancers, paying particular attention to a miniature Venus with tilted breasts. Brass tips covered each nipple, from which dangled green tassels a foot in length. She had very straight shoulder-length red hair and wore transparent green chiffon trousers.

After the dancing was over, Parker said to Compton; "That bitch had hair as red and about half as long as Laurel's."

For a split second, Zero fingered a table knife. Then he dropped it with a thud. Laikenhauf or not, he was aroused to retort, "How the Hell would *you* know?"

Parker laughed long and loud enough to worry the other three men, especially when they had caught Zero's fiery expression. The Colonel ignored them, reached out to grip Compton's shoulder and said in genial tones; "Come to my tent. Eight tomorrow morning."

Of course, when Parker stood up, it was time to go, but somehow they became divided—four to one. Zero wished Parker and the others a polite good night, sat back down at the table, and peered into his billfold.

He could not give the waiter a forbidden greenback, and of course, no foreigner had a right to receive military script. The only French franc note he had was a five-hundred—a generous fee—but Zero was in no mood to waste time. He replaced his billfold in his pocket, glanced at his gold chronometer, and settled to wait until the waiter reappeared. He looked neither right nor left and, therefore, did not notice when Abach emerged through the swinging door of the kitchen.

The doctor made his way to an empty table in the back shadows of the large room. He was tired, and anxious to get a meal and go to bed. But he was satisfied with his night's work. He had an idea where the trouble lay and that by noon next day, the mystery would be solved.

By that curious alliance wrought of having seen the doctor in the kitchen, the waiter approached him with professional solicitation and took his order. While he waited Abach thought of Parker and of the curious uneven aging process which left a face like Parker's virtually unlined at forty-seven years old, although the creviced wrinkles held a perpetual convention across the back of his leathery neck. Abach thought: Parker is fierce, honest, and abused by life. He has a sun-squint and a good start on skin cancer. Unloved by his wife. Two daughters, one just married, and Parker dreads the natural aftermath—the role of grandparent. Why do people tell doctors everything? Well, at least, I'm not a chaplain.

Abach thought next of the letter he planned to write to Laurel, and then, of Zero's clumsy apology that afternoon—anent the breach which had grown over his note to Laurel the previous January.

Then he glanced about the dining room and saw Zero Compton's back as he arose to acknowledge the descent of a young girl in a short plaid skirt and black turtle-necked sweater. Abach watched her cross the dance floor from the area of the ladies' lounge with swinging hips, whore-bud smile, and bouncing hair colored like Laurel's.

With incredulity, Abach saw Zero bend to kiss her hand, for all the world, a bleached gigolo. Abach recalled that September night in Paris when he had accompanied Zero to Pigalle, when Félicité Moreau and Guy de Brières invited them to their table.

At the transient BOQ, far into the night, Abach argued with himself that it was now incumbent upon him to accept Parker's proposal—whether Laurel approved or not.

9

Zero was in Parker's tent at eight o'clock the next morning, but he waited five days before writing Laurel a letter:

"My dearest, Parker reports well on the hospitality of my house. He had me in the command tent the other morning for cross-examination. Cross-examination first about the troubles with Beaumonde Franco-American relations, which he understands are at an all-time low. We spoke of rent gouging, black market in cigarettes and gasoline, tire slashing, and this year's crop of G.I. bastards.

"Next, he asked if I were Base Commander what my first act would be to improve things. I said I'd stop that business of a C-47 carting everybody's pay-day dollars to Brussels to get a higher, illegal exchange rate on French francs. By God, he was livid when he heard the pilot gets one percent of the gross (so I didn't tell him Fritsch sent me twice—ha-ha!).

"Next, he gave me a snow job about my combat record. Said the French worship heroes and champions and since he doesn't need to bow to anybody in the medal department, I have no comment to make about that, but he is loaded with gossip about my luck at French shooting clubs and the status of Guy and Michel. Titles.

"He had a couple of nice things to say about you, and the house, after getting off to a bad start. I have the impression that you and Michel must have run him through the wringer backwards, or something equally lovable. What happened? Anyway, his wife is afraid to come to Europe. She was at Pearl. Parker makes no bones about his allergy to France. He says I can relieve him of F/A cocktail parties and wreath-layings. I'll be his executive officer upon our return to the Base. Between you and me, my honest-to-God opinion is that Parker is worried about getting his star, but still unwilling to kiss French asses. I think he wants me to get him a Croix de Guerre or a Palm Leaf or both.

"He said you'd help me in this job. I guess he likes you. He intimated that he'll fix me an early promotion if I cut the mustard and I've been thinking all day how we'd have done a few things different if I could have foreseen such an assignment. For one thing, I wouldn't have held up Hachère's rent to force the bastard to put in a hot-water heater. What's a couple hundred bucks against an eagle? Get smart, Laurel, and sweeten the old boy up before I get back. Michel can help. So can Vervins. But don't *tell* anybody yet. Wait 'til they're needed. Love, Zero."

And then he added a postscript: "Have the Hachères over *before* I get back. Six courses and a bought dessert will make them forgive anything, and if all else fails, apply your charm to pretty Paul. Abach was here, playing detective to a microbe. He has agreed to Parker's invitation to take command of Beaumonde AB's hospital. You know, Laurel, he's so God damned sincere. I feel like an ass for the way I treated him last winter and I told him so. And I'm sorry for everything I said to you about him. It's a mess down here. So stinking, so filthy hot. I can hardly wait to lay you."

Laurel went to her desk and took the telephone down to call Paul Hachère and apologize, but changed her mind and decided to write a note.

She thought about Zero in charge of Franco-American relations in the Beaumonde area. Here was her chance to enlarge, to improve, to change the tangled, mutually faulty situation. What if she had to be nice to Paul Hachère and his father? What if she had to pretend cordiality toward the gravy-stained, body-odored matrons of upper Beaumonde? What did it matter as long as opinions of Americans and therefore America were improved?

Yes, thought Laurel, this will be worthwhile, but Zero is wrong about one thing. People at Michel's level have nothing to do with the local Franco-American situation. Michel's a detriment to this scene. Even Americans find him ridiculous.

Late that afternoon she was upstairs when Olande came to say that the Marquis de Berteaux waited in the salon. Laurel dallied a half-hour in her room, unable to decide how or whether to reveal Zero's new job. When she descended the stairs, Michel was receiving at the front door a very large carton from a special delivery mailman.

Knelt on the salon carpet, Laurel managed to open the box and tuck the enclosed card into a pocket before Michel dropped beside her and grasped the lid of the large carton to stare at the label. She heard him whisper in astonishment: eleven kilos!

She studied the mass of rose heads, walked to the mantel, not having glanced at the card but knowing the tribute came from Guy. His presence seemed to fill the salon as realistically as the scent of some twelve or twenty dozen roses.

With her back to Michel she carefully withdrew the engraved card and read Le Comte de Brières. A thrill washed over her before she turned the card over and read in his handwriting; "Forgive me. It was impossible to celebrate your marriage." Immediately, Laurel swooped down and tossed the card into the flames, which seemed to lick out at the hem of her skirt in protest.

"What did he say?"
"He said hello."

"Tell me! Tell me!" His tone was knife-edged. She knew before she turned around how he would appear—the old glitter, the impish greed; he would be half out of his seat. She faced him slowly, determined that he should break the silence if it was broken.

"In Paris they say he is stricken of you!"

"They are always whispering in your ear, aren't they, Michel?" So that's why he had not been at the house for three days?

"Laurel, is it the same for you? I promise never to betray you!"

"Whose side are you on, Michel?"

"Yours, of course," he replied glibly.

"No, Zero's or Guy's?" Feet braced lightly apart, she faced him from before the mantel, her smile amused but contemptuous. Totally self-serious, he replied that Guy was his oldest, truest friend, but there was no one in the world whom he loved more deeply than Zero. He represented in a man everything valuable, worthwhile, and enviable.

"All things done," sighed Laurel, "then they are equal?"

"I suppose, but why?"

"You took a terrible chance, building up this fantasy between Guy and me—a chance with their regard for each other."

In disgust, Michel stood up and rammed his hands deep in either pocket. "You don't pretend a woman could come between two men like that?"

There was no doubt of the mockery in his eyes; Michel hated women. He had spent three days in Paris, he said, persuading Guy he could scarcely face the Comptons again without making a hurried and tangible apology. "I suggested he send roses—but he sent eleven kilos. Eleven kilos. Laurel, he's wild!"

Oh, God! she thought. I might have known—Michel badgered him into it.

"I'm worried about him, Laurel. I—what I shall say must be excluded from our amusing enmity. Laurel, tell no one. Guy doesn't go out—even when girls telephone him."

"Listen to me, Michel! You brought him to Monceau but this is my house—*my home*—and I never want to see Guy in it. You're not to show him where it is, or tell him he's welcome, or ever, ever mention my name to him again!"

"Laurel, when you're angry, you're as fine as a thoroughbred filly!"

She saw, there was no question of it, admiration in his eyes. But what did it mean?—gone with the wind in the next five seconds!

At dinner, she reconsidered the strange look on his face as they sat across from each other. Near the end of the meal, she noticed that his hands were marvelously clean. His nails were groomed for the first time since she had known him. As he caught her absorbing this, his lips spread in a frank, affectionate grin.

"Michel! You've had your teeth cleaned!" she cried in childish surprise.

"Yes," he sighed with subdued pride, "the first visit I've made to a dentist since I was stationed in England."

Back in the salon with coffee and cognac, the pair began racing through one of their intellectual discourses. Laurel led him into a discussion of the personal trials of Oscar Wilde but Michel switched to Spinoza and Kant, batting deft questions far afield where she dashed about, trying to make an out with every answer.

He spoke of Browning, Byron, and the Victorians, afterwards catapulting into modern art with an inquiry about Picasso. Laughing at Laurel's incorrect reply, he rode victoriously through two more demitasses and three cognacs before she asked his opinion of Wagner's symphonies.

"Touché! I know damned well he never wrote a symphony, but I'm going to bring you a book on Picasso!"

And so they went on, Michel drinking steadily of Zero's brandy, Laurel moving now and then to the piano to break the monotony of his voice. Near eleven, he ordered her to have the maid bring more wood. "It's bitter tonight. Uncommonly so for the end of September."

Olande left a bit of snow on the small logs in the basket. After a hasty look out the window, Laurel understood the significance of the snow. It meant that Michel would have to spend the night. The hill would be too slick for him to drive down and the sanders never began their chores before seven A.M., and, after all, this was the first snow of the season.

Later she said, "You know you can't leave here tonight. Why don't you go on up to bed?" He did not reply.

She regarded him through lowered lashes, fully aware now that he was drunk, that she could never get him up the stairs by herself, and that Olande had long since gone to bed.

"Laurel, your smile is one-sided. A gloss-print Mona Lisa." His eyes were closed. One arm relaxed across his body in the beginning of sleep. She waited until he began to snore. Then she arose and went to bring him cover.

In the deathly quiet house, she sat down at Monsieur Hachère's great roll-top desk in the library and filled a wide-pointed pen with jet ink. Then, she selected from one of the pigeon holes a thick white folded paper unjustly dubbed an informal, for the regally simple line of black engraving was imposing—Mrs. Zeno Richfield Compton. Inside, she scrawled, "My dear Guy . . . ," and then gave up.

Going up the stairs, she coped with a nagging sense of guilt. I can't have a man staying here all night with Zero gone—I mean—not regularly. I've tried every way in the world short of seduction to shake Michel Berteaux. God, how simple my life seems in retrospect before I met him! Zero's wrong about his helping the Franco-American mission. He's wrong! I know it in my bones. If only I could blast him out of our lives! If only . . .

10

In the morning Laurel saw that the snow had been heavy. With glee, she pictured her children's pleasure at playing in snow. She herself had never outgrown a Louisiana-born sense of festivity at the sight of white ground-cover. The bland, rather tasteless bowl of snow sprinkled with vanilla, sugar, and cream was an annual ritual with her, whenever locale afforded it.

She swung off the bed and slipped her feet into high-heeled black velvet mules. Immediately, she slipped them off and got out of her tight-cuffed ski pajamas, then wrapped her body in a wool robe printed with leopard spots. She cinched its gilded belt so tightly about her waist that, looking down, she saw the profiles of her hipbones and wondered whether she ought to try to gain some weight.

Feet ensconced again in the black mules, she sped to the vanity and began brushing her tangled hair. Idly, she lit a cigarette and wished that Olande would arrive with coffee, but just then, a hard, rapid knock hit the door.

Michel said: "Open up! I've the coffee!"

She glanced down at his wrinkled trousers and up at his red-veined eyes which seemed visibly to ache. Helplessly, she laughed at his painful, apologetic grin. "You're a fine example of French nobility!"

He took a deep breath and every item on the silver tray rattled. "I'm sorry, Laurel, but let me tell Zero myself."

They passed the morning with coffee and conversation, Michel taking over amusement of Chris. Laurel consoled Brick upon his noon arrival from school. The child was furious that the sun had destroyed the night's snow.

"Keep him out of school this afternoon, Laurel, and we'll all go for a drive."

Within the hour, they were speeding down the highway out of Beaumonde. She smiled at Brick, who pressed his nose to the window in the back of the Simca and mimicked the sound of its motor. Then she shifted sleeping Chris in her arms and glanced up as Michel took a right turn onto a two-laned path.

A quarter-hour later he parked the car in twin ruts and, after Laurel had arranged a sleeping child on either seat, she followed him some yards down a boggy path marked by naked currant bushes as tall as her shoulder.

The small clearing was ringed by ancient birch and oak trees, centered by an oval pool of clear water—a spring, decided Laurel. Beyond the slue lay a mossy patch of earth laced with thin crevices of snow and backed by a wire fence. The vines and brambles tangled against the barrier were brown and dead, although a few leaves of honeysuckle shone stubbornly green.

Michel, hands on hips, waited for her reaction. "Well?"

She said slowly, "In summer, it must be a satellite of Eden."

"Look at that old tree, Laurel—there, the one with its feet in the water."

She eyed the ancient boughs admiringly. "In America, we call it a green bay laurel."

"Why?"

"I don't know."

Their gazes met. She turned around, the space between them a few inches. Like a pair of moths finding themselves caught in a single web, they stared at each other without mobility. She felt that some perverse intimacy apparently had mushroomed during their prolonged conflict. His hand drew up. In that instant, she would have sworn a glaze of passion blurred his eyes, but his hand came to his own face. He pushed in his nose with one finger, stuck out the tip of his tongue, and pulled at the skin of his Adam's apple to make his tongue shoot back into his mouth. This was a silly trick which her children found hilarious.

They left the forest pool and returned to the car and to Beaumonde—up and down the winding hill road, around the lower base of town again and again, for Michel refused to stop the car until the children were done with their sleeping.

Laurel retired upstairs the minute they were home. She spent an hour bathing and dressing. When she returned to the salon near five o'clock, Michel was reading a French copy of *Aesop's Fables* to Brick while Olande fed Chris in the kitchen.

Michel halted his reading long enough to request a drink. He said little more to Laurel throughout the cocktail hour, or during their early dinner, devoting his attention rather to the boy. By eight o'clock, there were two sounds in the house—the cuckoo clock's pendulum and Laurel's indifferent piano-playing. She was in a quandary. She did not know how to tell him that he simply had to go home—he could not remain another night. He sat reading *Time* magazine, lounging as comfortably on the sofa as if he were a permanent resident of the house.

She got up from the piano bench, ambled slowly across the room and planted her back against the salon door, one hand lightly holding the knob behind her. Discovering the silence, he glanced up. His gaze darted immediately to her gilt mules, up the line of sharply fitted velvet trousers of bottle green, over the starkly white jersey blouse—discreet of long sleeves but daring in cut, for it crossed without a fastening and tied in the back. Her taut, partly bared breasts pouted in white relief like a bisque of Venus. He took a long deep breath and swallowed.

"Michel . . ." How could she frame her statement to best effect—"you must go now—you've been here quite long—you've. . . ." Again, she said, "Michel. . . ."

She flattened her back against the door as he got up and came deliberately toward her. Laurel's pulse raced in her ear when his hand swung up and moved above her head to brace him against the door. Their eyes held—scarcely a foot apart.

"No wonder they're telling tales in the Beaumonde cafés about some American woman trying to pull some Frenchman's hair out in her own living room!" His eyes were clear, amused, and unmistakable in their certainty. He bequeathed one frank glance upon her bosom. Then he smiled tolerantly. "Go upstairs and put a pin where it belongs in that blouse while I set up the chess game."

On fire with humiliation, she fled up the stairs two at a time, peeled to the skin in her bedroom and plopped between the covers, not bothering to turn on a light. Raising her head from the pillow, she withdrew the pair of tortoise-shell pins and threw them vehemently out to the floor. Jaw clenched in furious decision, she vowed not to leave her bed until Michel was out of the house—a vow impossible to keep, for, when she descended the stairs at six-thirty the next morning, (too full with sleep to lie still longer), a cloud of acrid French tobacco smoke fogged the hall.

My God! He's slept on the couch again!

Laurel stood before the salon door and opened the leopard robe to wrap it more tightly about her. She pulled in the belt one notch and, priming herself for what must be said, flung the door open on the motherlode of smoke—but Michel was not in sight.

"Laurel? Laurel?" His voice resounded from the kitchen. "Is that you? Hurry up! I can't find the coffee!"

She turned, face pensive. Why the Hell should I care how long he stays? I tried to get Zero to send him away—how many times did I try? And how far did I get? But I'll be damned if I'm going to stay stuck in this house all day long with him again. I'll just tell him—tell him. . . .

"Good morning, Michel!"

"Hi!" he said with his back to her as he carefully ran tap water into a measuring cup before adding it to the slender, spotless chrome percolator.

From the apothecary jar she handed him, he spaded out six turns of grounds before plugging in the electricity. Then he sat down with a pleased sigh. Her eyes landed on a neat crease in his trouser leg and darted up to his face.

He said, "After you deserted me last night, I went out and brought in my bag." He chuckled and ran his tongue over his upper lip. "It had been in the car since I left Paris. Laurel—I'm sorry if I hurt your feelings." He waited for her to reply, but she watched him without expression. "If it helps, I'd have said the same thing to my mother."

When Laurel declared in midmorning that she had to go marketing, Michel did not wait to be asked. He grabbed his jacket and black beret to go with her, and in front of the house, persuaded her to drive on to Redan to the poissonnerie he frequented. She maneuvered him into a restaurant on Redan's square at lunchtime, where he was obliged to take the check.

Rather heady from the wine, she decided upon a direct approach. "Michel," she said in a very low voice. "When are you going home?"

The imp lighted in both his eyes. Brows arched, he replied: "The first time you bore me."

11

Michel had grown restless. That night at dinner Laurel suspected that he had at last run out of something to say but he began to relate an event of which he had meant to speak to her earlier, he declared. A fête given by the mayor of Coucy. "You know Coucy. It's only five kilometers west of Noël."

"Yes. That's where Ruth and Jack MacDonald live."

"Be quiet! That's what I was going to tell you—about meeting them."

She tried to tell him that he had met the MacDonalds at the anniversary party in August, but Michel argued: If that were true, then he hadn't realized at the time how much he liked them! "Although I must say, Laurel, MacDonald seems a bit of a barbarian as far as education. Don't American men ever go to college? Do just you women get brought up properly?"

"Jack's from a town called Spokane, Washington. People talk that way out there. If you really want to know, he has his Master's. Psychology. Abnormal psychology, as a matter of fact."

He downed the last of his coffee and sprang up to pace the floor. "Well, he should have majored in speech, but I like his wife. She says you're the most admired of all the American women—the way you run your house and help people. He watched her from the side of his eyes. "Of course, I don't believe her for a moment."

Laurel reached down to flick a tag of lint from her skirt. "Why?"

"I've seen how you live for two days."

She longed to reply: It's God's own blessing that no American has come near! Aloud she said, "I made up my mind the day I saw this house to inject some light moments in American lives."

"Ruth says you feed more American women lunch than the Officers' Club feeds men."

"You sound jealous!" she smiled.

"Well, if you wanted to be with Americans, why did you bother coming to France?" he said petulantly.

"I give the Beaumonde ladies a turn, too," she argued, shifting her feet into the chair.

"Beaumonde ladies? There's no such thing!"

She said ten of them had come to tea. Madame Hachère, Madame Risseau, Madame. . . .

"Laurel!" he screeched in fury, "How many times must you be told to cut off these Beaumonde leeches?" She noted the distended veins in his temples, the furious reddening of his whole face. Oh, if Zero could see him now, coiled to strike his fangs into the hierarchy of fair Beaumonde!

With careful nonchalance, Laurel lighted a cigarette. "As long as I'm an American in France, I don't have to limit my associations to any strata. Besides, Michel, I feel obliged to demonstrate democracy in action. The society of Beaumonde. . . ."

"There's no society in Beaumonde!" he shouted.

Laurel sat up straight in the chair, her feet shifted to the floor. "You bore me! I've never been a member of society in my own country."

"Liar!" he cried.

She was on her feet, glaring at him. "My family was *above* it!"

"Your sense of modesty is rarely so perverse!" It was Michel at his worst. Marquis de Berteaux. Effeminate Mephistopheles.

Laurel took a step toward him, and another. It was time to employ the only means certain to annihilate him from her radius, from her house, and from her husband, for Michel, she was certain, would fear her telling Zero his catastrophic secret, should she prove it!

Moving toward him, she had never been more positive of the facts. He had no inclination toward men. He abused womankind to protect himself. If no woman discovered he was impotent, how could he possibly be exposed?

She had one idea as she approached him—that, regardless of how hard it was to do, or what crushing of pride it entailed, she had only to entwine her hands behind his neck and that, once he recovered from his shock, and regained co-ordination, he would get out of her way and keep out of it for the next two years.

Perhaps he divined her intent, or perhaps anger overcame him. At any rate, just as Laurel pressed her palms together before her and inhaled a deep breath, Michel stepped aside, circled her, and strode out of the room. She heard his footsteps on the stairs, and then, overhead in the spare room. There was a silent break in his descent—the umbrella stand creaked in the downstairs hall.

For a long time after he went out the front door, she stood there, supported by the mantel, thinking her mother was right about one thing. What you expected to be most difficult was often easiest of all. She was rid of Michel.

Next day the Hachère men were coming to dinner. This was the result of Laurel's apologetic note to Paul. (The Hachère ladies were reported to be in Paris.) Dressed and waiting, Laurel poured out three ounces of brandy, which she took into the salon. The liquor vanished in less than fifteen minutes, but still her dread of the evening lingered. She felt warm, a bit lightheaded, uncommonly nervous, and not at all surprised when the smirking pair arrived early. She had just served them highballs when the unexpected happened. Michel burst in, greeted his compatriots affably, and said to Laurel he had heard during the afternoon that Zero's return date had been set.

She said, "No one has told me anything more definite than mid-October."

As Michel dropped into a chair, she started out of the room. "Where are you going?" he demanded.

"To have Olande set another place."

"I can't dine here tonight!" he said in a tone which seemed to imply the whole world knew why.

"You can't?" She coolly took a sip of the new glass of brandy. "Why not?"

Michel's words flowed deliberately. He had dined, to tell the truth, at a restaurant in the Redan square. She knew he was lying.

He accepted her offer of a drink and launched into a discussion with the Hachère pair of the coming agricultural fair in Beaumonde. When this subject was worn out, Laurel devilishly renewed the question of his dining with them.

"I've a marvelous veal roast with garlic stuffing, and green beans done in the same pan. Ah, Michel!"

An ugly twist caught and released a corner of his mouth. "I'll tell you what!" he declared. "You begin your meal and I'll move into the dining room with you so dinner won't be delayed. I'll just finish my drink there."

She imbibed thoughtlessly throughout three table wines, observing how pleased Papa was to be in company with a Marquis, though Paul managed studied unawareness. He did not address Michel in third person as his father did, nor wait for the Marquis to pass first through doors. It was an evening Laurel never wanted to repeat, she concluded, as she drained the last of her eighth glass of wine and edged her chair back. She felt extremely unsteady as she got to her feet, but once she began to walk, equilibrium settled.

She downed four cups of coffee in the salon. Smoke from three cigars—she had passed Zero's Dutch Havanas generously—was making her dizzy. But she sat very rigidly and gave no sign.

Near eleven, yawning Papa declared that it was time to leave. In the salon, Michel made no pretense of getting ready to go. He shook hands with both men while Laurel brought their coats, and he helped the older man into his before their hostess escorted them to the door.

Laurel leaned against the wall and closed her eyes, as if she were waiting for the afterglow of their lavish good nights to evaporate. She had never been drunk before, which accounted for her puzzlement. If I had really drunk too much, I wouldn't be able to walk and talk and see straight. But I have a terrible sensation in my brain—as if there's a layer of fly paper between my ears—as if the gears in my brain had run out of oil and been sprinkled with sand.

She squared her shoulders and aimed for the salon door, got through it and safely to the couch where she tried not to flop as she sat down.

"I've tried hard to school you as properly as any Parisienne," said the voice. Laurel glanced up as high as his pacing feet. Michel was feet and knees! No body. No head. Oh—but a tongue! She closed her eyes; the blackness swerved dangerously.

"You've been in France long enough to drop this naïve tourist role and cut off these God damned yokels!"

She frowned pensively and stared at the coffee table. "You shoot with them on Saturdays—you belong to their—their Club."

"I'm a patron!"

"Patron saint."

"Shut up!"

"Whadyou call it when you drink champagne with them after the shoot?"

"It's a patron's duty. Not a social tie." Then she heard his snarl: "You're drunk!"

Laurel closed her eyes and fell face down across the arm of the couch. In slow alliterative sing-song, she chanted: Misogamist—misogynist—masochist—Michel. When she stopped singing, the silence terrified her. She ran in spurts, redirecting her aim until the salon, the stairs, and the second-floor hall were behind her, until the solidity of her bed lay beneath her.

She was thinking how cool the green of the taffeta spread felt. Then the light came on in the room. Michel's voice had followed her! "Laurel," he mumbled in irritation, "you can't let a maid find you in the morning like this." She longed to tell him to get out, but speaking was too much trouble.

He parted her hair to find the concealed zipper at the back of her neck. Awkwardly, he drew the dress down over her shoulders. She heard his steps circle the bed. The light went off. Too modest to look. Her mind formed the word pansy.

The taffeta spread made a swish as he turned the covers back on one side. She remained limp as he dragged her until her head was reasonably near the pillow. But what happened then was to her fogged mind a perversely absorbing nightmare.

Helpless little kisses as fluttery, as airy, as ineffectual as a butterfly's pass at a daisy. Then clumsily, he inserted into the black chasm some innocence of a lost child. "Help me! Laurel, help me!"

Gradually, she conjured a vision of a woman flailing in a red molten pool of bottomless quicksand. In a seizure of tumescence and organic mania, the faceless female panted in sobbing screaming sighs with only Michel to save her.

Laurel was awakened at eleven next morning by agony at the base of her brain. She wiggled one toe and felt quick protest in a hip joint. Her body was bruised, furious, and ailing, but memory was clear. She turned to the wall, into the pillow, to the ceiling—turned achingly, reluctantly, trying to blot out that memory.

So great was her dread of facing Michel that on the fourth day afterwards, hearing the muffled sound of the door bell and recalling that both maid and children were out of the house, she darted up from her bath water as if to run and hide.

After a few days she could move without wincing. She could even speak coherently and sit still, listening to Olande or the children or American wives. But a strange alteration had come over her. Often when she was alone a weird little phantom suggested its inhabitation of her body. What had happened to the real Laurel?

12

Laurel had not seen Michel for eight days. Then he turned up at the airfield where she was awaiting Zero's return from North Africa. She watched with apprehension as the Frenchman sped toward her, smiling before the waiting Americans. He kissed her hand with a flourish.

"You'll start a scandal," said Laurel in French. Ruth MacDonald's brown eyes showed amusement at her friend's statement. As Ruth and Michel greeted each other—he shook Ruth's hand—Laurel examined with dull surprise her feeling of anticlimax.

At a safe distance, the first light-bomber from a formation of four twin jets was parking. The great rumbling hiss of the engines died. The bubble canopy shot open. Parker stepped onto the wing, got to his stomach and slid carefully to the concrete ramp. Meanwhile, from the co-pilot's side, Zero arose, sweeping off his helmet and parachute harness in a single motion.

He rolled his neck in a circle, then brought a determined palm over his face from nose down. Laurel sensed his effort to dispel a feeling he still wore the irksome oxygen mask. And then, she felt an echo of elation. How good it is to see him!

By six P.M. the salon at 14 rue Père Marquette vibrated with well-wishers. There were the Risseaus, Hachères, Martins, Monsieur Vervins and his son, newly arrived from Algeria. There was of course Michel. And the MacDonalds, Edneys, Woods, Stevens, and Colonel Parker had accepted Zero's quick bid to come by for drinks.

Shortly before eight, the guests began to vanish but Zero invited Vervins and his son for dinner, as well as Parker and Michel. Afterwards, as the men spoke of Zero's new task, in the area of Franco-American relations, Laurel performed her duties at the coffee tray. Then, she attempted to depart upstairs, but Zero objected adamantly, "I'm not ready to let you out of my sight yet!"

Laurel sat down with her knitting, though it rested in her lap while she studied Zero. The admiration she had felt that afternoon, as she watched him braced against the sky on the wing of his plane, still lingered. Of course, she was beyond deluding herself: theirs was relegated to the common garden variety of American marriages, weeded now in dual adultery.

She held no hope of falling back in love with him. No, she reminded herself quickly. I was never in love with him, or his promiscuity would have broken my heart. Whatever I felt for him at the beginning had to do with what some people call sex appeal. Zero's more susceptible to that sort of thing than I am. Probably, that's what drew him to me. That's the answer. But we have two children, and an obligation to keep our home together. If physical love was our original tie, then why not try to rebuild on such a foundation?

What was it Abach had said—"if this is a good example of what Zero has had to put up with. . . ." Laurel began to knit, her teeth often sinking into her lower lip, as she waited for the men to go. Parker left at ten-thirty. Vervins and his son followed. Immediately, Zero and Michel switched their topic to the coming hunts at Noël to begin the first week of December. House parties. Two, three, four days at a time. But Laurel did not really listen.

When the cuckoo announced eleven, Zero stood up and said to his guest; "You and Laurel carry on. I'm half-dead from the flight." At the door he looked back. "Stay the night, Mike. It's late and there's plenty of room."

Laurel picked up a cigarette and Michel dashed across the room to light it. When the flame died, he bent further until their eyes were level. He said, "I don't give a damn that you forced me to dine with Vervins, but that son of his is a. . . ."

She retorted, "Zero asked them."

"Ah!" he said, "You call that passing the buck in American. I know."

With contempt in her eyes she said, "You've got to get out of here, Michel. . . ."

He lifted both brows in arched surprise. "Zero asked me to stay. This is his house."

"It would serve you right if I told him."

He sat down in Zero's chair. "You could, but it might hurt you. In the first place, he knows how we love to fight. He wouldn't believe you. He's American. And I'm his friend."

She arose from the couch and went to the mantel. "Your middle name should have been Lucifer." She braced her elbows on the mantel and cradled her chin in her palms. Michel came to the opposite end and imitated her pose.

"Laurel," he said in a low voice. She watched him close his eyes and inhale. "Laurel, I've decided to paint you." He waited for her reaction. She laughed, seeing how absurdly serious he was about his talent and its expenditure. She turned around to face him, and he closed the little distance between them, clasped his arms lightly about her waist.

"Let me go."

He laughed, released her, and backed away. She watched him light a cigarette, take three or four puffs and toss it into the fire. Then he walked to the door, apparently ready to go upstairs to bed. He halted and said, "You'll come to me when you're ready."

"For what?" she said through clenched teeth.

"For a sitting. Laurel, I promise you it shall be a masterpiece. My chef-d'oeuvre of gratitude to you—and no one but us shall ever know. Laurel, I shall paint you and arrive, really arrive, as an artist, but more important, you've shown me that I can marry now—when I find myself a wife."

She stood very still, her face hidden in both her hands. His lips felt cool against her brow as he said tenderly, "Good night, my dear Laurel. Now, you'd better run up to Colonel Compton."

For a week, Laurel enchanted her husband with a connubial existence at times savage. Such belated bliss might have lasted except for Zero's affair with bourbon the eighth night after his return, the night they attended a rather bacchanalian spree in Parker's suite at the BOQ. The party was not memorable. Misfortune occurred when, in the height of ardor, Zero uttered the name Chia. Unaware of Egyptian dancers at Corliss Air Base, Laurel guessed wrongly that the name sounded Italian. Zero had spent a night in Rome on his return, and who could remember how many nights in Naples or Genoa or Rome the past year?

This episode inhibited her matrimonial campaign. The morning after Zero named Chia, she laid plans to decorate the empty bedroom containing the gold marble fireplace with its Latin motto.

She stood in the middle of the bare room that October morning and envisioned, one thing at a time, what would be done to her room. My room? Yes. We're getting of an age to esteem a little privacy. I'll think of some way to persuade Zero to agree.

She would find un lit à baldaquin with a wall canopy, perhaps

—the bed must be covered, the canopy draped in olive velvet with silk fringe of gold. She would bring the Limoges medallioned game table up from its ignominious corner in the dining room.

I'll use the same olive velvet at the window, and I want a chaise longue in gold brocade. The Cloidon clock will go on the mantel, and I'll use a small Aubusson, and I think I'll bring up the Degas from the salon. Zero will be relieved. He doesn't care for anything borrowed from Paradis, anyway. And this will be my room—mine.

13

One day when Laurel was driving Brick home from school and about to park the car, she spied a fracas in her courtyard. A Gypsy faced Olande who was braced across the stoop in an air of distress. Laurel turned to Brick and said, "Wait here in the car for me—just a moment—and don't touch the gear or anything."

She closed the car door and hurried toward the house. Olande was scolding the Gypsy furiously for entering the gate without permission. The Gypsy grumbled, but Laurel saw that she was prepared to depart on an instant's notice, for one hand held out an assortment of ribbons and laces, while the other clutched the open edge of the gate.

Laurel took a step closer and saw now Mr. Candle, the great Weimaraner dog. Abach had arrived—surely, surely! Laurel laughed, knowing the strength required of Olande to restrain the beast, who seemed determined to have a pass at the gracefully dangling ribbons.

The dog twisted and lunged forward, bound for the Gypsy's wares, while Olande moaned and rubbed her pinched hand. The woman slipped through the gate. Mr. Candle reared against it, snapping the catch inadvertently by his weight. Saliva foaming and dribbling from his mouth along with a purple satin streamer and a morsel of Brussels lace, he eyed the Gypsy.

"See what bad luck comes of trespassing!" cried Olande.

The Gypsy straightened her array of ribbons, and snarled quite close to the gate, brave behind the barrier, "Why don't you go back to Germany! Ah, wench, I heard you say 'come' to that monster!"

"'Come' is an English word, sale bête! And I'll go back to Germany when you return to Spain!"

Laurel wished, for a moment, they were both in Argentina. To the Gypsy, she said, "Be gone, Esmeralda!"

"A curse on your house!" snarled the crone with an air so falsely ominous and grandiose that Laurel was troubled not to laugh in her face. Gypsies had camped on the south tip of Paradis' land every winter since she could remember. But the toothless French one played her act. She drew her shawl in on her free shoulder and spat on the ground. Then, with the blunt end of her black cane, she drew a line between them in the sand and gravel.

Willing to play along, Laurel drew the index finger of her right hand beneath her nose. Not once had their eyes left each other. Laurel said, "You need no curse. Your mother wore tin earrings and your father pulled his wagon with a milk cow."

When the American turned to enter her gate, the maid stood beside the upright dog. Her face was a mirror of sick dread. "Oh, Madame! Surely, surely, you do not understand!"

Laurel turned from her and bent slightly so that her eyes were level with the dog's, the gate between them. She said to him, "Well, old friend?" He gave a delighted bark and lashed his apple-red tongue between the grills three or four times. Laurel turned her cheek within reach and he kissed her joyously.

"Oh, Madame!" cried Olande, frightened and impatient. "May I please run catch her and buy twenty francs' worth of something?"

Laurel straightened, surprised. "Why on earth?"

"It's bad luck, Madame, not to buy something from a Gypsy."

Laurel came through the gate, commanding the seventy-pound dog to Sit! for it was obvious that his enthusiasm was temporarily boundless. He sat, lifting one front foot, then the other from the ground—as if it were scaldingly hot. Laurel bent to pat his head and scratch beneath his chin. "Olande, are you really afraid of Gypsies?"

"Well, I—yes, Madame."

"What if I told you sorcerers are mentioned in the same paragraph in Revelations with whoremongers, murderers, idolaters, and liars?"

"I—Madame—are you sure?"

Still bent to the dog, Laurel glanced up at her with a smile. "Ask Monsieur le Curé tomorrow morning, and now, go get Brick from the car—but Olande, is Dr. Abach—is he here?"

"He did not sit down, Madame."

"No suitcase?"

"No. Just the dog."

"Well, go get Brick and say to him that he has a great surprise. Olande, is he not a beautiful dog?"

The maid frowned down at him. "Yes, Madame—but. . . ."

"But what?"

"He is too wise. He knows I am afraid of him. This hour. . . ." She halted and bit her lip on a deep breath.

"This hour what?"

"While I was upstairs with Chris, the dog ate three pounds of boned turkey from the kitchen cabinet."

"A gourmet, uh?" Laurel said to the dog.

"A gourmand, Madame."

Mr. Candle had stopped his dancing. He eyed one and then the other as if he understood each word and awaited the verdict. Laurel viewed the maid coolly. "Perhaps he was hungry. Now, get Brick from the car while I take the dog inside and get him calmed for their meeting."

Laurel had had enough for one morning, but shortly thereafter Madame Hachère arrived on some thin excuse of needing her November rent a few days early. When Laurel demurred, Madame confessed. Her husband had plans to use the hundred dollars for some foolishness of his own. As one woman to another, as one wife to another, she corrected herself, couldn't Laurel understand?

Laurel then recalled that the garden was to revert to the premises at this time, and so she paid the landlady her rent, saying that she would like now to have the key to the potting shed since the area badly needed cleaning for the winter.

Madame Hachère pursed her lips regretfully and said; "I do not know how to explain. Madame Compton, I cannot give you that key. You see, Raoul, my ancient gardener whom you have seen here sometimes, was the manservant of my husband's mother when she resided in this house. He was furious that we leased it to Americans in the beginning. And he is very old, and must be humored."

Laurel found it the most unlikely of stories, coming from a Hachère. Almost sarcastically, she said, "Then am I obliged to ask him?"

"Oh, no!" exclaimed Madame Hachère. "But I could not offend him. You see, those are his tools in that old shed. Really, they are useless and you would not want them. Why don't you buy some of your own?"

Ah, decided Laurel, French vengeance—ladylike but emphatic! She's retaliating finally for the embarrassment over the hot-water heater, and for my having sent the rent by a servant afterwards. What would I give to be able to say that—but Zero has the wrong job now.

"Olande!" called Laurel toward the kitchen. When the maid appeared, Laurel said too lightly; "Olande, the garden will become the property of the house in a few days, and Madame Hachère is too nice to go and fetch the last of her vegetables. If you don't mind, run down and get those four potatoes near the east fence. And by the way, tell your husband tonight we'll have to delay cleaning the shed because the tools belong to Raoul, who does not choose to have them used for American purposes."

Laurel turned away from Olande to an appalled Madame Hachère. She said to the landlady, "Ah, Madame! The whims of the old are often like the whims of the very young, don't you agree? Well, excuse me, now! I must get up to my sewing."

The truth of the matter was that Laurel's sewing was long finished. All items within the house destined for her room were in place, except that she still had to go to Soissons and pick up a loveseat and matching chairs from the upholsterer.

She returned in late afternoon with the furniture, pleased by the work that had been done. At her doorstep, however, Olande waited with that special expression for which Laurel had found no mental description more apt than important distress. Reluctantly, Laurel asked, "What is it this time?"

"Monsieur Hachère."

"Ah!" said Laurel gleefully, thinking of the domestic crisis implied by his wife. "He came to have me pay *him* the rent?"

"No, Madame. He telephoned first to see if you were in."

Laurel tensed mildly, "He wanted to see me?"

"No, Madame. I think he wanted not to see you, for he arrived with old Raoul and the two younger Hachère sons within ten minutes after his telephone call."

"And?"

Olande wore the face of neo-tragedy. "While Monsieur Hachère and Raoul removed seventy-two dahlia bulbs from the courtyard and first garden in the rear, the two younger men gleaned seven and a half bushels of apples and winter pears from the garden."

Laurel was surprised that she felt no anger. "Olande, I'll bet you made A in arithmetic!"

"Oh, Madame!" wailed the girl. "I was afraid you'd blame me."

"Don't be idiotic!" scolded Laurel.

"But there's something else. It's in the afternoon paper."

"How could it possibly concern us?" Laurel had her hand on the bottom stairpost, impatient to take the garden problem upstairs before she exploded in the girl's presence.

"It concerns Monsieur Risseau, the Hachères' attorney. Madame, it says in the paper that he has processed to a successful conclusion a case against an American airman who gifted a French family—a benefactor, the sergeant claims—with an American appliance. It seems the sergeant left the appliance with the French family when he transferred to Germany because they had been kind to him and his family. But a neighbor reported them and the sergeant and the French family have both been found guilty of evading French customs. Risseau proved to the court's satisfaction that the sergeant sold the apparatus."

Appliance? Apparatus? Laurel thought of the American refrigerator left in the basement of 14 rue Père Marquette, secured from the Frakes by Risseau for his daughter's wedding gift. Laurel asked, "What was the punishment?"

"It says in the paper the sergeant was fined the equivalent of four months' pay."

"And the French family?"

"They were forgiven because—well, it says in the paper their son has tuberculosis. A minor son."

"What was the appliance, Olande?"

"Well, I did not wish to anger you, Madame, but it was of course a refrigerator."

"Of course," replied Laurel, waiting—still waiting to feel a bolt of thunderous wrath. But the day had too many meanings, she thought as she labored slowly up the stairs. The Gypsy. Madame Hachère. Raoul's tools. Papa. The dahlias gone before next summer. And finally, Risseau processing in dignity a "crime" he had himself successfully committed, knowing no Frenchman in Beaumonde was courageous enough to report an attorney.

Laurel undressed and bathed, routinely, effortlessly. She admitted a tired, philosophical acceptance. None of what had happened today was peculiar to France. It could have happened anywhere in America, she told herself as she brushed her hair before the mirror.

Leisurely, she dressed for a gala evening. The ball to welcome the Squadrons home from North Africa had been postponed twice because Parker had been called both times to Headquarters in Germany. She regarded herself in the mirror as she straightened the discreet sleeves and shallow décolletage of an expensive black dress. Adding a bib of white pearls, she tried to remember how old the gown was, whether it had been bought the year before or the year after Brick's birth. At any rate, it was the kind of dress any woman relied upon, classic enough not to discourage intimates and rich enough to impress outsiders.

Zero entered and flung his hat on the bed. She glanced in the mirror and said, "Hi!" The bed creaked then as he flopped across it, face down, his legs hanging over the side. "Had a rough day?" she said softly, companionably.

"A regular bastard." He raised up on one elbow and braced his jaw with a palm. "Laurel, I can't find a place to grab this job."

She took a guess. "Risseau and his refrigerator case?"

"That's among the lesser perils at the moment."

She fastened the beads and put on one pearl earring. "I could have told you that day we had the toasting of the verbal rent contract up at Hachères."

"What do you mean?"

"He told you he explained your joke about the potatoes to Hachère. He was lying."

"Oh, Christ! I knew that." Zero sat up and rubbed his face with both hands. Laurel watched him then take off his uniform blouse.

"How?"

"By the change in your eyes when Risseau answered. You know, Laurel, you're an open book."

She swung around on her little dressing-table stool and Zero's eyes took in her dress, her pearl jewelry and came back to her lips. "Laurel, you're gettin' too God damned old to wear black and no make-up."

She laughed. "Thank you, kind sir!"

"I'm serious. Besides, tonight is no night for black. You depress me. You look like a patron of the society to preserve classical musicians or something. . . ." He was peeling off his clothes now, hurrying to get to the tub. Her eyes lighted as she thought of the copper lamé creation she had hidden away and of how Zero would look when he saw her in a dress slit from thyroid to navel.

Her amusement growing, she went into the spare bedroom and got down the carton from the top shelf of an armoire. Then, with him safe in the tub, she wiggled into the elasticized sheath and straightened the shoulders and long sleeves.

Laurel knew before she stared into the full-length mirror of the armoire that the dress was indecent. A dress for a woman fighting to regain a husband, or for a girl whose swain lacked courage to propose. Staring at the mirror, she gasped. Like mermaid's skin, the fine mesh clung to each curve and hollow from hip upward. Minus button, bauble, or trim to distract the eye, the garment was one masterful stroke of cut and drape.

Well, she smiled to herself, it would be a good joke on Zero, though certainly a woman would have to be in desperate straits to exit from her own front door in such a gown.

To add to the effect, she bent before her dressing-table mirror and painted her lips with an orange lipstick. Now, she took down her hair and parted it in the middle, braiding the two halves to bind them around and around her head. She stood before the mantel in their bedroom when Zero entered naked from his bath.

He blinked twice, seemingly speechless. "Laurel, you look like Medusa on the rocks."

"You have me confused with Scotch," she said, not moving.

He came determinedly toward her, his gaze riveted to the slender exposure between her breasts. His fingers slid beneath either side of the molded opening. His hands cupped her breasts and he seemed everywhere at once—his mouth and his hands as he breathed her name heavily and longingly. She laughed, "Not now! You've got to dress. So have I!"

She leaned back, away from him, waiting for him to decry her lipstick, but his lids were heavy, half-closed. "Laurel, you're the most . . . Laurel. . . ."

"Let me go!" she laughed impatiently. "I've got to change. I only put this on to—to. . . ."

His arms fell away from her. He stepped back in surveyal. "Laurel, wear it for me."

"Why, Zero!" she replied incredulously. "It looks evil!"

"Oh, no!" He began to chuckle. "If that's the case, I wouldn't have bought it." She glanced down at her flat abdomen and the narrow slit over her bosom. "Laurel, when I look at you in that thing, I don't feel thirty-six years old—I feel—well, nineteen. . . . Laurel, wear it."

"Zero, what will Parker and the others think?"

His hands flew to his hips. One brow lifted in smiling emphasis.

"By God, I'll do a lot to salve Parker, but you're not dressing to suit him—not *yet!*"

Laurel bit her lip, wondering how to remind him that Abach was on the Base, and, in all probability, would be attending the party. How anxious she felt to maintain the improved relationship between him and Zero. She turned away and picked up an emery board from the dressing table. She heard him open a drawer, and heard him say, as if he read her mind, "Abach's not coming to the shindig. He took O.D. so the other doctors can all attend."

"He would," she sighed.

"What?"

"Nothing. Nothing at all." She dropped down to the stool before the dressing table and watched him draw on his shorts and T-shirt. "Zero," she said pensively, "Madame Hachère came today to demand the rent."

"Well?" he said without looking up.

"Three or four days early."

"Get a discount?" he said smartly.

"No, just a door slammed in the face, so to speak. She refused to give me a key so we can get a rake and hoe out of that tool shed."

"Well, Christ! Don't be as chinchy as they are. Buy some."

"Papa Hachère came and took the dahlia bulbs up this afternoon while I was gone."

He drew on both black socks before he answered. "Seems like they're his—if that's what he wants to do with them."

"He had all the apples and winter pears picked, too."

"They're probably wormy, anyway."

"Zero, there was a Gypsy woman here today. Came into the courtyard without ringing the bell."

He glanced up at her, brows lifted. "Have any trouble shaking her?" Laurel shrugged negatively. "Well, what else?"

"Nothing."

She became silent as Zero slipped his arms into his tux shirt and sat down on the bed so she could insert the pearl studs without her having to reach up. Carefully, she tied his tie, ignoring with a smile the playful tweaks he employed here and there. She thought: Oh, if only his mind was as susceptible as his body where I'm concerned. In nine years and these months, I don't believe we've ever had what they call a meeting of the minds. Truly, we live in separate worlds. Always have. Probably always will. I could tell Guy what's happened today, and he'd listen, and tell me what to do.

14

Parker beckoned to Zero, who rose and left Laurel alone at a table in the shadows. She studied the assembled officers and their wives and could recall no missing American, except Abach, although a group of four tables extending well into the middle of the room was still empty.

Suddenly, on the side opposite the bandstand, she caught sight of Paul Hachère emerging from the cloakroom, followed by his parents, the Risseaus, Martins, Clau-Bouvilles, and other couples, who were being ushered to the four tables by Monsieur Duprée, senior civilian employee of the Base, and the man who had invited Zero to his very first French trap shoot.

Laurel tensed at the sight of the mammoth, Rembrandt-proportioned beauty in mink-collared ivory brocade. Duprée and his wife stepped back while the officious matron fingered her diamond necklace and directed each member of the French group to his or her position at the tables. Duprée was merely the sham host; the hostess was Belle Tricot!

Laurel had never seen her, but any doubt she might have had as to the woman's identity was negated by a glance at Paul Hachère's glowering expression. Hastily, Laurel's eyes searched for Monsieur Tricot, who by rumor seldom appeared in public with his wife. (His position as Commissioner of Public Utilities for a six-state area was appointive out of Paris and had survived six cabinet failings—a distinction which placed him notches above a governor!) But Laurel located him by his handsome English dinner jacket, his look of tolerant scorn, and by the fact he alone disdained looking at Belle Tricot.

Laurel turned her back on the seated group and bowed her head in racing thought. She saw even in the unlighted niche the ripple of the copper lamé as her weight shifted from one hip to the other. Why did I let Zero talk me into wearing . . . but what does it matter? I don't care what she thinks—after all, I've never met her. . . .

Unwillingly, she thought of Michel's recent statement that a roll in Tricot hay would better an American officer's housing situation. Laurel did not doubt this and she knew for a fact that some American wives in Belle Tricot's coterie shopped at both Commissary and PX for the French woman, affording her illicit luxuries in exchange for social favors. Fritsch, Parker's predecessor, had made an astounding exception to Base policy, and granted both Tricots laminated entry passes—much like those Laurel and other wives carried. Parker was stultified to learn that either husband or wife could therefore come on the Base any time, even during rigid alerts, and that withdrawing the passes would be hazardous, because Tricot's supervisory position covered not only water, electricity, coal, and fuel oil but affected the prices and contract particulars at annual renewal. As the Base Judge Advocate explained to Parker and Compton, it was a situation.

Memory of these facts did not help Laurel's pique, for it nettled her to be there unseen in the wrong dress. When Zero returned with Parker, he said, "The three of us have to sit at Duprée's table. He invited us."

Parker snorted in good-natured surprise, "Me? With that Tricot woman and her stooges? I should live so long—in my own Club!"

Laurel's chuckle seconded his stand, but Zero was annoyed. "Sir, it's none of my affair but. . . ."

"That's exactly my point," said Parker. "I'll see you around!"

Laurel studied his back enviously as it grew smaller and

merged into the anonymity of the crowd about the bar. She looked petulantly at Zero. "No."

"Oh, Christ!" he exploded, taking her by the elbow. "What makes you think we have a choice?"

For a time, the eddy of greetings exchanged with the French group absorbed her attention. Every person about Duprée's table had stood up as the Comptons approached and greeted them courteously and enthusiastically. Zero, in unexplainable confusion, presented Laurel to Monsieur Tricot instead of vice versa. Laurel saw that the error did not escape the suave fellow. His English was fluid and flawless, but ridicule seemed bottled in his eyes like Seltzer contained beneath a cork. She was on the verge of accepting Papa Hachère's offer of his own chair when she realized that Madame Tricot, whom she had still not met, stood—immobile and silent as the Sphinx—beside Papa.

For an instant the two women weighed each other. Then, Belle Tricot extracted from her gold-mesh bag a pince-nez. Papa Hachère said, as he lifted his chair and set it back to the floor, "Surely, you two charming ladies know each other." Laurel nodded. Belle Tricot said an icily toned, How do you do?

Then music blared forth and Duprée was on his feet and behind Laurel's chair to ask her to dance. He chatted interminably; she nodded. Next came Paul, who, as she knew, believed that in dancing the hold was half the battle. Martin, Risseau, Clau-Bouville, and others followed, and finally a sturdy, expensively lotioned Tricot, who held her on his paunch while his feet executed featherweight turns. At least, she reflected, he saw no need to talk!

Over the shoulders of her dancing partners, Laurel saw the unfairness of Zero's entente, for he had not danced with a single one of the French matrons. She knew he had no intention of doing so, even if they had not been buxom, cloying, and, generally, ten to twenty years his senior. He wouldn't have danced with them had they been the maenads, she reminded herself scornfully, but I've had enough of being lend-leased. When I get back to that table, I'm telling him: I'm going to the wagon or the outhouse or the restroom or somewhere. I've *had* it!

At first Zero pretended he didn't understand her beckoning

glance, but she had scarcely reached the bar area when he began to rebuke her. "My God, Laurel! What did you tell them?"

"Zero, you've no business with this job unless you're going to wedge in some language lessons. I simply told them I was dying of thirst, that I hadn't had anything to drink all night, and I was going to the bar for quicker service."

When he made no move to get her some kind of drink—in truth, Laurel would have been happy with water, so great was her thirst—she worked her way between a pair of broad backs at the bar and caught the bartender's eye. Soon, with a martini in each hand, she turned about and wiggled out carefully to keep from spilling the full glasses. She was about to remind Zero to pay, when she caught sight beyond him of Madame Hachère, who was waving the fingers of one hand in timid familiarity. A bit less courageous, thought Laurel, than when she's standing in my hall telling me why I can't have the key to her tool shed.

Now, over Zero's shoulder she saw a glowering Madame Tricot, who undoubtedly was aware of Laurel's attempt to slip away. I won't, she declared silently—I won't grease them up for the remainder of the night. Zero can if he must, but I won't—not tonight!

She took a quick push to the left, spilling martini over the rim of the glass, and decided then to sip off the excess. She saw Zero waiting for her to move on so he could follow. Then she came even with a noisy table occupied by Regina and her husband and several others.

"It's time for a toast," shouted rarely gregarious Edney. He stood up, the neck of his champagne bottle aimed at Laurel's glass. She held it still while he poured, and while Zero moved in closer, extending his own glass.

"Chugalug!" shouted an officer whom Laurel did not know but Zero apparently did. The two men clinked glasses. "Chugalug!" the stranger returned to Laurel.

Around the table, glasses were tilted, but Laurel only pretended to gulp. They sat down with the revelers, and in the next hour, Laurel drank very little, although her laughter was merriest of all. She had almost forgotten the dreary French until Paul Hachère approached to ask her to dance. Zero answered yes for her, and the pair eased onto the dance floor. Paul said almost at once, "Laurel, I congratulate you! I never thought I'd see the day when anybody had the courage to affront Belle Tricot."

"Why haven't you, long ago?" she said airily.

Paul shrugged. "Don't think I haven't thought of it, but surely you know by now she owns every sou of stock in my father's agency."

This had not occurred to Laurel. Half-embarrassed, she spoke her next thought, "Paul, why does she hate me?"

"Why, what makes you think that?"

"Oh, the way she looked at me through those glasses."

He laughed. "No French woman is going to wear ordinary glasses. Don't you know that?"

"I've heard, but, Paul, I feel it in my bones. She and I are enemies."

"I told you before—that Malmarquis de Berteaux."

"This isn't the nineteenth century."

"Well, *tell her!* Laurel, Berteaux sleeps and dines too often at your house. And the postman tells her maid every time you get a letter from Berteaux's mother."

Why, the indiscreet devil! But Paul had one more thing to say, and it hardly concerned the ubiquitous little postman. "Laurel, you mustn't taunt her. She can be rather mean. Last summer when she heard my parents were about to rent the house to you, she told them a fantastic lie about seeing you holding hands with some fellow in a restaurant in Paris."

Near midnight, she glanced about the table and then over the room, and last, toward the bar. How long had Zero been missing? She turned to Louis Edney, whose rare intoxication had stabilized at a rather uncertain stage, and asked him where Zero was.

"I'm taking you home, Laurel. Tell me when you're ready."

"But what's happened to him?" she demanded almost irritably.

"Fire." He smiled inanely.

"Where?" she frowned.

"Some farm around."

"But what has that to do with Zero?"

"I'll take you home. He'll tell you in the morning."

"OK," she said through rather narrowed eyes and a calm smile, although she had no intention of allowing Louis Edney to drive the extra distance in his condition. About a half-hour later, she reached the cloakroom undetected, she believed, and put on her sable coat. As she made her way toward the car, relieved that Zero had apparently gone wherever he had gone in a staff car, Paul Hachère ran to catch up with her.

"Laurel! Laurel, I'll drive you home. Zero told me if Louis Edney drank too much, I could do it."

"Where's he gone?"

"Edney? Why, he's inside. I think he'll. . . ."

"No, Zero."

"Oh, Parker sent him off to Nouilly."

"But that's Edney's village!"

"I know. He had to go a bunch of places. He'll tell you about it in the morning."

What was it? she asked herself. A conspiracy to keep his mission a secret?

Laurel smiled so flatly as she declined Paul's offer to take her home that there was nothing left for him to say. He stood with his feet braced apart and waved her off from the front of the Club, as if she were charging away to Antarctica, but Laurel drove only three blocks—to the dingy, dismal wooden hospital.

She parked her station wagon between a pair of blue ambulances and entered through emergency doors with a vigorous swing that left them echoing in smaller and smaller arcs. She knew Abach would be in his office.

15

A pot-bellied coal heater stewed acrid coffee while heating the stuffy room. Feathered by light from his desk lamp, Abach turned his face as she came into the open door. "The kids OK?" he said tensely.

Laurel said without slowing down, "They're better than I am."

His swivel chair creaked as it swung about. He was on his feet, searching her face while he held her lightly by the shoulders. She waited for him to release her; she had spied the neat metal cot behind his chair. Its taut olive-drab blanket seemed a wonderful surface to fling her tired back.

Abach watched her stretch out and gather the rich fur around her. When she looked up at him, he was taking a roll of elastic bandage from a glass-doored cabinet. "Put it away!" she chided. "You can't mend my wounds with that!"

He came over and sat down with ease on the foot of the cot. "No," he chuckled, "but I can sure as Hell protect your reputation if that night nurse comes in to get a swig of coffee. She knows I'm no psychiatrist and this *ain't* a couch!"

"Where am I hurt?" asked Laurel.

"Oh, let me see!" He turned his face thoughtfully to the board ceiling. "A sprained ankle. That's simple. Impersonal." Idly, he placed the start of the binding beneath the arch of her right foot and brought it up deftly, expertly twisting and wrapping three rounds, whereupon he paused, holding the remainder of the roll in his hand, as he asked whether the dog had knocked the baby down yet. She shook her head. "You'll have to watch Chris, Laurel. He and Candle on the stairs at one time. . . ."

"I know. That's why I put gates at top and bottom of the stairs."

"But the boy'll be opening them soon."

She eyed him stolidly. "You'd make an awful father."

"Why?"

"You're a bigger worry wart than I am."

He shrugged and took two more turns at the bandaging. "That's what comes of patching up too many."

"Nuts! You ought to know from some of the things we survived—kids are made of rubber."

Silence fell between them. Eventually, she broke it by asking abruptly, "Where's Zero?"

Abach replied without hesitation, "A couple of airmen from Installations Squadron set fire to Vervins' winter hay supply while they were walking from Nouilly to Beaumonde."

"How do you know that?"

"I walked over to the Officers' Mess about a half-hour ago to fill up my coffee pot. Parker was there, trying to get thoroughly sober before he went into the Police Station, I guess."

"Why did Zero have to go?"

"He represents Parker. What interests me more is why you're here."

Laurel raised herself up to a sitting position and eased back against the wall. She pulled her coat quickly together and began to talk in earnest, telling him of her difficulties with the Hachères—even to Paul's two visits. She told him about the dance that evening and of her withdrawal from the French contingent.

Proceeding more slowly, she explained as best she could Zero's near-indifference when she tried earlier in the evening to discuss the abuse of the Hachères. "Abach, I don't know what I came here to say, except that I can't seem to find my place. I can't live up to a role I don't understand, and worse still, I've lost my enthusiasm for trying."

He was thoughtful in the little silence, perhaps waiting for her to go on, but when she did not, he asked a simple question, "Then, what do you want?"

"I want to quit worrying about the French. I want to go back into my little shell with no obligations except house and children."

"You could accomplish that back in America."

"That's exactly the point. Abach, every time I look deep enough into truth, that's all I want—I want to take Chris and Brick and go home. I'm not the same person I was when I came over here." She paused. "Abach, I want to go home and learn to be the way I was, before it's too late."

He refused to take her seriously. He offered what he teasingly called a prescription. It involved an hour's talk during which he made an attempt to give her a new viewpoint towards the potentialities around her. Laurel heard him out, interrupting only to clear a point now and then, and when he was finished, she tolerated between sudden yawns his completion of the bandage.

When the two hourglass-shaped brads held the end of the wrapping taut, she dropped her feet to the floor and slid the free one into her shoe. "You're a fine doctor," she chortled as she bent to pick up the other shoe.

He did not look at his handiwork as he protested, "Why, it's a superb binding job. I never saw better!"

Laurel limped toward the door on the one spiked heel. "Just the same, I'm glad that nurse you mentioned spared us undoing." She turned back and regarded him affectionately. "Come on! You did this to me! You can just help me creep to the car!"

Affixed on his arm, she went silently down the ghostly corridor, through the dispensary and out to the car, and when the door was closed and the window newly rolled down, she said to him in a whisper, "In the first place, unless there's a fracture, a good doctor always bandages a sprained ankle with the foot hanging in down position. Edema. Lymph glands. Et cetera." She cleared her throat in lordly emphasis. "Look it up!"

"And second?" he tossed his head back in mock rebuttal.

"Second? I think you're losing your mind, Abach. You forgot to have me take off my stocking."

16

"The number three cleaning girl in the BOQ is pregnant by an American sergeant with a wife and three children. A gendarme was poisoned two nights ago by his mistress in Blaineau, but the police called it suicide because the whole village knows this gendarme had abnormal tendencies in bed. What else? Unholiest of rumors—bread prices will be raised five francs a kilo by the French government in about three weeks."

"Aw, Laurel!" Zero guffawed, "For Christ's sake!"

"Keep laughing," she retorted.

"I hardly see you in the guise of Mata Hari!"

"Zero! You make me sound so absurd! Can't you understand? Here's part of France all around us—people breathing, walking, cohabiting, dying, marrying, grumbling, and enduring Americans." Her voice lowered; her eyes brightened in sincerity. "Paris seems remote now. But I'll bet you five hundred dollars to a doughnut that the day we leave France, I know the Department of Gregny better than any American ever has."

"My God, Laurel! It's a wasted effort! It's not worth it!"

"I don't care," she argued stubbornly. "It's like looking at your own child and knowing it isn't the prettiest or the cleverest. But it's still yours and it's your duty to accept it." Why not use Abach's exact words? "And you can't love it if you don't even know it!"

For nearly a fortnight, she had thrown herself wholeheartedly into Abach's suggestion that she concentrate a while on blending herself into the local scene. Dressed in dull grays and flat, rustic-turned French shoes, her head bound in a scarf, she appeared a typical Beaumonder en route to ten o'clock shift at switchboard or cash register on the Base Américaine those mornings she rode the free military bus, with her nose buried in a Beaumonde newspaper. She wore very dark French-made glasses and sat, when possible, beside some sober G.I.

Instead of her former quick glimpses at headlines and advertisements in French newspapers, she had begun to force herself to read what concerned France. She had no bent for economics, politics, or sensationalism, and generally, the French news could be classified in these categories. However, she persevered.

Zero had been absent, preoccupied or exhausted for two weeks. With his flying and the comings-and-goings of Michel anent the hunting season which would soon be in full swing, Laurel had no chance to approach Zero on the broader aspects of Franco-American attitudes. The evening she proposed to have a quiet chat on the subject, he rolled his head tiredly in his big armchair. "Laurel, for Christ's sake, I'm sick of the word Franco-American. I wish it was still a label on a spaghetti can—the way it was before we came over here!"

Apparently, though, her interest touched a chord in weary Zero. He told her about the investigation he had just completed, that concerning the two airmen who had ignited Vervins' hayshed. "Kramer and Schiller, Laurel. A fine pair of upstanding Americans. God damn it to Hell! Kramer sat picking his nose during every interrogation, and when the policeman had Schiller undress for routine frisking, his socks stank so God damned awful, you couldn't even smell the mildew in the Beaumonde jail."

Laurel interrupted. "But you got them out of French jail that night and took them back to the guard house?"

"Yes," he sighed deeply. "But let me finish. They started drinking red wine in Nouilly. Place doesn't even have a café license. Some damned butcher who sells vin ordinaire in his back room at night, sells it at fifty cents a glass to drunk G.I.'s. He pays sixty cents a litre for it—oh, well. They tanked up pretty good, but things were dull. No girls came in. Nothing to do. So they decided to go back to the Base, to the Service Club. Schiller objected about the time they hit the back gate. Not even any beer at the Service Club. So they walked on through the Base and went out the front gate this time—headed for Maxia's in Beaumonde—you know, that dive across from the Gare.

"Schiller says they went in that filling station café, the one with kerosene lamps and those Danish beer signs. It's run by an Algerian itinerant, Laurel. He just moved in at the end of harvest season with a family of French Gypsies who own it. Anyway, Kramer and Schiller went in to have a beer and they had three or four, I guess. Schiller insists he doesn't remember what happened after they left the place, but Kramer made a full confession. He claims it always does something to him to see a full moon in the fall, says he gets homesick for the country because he was raised on a farm in Iowa. He said it'd been eating him a long time the way the French use those short-handled hoes and the way they underplant and rotate crops and mulch their soil. All a lot of God damned tommyrot, according to him, and a waste of time and earth. Anyway, he says he got to thinking about how good a bonfire smells and how a hay fire lights up the countryside. . . ."

"Zero, he sounds like a candidate for pyromania!" said Laurel.

"I guess not." He grimaced. "He didn't have the guts to set it himself. He dared staggering old Schiller."

She thought it all over a minute. Then she said with scarcely felt cheer, "Well, at least, Vervins' hay was fully insured. Zero, it was fine of him to come here the next day and ask you to go light on the two men."

"Yeah, he's a prince. But unfortunately, that wasn't the point. You see, there's the local election coming up the end of this month, and before this happened, we had a chance of seeing the Mayor out of office. Now, he'll be reelected—him and his anti-American buddies."

"Well, at least, he's anti-Communist, too," she said.

"Aw, you're smart enough to figure out by now that when a Frenchman hates Communists *and* Americans, he's a real loggerhead."

Laurel eyed him thoughtfully. "Why does the Mayor hate Americans?"

Zero shrugged. "Nobody seems to know. He's just that way." He looked too tired for her to speak her mind. What Zero meant was that the information had not been readily available and so no one had made a project of finding out. After all, did a Frenchman have to have a reason for hating Americans?

Laurel's answer to herself was a defiant yes, but she said no more, as she glanced down at a stack of periodicals at her feet. She couldn't pester him just now with synopses of her reading.

Zero stood up, yawning. He smiled at her affectionately. "You're so God damned smart, why don't you make a project of finding out?"

"Finding out what?"

"Why Mayor Cravet hates Americans?"

Her frown was quick and annoyed. "How could I do that when I don't even know him?"

Zero kissed her good night—kissed her on the forehead—and went out of the room. Abach was wrong! she reviled herself. Suppose accidentally I found out why Cravet hates Americans? I couldn't change his attitude.

The next morning, Armistice Day, Zero left for Verdun before eight A.M. to participate in a wreath-laying and luncheon in Parker's stead. At eight-thirty, Olande and Francis took the two children by train to Olande's village for an overnight stay with Olande's parents. Laurel's plan to lunch with Abach went awry. A corpsman telephoned before nine A.M. to say there had been a bad collision—five victims—surgery three hours already and probably Dr. Abach wouldn't be free until midafternoon.

It's a lonely business, reflected Laurel, as she struggled through her first morning entirely by herself in the Beaumonde house. Then she said it aloud to the friend who followed her on all-fours from library to kitchen to salon to courtyard. Mr. Candle obviously missed the maid and the children. When he gave an exclamatory bark soon after the cuckoo sounded ten A.M. she went into the courtyard again. From the distance below the hill, she heard a rumble which became identifiable as she and Mr. Candle sat on the front stoop. They heard the roll of dirgeful snare drums. The veterans and veterans' relatives were parading heavily up the hill to lay their wreaths at the foot of concrete Miss Victory in the little park to the left of her house.

The French don't forget their dead as we do, thought Laurel, as she tried to remember how many years it had been since she had laid a wreath on any grave. Of course, she thought next of her brother, still not dead in her mind. Peter, she reminded herself with growing morbidity, will never be more than twenty-one. Twenty-one years old.

The slow, surging panic of avoided reality began to seep into Laurel's middle. Her arm bent tightly about the steely shoulders and chest of the massive dog. I should have gone with Olande and the children, but they don't need me. I should be with Zero, but he was afraid there might not be any other women. Involuntarily, her heart poured into her brain the surprise of prayer: God in Thine Infinite Mercy, show me where I ought to be!

Slowly, Laurel moved toward the gate, watching between the bars until the hundred or so dark-clad marchers had moved leadenly past. Her head uncovered and no coat over the thick gray knitted dress, she bade the dog wait, whispering and entreating him not to bark when she closed the gate.

She fell in behind the crippled and aged stragglers, noticing that no eye allowed itself the turnings of curiosity this day, this occasion. In the park, she remained in the outer fringes of the semi-circle, going through the motions of their services to the lost. And when they marched back past 14 rue Père Marquette, Laurel separated from the mass and re-entered her own gate.

Scarcely had she finished patting the dog, however, when her gaze lighted on a blue handbill from which he had already chewed one corner. An efficace du logement—a protest against the number of Beaumonde houses and apartments being occupied by Americans. A movement was afoot to force all Americans to relinquish their Beaumonde houses or face an organized—the word *legal* was used redundantly—effort to have authorities far above Air Base level order them to vacate the city of resident Americans.

Laurel paused and stared up at the façade of her dwelling, as if to assure herself it was still there. She studied the paper which enumerated the five resolutions expected to be passed at a citizens' meeting the coming week before the Hotel de Ville. Her eyes widened at Cravet's signature, but something more than dismay gripped her heart as she read the attesting list of unions, political parties, and veterans' societies who would be represented at the meeting and who apparently were in accord with the protest. Laurel's heart literally skipped a beat as she read the names of three local priests, including Olande's beloved Monsieur le Curé of lower Beaumonde, and the Catholic MRP chairman of the region, and finally, the names of Madame Martin and Monsieur Risseau, whom the paper described respectively as "Beaumonde's widely known lady authoress and Beaumonde's leading attorney."

She ran inside her house, sat down at the typewriter, and quickly wrote the salutation: Dear Guy, ...

With compulsive speed and without restraint, she told him of her situation, beginning with the unpleasantness with the Hachères. She included Belle Tricot, Vervins' hay incident, and finally, her research resulting from her talk with Abach. She did not mention the source of inspiration, because it would take too much space to explain Abach's role in her life.

In truth, she did not worry at all about what she said, or the way she said it, for the writing of the letter would serve its own end. Laurel knew that to get a quandary on paper often resolved it. Certainly, she could not *mail* the letter.

If she needed any proof of this, it came in her own surprise at a rereading of the first three pages, for, in trying to portray to Guy the kind of Americans who advanced an opportunist like Belle Tricot, Laurel freewheeled some ideas she did not realize had been in her own head:

> Ruth MacDonald is one of the few women capable of withstanding a society dame in France. She said to me: "I've had one lunch at her house and she's awful. A French DAR. I had to have a way to insult her nicely and permanently, so I just never repaid her invitation."
> Liz Wood has the kind of individuality which eliminates her automatically from the Tricot circle. She treats God damn like an adjective, weighs ninety pounds, smokes like a train, and drives ninety miles an hour in a Volkswagen on the roads between here and Paris. (I survived one trip with her!)

Helen Stone and Martha Giscewiecz, however, exchange both dinners and luncheons with Mme Tricot, and regularly include her in American functions. I do not know how to explain to you this type of American woman. These represent the more admirable half of the Tricot victims—those ambitious goodwillers hellbent on going native with French uppercrust, and to them, in Beaumonde, that is Belle Tricot.

But I have saved for the last example of Beaumonde Air Base officer's wife the one who supplies (I suspect) Belle Tricot with the tidbits of information to which she has no right—the forecast of a Squadron's target capability this month, or the date of the next escape and evasion exercise, and also, enough details of the secret evacuation plan for dependents that Mme Tricot makes jokes about the twenty items we are all supposed to keep on hand at all times in case of war. I cannot much blame Mme Tricot because the list includes toilet paper and a camp cook stove, and I am intrigued to imagine terrified, escaping American mothers running back to the basement to gather up such "essentials."

Such a person is Susan Crandall, who arrived in France with her two teen-age children and a curiosity about whether reconciliation with her husband would work this time, but Harrison seemed unable to change his old habit of bedding down at random. In no hurry to quit him overseas, Susie is apparently devoting her tour in France to enjoying her sorti in Beaumonde "society." Society to her, you see, is as clearly defined as ground staked inside a fence. You will not likely understand, Guy, what a woman with Belle Tricot's material affluence represents to an American like Susan Crandall. Nothing in her background and possibly little pictured in her future could compare with the approval of Belle Tricot.

It's good material, thought Laurel with pursed lips as she read what she had written; and of course, there was no harm in pouring it out since the letter would never be mailed. Release was therapeutic, she repeated silently—but Laurel's shoulders were aching from the uncomfortable chair and the length of her effort. With speed, she moved to finish:

Back to the question of discipline for the two airmen who ignited Vervins' hay supply, each received a sentence of six months at hard labor. One received or will receive a dishonorable discharge, the other will be retained because he confessed. I share the opinions of other Americans that Zero went too far in making examples of the pair, but on the other hand, I am sorry for him because no precedent has been established in this type of liaison and much of what Zero will do is pioneering and must therefore be sometimes wrong.

His main reason for severity at this time is the coming election. Cravet (R-S) is up for re-election. The American-flavored candidate is an MRP named Maynardie, of whom I know little, and the third candidate is a Communist named Audran.

Cravet is the kind of official who makes the most of every bar brawl in which any American can be implicated. That, unfortunately, is the majority of bar brawls in Beaumonde. He keeps the mails hot with letters to Base officials and the American Embassy. He puts proclamations in the newspapers, and influences taxes levied on Americans. Colonel Parker, the Commander of Beaumonde Air Base, said to me he is certain Cravet would like nothing better than to provoke some incident by which he could declare the whole city of Beaumonde off limits to American airmen. This was done last year for a period of three days in which Americans like myself and Zero could go only to and from their own houses. Other Americans could not enter the city to visit us, and the children had to be taken out of French school during that time. Can you imagine anything more unpleasant?

Laurel wrote of Brick's school and of the handbill against Americans living in Beaumonde houses and apartments, and even of having broken the lock on the tool shed in broad daylight while Olande screamed in horror—not at the advent of the dread policeman (Laurel knew lockbreaking was a serious crime in France) but at sight of rat calling cards among the debris in the cobwebby potting shed where not a single garden tool lay.

She had written two hours and nine single-spaced pages before there was nothing else to say . . . except:

I close now, dear Guy, having imposed upon you all the transitory griefs of my November heart. I am not lost to their transience, for I no longer take myself so seriously. By next November, perhaps I shall be back in America or transferred with Zero to Turkey. So I must view France from a reasonable distance!

At any rate, you will be good enough not to tell Michel I have written you, and I ought to say here that Zero has discouraged me from such open and lengthy expressions about the situation here. I believe there is only one motive which would bring me the rashness to mail this letter to you —and that is if I believed you could answer one question for me: Why does Cravet hate Americans? But you are too far from it all, and bless you for choosing roses. As ever,
LDC.

Laurel heaved half a sigh before the doorbell rang. It was the messenger from the railroad station who handed over a small parcel about the size of a stationery box. When she had locked the door, she wandered into the salon and sat down in the Gainsborough chair beside the hearth. Carefully, she tore the wax seal from either side of the little box and lifted the lid to discover a miniature wreath fashioned of glossy holly leaves and tiny, tiny red rosebuds.

Hot tears dropped and disappeared into the closely woven foliage. Laurel's heart twisted in grief as fresh as the scarlet buds. Guy. No card. No word of sympathy. Just Guy reaching out to say without a word that sympathy was predestined.

The post office doors were locked, but she dropped her lengthy billet-doux into the metal container before the entrance and turned away, aware of a new heaviness, one unanticipated until now. The awful, awful waiting.

17

Fontaine, the postman, whose route included both the Tricot and Compton houses had no intention of doing away with a piece of mail. Such a misfortune had been the fault of Jeannette, Madame Tricot's maid. That morning, November 14, he placed the letter in the inner pocket of his midnight-blue serge uniform, but later in the same day, he transferred it to a safe place beneath the hard disc lining his red-piped cap. There, his wife would not find it.

Next day, he accosted Jeannette as she brought morning bread through the Tricot gate. For a month she had refused to meet him at their old rendezvous, the slender café two blocks from the depot, but, as he expected, the idea of peeking at a letter such as he described won her.

He sat across from Jeannette by nine that evening, agreeing that the weather was too cold for wine or beer. She asked for hot chocolate, and Fontaine demanded not a cup but a pot of tea, saying to the girl that he found it an expedient way to steam open the letter. "After all," he whispered prudently, "there's no harm in having our fun with it, but tomorrow it shall be delivered. I shall fulfill my oath!"

Opposite him, Jeannette idly stabbed her pompadoured roll with one stem of her large, black-rimmed dark glasses. She watched him work cleverly with the glued lip of the envelope until it was open, unmarred. Fontaine's joy went gray as he unfolded the letter. Neither he nor Jeannette could read a word of English! Apologetic, feeling almost unmanly, he reddened and sputtered, but Jeannette's mouth, a Hollywood-styled, elliptical

"O" of congealed layers, rounded in a fantastic idea. La Tricot spoke English better than a queen and would be abjectly grateful for this particular letter.

Fontaine shook his head emphatically. Jeannette grabbed at the letter and he tried to stand up in the booth to get the sheets from her hand, but the girl purposely tipped over her chocolate cup and the liquid frosted the half-dozen written pages, with a surrealistic design.

She began to rebutton the top three buttons of her pale pink Orlon sweater over her flat chest. Then she flounced out of the curtained booth while Fontaine shook off all the liquid which would depart from the pages, then folded them in halves and put them inside the dry envelope.

At the railroad station, he paused casually to exchange a few words with Cambot, the crazy chestnut vendor—a bucktoothed dreg of humanity feared by most of Beaumonde. His grotesque and soiled black garments went with his distorted speech, but Fontaine treated him without condescension. Quick-witted, the little postman had a knack for understanding the swallowed words. He prided himself on not tossing the pauvre homme salutations or one-franc coins as a scrap of food is tossed to a mange-infested cur.

To Fontaine, Cambot was a half-blind eccentric who could afford to treat humanity with the independence of a king, for who else in all Beaumonde could repair a slate roof? It was a lost art, and no one knew what invoked a Cambot "yes" but everyone knew, if Cambot refused to come, a slate roof went on leaking.

This November night, however, Fontaine was scarcely thinking of his own solid slate roof. Heaving continuous little sighs as he stood four or five minutes with wheezing Cambot, he remarked in fashion immemorial that the weather was quite cold for November. Cambot grunted his reply and turned his back so that his urine could not splash his roasting wares. Seeing this, Fontaine quickly dropped the damp, limp envelope on the encrusted grill three or four inches above the red coals and sped away into the night.

Despite a cleft palate and worsening cataracts, Cambot had

hearing and sense of smell far more developed than average. Not only did he hear the postman's relieved whistling but also Cambot had heard the thump of something on his treasured grill. In the same instant, he smelled a brown odor—dark brown, his mind informed him, like scorching chocolate. With bare, wrinkled hands, he raked across the hot grill and plucked the first corner of the envelope he felt, slammed it steaming into his pocket and felt warmth through four layers of cloth.

18

The day before Thanksgiving, while Olande steadied the chair, Laurel hung her Degas painting in the finished third-floor bedroom.

"Madame," said the maid, "I never dreamed when I was young that I would have the fortune to work for a family which owned a Degas painting."

Laurel thought: when I was young. What was Olande now—twenty-two? twenty-three? Laurel moved to the window and stared down at moss-rimmed bricks three stories below. "My brother used to make me cry when we were children by saying I resembled that girl."

"Your brother, Madame? I didn't know—where is he now?"

A shadow veiled Laurel's eyes as she studied the painting. "In Heaven, I trust." A taut silence stretched between them. "The war, Olande." Still, she stared at the picture through the servant's audible gasp. "He was twenty-one, Olande, and people kept saying how fortunate that he left no wife, no children, no fiancé. What do people mean when they say how fortunate it is that a life has been snuffed out before it had time to complicate other lives?"

Laurel turned her back on the girl to hide her own tears. When she faced Olande, she saw the steady trickling from the brown eyes. "I did not know, Madame. Ah, excuse me!"

Laurel smiled earnestly. "Do not apologize. My grief is like that bomb scar on the back of your leg—healed, but always present."

Olande asked rather timidly then how she had guessed the scar to be from a bomb. Laurel replied with a question about the arrival of the Americans at Beaumonde in 'forty-five'. People lined the streets that day to welcome the tanks and jeeps, Olande declared. Women threw dahlias and roses, although the Americans atop the vehicles kept asking for tomatoes.

"Where were *you* that August day?" Laurel asked.

"At my parents' home, five miles from here. It is odd that you speak of it just now, Madame, for only a moment ago I was thinking of it. The cast had been off my leg for two weeks. I felt strong, but my sister was by then ill. The day of Liberation, the doctor came to see her and said she must have meat to recover. I spent the morning in the forest gathering snails and I found six dozen, Madame! Imagine! I can't eat a snail to this day— because I cleaned them all and I was standing in my mother's kitchen, thinking how quiet the country seemed and how slick snails were. Just then, I heard the first siren from Beaumonde.

"Without being told, we knew what it was. My father went at once into the cellar and brought back a bottle of Calvados buried in that floor several years. We drank toasts with the neighbors off and on all afternoon. You see, Madame, everyone had hidden a bottle toward that day—wine, cider, champagne, or something."

Olande's eyes rimmed again with tears. Her lips trembled. Laurel felt a tightness in her own throat. "Near dark," the girl went on, "after the courier had come to our village with the official news, I remember dear Papa's toast. . . ." Olande crossed herself. "To the end of all our troubles, he said, to the new France!"

The sound of the doorbell arrived with perfect timing. Olande bounded athletically down the stairs, two at a time. At the end of the first-floor hall, she paused to wipe her face with the corner of her apron, and contrary to habit, she swung open not the entire door but the hinged glass pane.

From the black-iron scrollwork barring the rectangle outside the glass pane, the dread white gauntlet shot through with its unsealed envelope.

"Mon dieu!" cried Olande.

"Don't be a fool! I won't bite!" said the uniformed policeman. Impatiently, he extended the envelope a bit further. "Mon chat! Mon chat!" he implored in his hurry to be gone.

Olande replied indignantly. "I am a married woman, Monsieur!"

The agent said, "It scarcely matters since I am busy every night for a month, but won't you please hand this to your American?"

He dropped the envelope and withdrew his arm. Olande caught the grill work in a death grip and shouted, "Monsieur! Monsieur! I tried to warn Madame not to break the Hachères' lock for they are evil people. See! See! *Are they not!*"

He was gone, without looking back. Olande closed the glass against chill. Ah, grace of God! Poor Madame! The maid bit her lip and studied the envelope, front and back, seeing it was not sealed. Extraordinary courage was required of her to withdraw the printed form. To her relief, it was not a summons into court, but merely a complaint. Certain of what she would find, she extracted the sheet and saw the name—not Madame Compton but Olande Faure Soleil. Breathless, white of face, she dropped to her knees and said two Hail Marys.

Laurel found her there with the complaint dangling in her hand. What neighbor would have reported the girl for leaving garbage containers on the street curb past nine-thirty in the morning—in violation of an obsolete Beaumonde ordinance?

Determined to settle the matter herself, Laurel said next day to Michel after Thanksgiving dinner, "I've a complaint against my maid for leaving garbage cans on the curb too late in the morning. Can you telephone whatever office issues such things and say that I understand now, and it won't happen again?"

"Certainly," he replied with alacrity, "if you'll promise not to tell her I did. I don't want her badgering me the rest of my life when you're back in America!"

Immediately, she handed him the complaint and he pocketed it, no more being said on the subject. He and Zero spoke of little that evening except a hunt the previous Monday at Noël. After they had exhausted the topic Michel announced that, because of the rich game crop this year, he had decided to hold an extra hunt for a group of Paris marksmen. He turned to Laurel. "You'll come this time because I'll be having a dinner the first night."

She asked guardedly, "There'll be other women?"

"No," he replied, "but I'd like very much to have you at the table."

She appealed to her husband, "Zero, do you think it's imperative? I'm terribly out of place in that kind of crowd."

Zero thought about it a minute before saying, "I think she's right, Mike. Let's save her for the real McCoy!"

A few days later Michel arrived at 14 rue Père Marquette and announced, "Laurel, I simply can't do it."

"Can't do what?"

"Order food, dicker with caterers, referee servant quarrels in the kitchen, keep conversation balanced at the table, and serve coffee after dinner. I don't even know when to gesture the diners away from the table at the proper moment—the way you or my mother does."

"You need a wife," she said dully.

"You proved that to me once before."

She gave him a withering glance. "Michel. . . ."

"No, let me speak!" he interrupted. "You can see very well I need you to act as hostess."

"Michel, your mother could get away for three or four days at a time." Laurel's eyes narrowed. "I'll bet you didn't even ask her to come!"

"Why, of course not! You don't suppose I want an old lady at my parties? Laurel, you've got to do it!"

She was on the verge of saying yes when, in her mind's eye, she envisioned Guy's face at the table—Guy relegated to some minor position while she sat trapped in hostess position across from gloating, self-absorbed Michel.

She raised her lashes and regarded him. He broke into an amused grin and said, as if he had read her mind, "Guy turned down the first hunt on some thin excuse. So I didn't give him a chance on this one."

She picked up a cigarette and lighted it slowly in pretense of inward calm. "Why on earth should Guy's presence or absence affect my answer? You know perfectly well, Michel, that I'll be obliged to do what you say so you won't bother engaging Zero's influence to get your way."

He had, he now declared, another favor to ask. Several wives had unexpectedly decided to accompany their husbands, which left him short of adequate sleeping space since he had refurnished so few of Noël's bedrooms. "Laurel, what I'm trying to say is this, can you lend me two bedrooms?"

In a joking way, she replied, "You don't propose that we bring two rooms of furniture to Noël?"

"Why not? You moved it across an ocean! Zero's got enough rank to ask for a truck and a couple of men to bring two beds and chests.

"No," said stunned Laurel.

"Then I'll rent a French truck!"

He eyed her a second or two before he left the salon and walked to the foot of the stairs to yell for Zero.

It would be simpler, Zero announced, in fact it would be a privilege to host Michel's overflow here at the Beaumonde house. Laurel sought frantically to get his eye and signal error, but he was intent on Michel. "After all, Mike, it should give a sensational touch to your party. You'll have those Paris Galahads falling over themselves to get to spend the night at Laurel's."

Under visible strain, she nodded her good nights and left the room, but she was the essence of composure a few evenings later when Michel's chosen pair arrived—Count de Méttinger and a Berteaux Baron named Maximilian, one of Michel's younger cousins.

Their sojourn at 14 rue Père Marquette went off very well. However, less than an hour had passed since de Méttinger and Max Berteaux were on their way back to Paris the morning after the hunt, when Michel reached Laurel on the telephone.

Through some mysterious confusion, he claimed, six of his guests understood the houseparty included a fourth evening. "I'm stuck, Laurel! Stuck! The gardener's wife can arrange a cold lunch, but what can I do for dinner? I've no cook, no waiters. It's too late anyway to place an order with a caterer. . . ."

Bluntly, she mentioned the restaurant on Redan's square, and the Écu in Beaumonde, but Michel lost patience. "None of them has ever seen inside an American house. These are Parisians, Laurel! Think how well you could represent your country! They'd remember one night at your table far longer and more happily than a dozen speeches! Now, don't be rushed into saying yes. Think about it, and call me back."

"Why think about it?" she said icily. "You've made the legitimate appeal. But dammit, don't come before eight o'clock!"

"What do you *mean*—no cocktails?"

"That's right! Not when *I'm* doing the cooking. And *goodbye!*"

Laurel had conceived a solution to this new impasse—at least, to forestalling its recurrence. It was not gracious or easy, because she had liked instinctively the three women now remaining at Noël, especially Geneviève Vernes who was near her own age, who dressed with elegant restraint, and who spoke impeccable English. She reminded Laurel, in fact, of someone she had known at some time or other, but could not recall in the rush surrounding the formal breakfasts, high teas, and banquetlike dinners at which the few women were stretched too far apart at the table to converse with each other.

Nevertheless, Michel's audacity had to be reined. There were dozens of ways to disconcert a French person at an American table. Fried chicken to be held in the fingers at buffet. A champagne cooler filled with crushed ice, carbonated drinks and canned beer—all dripping and difficult to maneuver while standing up with a plate of food and a knife and fork. For dessert? Not pie. They could call it a tart. Why not a caramel apple—a red apple, sticky and mounted on a little pole? And all buffet style, because no French person was accustomed to any item of food larger than a canapé unless he was seated!

Michel however set a triumphant example of everything from

how to grip fried chicken properly to the easy custom of sitting on the floor with his plate at the accommodative height of the large coffee table. He led his compatriots into a gay, expectant curiosity toward every novelty of the evening, assembling the three women about himself in the kitchen after dinner where he copied for them recipes from Laurel's treasured metal box of family cookery secrets.

As for the men, they were clustered in an elliptical circle about Zero's gun collection, which was laid out amid the library floor—and one exhibit soon followed another. Gun trophies. Scrapbooks. Medals. More drinks. And finally—Laurel could tell a room away—the unboundaried world of dirty jokes.

Exhibition was the word which came to her mind. These Parisians were seeing America through a new peephole. And nobody stayed until three A.M. anywhere unless the view was agreeable.

19

Through the night, Guy mumbled periodically in Italian or Spanish or French, sometimes rolling his head from side to side among the pillows of the baldaquin bed. In the brocade chaise brought bedside at the start of her vigil, Laurel straightened and stretched, her face nearly as pale as Guy's above the black of her long-sleeved sweater and velveteen slacks.

Wordlessly, she prayed that when Guy awoke, he would be lucid. She arose and walked to the window, opened it, folded the iron shutters into daytime position, and peered into the opaque fog now tinged with blue promise of dawn. The wet chill was piercing.

"How did I come here?"

She clasped the window quickly and darted to his side, recoiled into the chaise longue and swung her feet beneath her body while she lighted a cigarette. "Your car is parked in front, but the windshield seems a bit the worse for wear." Nonchalant. Sophisticated insanity. As if it had happened a dozen times.

Guy's eyes took in the displacement of the chaise, her costume, and the color of morning framed in the fogged glass. "The fog. A fellow in a small truck backed out in front of me. I don't remember after that—but, Laurel! The trouble I've caused you."

"If we're going to spend the day in regret, let's start with the bump we found on your head."

Guy frowned tiredly. "We?"

"The maid's husband, Francis. I was going to call Abach but Francis felt your pulse, examined your breath, shined a flashlight in your eyes, poured a glass of brandy down your gullet, and assured me with utter male superiority that you would live—if I got out of the room and let him dress you in pajamas."

Laurel tossed the burnt match across the room and watched it sail into the fire on the hearth. "In fact, he did a nervous little dance every time I got up again to call the doctor." She made a bland face to mimic the laborer's innocent glare and copied his accent: "Monsieur le Comte will be humiliated to have a strange physician—French or American—in someone else's house. Too much of a drama, Madame!"

Guy's smile was weak but convincing. "I must thank that fellow." He glanced down at the robe he now wore in bed.

"It's Zero's. You felt so cold I thought you were dying of the bed's temperature." In renewed alarm, she exclaimed, "Let me call Abach. He wouldn't tell. He. . . ."

"No, Laurel," he replied with authority. "It isn't the bump. I have a damnable head plate, a war souvenir. And I must have scored a bull's eye last night." His fingers traveled along the edge of his hair. "Laurel," he said in a different tone, "what time do you Americans get up in the morning?" She eyed him solemnly. "The way you were waiting when I woke up, I had the impression you'd been here all night."

Teeth hard against her lower lip, Laurel arose and crossed to the fireplace. Wearily, she clutched the cold mantel ledge with both hands and sagged until her forehead rested on her hands. Unseeing, she stared at the friendly fire. She bent then to lift two remaining sticks of firewood to the dying flames. A slim toe hidden in brilliant green suède kicked the fresh log so violently that coals showered upward.

"Laurel, come here!"

She flung her unbound hair between her shoulders and went obediently. Determined to avoid his eyes, she regarded the crocheted lace of an ivory linen sheet. Guy said softly, "You've paid an awful return for one cup of tea!" He reached out and took one hand. "And sassafras tea, at that!"

Laurel withdrew her hand, feeling very much an adolescent. "A friend in need—I mean, greater love hath no man." She laughed ineffectually. "Et cetera!"

"Look at me, Laurel!" Helplessly, she lifted her face and found his caressing eyes, his loving smile. "Love suffereth long, and hath great circles under its green eyes. Laurel! My tired Christmas-eyed angel!"

She took two steps back, her gaze on him laden now with something like fear. "Let me call Abach, Guy! You're not yourself!"

"Then who am I?"

Tension linked them an instant in silence. Guy turned away from her pleading gaze and wiped irritably at his right temple. "Laurel, I must rid myself of some vision I suffered last night. I have not seen a desert in my life, yet I was completely lost in one, sun burning my skin, sand blowing and blinding me. I walked an interminable distance. Sand. Heat. Thirst. A very dry Hell. But in the distance, I saw a bright haze.

"When I came near, the haze had a face and long hair. A woman with hair like yours, twining over her shoulders the way yours is now. I implored her to give me a glass of water, and I called her Venus because the pink aura reminded me of a Botticelli painting. . . ."

"I know the painting. In school, we called it Venus on the half-shell. Guy, what did Venus say?"

He regarded her thoughtfully. "My head claims that she screamed, but my heart pretends she wept. Laurel, I cannot remember."

Just then, Olande burst through the door without knocking, carrying a tray with coffee. She waited beside her mistress with an unnoticed cup. Guy told the maid to set the cup on the table, and then, having accepted his own, he nodded and somehow inflected his Merci! with such finality that the reluctant girl was obliged to exit without even glancing back.

Laurel crossed the room, roaming irritably from window to hearth and blowing smoke, through which her head moved before the cloud could dissipate. Guy said guardedly, "Zero is not in this house?"

Her voice seemed on the edge of tears: "No! He's in Germany." She took up the cup of coffee and swigged half of it, scalding as it was. The cup jangled against the saucer as she set it on the Limoges table and stared at him. He had fallen back against the pillows, apparently lost in concentration as his fingertips glided from forehead to chin, measuring his morning beard.

Brick burst in suddenly, delighted to find his friend. He gazed quizzically from Guy to Laurel and asked matter-of-factly: "Laurel, why is Uncle Guy in your new bed? Has he got tonsillitis?"

"Brick, go tell Olande to give you a cup and I'll make your mother give you some coffee!"

The boy was already at the door when Laurel called out, "Bring two cups and help Chris up the stairs when you return. Don't let him fall!"

Later she lay curled in the chaise now returned to the windowside. Guy, still propped in the bed, asked quietly: "Laurel, what are you thinking?"

Her gaze darted to the mantel's motto—We have all been mad once. She heard his laugh flicker like a shrug. Stifling a yawn, she eased her neck and head more comfortably into the tufted softness of the sofa.

When she awoke, the Cloidon clock on the mantel said two-thirty. The color of the window said afternoon. The bed was made. Coffee cups had vanished. A magenta-satin down comfort half covered her.

Guy was gone.

20

Twenty people mingled about Noël's fireplace well after dinner. Coffee and brandy finished, they began to cluster in twos and threes in the reception hall until the hum of separate conversations were like tuning sections of a symphony orchestra.

Laurel listened. Dulled with daytime sleep, she remained with her back to the room, half-hidden in one of the deep fireplace armchairs. Guy dropped into the opposite chair, but they said nothing until the last bystander moved out of hearing range.

"Are you well?"

"I am tired," he answered, "and the headache is not quite gone, but it will be all right by tomorrow. Laurel, I feel sad when I think of the trouble I have caused you. Especially since Zero was away."

Michel's brother Philippe sauntered over to engage them in light conversation. The moment he walked away, Guy resumed, "What did Zero say?"

"He said the weather was so vile that he was on instruments every mile of the return flight. He said that I had not slept until five o'clock in the afternoon since our honeymoon. Then he said, 'Get up! We're due at Michel's in half an hour'."

"You did not tell him. . . ."

"No. What did Michel say?"

"I told no one. Certainly not Michel."

"But the car—the broken glass?"

"I spent the afternoon at the garage. The windshield is new and Michel apparently presumes I arrived in the area this afternoon." He laughed without humor. "I'm scarcely noted for preoccupation with the calendar, Laurel, or for punctuality."

"Rebellion against regimented authority," said Laurel idly, not thinking as she spun her empty cognac glass twice around in both palms. "Well, we both seem extremely clever—with no reason at all. It isn't as if Olande and her husband and my children weren't under the same roof. . . ."

"Laurel, why did you stay with me all night?"

"What do you expect me to answer?" she cried out.

"The others will hear you!"

"Well, let them!" she blurted in a more muffled tone. "How would you like to sit beside a bed all night counting heartbeats and bargaining with the Almighty against the mayhem you possibly are committing by accepting a peasant's advice on the discretionary protocol of French nobility?"

Persevering in his relaxed pose against the leather chair, Guy sighed, "I had hoped the reason was somewhat different."

"Stop it!"

"No, Laurel. I will finish. I am not sorry I stumbled out of the fog to your house, but I will not come again, not even to Noël— if that is what you wish. I would die to preserve your happiness, or to save you from misery. You know that, but I am no school boy. Laurel, don't banish me unless you mean it!"

He was leaning forward now, whispering in urgent softness. Her teeth pressed her lower lip so hard she admitted a faint taste of blood. Then, as if he had been catapulted from outer space, Michel popped up over the back of her chair, leering at Guy, "What's the matter? A lovers' quarrel?"

Guy grinned with a force that made Laurel wince, but Michel leaned further over her and flipped the cigarette from her right hand. Then he lifted her fingers to his lips, his eyes continually on Guy and mocking as he planted a row of precise kisses from her wrist along her forearm.

"Look at him, Laurel!" he said. "Isn't he long-suffering behind that cinema smile? And you know, inside he burns hotter than the molten glass at St Gobain!" Laurel tugged to free her arm but he held on, "Don't expect too much of him. His goddess is honor. The Victorians knew nothing of transmutation."

Rage, fright, and humiliation surged through Laurel, as she continued her attempts to free herself. Guy quietly cleared his throat. Laurel watched his glance swing above her head as Zero shouted affectionately, clapping Michel across his bent shoulders, "Hey, Berteaux! Unhand my femme!"

21

Fog descended so heavily by Thursday morning that the day's shooting had to be canceled. Philippe came to call on Laurel. She was genuinely fond of him, but her effort to listen above her personal turmoil was increased by his repeated praises of the wartime escapades of his brother.

Laurel paid polite heed, nodding or dissenting in the required places and remarking abstractly that the scenes described by Philippe tied in with various tales Michel had told in the past, although there was a great contrast in Michel's offhand account and Philippe's tendency to pedestal his brother's heroic achievements.

By the tea hour, she could bear no more. In the gentlest of voices, she asked Philippe why he had spoken continually of Michel.

"Laurel," he smiled in mixed shyness and relief. "May I be completely honest?" She nodded quickly. "My mother has given me a quest I find difficult to fulfill. She asked me to learn of you whether there is some eligible, refined American girl. . . ." He paused, reddening. ". . . you see, there are many changes in him since you and your husband befriended him. I do not need to recount those obvious and physical. But there are changes you may not be aware of including regular and dutiful visits to

L'Alouette. Now, how shall I tell you? My mother has no hope that there is already some girl, but she cherishes an air castle of a hope that you may find one for him because she worries already that when you and Zero return to America, Michel will fall back into his old ways. Laurel, what else can I say?"

"It is quite enough," she replied. "Tell Véronique I agree entirely with her, that I am flattered, but that Michel expects to discover his own wife entirely on his own. I think no one must interfere." Laurel paused a moment. "It is my own opinion that marriage to an American would be a catastrophe for a man of Michel's will."

They regarded each other in grave candor. Sympathy undercut wisdom as Laurel leaned toward him and said, "If I tell you a secret, will you promise not to tell anyone, not even Véronique?" His eyes assented solemnly. "Michel confided to me a while back that he is going to look for a wife."

She could not miss the speed and depth with which Philippe blushed. His hands rubbed each other consolingly, and he stammered as he spoke, "He has—has—has cost you a great deal." One hand pounded—a fist in a palm. He glanced full into her eyes with great meaning. "It is a generous, kind thing you have done for him. God knows he doesn't deserve it."

She was on her feet, pacing like a snared young tiger. Then she paused before him and said without guile, "Philippe, does it show?"

He caught her hands and held them firmly while he planted a soothing kiss on her cheek. "No, dear heart! But I know my brother. No victory is real with him until it is exposed."

"To the world, I suppose," murmured Laurel.

"Don't be childish! He's a bit too French to account names, dates, and places to any human being, but Guy and I had seen what was coming for a time. In all our lives, no woman had inspired Michel to such venomous outpourings. You represented total challenge to him, Laurel. Ask Guy to explain it to you sometime. He understands Michel much better than the rest of us, and he is able to express himself in all situations."

Laurel withdrew her hands from his grip and sat down to light a cigarette. Curiously relieved, she found courage to ask the question in her mind. "But you and Guy both understood how nearly I've hated him?"

Philippe seated himself on the couch and began to pick at the cuticles of his nails. "Yes. But you see, Laurel, Guy said to me four or five years ago that the right woman would break Michel's self-contempt someday and recently he confided to me that Michel had met the right woman."

Unexpectedly, she broke into brief tears. Philippe sat quite still until her composure was restored, and then he said, "Laurel, I did not mean to make you sad."

"You don't understand how it feels to be a pawn in a foreign chess game. With people you love predicting. . . ."

"Laurel," he interrupted, "you surely understand that I regard your sacrifice as poetic. And Guy's as—as. . . ."

"Guy!" she shrieked. "What did he sacrifice? Oh, Philippe, you're a fool! A blind, romantic fool!"

"Free opinion is man's birthright," he said in hushed restraint, "but, Laurel, Guy sacrificed more to stand by and know what would happen. Laurel, don't you understand? You are the only woman he's ever loved."

She sat upright, hands gripping the delicate arms of the Louis XIV chair. "Philippe—I . . . you must. . . ." Her words trailed off at the creak of the front door. Zero's voice blended with Guy's in healthy laughter. Then Laurel heard a third voice. She straightened in the chair, leaned back in pretended poise, and let her hands fall on each other.

Zero opened the salon door and held the knob while Guy and Abach bartered briefly for one to enter ahead of the other. Guy came first, walking directly to Laurel and lifting her hand for a greeting kiss. Abach turned toward Philippe, who stood up, weighing the stranger. Laurel said, "Abach, this is Michel's brother, Philippe—Count Philippe de Berteaux. This is Dr. Samuel Abach, Philippe—a friend from Louisiana."

They shook hands and Philippe sat back down. Guy's feet and legs were very much in the corner of Laurel's vision because he stood but a few feet from her chair, leaning against the mantel. Abach dropped into the Gainsborough chair across from Laurel. When she finally met his eyes, he gave her a searching look before he glanced up at Guy. "I meant to tell you at lunch, Guy, your color's a great deal better than it was last fall."

A wild gush of resentment broke inside Laurel. Zero and Guy. Now, Guy and Abach. Who am I? The imbecile stranger?

Guy wafted to the piano and sat down while Laurel concentrated on maintaining mannequin composure. "Zero," she said rapidly, "I'll go and have Olande make some more tea. All three of you must be frozen!"

"Tea!" he exploded. "Christ, we may be frozen but we're still red-blooded. Tell Olande to bring in some—no, not whiskey. This calls for a celebration. Let's break out a bottle of Chimmery— some rose champagne, eh, Guy?"

Guy smiled above his playing and nodded without a word. Laurel arose, meeting Abach's amused eyes. "What's the nature of the celebration?" he asked whimsically.

"Why, it's obvious," she said with only the faintest tinge of acid. "In all these years, I'm finally about to get yours and Zero's feet under the same dinner table—and don't say you can't stay!"

"Can't stay?" echoed Zero. "Parker said at lunch Abach's been working twelve hours a day since he got here and he's not to set foot on Beaumonde Air Base before Sunday night!"

Abach's smile was inscrutable. "What *is* today?"

"Thursday," said Laurel.

Zero dropped down on the piano bench beside Guy, and Laurel heard him say, "As I was explaining, if they made an air-to-ground attack, we figure the maximum time to move west of the Rhine is no more than. . . ."

Laurel sailed from the salon and marched to the kitchen, staring on her arrival there at the simple face of her servant so long that the girl was disconcerted. "Madame, what is it?" inquired the questioning voice.

"In a word? Olande, it's envy."

Laurel had never felt so continually superfluous as she did by the end of a lengthy dinner that Thursday night, until Zero and Philippe decided to settle a minor argument about telescopic sighting—in the library. Then the salon seemed suddenly more soothing, as she glanced from Abach to Guy, who sat on opposite ends of the coral sofa.

"You've known each other a very, very long time," said Guy, as if to himself.

"Twenty-eight years, more or less," supplied Abach. "I remember the first day I—well, not the first day I saw Laurel, but the first day I remember with her, we buried a robin, caught three brim, and set a tool shack on fire trying to fry the fish in a Teaberry coffee can, and I decided she was as much fun as a boy."

Her eyes sparkled deliciously. "But then he declared war on me, conscripting all the colored waifs on both plantations, and I rode into battle with a sugar sack flying on a broken cane pole, hollering I was Joan of Lorraine. . . ."

"And I told you your horse was too black."

"And, Abach, do you remember Peter deciding he wasn't on my side because that put him in command of a woman and then he showed both of us, when all the little black devils followed him to the swamp because he could play a French harp."

The sound of Guy's laughter jerked both Abach and Laurel back to the present. Abach said to him: "It seems a helluva short distance between play war and the real thing when a person looks back."

The two men were still talking about the war when Zero and Philippe returned.

22

Laurel glanced at her watch: three-fifteen. She parked the long station wagon beside an elegant black Citroën before the moss-roofed stone building. Beaumonde's police station. And she thought with tense irritation: What a thing to be doing on December twenty-third!

Getting out of the car, she noticed wisps of fog coming from the lips of the two men who sat in the adjacent car. The driver wore an ordinary Belgian greatcoat of olive drab felt and a brown béret, and the other was hatless, but his natural cashmere topcoat was a mark of luxury seldom observed in the northern area.

Laurel slammed her car door and, to avoid slipping on the filthy gutter ice, took a broad step to the cobblestoned walk, so worn as to appear hand-polished, like the freshly shined brass handle in the rotting oak door.

As she reached for the door handle, Assistant Chief of Police Lefèvre exclaimed behind the wheel of the official Citroën, "Look! An American woman!"

His superior, Charles Saint-Agneau, jerked his head around on his stub of neck, in time to glimpse the shape of round hips defined through her belted trench coat. "Probably she brings Christmas razor blades and chewing gum for prisoners. Americans develop enlarged hearts at Christmastime."

Lefèvre shrugged negatively and reset his béret. "She carries no basket."

Agneau duplicated the shrug. "Perhaps she comes to renew her identity card." Inside his overcoat and jacket, he found a cigarette. Lefèvre flinched as the Chief scraped a wooden match across the gleaming dashboard, but Agneau did not notice. He inhaled so rapidly that his cigarette soon glowed red half an inch. Then he dropped the match to the floor and tamped the flame.

Lefèvre opened the door on his side. "Sir, forgive me! But should we not go in and post these holiday shifts?"

The two spanned the cobblestone walk in three steps. They went through the decaying door, Saint-Agneau proceeding directly up a flight of steps so worn that each retained an oval lake of the afternoon's second mopping water. At the turn in the walled landing, he shot one brief glance down at Laurel Compton's neat back and sped on.

Lefèvre did not go upstairs but turned right and passed inside a swinging gate. He walked behind the desk sergeant and looked over his shoulder at the creased, unfolded paper. Then he peered through the bronze bars of the sergeant's window.

He glanced back at the official paper, noting now with alert interest that it was a subpoena. He read her name, and the name of her husband; then, Lefèvre's eyes narrowed on the printed form. He realized what was missing. There was no stamped serial number in the blank provided for that purpose. Something was amiss! A bad joke? or a crooked trick?

"I'll take care of the lady. It's time to telephone the health nurse and find out if she'll be making her rounds the usual time tomorrow and Christmas Day." Lefèvre flung his head back, eyes on the red-headed woman, and said to the sergeant, "Since it's almost Christmas, you can go use my office to make the call."

He glanced down studiously at the paper, and when the heavy footsteps had departed behind him, he asked Laurel Compton, "Where do you believe this came from?"

Laurel liked his freckles, his effort to maintain severity, and his strawberry-colored hair. Forgetting her dilemma for a moment, she sparkled, "I'd like to believe it didn't come from here, but I don't believe in the Père Noël. I haven't for several years."

Watching her mouth intently, Lefèvre nearly smiled. "Have you a neighbor with whom there's trouble?"

She shrugged thoughtfully. "The old woman on my right won't say good morning, not even in answer to my older son. But, then . . ." She shrugged again in unconscious propriety to the subject. ". . . in France, an American learns. . . ."

"Yes," he said curtly.

Encouraged by the grip with which he held the paper, Laurel burst forth in narrative—unplanned, involuntarily gestured. Three times in the first half of December, the police came to 14 rue Père Marquette with anonymous complaints. The first and third concerned the maid's husband, but the second was unjust—Olande's violation of an obsolete regulation.

She did not say to the plain-clothes man that the Marquis de Berteaux had patched up one complaint or that Francis' offense both times consisted of making too much noise starting his motorcycle at five-thirty in the morning.

Laurel simply moved on to the real mystery, her receipt three days earlier of this subpoena which claimed she must appear in January court to pay eight-thousand-francs rental tax on 14 rue Père Marquette, plus a fine of some thirty-six thousand, the penalty for being late about sixty days. In present exchange, about three hundred forty dollars!

"What I don't understand, Monsieur, is this line typed across the bottom, 'Prior settlement is the privilege of defendant.' If I am a defendant, what precisely is the charge? When I use the pronoun 'I,' naturally, I speak for both myself and my husband."

Lefèvre regarded her narrowly. "What does your husband say to this paper?"

"I am deeply embarrassed," admitted Laurel, "to admit he knows nothing of it."

"Why did you not tell him?" asked Lefèvre, as if such a question was in line with official perusal.

"Because he is at the moment in a position—an assignment incompatible with anger, Monsieur. Or perhaps because I love France. And he does not. Not always."

Discouraged now, she braced her gloved hands on the counter before the grilled window and inhaled a sigh. "Why then did you come here?" demanded Lefèvre.

"Because a British friend of mine swore on the Union Jack that Directeur Saint-Agneau is allergic to bribery. Am I permitted to see him? Is he here?"

Lefèvre folded the paper and dropped his hands. "By appointment. Perhaps a week. But if you will wait, perhaps I can help you."

There was no chair, no table, no bench—only a brightly gleaming bronze cuspidor—on the nonpreferred side of the partition in the police lobby. Hence, Laurel stood while Lefèvre sped back through the swinging gate, past her, and up the stairs with preoccupation that allowed him to splash without noticing through the placid stair pools.

In the Chief's third-floor suite, terse sentences passed between the two men before Agneau went to his desk and buzzed the downstairs desk. He wanted the dossier on 14 rue Père Marquette brought at once.

Laurel heard this, and watched the desk sergeant disappear up the stairs with a brown folder. He reappeared in about five minutes, empty-handed, and she saw him leave the building, gallop in a straight line to the Bureau of Tax across the Square. Soon he was back, red-faced, not willing to glance in her direction. The sergeant flipped a switch on his intercom box and said, "Sir, the tax clerk refuses to surrender the dossier on 14 rue Père Marquette without your written request. Regulation."

Receiving this news, Saint-Agneau himself picked up a telephone from his desk and called the property-file section across the street in the Bureau of Tax, and soon, he was in conversation with the Directeur. At this level, it took no trouble at all to determine that no rental tax statement could possibly have been issued on the house in question since the present tenant had lived there less than half of the required year.

Saint-Agneau thanked him, hung up, and turned to Lefèvre. "Three minor complaints in a matter of weeks," declared the Chief pensively, "and one fine paid. And now this forgery." He walked to his desk and sat down with the brown folder from his section's files. Slowly, he turned through the few papers. Then he slammed the folder shut. "The Comptons, one or the other, or both, have enemies."

"Sir, I took the liberty of inquiring a moment ago . . ." Lefèvre hesitated with a sheepish grin. ". . . whether there was a difficult neighbor."

Agneau's glance shot to him with alert hope and as quickly hope died. "Ah!" he sighed, "no neighbor would dare to instigate a false subpoena. Besides, Hachère, Risseau, Martin, Tricot—all the influential pretenders live on *top* of this aching hill." He sat a moment, pursing his lips in silence. Then he said to Lefèvre, "What did she say?"

"Something about an old woman on the right who wouldn't say Bonjour."

"On the right," mused Agneau. "That would be—number sixteen. Lefèvre, get on the intercom and have the sergeant look up the master ledger for the name of the complainants while I telephone the Tax Directeur and find out who owns 16 rue Père Marquette. . . ."

Already, Agneau had the telephone in hand as Lefèvre lunged to the speaker box fronting his desk, and soon the two policemen confronted each other with new certainty. The complaints had been signed by one person, the elderly housewife who tenanted the adjacent dwelling, but what made the farce more entrancing, 16 rue Père Marquette was the rental property of Madame Tricot.

Saint-Agneau sat quietly for a long moment, pondering the puzzle. When Lefèvre could abide the suspense no longer, he spoke almost timidly, "But, Sir! How would a respectable lawyer such as Risseau or Martin dare enter collusion in any form?"

"Have you no imagination, Lefèvre? This was probably the result of some fourth bottle—a party plan to nettle the Americans. Risseau nor Hachère nor Martin—none of them would dare take a second step in such a ruse."

"But if Madame Compton or her husband had gone to Martin and simply paid?" asked Lefèvre.

"Why, he'd have taken the money and felt no fever of conscience whatever. They'd have spent it to celebrate success of their coup! Lefèvre, can't you get it in your head that a bow from the waist and a charge account at a tailor's don't turn a man into a gentleman?"

"But, Sir! What's our next step?"

"To give the American woman comfort without intelligence."

"Sir, you can't afford to offend Madame Tricot in our position. I mean—that is—Monsieur Tricot exerts a very strong in. . . ."

"Lefèvre, he exerts influence in every direction except his own house. Of all these people, he alone is a gentleman, but that does not provide him much knowledge of what goes on with that wife of his. You know the saying," Agneau smiled broadly, "there is no wind in the eye of the storm. Lefèvre, I'm going to tear that subpoena in half. I want you to take the half with Martin's own stamp on it and mail it in an official envelope—mail it at the post office where none of the men here will have a chance to see it."

"To whom, Sir?"

"To Madame Tricot."

"And the other half?"

"You will give it to the Compton woman before she leaves here."

Vigorously, Agneau picked up the printed form and ripped it in half. Then, he opened his middle drawer and selected a rubber stamp. Across the back of the paper, he stamped INVALID. Then he took a pen and scrawled hurriedly beneath INVALID two words: Joyeux Noël!

He pushed the two halves of the subpoena forward on his desk toward Lefèvre. Agneau, without a word, then took a bottle of Calvados from the bottom drawer of his desk and swigged three quick gulps before handing it to dumbfounded Lefèvre. The latter constrained thirst to an equal number of gulps and handed the brown bottle back.

"Do not speak my name to Madame Comptom, but say quite clearly that you advise her to retain this torn paper."

Lefèvre's face softened in a pink glow. "Sir, why don't you take it down to her yourself? She is very beautiful. Very radiant. Very raffinée. . . ."

Saint-Agneau replied, "It is a pitiful thing to watch a bachelor at Christmastime, Lefèvre."

In mid-December, a military ship departed the Port of New York with a secret cargo, which was unloaded at Bremerhaven on December 22, swiftly convoyed by truck to Beaumonde Air Base, where volunteer airmen made packages of the surplus foodstuffs—dried milk, beans, sugar, flour, cheese, and canned meat.

An airman in fatigue clothing appeared at Laurel's door and said that Colonel Compton awaited her in P-14, the huge new concrete warehouse on The Base, and that she must come immediately.

"But it's such a silly thing to fall in a classified category," she said to Zero, when he explained that the fifteen hundred sacks of food were destined for the needy. Zero replied that the Communists would have seized the matter for propaganda, purporting the food too old to be consumed by Americans, or that the Yanks were again buying the French.

Other wives of officers, those who lived in outlying villages, arrived at the warehouse and were handed lists of recipients. By the lists, it was apparent that the task would require of them not much more than half a day if the trucks were loaded on time, for while Ruth MacDonald's list included thirty-two names, the average for the smaller villes was no more than a dozen.

The first delay came from Laurel, to whom Zero had handed Christmas greeting stickers the women were to paste on the filled sacks spread in neat rows over the warehouse floor. Laurel called Ruth MacDonald aside to have her read the message—twice: "We who have much wish to share our abundance at Christmas and the New Year with you who are unfortunate." This was what it said in French!

Ruth said instantly, "We *must* explain to Zero. Laurel, my God!"

"There's no use explaining to him. He'd say there isn't time. But you go to Nouilly. Take two or three gals with you and tell them to scour Nouilly and the next two villages, and to use Regina Edney's name everywhere they go. Damn her for going off to England! She'd swim back if she knew about this."

Fortunately, Zero was too involved in truck routing and asides to Parker to have learned of the crisis in seals. By nine-thirty, the Washington stickers were ashes in the furnace and the neatly affixed French "papillons" stated in familiar symbols a message the lowliest educated French person could absorb.

Zero saw too late: "Christ-a-mighty, Laurel! How they gonna know it's from Americans?"

She took his elbow and gently turned him away so that the group of women would not hear and laugh at him. "Zero, suppose you'd been in need of food for a week or a month or a decade and a blue truck with a G.I. driver stopped in front of your house. . . ."

"OK. OK. OK. I get the message!" he said hurriedly.

One by one the blue trucks departed, either carrying an American wife beside the driver, or being led by one in her own car. Standing on the loading dock of the big warehouse with the chill fog swirling down her collar, Laurel realized she was the only woman left. "But, Zero, we still have four trucks?"

"Sure, we got three hundred and twenty sacks for Beaumonde alone. That's your and my baby!"

Parker climbed into the station wagon with both Comptons, handing Laurel a multi-paged Beaumonde list which civilian Duprée had compiled under classified status—God knew exactly how. God and Duprée, said Parker.

As the convoy rolled slowly toward Beaumonde, a jeep followed them. Laurel said, "Who's in the jeep? The French address-finders?"

"No," snorted Parker affectionately. "That's the photographer and his assistant."

Still unbelieving that some French aid was not awaiting them to find the addresses, Laurel said, "Zero, it would take us and four American truck drivers ten days to find all these places."

"Aw, Laurel! You're too modest! You know Beaumonde like the back of your hand."

"Zero, listen to me! Regina says some of the poorest people in Beaumonde live in those caves on top of the cliff—the dirt caves you can't see because of the city dump. They're on the opposite side of the hill from us."

"Everybody knows Regina Edney is a congenital liar."

"Zero!"

"Well, it's the God's truth."

Her lip tightened. "It's Christmas Eve. I don't mind helping but I want to be with my children, and besides, I promised Olande from noon off. Zero. . . ."

But the convoy was in the fringe of the lower city. After a half-dozen stops and inquiries, they pulled close together before an unnumbered hovel in one of the worst of the tenement sections. Laurel explained to the trembling old woman the mission, the gift. Tears streamed down the gnarled, unwashed face. Laurel stepped back. The photographer moved up and asked her to tell the woman to please stand still. He turned to Parker and informed him where to stand, how to place a hand forward on the sack. He yelled to his assistant, "Get a load of those tears! This might make *Stars and Stripes!*"

Laurel sped away, trying to dismiss what she felt. She got back into her car as the sixth flashbulb went off toward Parker's posterity. When Zero climbed in beside her, she made no preliminary approach. In fact, the moment solution occurred to her, she demanded that they go to the French police because nobody else had as complete knowledge of Beaumonde addresses.

"Atta girl," praised Parker exuberantly, "but first, you'll let me off. I've managed so far to avoid meeting that Chief Saint Agnes or whatever his name is—since I've cut out this crap of issuing honorary passes to the Base. Wait a minute, Zero! I'll get out and have the photographer take me back to the Base in his jeep. That way, I won't slow you down."

He leaned across Laurel to shake Zero's hand and to wish him a Merry Christmas. Then he kissed Laurel on her cheek.

As she got out in front of the police station, Zero yelled after her to hurry, because the four big trucks practically covered the town square. Again and again, she gave her explanation inside the police station, being handed to a somewhat higher level each round until at last she stood face to face with a small, bullet-headed Frenchman in his third-floor office.

"I cannot have understood!" he exploded after her tale.

"Yes," smiled Laurel, "there are four trucks below, and three hundred and twenty sacks."

She heard the door open behind her and saw Agneau's surprise; there had been no knock. "What does he say?" demanded Zero. She whirled to discover his Colonel-Compton scowl, and quickly turned back to the Chief of Police.

"May I present my husband?" The Frenchman got his hand out first and the two surveyed each other for a moment. Then Agneau went behind his desk and sat down. Laurel caught the rebuff—she was standing—and her heart sank. Damn Zero and his gruffness when decorum was the yeast in French dough!

"Laurel, tell the bastard to say something one way or the other. Push him to the point! Tell him we got three hundred sacks down there waiting and four truck drivers who have a lot better way they could be spending Christmas Eve!"

Saint-Agneau got up from his desk and walked to the window. Staring down at the street, the trucks, he said without glancing at either Compton, "Ah, Madame! Why did you not come to us a week ago with this list? We could have synchronized the routes into a pattern." He faced Laurel now, as if her husband had departed. "Why have you waited until Christmas Eve when I have scarcely half my force on duty?"

"Sir, it was a secret."

"A secret!" he shrilled, his face livid. "It is our business to guard secrets!" She knew now, knew beyond a doubt, that Saint-Agneau did not care to hide his disinclination toward Zero, that he did not approve of his bursting in, and that his ear was not deaf to English. Oh, my God! "It is too bad," sighed Agneau, in a new tone, "for it is a wonderful thing you have proposed to do."

Her heart dived. There was no mistaking his resignation. She pulled her coat together and took a deep breath. "Perhaps I was wrong to have come, Monsieur, but I was sure that if it were at all possible, you were the one to help us."

"Help you?" he exclaimed, his hands taking flight. "Of course, we will help you! That is not the question." He flipped the switch on his intercom and demanded at the top of his voice, "Send me Barbier on the double!"

24

For three days after Christmas, Laurel was sick with a cold and still suffering from the Christmas Eve experience with Beaumonde's poor.

Barbier, the Chief's hand-picked policeman, had led them through cobblestone alleys and into garrets where the elderly, feeble, derelict greeted him by name, and where he replied in familiar terms. Over and over again in dark halls on second, third, or fourth floors she had observed in haggard faces also that peculiar horror with which the French can react to the uniform of police. Even when they understood the nature of his call, and that the sacks contained free food, there were varying reactions.

One elderly woman nearing ninety kissed Barbier on both cheeks and then, fingering a grapefruit-sized growth which protruded from her neck, she inquired whether the American would be offended if she kissed him. Laurel stood translating behind her words to Zero, who bent down before the poor woman finished her question. She flung her arms about tall Zero's neck in total, reckless abandon. The tiny woman backed away and hurried a spotless linen handkerchief edged in incongruously fine lace to her streaming eyes. When they were back downstairs, Zero pressed a five-thousand franc note into Barbier's hand and pointed up the stairs. Whistling, Barbier ascended to deliver the money. But it was too much for Laurel. Less than a third of the way through the project, she doubted her ability to continue, for fear her heart might burst.

In a third-floor garret, she had her first close look at legendary

Cambot, the chestnut vendor who fired one-word questions at Barbier, while Laurel glanced over his shoulder at immaculate, bleached boards of the floor. There was a cot, a neat writing table bearing an oil lamp, some stained sheets of handwriting and, of all things, a new French-English glossary—and a magnifying glass.

Here, Barbier turned to Laurel and explained that Cambot declined the food. He had plenty. "Tell him," said Laurel, "that I observe with woman's eye how he studies English, and that he might therefore find pleasure in cheese, beans, and meat which have come by ship from America. And tell him, it is true, my elder son is permitted to buy a cone of his chestnuts for each bon point he brings home from École Maternelle!"

Barbier had not time to say a word before Cambot's hands were outstretched. He took the sack and bent from the waist. Laurel looked at the crown of his Germanlike chimney-sweep hat, which appeared for all the world as if a herd of elephants had recently passed over it.

As for the caves Regina had mentioned, they had doors, salvaged or stolen from dumps, but no floors and few furnishings. The inhabitants listened suspiciously to the policeman's story, their eyes not leaving the brown sack once its contents were explained and understood. This had been the worst of all to Laurel, for such people had not received the sacks. They grasped, clutched, grabbed, seized, and ran back into their holes like human rats edged out of the race. In one broken door, she heard a key turn as she, Barbier, Zero, and the truck driver walked away.

Perhaps the only inspiring interlude of the long day had been in a French orphanage where several sacks and three small barrels of refined sugar were left. There were twenty-seven children living in the ancient building, which was large, clean, and clinically furnished, but she was stricken with the impersonality and the curiosity in childish eyes.

Again and again, Laurel glanced back at a blue-eyed baby girl of eight or nine months dressed in a charcoal sweater several sizes too large; her shoes were sturdy, but *one* was *brown* and *one* was *white!*

"Laurel," whispered Zero as he caught her beside the crib and touching a spot of too-high red in one chubby cheek, "don't cry. It's Christmas! Christmas Eve!"

She looked up at him through a blur of tears. "I'm sorry, Zero—it's just that . . . that I begin to doubt God when. . . ." A sob clutched her throat, but she waited to go on. "Zero, look at her sweater. Gray on a baby. And shoes—not really a pair—and . . . Zero. . . ."

He peered closer at the smiling baby. Through a sudden frown, he asked, "What's the matter with her mouth?"

"It's a harelip. Oh, God! Zero, Christmas is gone—gone. . . ."

"Come on! You'll feel better. I know you're tired. My bones ache."

"Zero, I want this child."

"A thing. . . ." Laurel knew he was about to say, A thing like that? But he quickly amended, "You wouldn't have any more chance than a snowball in hell of adopting her."

"Why?"

"We're not Catholic. This is France. Come on, Laurel! The driver's waiting."

Soon after Regina Edney returned from her English holiday she arrived at Laurel's house, having already learned of the Christmas charity project.

When they had exchanged greetings, Regina asked what time Laurel and Zero had finished their tour Christmas Eve. Seven-thirty or eight, answered Laurel dully. She went on to say that afterwards on the same evening she'd gone to pick up a rocking horse at the tobacco store.

"Rocking horse? Tobacco shop? I say, Laurel!"

"Well, why *aren't* you a mind reader?" Laurel explained that the toy had been sent from a friend in the States in too thin a carton, that Francis took it to the erstwhile carpenter in his terrible little café. The man repaired wooden items.

"And the reprobate charged you three times what the repair was worth?" chuckled Regina.

"Not only that. He tried to keep the change. Why do they think Americans can't count French money? I kept standing there. Waiting. Waiting. Waiting. My hand out. He finally simpered, 'You are strange for an American,' and he let me carry that heavy toy out to the car."

"Well, good riddance!"

"Oh, that wasn't the last! When I got it loaded in the station wagon and was about to drive away, he came running out and knocked on the window until I rolled it down."

"Cigarettes?"

"Yeah. American cigarettes. A French tobacco man! 'Madahm! It is the Eve of Noël and to drive such a car you must be very rich and I am very, very poor.' Before he could say cigarette, I remembered Michel had left a half package of his Pélouses on the seat."

"You didn't!"

"You should have seen that face when he caught sight of the blue package! French cigarettes! Oh, brother!"

Laurel lighted a cigarette, her third in the half-hour Regina had been there. Cautiously, Regina mentioned this. And then she said, "Laurel, your nose is red. And you're not willowy anymore. You're bloody thin!"

Laurel's smile was enigmatic. "Psychosomatic symptoms. I saw too much the day before Christmas. Regina, how could you get new shoes for twenty-seven orphans without using your own name? I mean, get the children fitted and all that, without the staff knowing where the shoes came from?"

"Well, I suppose you could sell the Officers' Wives' Club on a project like that."

"Three or four times a year? Children's feet grow fast."

"Well, no, our club doesn't have that kind of welfare money. But Laurel, you mustn't let what you saw get you down. It's been going on for centuries. Besides, the French government takes better care of its orphans than most countries. I bet you didn't see a single child *without* shoes?"

Pensive Laurel nodded. Regina bent to her perpetual shopping bag and took out a folded newspaper. "I think you may as well see this now. Maybe it'll take the martyr-complex out of what you did!"

Frowning at Regina, Laurel accepted the paper, which was already folded open to a half-page spread with a sizable headline: AMERICAN FLYERS OF BEAUMONDE AIR BASE BENEFIT GREGNY POOR.

Laurel's eyes flew over the picture of Parker handing the sack to the first woman, and the caption: "Commander of Air Base gets his picture taken handing out first sack." At the top of the whole spread was a letter purportedly signed by Parker, a letter in which every step of the charitable maneuver was described in flowerful, loquacious French in contrast to the intense restraint of French journalism.

Laurel faced the indignity. Neither Parker nor Zero read French. It was obvious that some minor employee down the line had seized the opportunity to see his bad poetry in French print! In fact, some of it was plagiarism for the final sentence in the letter had been copied almost verbatim from the discarded Washington stickers: "We who have so much welcomed this chance to share with the good but unfortunate poor of Gregny our bountiful material blessings."

"Well," said Laurel with dry disappointment, "this bit of back-patting will get many a French horselaugh today."

"Yes," sighed Regina, "it's the kind of clipping that a Frenchman will mail to his cousin who doesn't live near an American Air Base."

With the paper tucked back into Regina's shopping bag, they sat in uncustomary silence. What was there to say? Then, unexpectedly, Zero burst into the house bearing the same newspaper. "Hey! Hey!" he said affably. "You two see we got a half-page spread?"

Laurel gave Regina the kind of warning wink which said, No use explaining!

Regina had scarcely left 14 rue Père Marquette that afternoon when Zero mentioned through sips of bourbon and water that he had a houseguest arriving a few days ahead of Michel's January 2 hunt.

Laurel knew that Michel had asked them to make room for two more guests, and that one of them would be a rich Parisian bachelor of middle-age named Jean-Paul Cochinereau. Michel had been uncertain, however, who the other would be.

"Laurel, I want to get Guy away from Michel long enough

to put across my interest in Spanish goat hunting next summer."

"Guy?"

"Yes. You see, French people are nearly obliged to spend the holidays with their parents—like Michel is doing at Normandy."

"Guy *can't* come before the hunt. He'll have to be with his mother at Reims through New Year's Day, anyway."

"Well," grinned Zero, "you'd better tell him that, because I called him this morning—at Reims—and he's coming here the thirtieth."

"Why, Zero!" She sat up straight in her chair. "That's Monday!"

"And this is Saturday!" he said mockingly. "I'm waiting until Monday morning to sign out on ten-days' leave. I'll be here the whole time!"

25

On Monday morning, Zero drove to the Base at seven-thirty. When he had not returned by ten A.M., Laurel supposed that Parker had detained him unexpectedly, but still she had no doubt that his leave would be realized, for Zero had put in a year with no relief longer than the week's stay at L'Alouette the previous summer.

She was sitting at the desk when the telephone rang. Zero said without a moment's delay, "Don't change our plans, Laurel!"

Foreboding welled up. She recognized the tone of voice that Zero used when he dared not speak freely. It could only be one thing—the irksome alerts. Maneuvers which lasted from twenty-four hours to a week; a week had been the longest, and while dependents could come and go to the Commissary, or Officers' Club to wait on the odd chance that one's husband would lunch or dine if he could get away from his duty post, no airman or officer could leave the confines of the Base until the all-clear siren blew. Even Colonel Parker could not predict the beginning or end of such a state, for the alerts were instigated in German Headquarters.

"Don't change our plans, I said."

"I have no plans," she said through her numbness.

"Hold steady, Laurel. I may be free before the others if Parker can contact Headquarters and pretend my presence at a VIP hunt has diplomatic ramifications. Franco-American."

"I'll telephone Guy now."

"Why?"

"To have him postpone coming until you're free."

"You won't do that. I plan to get free. Besides, Laurel, you'd insult him."

"Zero. . . ."

"Laurel, I've got to go. We each have two minutes on this telephone in the Club. Oh—Abach says hello. You ought to see him in a helmet. Good-bye, Laurel—and cross your fingers, and your toes, too. Bye."

Laurel was standing up from her chair by now. The moment the telephone was back in its cradle, she began rummaging wildly through the pigeonholes of the great desk, hunting in vain for her address book. But of course! Zero must have taken the small book to make his call from the Base to Reims the previous week, and had forgotten to put it back in its place.

Undaunted, thoroughly convinced of what must be done, she grasped the telephone and got the long-distance operator, who subsequently reached information at Reims, but the Chimmery number—alas!—was restricted. It could not be given out.

Don't change our plans. . . . Zero's never asked himself what Guy means to me or toward me. As jealous as Zero is . . . Abach. . . .

Don't change our plans?

Suddenly, she saw Guy's face. Surrounding the beloved image was Zero's reassurance that he expected to be free. She arose, almost ran up the stairs, and hurriedly began the tedious process of washing and drying her hair.

At seven that evening, however, Zero was still not home. She went into the dining room and removed the third place from the table. As she entered the hall, a single knock came from the front door. She swung it open, whispering facetiously, "Monsieur le Comte!"

The moment of silence was marvelous, as was Guy's laugh. "Well, Madame Américaine! What's the matter? Open your eyes! *Now!*"

"I am afraid."

"Open your eyes!"

Reluctantly Laurel opened her eyes: As always his head was bare, but there were snowflakes lingering in the black hair. "You're Père Noël," she whispered.

"Who else?" he answered gaily. "Here!" Through the top of the plastic box, she gazed upon a double handful of purple violets.

As he raised up from kissing her hand, Laurel said, "I'll call Francis to bring your luggage. Perhaps you'd like to go up? Dinner won't be until eight. . . ."

His eyes interrupted her. She had never seen them so merry. "Dinner is always at eight," he mimicked, "and I don't want to go up. I want to follow you about and help you do whatever you're so intent upon!"

Banded by candlelight and words, the two moved effortlessly into rapport. "It is a shame about Zero and that awful maneuver," declared Guy. "He has no luck, missing such a dinner. Even my mother's chef cannot make such a galantine."

"I made it," twinkled Laurel.

"Ha!" He fell in with her teasing tone. "Where would you learn such a thing?"

"In a kitchen."

"Never!"

"Yes. A Louisiana kitchen."

He leaned around the flaming candles to regard her with solemn eyes, "Laurel, do you think I care if you can cook?"

"I think you're ungrateful! I *like* to work in a kitchen, Monsieur le Comte!"

He grasped the heavy candelabra and set it aside. "No," he whispered, "you don't belong in anybody's kitchen."

Olande entered and Laurel watched her set a demi-bottle of iced brut near Guy's hand. Candlelight reflections danced in the cut-glass crevices of the cooler, even in particles of ice caressing the dark green bottle. Guy bound a napkin tautly about the wet bottle. He poured a pearl's depth of champagne into his glass, filled hers, and then his own. "I drink," he said laughingly, "to the first Frenchman who tasted the blood of the grape from this glass!" Their goblets touched. "Perhaps he was a king!"

The two began to laugh, careless loving complete laughter with its accompanying gaze to lock out tomorrow; laughter more intimate than any kiss, so intimate that Olande, hearing this from outside the dining-room door, turned back with an exhausted smile to return the coffee pot to its warmer.

Near midnight, the servant raised up once more from the kitchen table, awakened by distant sounds of Monsieur le Comte's footsteps as he paced slowly, regularly in the room directly above.

Olande wandered on kitten feet down the first-floor hall to the dining room because it lay just below the master bedroom, and sure enough, she heard the telltale click-click of Madame's high heels and the multi-sounds of the great dog's claws as he loyally followed her pacing.

Yawning heavily, she returned to the kitchen and took her diary from the top of a stack of empty egg cartons in the pantry: "The ways of the rich are sometimes poor," she wrote, biting her pencil eraser a moment before she finished: "—as if Nature can be cheated."

26

The next morning Laurel awoke feeling guilty. While she and Guy had soul-searched the night away, Zero had likely stood guard duty. She told Olande she was going to the airbase and hurried out the door without seeing Guy who was apparently still sleeping.

"There's a hot rumor we may be free by tomorrow," said Zero, as he sat with her in the Officers' Mess.

"You haven't seen Parker?"

"I can't get to him. They say he's as tense as a lightning rod, and about as receptive to conversation. Laurel, I can't even get a God damned clue to the reason for this Class II alert. It's not like the others. In fact, I don't know how you got on Base. I read a half-hour ago on the Squadron bulletin board that dependents would remain off-Base until further notice—except medical emergencies."

"Well, you're looking at one." She grimaced. "I all but told the guard I was having a slight miscarriage. Zero, what's a Class II alert?"

"Material sabotage. I shouldn't tell you that. But what the Hell?"

Laurel said, "I heard that the fence was cut in three places the last two nights."

"Doesn't mean a damned thing. Those beet workers cut it when they don't want to circle the Base on their bicycles."

"What would happen if the throttle linkage on a jet wasn't safety-ed?"

Zero's eyes narrowed sharply. "You're crazier than Hell!"

"What would happen?"

"Normal take-off. Three—four—maybe five minutes in flight before pilot control vanishes."

Laurel paled. Five planes, she said, were found that way the previous morning. Zero stared at her, his eyes protruding in astonishment. "All in the 104th area," she added heavily.

"Jesus God! So that's why the ramp and hangar are barricaded. Sure! It fits. The Commies got twenty-seven new seats in the Assembly, but the NATO renewal was ratified anyway. Sure, Laurel! Five crashes would have demoralized the crap out of all of us! Why, the fanatic bastards!"

He pushed the plate of congealing spaghetti away, all interest in food abandoned. She watched his rapidly changing expression, anticipating his question. "Laurel, where'd you crack these chestnuts?"

"The prize in a box of Crackerjacks."

"You finally hit three cherries on a bus ride!"

"Zero, I'm afraid."

"For Christ's sake, Laurel! You'll give us both a chill. Go on home and play the piano with Guy, or read books, or talk to the children. You know, if war broke out tonight, there probably isn't a man in France who'd come nearer getting somebody out safely than Guy. I've read a security file on him. Laurel, there's nothing in the cloak and dagger business he hasn't done."

He stood up and pushed in his chair. "Come on! You better get out of here. It's depressing." Together they walked to the cloak room, its entrance blocked with metal helmets, oxygen masks, and pistol belts, where Zero now retrieved his gear from the stack, a piece at a time.

Driving the station wagon from the Officers' Mess to the gate, Laurel eyed rain-soaked G.I.'s in defense positions along the perimeter road. Extra sentries spiked the massive heating plant, while airmen with forty-five caliber pistols in cartridged belts stood at ease every fifty feet up and down the spur track leading into the Base.

During the twelve-mile drive between the guard gate and 14 rue Père Marquette, she retraced the information gained in the Officers' Club kitchen. There she had found Regret, the young chef, who welcomed her. (She had taught him to make American apple pie and he was grateful.) Regret brought a bottle of Cinzano and one glass. Obliged to accept this tribute, Laurel sipped slowly, smiling as if she did not detest Cinzano, while some yards away, the kitchen staff busied themselves frantically to ready the lunch service.

Keeping an eye on the workers, Regret quietly answered Laurel's question. At one point, she apologized for her ignorance of motors, whereupon he brought pencil and paper to make a crude drawing. She stuffed the paper into her sleeve while Regret said loudly, "I am a Southerner, Madame, and these beet diggers tell me nothing, especially since night before last when I removed four exquisite Châteaubriands from the brassière of the Nouilly wench when she left her shift."

Laurel drained the glass and moved to the hall to get her coat. For the eighth or ninth time, Regret said, "How shall I ever thank you, the most gracious lady of Beaumonde?"

She looked him straight in the eye. "You might possibly forgive me if I ask a rude question. How did you learn such a thing as you have told me?"

Regret shrugged, pursed his lips and went through all the French motions preliminary to confiding, "I belong to a club of making model airplanes. My roommate in Nouilly is also a member, and—you may find it very indiscreet of me, Madame—I give him coffee and brioche here in the kitchen each morning."

"He works on the Base?"

"But, of course! He is a mechanic in the 104th Squadron hangar."

When Laurel entered her salon, Guy was stretched out on his stomach, his great length seeming to bisect the room. On either side of him, a youngster mimicked his elbowed posture. Laurel had no trouble seeing that Brick had badgered Uncle Guy into reading some of the dozen books brought from Paris.

Quickly, she left to hang her coat and rejoin them, her mood already uplifted. But Guy had not finished half a story when Chris crawled into his mother's lap and fell asleep. She carried him in her arms as she went to answer the telephone. The first thing Michel said was, "Is it true that the men have not been off Base since Monday morning?" She laughed and asked him at once whether he was an agent. Michel then said, after a burst of denial, "Cochinereau called this morning. He'll be a day late getting here. You don't mind?" Laurel said nothing. "I haven't been able to reach Guy," he explained, "but I'm almost sure he'll be coming. You don't mind keeping him this time?"

"I don't mind anything, Michel, if Zero can just get loose."

"Well, I don't give a damn about any of the men, but you've got to be here."

"Why?"

"I don't know, Laurel. I've never had all these Belgians before. I'm nervous as a cat, and you're my—my symbol of success. Well, good-bye!"

"Wait a minute, Michel—you mustn't . . . I mean, don't drop by tonight—that is. I'm going out to play bridge with some of the other wives. They're all terribly nervous over this alert, and I suspect you may know why. Good-bye!" And she replaced the receiver before he could reply.

Upstairs, she carefully covered the child in his crib. Then she went into her own bedroom, hers and Zero's, and sat down in the chair near the window to watch sparse traffic winding up and down the hill.

Near five o'clock, Brick rushed in to ask why she was there. She hugged him with extra fierceness and asked whether Uncle Guy was still downstairs. "Yes, Laurel. He sent me to find you."

Smiling, she arose. They had no more than settled in the salon with Guy at the piano, not really playing but idling, when Brick began to chatter. "Uncle Guy, you know what? Tomorrow, Chris and I are going on a train trip—five miles to Olande's village. We get to stay two nights. Do you know her Maman, Grandmère Faure?"

Guy's hands were on the boy's shoulders but his eyes flew to Laurel's, and then back to the child's. "Non, but perhaps someday you would take me to meet her. What does she cook best?"

"Mocha gâteau," replied Brick earnestly, running his tongue tip over compressed lips.

"Why, we're having that tonight!" said Laurel. "Brick, would you consider dining at the table with Uncle Guy and me?"

He turned from his friend and straightened his shoulders manfully. "Well, yes, if you want me."

She smiled. "Then, do me a favor and go tell Olande we want dinner moved up an hour earlier."

Laurel was pacing up and down when Zero entered the Officers' Club next day. "You look distressed," he said, as he kissed her on the forehead. "Is something wrong?"

"Oh, Ruth MacDonald telephoned me from here this morning to say the embargo against dependents entering the Base had been lifted, but I might have known it would take a Presidential order to get a Frenchman in here now."

"Where is he?"

"I took him back to the house. He's going to help Michel walk the runs this afternoon, and finish cards for the hunters to draw their locations tomorrow morning."

Discovering that neither of them had any appetite, they agreed to forego the congested dining room, which was filled with chattering couples. After Zero deposited his green helmet, webbed cartridge belt and olive-drab raincoat, the two settled in a remote corner. Laurel burst out, "Zero, what *shall* I do tonight if you can't get away?"

"Why, you'll go on to Noël with Guy and do the best you can to make my excuses to those people, who will find it unthinkable that I'm not present when I accepted a hunt!"

"Oh, that's not what I mean. Olande and the children left this morning. I took them to the railroad station at eight o'clock."

"Laurel, for Christ's sake! You know as well as I do Guy's not going to bite you! Besides . . ." His eyes twinkled comtemplatively. ". . . he's the last man on earth you'd go to bed with."

"Zero!"

"How'd the New Year's Eve dinner go?"

She sagged in anticlimax and tried to think. "Brick ate with us. Nine feet tall, he was! Baked ham, black-eyed peas, cornbread, and coleslaw. A regular Louisiana New Year's spread—except for a mocha gâteau."

"Guy took to all that?"

"He didn't seem hungry, come to think of it."

"And after dinner, you played piano, and he played piano, and. . . ."

"No. We got to talking about politics and France."

"You? What do you know about French politics?"

"Nothing, of course. I asked him to run for king of France and his answer was a sack full of emeralds to buy Brick's, Chris's and my escape to Switzerland if a war starts. Then he bade me good night and went up to his room."

"Christ, Laurel, you're a panic! Next, you'll want me to believe he had the family gems dismantled and laid them at your feet."

She eyed him dourly. "No, as a matter of fact, he threw them on my lap. What do you mean, Guy's the last man on earth . . . ?"

"Laurel, let me make it clear. Guy de Brières could no more behave dishonorably than he could shrink in front of danger. I don't think you appreciate the kind of man he is, but then, women don't understand. . . ."

"I suppose not. But why is it you said Guy would be the last man. . . ."

"Because you've got a romantic complex that would keep your clothes on in front of him if somebody had a gun in your face. You want him to think you're perfect. Laurel, I don't mean anything—that's just the way I see it. So if I'm not worried, why should you be? Why don't you grow up and quit stewing, quit. . . ."

Dimly at first, she heard the series of siren blasts at one-second intervals. The sounds threw the room into waves of commotion. Mufti-clad officers began to dive into the pile of war accessories like women at a bargain sale. Zero was halfway out the front door before Laurel caught up with him, her face white, heart racing, hands and knees trembling.

He adjusted the catch on his gun belt and gave her last-minute orders, "Leave the house a couple of hours before the dinner since Guy's already up there. I don't want you alone on that road after dark, and you have him follow you home. He won't mind."

Laurel froze in her tracks and watched him grow smaller and smaller down the road. A quarter mile from her, headed for the bomb dump in the disbursed area, Zero remembered to turn around and raise his arm in farewell.

Zero, cried something deep within Laurel. Zero, come back! Come home with me—home where we belong! But the moment he was out of sight, she thought of the car, the drive home, and the coming evening.

In stockinged feet, she hung her wet trench coat in the hall and backed to the radiator opposite the umbrella stand, reflecting that she was alone in the big house. She rounded the lower stairpost then, en route to a hot, long, leisurely bath where she stayed the better part of an hour.

Feeling suddenly chilled in the cooling water, she stepped out and dried hurriedly, scampered down the hall and grabbed her leopard robe. She clutched the garment about her body to offset the chill and wondered fleetingly which hearth might yet have a fire, or at least embers on the hearth. Guy's, perhaps. And it was safe enough with him already ensconced at Noël.

Barefoot, Laurel sped down the hall and up the stairs to the lovely bedroom where she dropped cross-legged before waning ashes and coals. She leaned forward Indian-style and blew repeatedly until tiny flames danced with fickle promise. Spreading the unbelted robe, she bent her body half into the fireplace, but the warmth was too frail. She elevated herself to full height in a display of agility fit for a nymph and ran to dive headlong into

Guy's unmade bed, brushing off his carelessly dropped serge suit and a starched linen shirt.

Slowly, she warmed herself in the cold bed. Sleep came, tranquil until she jerked herself up, fingertips and soles of her feet numbed in panic. Mr. Candle waited, his tail wagging. Laurel swiped at her neck and touched moisture from his nudge, which had undoubtedly awakened her. She swept a wide span of red hair from half her face and eyed the clock: five-thirty. Now, all the way from downstairs, a knock reverberated.

She bounded from bed and ran to the door of the bedroom, only to speed back and lift Guy's suit and shirt from floor to bed. Then she flew wildly down the first flight of stairs and raced into her bedroom, there to toss shoes from the closet floor like a puppy uncovering a lost bone—until she located the second black velvet mule. The knock grew stronger, more rapid. Laurel circled the vanity table and grabbed both tortoise-shell hairpins. En route downstairs she wound her hair into a coil. "Wait a minute!" she cried sharply, setting the two pins securely in her chignon. Slowly, she swung open the door. Guy greeted her with a warm, half-apologetic grin.

"You were careless to forget your dinner clothes," said Laurel.

"On the contrary, I knew at noon when I left that I would be returning for you. So I did not take tonight's clothes."

"American women are quite accustomed to driving, and to driving alone—even at night."

He bowed in mock formality from the waist, and overdid a rare click of his heels, but the shadow of the hall caught his face as he whirled away upstairs.

A half-hour later, he closed the street gate behind her and turned to his Jaguar, but Laurel was already settling behind the wheel of the station wagon and had the motor running. He shrugged, came alongside, and said, "All right, you win! But I'm not yet enfeebled. Move over!"

She gathered in yards of lace and crinoline which rendered the Heims black taffeta gown so bouffant and, with a childish flounce, slid to the opposite side of the leather seat to stare out the window.

Neither of them spoke during the ride, nor through seven

courses of formal dinner, nor afterwards as they sat stubbornly opposite each other in the fireside armchairs. The moment Michel's English clock chimed twelve, Laurel left unobtrusively to find her coat. Michel followed. Over his shoulder, she saw Guy wrapping a white silk muffler into his black coat. She suppressed a desire to study the sheer elegance of his profile in contrasting black and white.

She turned to shake Michel's hand, saying she did not wish to dampen the party with a good night said before his festive friend. From the gun-cloak room, she went down a slender hall which bypassed the kitchen and slipped out the service entrance. She had rounded the house and moved to the front veranda where dim light aided a search deep within her handbag for car keys. From the dark, Guy came beside her, just as she remembered he had her keys.

"Give me the keys," she said, one gloved hand extended palm up although she did not look at him.

"What do you make of me, Laurel. A Montmartre pimp?"

Alarmed by the tremor in his voice, she nevertheless felt challenged to sustain her open hand. The front door of the château opened behind her back. Michel's voice fell upon them. "Another lovers' quarrel? Ha!"

Guy clutched her arm so decisively that she did not glance back as he urged her to the car. Unexpectedly, however, he directed her to the driver's side, and when she was seated behind the wheel, he closed the door, circled the back of the car and got in beside her, reaching over to insert the key.

Wounded pride assaulted Laurel. Gravel shot behind the rear wheels as she sped down the hundred-meter stretch to the gate. The road leading from Noël curved in the manner of a capricious little river, but she had driven it so often she could sense even the degree of bank in the sharper turns, and so she pressed the accelerator to the floor and held it there rigidly—three-tenths of a mile to the first bad curve and narrow bridge. She held her speed halfway to Beaumonde. At this point, she was forced to slow down because of intermittent stretches of ghostlike ground fog.

She had seen such fog on other rides. Zero, with his pilot's prepossession toward weather, liked to explain that this represented a concise example of variance between air and ground temperatures. It was only weather, Laurel reminded herself now. But tonight, the fog seemed something else, something which set her hands atremble, and then, the knee of her right leg, and finally, her ankle above the accelerator. From the corner of her eye, she saw Guy with his head against the back of the seat, eyes open, staring at the ceiling of the car. She glanced then beyond him and back to her left. Level fog stretched on either side of the road in lateral infinity.

Sweat broke out on her upper lip and on her temples. One finger of white doeskin glove burst at the index knuckle, causing her to swallow a wild laugh. She summoned the last of strained resources and unconsciously stomped the accelerator through the last three miles of the maniacal ride, blind to her buried desire to solve everything by fatal, irrevocable collision.

Before the house she abandoned the vehicle the moment it was still and fled without closing the car door, running like a woman trailed by a pack of ghouls. She heard Guy shut the front door, turn the key; heard the umbrella stand creak as he hung his black coat; heard the stairs under his weight. Then, something brushed into the crinolines at her knee. She sagged down and forward until her arms clasped the broad neck of awakened Mr. Candle.

Little by little, the lazy beast eased from her seated embrace to land with a final, satisfied thud on his back and across her lap, upside down. Indifferent to tan hairs which soiled black taffeta, or his weight crushing her crinolines, she scratched the dog's chestbone and cloud-soft ears. In the blind murk of her salon, she pondered the simplicity with which animals gave and received love, and regretted that she was human.

The cuckoo clock marked twelve-thirty. One. One-thirty. Laurel suddenly felt tired. Slowly, with the dog behind her, she labored upstairs to her room and lighted both dressing-table lamps, took off her four-hundred-dollar gown and dropped it indifferently across a chair where soon was added a small mountain of black lingerie. Like a sleepwalker, she moved to the closet, felt a garment on the nearest hook, and donned it.

Having freed her crown braid and brushed her long hair, she sat trying to recall what came next. Oh. Her nightly check on the children. She crossed the room to go through her door when darkness fell like a collapsing tent. Damn French electricity! Methodically, she retraced her path to the mantel and felt until she touched the small Dresden candleholder. She found and struck a wooden match, and when the flame was sturdy above the candle, she eased barefoot along the hall and fingered open the door of Brick's room, only to find the undisturbed bed. The children were with Olande in the country!

She whirled so quickly that the flame of the candle did not thoroughly revive until she passed the staircase a few steps off her right. Behind her there came a faint creak, no more than the second or third step down. Startled, she froze in real fear. Guy said, "I'm sorry if I frightened you. I went down to the library to get a book."

She sighed in relief, averting her gaze as she lifted the candle higher to light his face. She felt forlorn now, and awkward in the wake of the emotional tidal wave of the long day.

"Laurel," he whispered in a hoarse voice. "You're a vision—a pair of eyes, a mass of hair, and a cloud of gilt. You *are* from Paradise."

"And you, Apollo—had you an aegis, a lyre, a—a fig leaf, I should believe you were made in Greece. Where is your robe?"

"Button that robe and I may tell you!"

Their laughs came together and embraced in comfortable unity. "Guy?" He took the candleholder from her hand without their gazes separating, and set it atop the stairpost. Then he took her shoulders in his hands and regarded her with a firmness she interpreted at once as rebuke.

"I'm sorry for the driving."

"It did not matter. I would as soon die with you as live the way we must."

He brought her against his chest so that, bent a little, his chin rested on her crown. Laurel felt an indelible, almost unbearable tautness against his flesh, a thrill not imagined as she knew in her cheek the rhythm of his heart. She moved back from him. She tasted fear, exhilaration, and then plunged. "Guy?"

"Yes, Laurel?"

He clasped her hands lightly and planted kisses on her fingertips. With a soft, ominous, unmistakable inflection, she repeated his name. Her fingers curled pleadingly inside his palms. The question throbbed through their locked gazes until Guy offered by a turn of his head that refusal equally unmistakable.

"Why?" she choked, incredulous.

Guy released her hands and straightened, towering, arms falling loosely at his sides. "I would sooner abuse a child."

"Abuse?"

He stared transfixed as she rubbed balled fists at her eyes, sniffing furiously and reviling her weakness in weeping. She could not see the clenching of his hands below her line of vision, but when she was finally past convulsive weeping, she saw agony behind his sculptured features.

"Laurel, for me you are forbidden," he said quietly.

"In God's name, by whom?"

"I will not defile my love for you by evil."

"Evil? Guy, I did not will myself to love you."

"Laurel, try to understand!"

"Hell?"

"Laurel, no man is worth begging. . . ."

"You can't love me," she sobbed, her voice now a little girl's. "You love the image of your own perfection. It isn't me you can't defile. It's . . . oh, Guy! I would have asked no more than to be swallowed up by Hell as a fair price for your embrace—afterwards. But you . . . now, it will be lonely—and for nothing."

28

Around four that morning, Laurel heard the fresh, heavy wind arrive and as quickly depart. Behind it descended iced air too frigid to move, too frigid to bear cloud or fog. When the first slivers of navy blue pierced the iron shutters, Laurel dressed in layers of dull wool and ascended the many steps to the Cathedral yard atop Beaumonde's hill.

Behind her, Mr. Candle puffed twin jets of steam and broke immobile point to lift one paw then the other, rather than let his feet adhere to the frozen cobblestones. Nose skyward, the great dog eyed his prey in wistful menace, the pigeons in the hollow spires of the Cathedral, who chirped a hungry dirge and ignored the dog.

Laurel secured the wool muffler across her mouth and nose. The vicious cold still pinched cheeks and misted eyes as her gaze roamed the sprawling plane where chimneys began to pronounce the day in swelling bursts of spiral smoke—black and gray mushrooms birthing in the bed of winter's forest. A train yawned shrilly and, from a low tier of fiery vapor on the east, the red sun was a nomadic minx flirting behind pleats of a coral fan.

She climbed upon the foot-thick stone wall and sat down, her legs dangling over the trolley track some fifty feet below. She leaned back to brace her mittened hands against the rocks. Mr. Candle gave one exclamatory bark. Laurel turned as Cambot emerged from the Cathedral, moving in labored steps like a child's mechanical bear with its spring weakening. He seemed not to notice her or the dog but was aimed toward the alley between the lace shop and the poissonnerie. At the sound of a low whistle, Laurel turned away from sight of Cambot. She saw Guy leaning against the corner of the old Church. His face was pink with cold, his cheeks and chin and nose reddened. Bareheaded, he had but his collar to turn against the air. Laurel swung to the ground and ran eight or ten steps of the fifty yards between them before her steps slowed and his arms preceded him.

They stood a moment in silent embrace, before she started to turn away. Guy bent slightly, still looking into her eyes, and raked bare fingers beneath the dog's chin. "Laurel. . . ." he began through spurting steam, his own breath. At once, she shook her head, as if to remind him there was nothing to be said.

Arm in arm, the pair descended the Beaumonde steps. Upon their entry into 14 rue Père Marquette, Laurel had lost feeling —that temporary numbness of subcold which leaves skirted women with a sensation of having no knees. Guy followed her wordlessly down the hall, took their coats and hung them, while she began to make coffee. With the splashing water, she did not hear him descend to the basement, and had no idea where he had gone until, closing the tap, she heard those unmistakable sounds. Nothing on earth lent more reality to the natural demands of daily routine than the rasp of a coal furnace grate being shifted deftly back and forth while every pipe and radiator throughout the house echoed with metallic attention.

She glanced unintentionally at her elongated reflection in the side of the tall chrome coffee pot, startled by an embryo grin. *It's me. I'm making coffee. And Guy, my tall, dark, handsome, cloak-and-dagger lover who-won't-be-loved, is stoking a furnace. At this point, I should be leaping from the cliff or selecting the gun from Zero's cabinet—but life isn't that way.*

She set the percolator in its place and plugged in the cord, watching and waiting for the first feeble fountain to splash the glass dome. *But I'm not going to mourn what happened last night. Guy's not the fool I am—he could see beyond the moment. What would have happened this morning and this afternoon and next month and next year—a mad dive into bed—one ear cocked to the turn of a doorknob—or racing back and forth to Paris with one eye always turned back over a shoulder? Hiding.*

257

Hunted. Haunted by the need for concealment. He's above that . . . and even if I left Zero tomorrow—left him and got a . . . a divorce—Guy's a Catholic. Of course, he'd marry me. I know that. But then . . . then . . . new Churches—new priests—new confessionals . . . and no peace in his heart. I couldn't bear to watch him decay internally . . . no, I love him—more than a foolish moment. God, help me to help him!

At noon, minutes after the all-clear siren at the Base, Zero emerged before his house from a blue staff car, which waited while he changed to hunting garb. That evening Guy and Zero sat at opposite ends of a long table in the Noël dining room. Across from Laurel sat the host, heady with the velvet quality of his evening. The day's kill had been rich. Michel accented his pleasure at interludes with the same remark, "Zero's here. Now we're complete!" Zero's expression, thought Laurel, belonged to a man who found life superb, but she could not say the same of Guy.

After dinner the male guests busied themselves at Michel's direction placing dining-room chairs in rows across the foyer. He emerged from the gun room carrying an eight millimeter projector and tins of films while Guy set a small table behind rows of chairs. Movies of other hunts began as Laurel sat down in her usual armchair by the fireplace, well back of the audience. The twin chair across from her remained empty and she was grateful—for that and for the privacy of semi-darkness. Behind closed lids, she listened as avid hunters shouted recognition when a familiar sight flashed across the beaded screen.

"Laurel!" whispered Guy as he sat down opposite her and leaned forward, elbows resting on his knees, chin cradled in both palms. "Laurel, my angel!" His voice held urgency. "I have thought of little else today but your questions and your accusations."

Suddenly, her head throbbed in pain. "Guy, let's not. . . ."

"Yes, let's. I have gone down enough blind alleys trying to desert my love for you. Do you know that last night I had not gone downstairs for a book? I went downstairs to the gun cabinet and I opened the lock with a clip from your desk. Laurel, listen to me! I sat with the barrel of a twelve gauge in my mouth and flipped the trigger, but nothing happened and when I stood up and ejected the shell, I saw the drama. I had taken it from Zero's reloading stock—a spent shell waiting to be reloaded. And in the same time, I saw what I had taken no time to see—the scandal you would have—my mother's loneliness—my . . . Laurel, what does it matter what I saw? It was not meant to be done and so I came up the stairs, undecided whether to wake you, or to return to my room, and before I could decide, there you were. For a time I believed it all a vision. . . ."

She felt extremely dizzy—unable to comprehend all that he had said so rapidly, so easily, as if he were telling some third-person story. "Shhh!" she said.

"Why?"

"Someone may hear you!"

"Let them! If they hear, let them come and hear it all!" Even in the half-dark, his smile loomed dangerously. "I am done with caring for opinions, Laurel. I make my declaration to you now and everything hinges on your answer." For an instant, he buried his face in his palms. "Laurel, I know what it is like to be dead inside and to come alive when another person walks into a room."

"Guy, no. I can't bear it. I. . . ."

"Yes, Laurel, you've made me see that I have always been false, that I have been filled with delusions of moral grandeur."

"Guy, don't abandon truth!"

"Truth? There is one truth left for me, Laurel. You are my link with life. You must come with me."

She turned her head and watched the sight of the projector wheel turning, matched it with revolutions of the hushed motor. She saw the back of Zero's silvered head in the first row, and beside him, Michel's elbow resting possessively on his shoulder.

"Guy," she began in perfect control, "I hardly know how to explain without hurting you. Guy, for God's sake! This isn't the eighteenth century. It's the twentieth. I've wanted a good roll in the hay with you since the night I met you, but you turned me down. I'm not in the mood anymore—I mean . . . after all—I never had to ask a man before—much less beg."

As he whirled away into the dark, she sank further into the chair and felt enlarging malaise which had throbbed at her temples and the base of her skull these recent hours. She resolved to give no quarter to a painful shortness of breath, because she resented what appeared typical femininity. Why feign illness to dilute the last crisis?

However, when Zero summoned Abach to the Beaumonde house at four o'clock that morning, the doctor and his thermometer took a different view. Her temperature was a hundred and five.

"You'd better get down on your knees, Zero, and thank God we live in the age of penicillin."

"What is it, Sam?"

"Bronchial pneumonia, and don't call me Sam."

"Oh, Christ! I've had the rest of my leave canceled. Parker wants wheels up by eight in the morning."

"For the day?" asked Abach quietly, readying a syringe.

"No, four days. Cannes. Gotta look over the site for the new rest camp."

"Zero. . . ."

"Level with me, Sam . . . if it's too serious for you to take care of, we'll crank up and take her to Weisbaden General—right now."

Neither awake nor sleeping, Laurel opened her eyes and gazed at the vein in Abach's forehead which she knew would be distended. "No, Zero. Leave him alone. I'll be all right."

Abach slept at the Beaumonde house the next three nights. On the fourth morning he told Laurel she needed no further injections. He said she had him worried, though, because she had not asked when she might leave the bed, much less go out. She replied through a half-smile that she was beginning to enjoy her effortless life. "The children come to me. So does my food. Why, just think of the hours I save not dressing!"

Unbeknownst to Abach, however, she ventured about the house much of the morning after he left, and when Zero arrived at four that afternoon—a day earlier than expected—she was dressed and waiting in the salon. He drank a double bourbon. He seemed extraordinarily irritable but remembered to congratulate her on her quick convalescence, saying she looked as good as ever. When he returned with his next drink, she asked what he had done in Cannes.

His eyes flashed disagreeably. "You sound like you're checking!"

She laughed tiredly. "I'd forgotten all about it but Michel told me Félicité Moreau moved to Cannes." She waited for him to show some sign of interest or at least conversational acknowledgment, but he merely studied his drink. "Did he tell you about her?" she asked.

"Oh, you know how he rattles on. Half the time, I forget to listen."

"Well, he said she'd had some kind of financial reverse. Stocks or investments. Some financial collapse. She's next door to the poorhouse, according to him. I meant to ask Guy how much of it was true, but I forgot. Michel said she took a job as a hostess at the Martinez."

"Why, the son of a bitch! She's not a hostess. She's a switchboard operator. I saw her two days ago. You know Americans from here always stay at the Martinez. They give us rates."

"Well, I feel sorry for her."

"Oh, Laurel," he said with conviction, "I wouldn't waste my sympathy on her if I were you. She lives a pretty different life from . . . well, I mean she's out of Paris where her money-friends live. She'll do all right."

They sat for a time, and then Zero picked up a newly arrived hunting magazine which engaged his attention as long as the drink lasted. When he returned from the kitchen with his third, Laurel picked up her knitting and made a few heartless stitches.

Zero finished this drink shortly before the cuckoo struck six times from the hall, and in the next hour, he had a fourth.

When Olande announced dinner at seven—an hour early according to Laurel's instructions—he said, "God damn! Why the rush?" And he grimaced when Olande arrived with the second course of the meal—golden, crisp croquettes of salmon fenced in a ring of stuffed and baked white endive. Glancing at the tray extended beside Laurel in the servant's hand, he said, "God damn! Canned salmon!"

She took one of the croquettes, shrugging afterwards and saying, "Once a year won't hurt you."

Zero speared three of the golden balls and raked them onto his plate. "You know how I feel about canned salmon since you let that fifty-two pound King spoil when I flew it back from Alaska. And I *caught* it!"

"'Into each life. . . .'" said Laurel drily.

"And by God, you gave away two Reds I caught in the Sound."

"Zero!" she moaned wearily. "That was eight years ago!"

"Oh well! What the Hell? You're just like Michel, a God damned snob. You just naturally have no regard for anything unless it costs a lot of money."

Laurel laid her fork across her plate, indifferent to food before and now ready to forego it. "Zero, if we had a dinner date and you talked this way, I wouldn't go out with you again. Now, whatever's bothering you, don't take it out on me!"

"Laurel, I got plenty eatin' me. I got problems you don't even know about—problems coming out of my ears. Parker expects me to keep the Beaumonde liaison ironed out without a wrinkle, keep tab on the 104th—you realize except in name I'm still the one-o-four commander?—expects me to be a ready-teddy passenger-carrying pilot for him and all the sick women, and now he's put me in charge of building a rest camp at Cannes and running it when it's built—from here. Oh, Jesus. I came home, Laurel, to get a change of clothes. I've got to go back to Cannes for a week. I'm leaving here at six in the morning. And you want me to treat you like you're out on a dinner date?"

"Zero, I'm sorry. . . ."

"You sure as Hell are, and by God, I'll not be issued any more ultimatums. I'll say what I God damned well think in my own house and if you don't like it, you can blow it out your ass!"

She got up from the table and headed for the door without looking back. Bed felt good again. How strange, she reflected in the quiet of the room Zero would undoubtedly be entering any moment—how strange that his tongue no longer owned the power to hurt her. She had listened, but somehow what he said could not reach her.

She feigned sleep next morning through his good-bye kiss on the crown of her head, and having no reason to get up, she stayed in bed through lunch, and was still there when Abach popped in her door at half past three that afternoon.

He did not ask her how she was but said, "Laurel, you're young and strong. You've the body of a twenty-year-old. What's wrong?"

She slung the cover away a bit and raised herself on one elbow, frowning. "I have a knot here. You just reminded me."

He frowned, "What kind of knot?"

She made a face at him and fell back on the pillow. "If I knew what kind of knot, I wouldn't be asking a doctor." Abach moved swiftly to the bed and sat down beside her. "Probably a fibroid," sighed Laurel. The doctor planted his right hand over the spot she had indicated and his skilled fingers staved like a barrel upon the uterine development. He cleared his throat.

"Abach, am I one of those nice women who get the menopause in their early thirties?"

He took off his glasses and held them in his left hand, looking away from her as his other hand darted to the side of her breast and depressed awakening glands. She flinched and said, Ouch!

"Why do you say that?"

"Because it hurt!"

"No! Why did you mention climacteric?"

"Because I haven't had a period since the first of October or thereabouts." She frowned. "I remember it was somewhere about then. Before it snowed." Abach laced his fingers into each other and dropped his hands in his lap. He breathed deeply, solemn of eye, grim of mouth. She said, "Don't be a granny! I'm not afraid if it's a tumor."

"Laurel," he eyed her frankly, "you haven't got a tumor. You're pregnant."

He got up from the bed and went to the window to stare down into the street.

30

Laurel awoke next morning at six o'clock in a new state of mind. She had gone to sleep cuddling doubt of Abach's diagnosis: after all, no human being was infallibly right in all cases. But now there seemed no doubt. It was the eleventh of January. She was carrying an infant, and, no longer cajoling herself to believe it was not Michel's. She counted forward two hundred and eighty days from the October night.

No one—not Zero or Guy or Michel—would ever know, especially not Zero because she hadn't a doubt in the world that such a revelation would land her in divorce court to be shorn of her two sons. Zero must never know. Never. . . .

That January morning Laurel misconstrued nervous energy for renewed vigor. Before noon she gave Olande the remainder of the day and night off. Shortly after lunch she put Chris—now nineteen months old—down for his nap, and when the child awoke at three, she bundled him into the car, put the dog in the rear, and struck out to ride around until five when Brick would be done at school.

She drove up the serpentine road of the hillside, passed through the Square and down the narrow street past the Cathedral. Here her attention was attracted by a street fair. She left the car a half block behind the Cathedral and moved on foot toward colorful display booths, leading Chris slowly, the dog idling and sniffing as he followed. Laurel and her son moved past trays of buttons, belts, filigreed silver jewelry, strange kitchenwares, and tiny goldfish in plastic sacks of water which were strung head-high across one booth.

From time to time she glanced over her shoulder to make sure Mr. Candle had honored her command to "stay!" for she had sniffed far ahead fresh fish and animal meat, and knew the dog would be unwelcome any deeper into the area.

She was more than a half block from the dog as she held back to see what Chris would do about a charming discovery. Quite close to a little black goat, he tried to touch the steam exuding from the beast's nostrils. The animal stared woodenly at the ground below him, head dropped. Laurel eyed the tiny cart to which he was harnessed, a wagon piled high with dried lavender. His reins traveled to the hand of what seemed to be a dirty statue swathed in a wine-colored shawl. Something in the half-visible face nudged Laurel's memory, but the crone was not a remembered Beaumonde marketeer.

Chris squatted now at the goat's head and jerked off his right mitt. Laurel frowned as he reached out and tugged one or two of the goat's whiskers. She opened her mouth to scold him but the animal flailed his head up and down twice and was free. Chris had lost his grip, but quick as a flash, he reached back and grasped a handful of the long hairs and held firmly. Laurel was in the process of bending to slap his hand when the woman planted her foot against the boy's chest and sent him reeling backwards. In a nightmarish flash as the shawl fell away, Laurel saw the yellow eyes and a looped silver ring through one ear and realized it was the same Gypsy she had run down the hill! The crone snarled, "Thou beast who learned from Satan's lips to curse Gypsies!"

She raised her ebony cane and brought it sharply into the side of Laurel's neck. Laurel staggered backwards, terrified now, and tripped over her own son. In her effort not to land on the child, she went down atop a wooden case sprouted with twelve litre bottles of vin ordinaire.

Winded temporarily, she raised off the bottles and bent on her knees to whimpering Chris. Quickly she hugged his face into her neck, so he would not see the savage profile of Mr. Candle as he growled, braced his four feet backwards on the slick cobblestones, his deadly jaw teeth clamped on the soiled garments of the Gypsy.

Bystanders by now had ringed the scene. Laurel got to her feet, setting the child on the ground. She felt no pain anywhere except a severe bruise in an upper rib where one of the corked bottles struck directly on bone. Thankful to be whole and eager to get away, she gave a low whistle and Mr. Candle obediently loosed his jaws. Laurel heard a guttural shout, "She'll buy me new clothes, that one!"

Laurel melted into the crowd with the dog at her heels and a silent Chris beside her. Still trembling but otherwise steady on her feet, she waited some five or six minutes while a police agent listened to the gitane's sharp-tongued scolding. Then she escaped amid the onlookers.

At home she drank a double brandy and felt restored except for bruises. She drove with Chris to get Brick, and sat down at the kitchen table for plates of baked ham, baked sweet potatoes, and a salad of parsley and sliced tomatoes.

By nine she had a dull ache, low in her back, but that seemed unsurprising, thought Laurel, considering what had happened. At midnight she awoke with sharp little pains—miniature editions of labor, she recognized instantly.

Calmly she gave the Beaumonde operator the Base number, and Abach's BOQ extension. They spoke but three lines, and then time began to lose its dependability. It seemed only seconds before she heard the sharp tinkle of glass landing on the downstairs tile. Abach's answer to the locked door was to break the hinged glass pane and reach inside to the key.

Eternity seemed to come in his bounding footsteps on the stairs. Laurel heard them one after another and wondered whether he would ever reach her. She awoke in darkness, feeling his presence. "Sam, why did you bring me to this room?"

From the distance of the gold chaise longue by the window, he answered sleepily, "Had to put you somewhere while we did the housecleaning."

"We?"

"Me." He went on. "I want you up here away from the children, absolutely still for two days." From the blackness he asked then where Olande was.

"She'll be here by eight in the morning."

"You'll tell her the same thing I will. Relapse. Pneumonia."

"And the broken glass in the front door pane?"

"I've already nicked the dog's paw. She knows he's always trying to open the doorknob with his mouth."

Laurel lay effortlessly in the bed, watching great swirls of purple, red, orange, and green clouds push one another aside. When she awoke next time, it was a quarter before nine. She listened acutely and heard the front door slam and then the silence broken only by the distant dog-whine, Mr. Candle's protest at being left behind while Olande, Chris, and Brick departed.

She turned her head toward the gold chaise where Abach lay half-covered with the magenta comforter. She started to turn over, but too many areas of her body objected. "Abach, wake up!" He took one fleet look at her and then slowly sat up, working his shoulders and yawning as he reached out to the Limoges table for his glasses. "Abach, there's a baby girl in the Blery orphanage with a harelip."

"How old?" he asked, raising his arms high above his head and yawning again.

"Ten months—maybe eleven."

"Late. Not too late."

"Could you do it?"

"Not like Eggerton."

"Who's he?"

"Board man down at Paris. American Hospital."

"Would he?"

"You got a spare toothbrush around this hotel?"

"Would he?"

"I suppose. If we footed the arrangements and the bill at some French hospital. The bill for the room, but, Laurel, there's something else I want to talk to you about—when you feel stronger."

"I feel fine," she lied, "unless I try to move."

Abach stood up and said, "Where'd you get those blue marks on your back?"

267

"I fell on a case of wine yesterday afternoon—up at that street fair—with Chris."

"For God's sake!" He shook his head, running his tongue again over his teeth. "Old rubber-boned rebel!" Then he came to the bed but he did not sit down. "Laurel," he took her hand loosely. "I want Zero to send you home. You and the kids."

She muttered one word. "Why?"

"You know why. But if you need it stated, let's just say the best medicine I can think of for your problems right now would be an ocean between you and them. Nothing's as real when you're away from it."

She glanced down at their clasped hands and felt in his very grip the strength of his wisdom. "No, Sam. I moved into my own bedroom last week. I don't know whether I did it to punish Zero or myself. Anyway I'm in trouble with my own conscience. Losing this baby is like a reprieve, but I've got to give something back."

"Like what?"

"I'll tell you when I understand it." She gave him the best smile she could muster and withdrew her hand. "Now, if you don't think I'm going to die this morning, you'd better either call the Base or go to work."

"I called, at seven-thirty this morning. For your information, Madame Compton, I not only have come down with a slight influenza, but I have confined myself to quarters for three days —with friends to take care of me."

Laurel eyed him solemnly. "Parker's going to think you and I are that way."

"Well, where do we go from here?"

"I'll tell you, Abach, if you'll come with me. There's a four-year-old boy at Blery who needs an ear top."

"But that takes a plastic man."

"And a sixteen- or eighteen-month-old orphan with a clubfoot. And a woman who kissed Zero with a goiter as big as a grapefruit on the side of her neck."

"Probably nontoxic."

"You'll help?"

"No."

"Why?"

"I'm mending Americans as fast as they can wham their cars around telephone poles. Some nebulous idea of patching up northern France is a hopeless—and for me, rather conceited illusion."

"Why?"

"I'd have to envision myself spectrally, doctor with scalpel in portfolio."

"You said you'd ask Eggerton to do the harelip?"

"Sure. If he won't, I'll try. But on the condition you let the project go at that."

"Let's have some coffee now. You mind?"

Wordlessly, he left the room. Laurel purposely had sent him, for she needed time to think. If he refused to aid her plans, she had only to tell him flatly, to lie to him, that he left her nothing with which to fill her days in France except the making of tiretracks to Château de Noël, or—as long as it was a lie—to Guy de Brières in Paris.

BOOK THREE

1

It was the day after May Day, which had passed without incident save, according to the daily OSI account on the Wing Commander's desk, fourteen cases of tire slashings in six small villages (American-owned cars), and the uprooting of a horizontal kerosene drum which set fire to the kitchen of an American sergeant's domicile when the fuel drained in a rush to his air heater.

Parker and Compton sat across from each other in the former's new second-story office. Wing Headquarters was first of the concrete-block or "permanent" structures to be completed, although the new hospital, Base library and gym, and an austere little Chapel were in varying stages of construction.

Parker's body formed a loose angle, feet atop the glass of his broad desk, back laced against the swivel chair. He switched a dead pipe from side to side in his mouth. Zero sat edgily, somehow ready to spring from the straight-back chair on the opposite side of Parker's desk. Parker told him that Laikenhauf's widow would be arriving in Germany for a month's visit with her youngest daughter, new grandchild, and Army-captain son-in-law. "There's no landing strip. A tank outfit some distance from Fulda. But Whitmore told me on the hot line from our Headquarters yesterday he hopes to get her down to Bruchstein for a week and a few parties in her honor. At any rate, I'll try to let you know a day or two ahead when you and I have to go and for how long."

"Sir, I'd rather not. I know it's irregular. But she won't want to see me." Zero stood up, spun his chair around on one leg,

273

and sat back down with the back of the chair a stiff bib before him. He crossed his forearms atop it. "She was there the night in 'fifty when old Lacey's wife took a shot at me."

Parker's expression did not alter. He took the pipe from his mouth, eyes steady on Compton. "Everybody knows she was drunk. You know God damned well he's a broken man now from sanitarium bills."

Zero wore a dejected expression. "I don't know, Sir. Women are funny. You take a little thing like that wild slug breaking Laikenhauf's photograph clear across a room—and forty or fifty people seeing it—bad omen, Sir . . . to a woman—and the Chief not cold in his grave. Tell you the truth, Sir, for a month or so, I kinda had a chill when I thought about it."

"Aw forget it! Everybody knows Lacey's daughter is a divorcée. She knew her way around."

Zero Compton fell silent, having no more to say of the period he cared least to remember. But Parker was still probing his subject. "Women. Take Florene, my wife. Wouldn't think of coming over here because she's so God damned certain the next war will break out just like the one at Pearl. I was a captain— an old captain—expecting a promotion any day. I had protocol duty that Sunday—down at Ops waiting for a two-star general and his party to come in. Old Haines. He got killed at Leyte. Anyway, Florene was just coming home from a party and by the time she got across the field, the native servant had taken our kids. Florene walked through the Japanese part of town for two days before she found them."

Parker eyed Compton solemnly, chewing his pipe stem. "I never got home, never saw her before they were shipped out. Then in 'forty-four, I was sent to England as an operational observer. Ninety days, they say, and come back with a good critique. Well, I did—two years later. Zero, you can't imagine what it's like to know you're gettin' it on your second ride. Christ, the first six months in that dung heap of a prison, they couldn't get anything through their square heads except that I was a British spy." His face grew dark. "I used to lie there and think for an hour at a time about stupid simple things like the way a sheet smells after it's blown in the sun all day, or how a bar of Ivory smells, or the way clean dishes look stacked in a cupboard. God damnedest things, Zero. And I told Florene all that when we were back together. Like a fool I told her how it felt to scratch lice, or kneel naked on a broomhandle during six hours of interrogation, or how I'd get so panicky about what they were doing to me, I even jacked myself off in the dark now and then just to prove to myself I wasn't ruined for life."

Zero had lost all thought of himself. He stared rigidly at his Colonel. "A woman couldn't understand that, Sir."

"No. She moved out of my room. Some flimsy excuse of female trouble. Well, Zero, that's life."

"I'm sorry, Sir."

"'Sorry, Sir'? By God, you have got your teeth sunk in that next promotion, haven't you?"

"I hope so, Sir."

"Why?"

"You know as well as I do, Sir. An officer who doesn't get his first star by forty-five years of age—well, Sir, . . . it's an—an. . . ."

Parker came forward with his swivel chair to slam a flat palm on his desk. "An accident? Then, by God, I'd better have an accident before I leave Europe. If I don't, they'll force me to retire the following year, and Zero, I can't live and keep one kid in college and Florene in the swim at Lauderdale on a colonel's retirement."

The senior officer stared at Zero while sparks smoldered from his tired eyes. "Must be something to have a wife with no soap bubbles in her head about keeping up with—I mean out-doing the Dupont-Joneses."

"She's got her own flights of fancy, Sir. But we're lucky. Her father's mother left her a piece of sugar factory and a couple of securities. Ten or twelve thousand a year—if sugar doesn't break."

"Christ-a-mighty!" said Parker. "You realize the difference ten thousand would make to me right now? I'd tell Moyer to ram it. Compton, I'm sick of a team concept when you can't find two real teammates anywhere. It's been screw-your-buddy week since 1947. Take you and me—you're Laikenhauf too and I knew it before I saw you. Why didn't I come straight out and say, 'I'll take care of you these two years, don't worry!' But no—greed is contagious. I said in so many words, 'You get me a star and I'll find you an eagle,' and, Compton, the Hell of it is, that's just how I feel."

"Well, Sir," began Zero, "the way I see it, Congress doesn't leave much leeway for loyalty when ten or twenty wings at a time are cut out of the pattern. Even Laikenhauf never had a thing like that to deal with. The way I figure, when we start converting to unmanned aircraft and—well, the missile concept, an officer won't be able to turn his back on his own mother without taking a chance. The officer corps won't be survival of the fittest; it'll be survival of the quickest, the meanest, and the cleverest."

"You'll make it," said Parker with no inflection of flattery.

"Why do you say that, Sir? I'd appreciate knowing."

"Three things. Combat record. Laurel. And you're six-foot-five."

Zero knew when to change the subject. "Sir, I hate to keep harping but I feel uneasy. Things haven't been this quiet around the countryside since NATO bought land for this Base."

"What makes you uneasy?"

"Well, Sir, with a mayor like Cravet, you never know where to expect the next hole in the dike. . . ."

"Zero, he doesn't love us. He never will. But when there's as much good feeling as there is over something like this playground at the orphanage at Blery, he isn't about to jeopardize his position by downgrading us publicly." Parker paused to laugh. "You know, Compton, your wife pulled a fasty over that playground deal."

"How's that, Sir?"

"Well, I guess it's my fault. Sometime after the first of the year, I told her about the Wives' Club having twelve hundred dollars holed up in a welfare fund. She lit up like a candle and asked me how I thought it should be spent. I told her I didn't dare say because a Commander can't dictate to Wives' Clubs about their funds. But I told her what I hoped—that they wouldn't spend it on people who'd spit in our tracks the moment we walked away. I told her they ought to look into the orphanages in the area. Three of them. You know, it seemed to me a child would retain a lasting impression of America, regardless of future brainwashing, if Americans gave his 'home' a movie projector and films, or a record player and discs, or say, in the case of a thousand dollars, a yard of playground equipment."

"Then it was *your* doing, Sir?"

"Not exactly. I don't think you realize the weight your wife swings on this French grapevine—*and* the American. She put the bug in Ruth MacDonald's ear about the playground project, and Ruth, as President of the Wives' Club, got the idea approved. Zero, Laurel's got all kinds of things going with that orphanage —and plenty of French protection where it counts. The best I can find out, she must have got some influential French person with connections in Paris to forestall a cut in the orphanage's recreation stipend—you know, a thousand dollars' worth of playground stuff is quite a bonanza."

"Sir. . . ."

"Aw, Christ! Stop *siring* me!"

Zero arose and put his hands in his pants pockets. Parker's blue eyes on him were narrowed, unyielding. Zero turned his back on the Colonel and stared from the second-story window down to the parking ramp where a yellow starter tractor was fixing to prime a jet. When he turned back to Parker, the older man said, "You really don't have any humor, do you, Compton?"

"Sir, I hope you and I aren't around the first time one of those orphans gets maimed or killed on that play equipment."

Parker's face was flushed now. "We take a chance when we step in a shower. The French know that—they're not aborigines!"

"Well, if I'd known Laurel had anything to do with it, I'd have stopped it."

"You do and I'll have your ass!" Parker's face was livid now. Zero stared at him, jolted into the necessity of smoothing the scene quickly.

"Well, it's too late, Sir!"

"Thank God." Parker reached to flip five pages forward on his desk calendar. "The dedication is the fifth." He eyed Compton with preoccupation, his sudden anger discarded. "I think I'd better tell you some more, Compton, just on the odd chance you run into it by yourself. Laurel has a barrel a month of refined sugar coming in to a staff sergeant in the one-o-four—the one married to the French wife. They live up at Blery, the village."

"By God, I'll. . . ."

"No. You won't, unless you want those kids to go back to beet crystals on their oatmeal and in their cakes. You'll leave it alone, just like I'm doing, and somebody up in the Beaumonde freight office is. Zero, you don't fool these people, not for long. But one or two out of every hundred has a heart as well as a reporting pencil. Besides, Laurel's beautiful—and in France . . . well, you know."

Parker reached into his lower desk drawer and took up a folder. "I'm going to strain your loyalty, Zero, with a direct order not to repeat to a living human being what I'm fixing to tell you."

Parker hunted for the desired page, laying aside the folder as his eyes scanned dates and names beside a series of operations which had occurred between February and the twentieth day of April, at the French hospital in Beaumonde. The first on the list, one of a series of four operations, was on an infant with a harelip and cleft palate. Eggerton, from Paris had done the next with Abach's assistance, an improvement on a boy's ear. The third was a partial hysterectomy on a farm woman from Crecy who sold Laurel Compton eggs once a week. The fourth was the removal of a benign tumor from an eighty-seven-year-old widow in upper Beaumonde. Parker glanced up at Compton and said, "What do you think of Abach?"

"Best Goddam doctor in the world, Sir!"

"You know him well?"

"Pretty well. Doesn't exert himself to charm anybody, but he's dedicated, Sir."

"Especially to your wife?" Parker watched him closely. Compton's hands clenched. His jaw made a round ridge at the apex where it gritted.

"Especially, Sir."

"You can't really take a joke, can you, Compton?"

"You had a little too much to say about my wife the night we met, Sir, in Corliss. I . . . well, she's not *in* the Air Force."

"Too Goddamned bad, too. Seriously, Zero, you'll be in Cannes next week when this dedication ceremony at Blery comes off. I've got to be there because the Governor's coming. You don't really mind if I take Abach in your place? There'll only be Laurel and Ruth MacDonald and me, but I figured Abach could serve two purposes. Take your place and make my bread-and-butter speech. He speaks French fluently, you know."

Zero stared through the window. His brows came steadily together. A look of fleet terror flicked through his eyes as he arose slowly from his chair. Parker's back was to the window. He had not heard the black twin jet making its approach because it carried sound behind it, but Zero had seen the redundant dipping of the left wing. He knew—knew what was coming before flame burst like sprigs of ribbon behind the exploding pod.

Parker whirled and the pair watched the plane disappear a few feet above ground behind the new wooden barracks. Then a cloud of black-orange flame and smoke backdropped the entire barracks. All three telephones atop Parker's desk began to ring at one time, their sounds overcome by the raucous twang of the crash bell.

Zero was running, out of Parker's office, down two flights of stairs, out the door, across the ramp to the new fire truck pulling out of its berth from the first floor of Base Operations. Still running, Zero pounded twice on the mammoth red door and an asbestos-clad fireman flipped a lever which opened the hydraulic door. Zero mounted the cab without a ripple while the vehicle was moving at five or six miles an hour. Staring straight ahead into the holocaust some four hundred yards away, he clamped his jaws in tension until the explosion finally came. A sob caught his throat.

The fireman at his side flipped three foam valves into ready position, his face paling as the black tailpiece came free of fire and landed to the side, smoldering but absurdly unmarred.

"Red. Hunerd 'n fourth. I can see the num'ers—six-o-nine-five."

"Stone," sobbed Zero. "I told Edney the poor son of a bitch couldn't fly."

2

The first fatal crash in eighteen months—the first in the 104th—took its toll in morale. The five-piece orchestra imported from Amsterdam for the weekend played to three couples in the Officers' Club on Saturday evening and decided to forego the Sunday afternoon tea dance.

Monday morning Zero appeared at eleven A.M. for his daily briefing from Parker. When four or five minutes had gone by with no sound except Parker's attempt to fire his pipe, Zero said, "Sir, what was it you were gonna tell me?"

"When?" Parker knew perfectly well, but he eyed the younger man in pretended quandary.

"When the bells went off."

"I only wanted to be sure you didn't care if I took Abach to Blery, since Laurel was going."

"No, Sir. I don't mind," he said. "Why should I?"

"Don't let this thing get away with you, Zero. We've had a damned good record."

"I know it, Sir." Zero wiped a hand needlessly beneath his nose. "But I knew Stone—I let . . . I. . . ."

"You let Edney talk you out of it?"

"You know?"

"Edney makes a full account of that in his written report. He may be a sentimental fool, Zero, but he's no coward."

"I know it, Sir." Too restless to keep sitting, Zero stood up. "I think as much of Edney as a brother, Sir."

Parker squinted above the pipe smoke. "I feel that way about

Sam Abach." Zero met his eyes now in full attention for the first time in the interlude.

Zero said, unsmiling, "My wife and Abach have known each other since they were kids. Her brother, too. A sort of closed fraternity. Her brother's dead."

"I see."

"I doubt that you do, Sir, because I don't."

Parker grimaced and rounded his desk. He swung a fraternal arm around Zero's shoulders and turned him toward the door as they moved slowly along. "Zero, the only test is how you cope with it."

Framed in the door, Zero looked down at his Colonel with a glint of a grin, but his eyes were serious. "I could cope with anything, Sir, if I knew how to get Laurel to move back to my room."

Parker's chuckle ripped out unrepressed. He said without a moment's pause, "Hell, play it smarter than I did! Play like you're sick! That always melts them—you know, maternal instinct."

Zero Compton went directly from Parker's office to Abach's, surprising the latter not only with his amiable, unhurried visit but also with news that he suspected his liver was out of whack. A few black dots when he stood up too quickly. Lightheaded in the mornings when he got out of bed. And a dark-green taste on his tongue from morning to night. He left the doctor's office headed for home, having promised to lay off drinks for a week—why hadn't Abach made him stick out his tongue?—and to stay around the house the next two days.

Before Zero had time to reach his house, however, Abach had telephoned Laurel. "Zero's taking Stone's death out on himself, Laurel. You'll never believe it, but he came on his own a while ago to tell me he's got an upset liver. He needs to get his mind off himself and that crash. You'll try to cheer him up a bit?"

Instinctively, she thought of going to the master bedroom to turn the covers back and ready the room, but next, she realized Zero would be furious if he knew Abach had informed her.

In truth, Laurel felt compassion toward Zero, for recent days had not been easy for her either. Stone's French wife had declined aid from all the officers' wives except Laurel. At Mrs. Stone's request, she remained two nights, sleeping when the woman did, or helping tend the handsome infant, whose age exceeded proper limits defined in marriage papers by some three months. This gave Laurel no concern in her preoccupation with the child's tragedy. He would never know his own father.

Depressed by this, she doubted that she could go through with Parker's request that she talk with the young flyer's parents, who were telephoning by appointment from the States. They wanted their son's widow to bring her baby and live with them. Stone had been an only child.

Three times in the privacy of Parker's office, the swollen-faced widow interrupted Laurel's attempt to speak with the grieved father. Did they know? demanded Mrs. Stone. Did they understand when the baby came? Laurel saw it was impossible to resolve the woman's destination without stating the now inconsequential question, which she did as tersely as possible. To Laurel, the unrefusable answer lay in the heartbroken plea of Lieutenant Stone's father as he answered, "Tell Marguerite this is her home now. Tell her we wait, and beg her to give us a try, Mrs. Compton."

It was Laurel who accompanied the uncertain widow next day to Orly, having left in Parker's chauffeured car two hours after the Memorial Service. Zero had stood beside the car at the last moment, asking Laurel once more to get the girl to agree to his going, but when Laurel translated, Marguerite Loisye Stone stared straight ahead, clutching her sleeping baby.

Yes, Laurel felt sorry for her husband. Accepting the labeled bottle of pills Abach had given him, she quickly read the four-hour dosage and listened to Zero's explanation. Then perhaps he made his first mistake, for Laurel said to him, "Why don't you move into my bedroom? It's agreeable up there. You'll have a new scene to look at—the view of the marshaling yards is fabulous—and you can see Vervins' farm on a clear day."

Zero did not answer. He was in his own bed next day at noon when Abach dropped by to check on his progress. Laurel smiled as he complained, "Christ, Abach! What's in those pills? I feel like somebody's borrowed my knees every time I stand up to go to the bathroom."

Abach chuckled sympathetically. "It's called a cathartic, Zero. Sort of a diplomaed edition of Carter's Little Liver Pills. Didn't you ever get a dose of that when you were little? I'll bet you don't remember!"

Downstairs, seeing Abach out, Laurel expressed surprise that the pills were something stronger than sugar. "I started to give him those sympathy pills, Laurel, but then I got to thinking. Zero's pretty hard to fool. Besides, a man who hits the bottle as regularly as he does—well, a good catharsis won't hurt him, and I'll guarantee it'll be a week before bourbon tastes good to him again."

Abach started to go out the door, but he turned back, hand on the knob. "Why'd you sleep in a chair last night?"

She chuckled. "You're psychic!"

"No, I just noticed your official chair-sleeping comforter hanging on the lounge by Zero's window. Is he rolling and tumbling *that* much in his sleep?" Abach's eyes were mildly concerned.

"No, I thought he might need something during the night —you know, a glass of water or an extra pillow. You know. . . ."

Next morning, Zero came quite near asking the same question. Laurel returned to his room with the morning tray of coffee. He was already dressing, but he said the moment she entered, "I haven't been seriously ill. Why'd you stick to my side like glue?"

She blinked, noting his thinness, his gaunt cheeks. "Why—I . . . uh . . . old habits are hard to break. I'm not completely unfeeling."

"Why?" His trousers were suspended halfway between knees and waist as he studied her through a faint scowl. "Why? Laurel, why?"

She poured a cup of coffee, her back to him, and then turned around. "You were ill. You might have needed something." She smiled at him, relieved to note that he felt better. She followed him down the stairs and watched as he gathered his garrison cap and blue overcoat from the umbrella rack.

"You won't need that coat, Zero, not at Cannes!"

He slung the hat back at the hook, exploding, "Oh, Christ! I knew I forgot something. Laurel, I've got to pack."

Dedication of the playground at Blery orphanage—the ribbon-cutting and champagne fest—were postponed until May tenth in deference to the American tragedy.

At the appointed hour, Parker handed red, white, and blue beribboned scissors to the Governor of Gregny, who then cut the satin tricolors crossing the gate of the new playground.

With some difficulty, the Governor read a prepared speech of two hundred or so English words. France was humbled, he said in his crippled accent, by the magnanimity of American officers' wives at Beaumonde Air Base toward France's children. Parker, who had conversed with the Governor in careful German prior to the outdoor ceremony, responded to the speech with a nod and by glancing at Abach, who stood between Laurel and Ruth MacDonald.

The doctor touched Ruth's arm and the two stepped forward a few paces until they stood before the French Governor and his entourage, as well as the Mayor of Blery and his wife, and about two dozen others. In proper sequence of rank, Abach acknowledged the presence of French dignitaries and extended the regret of his Colonel and Mrs. MacDonald that neither could respond in the language of the country in which they had been so warmly received, *et cetera*.

It was a delightful speech, all agreed as the group moved across the cobblestone street toward the home of Blery's Mayor for the champagne conclusion. An hour or so later, Parker left in his staff car, while Abach drove Ruth and Laurel in his new Triomphe, first to Ruth's village, which was a mere four and a half miles from Blery.

As they headed into the great St Gobain forest—the short cut to Laurel's house—Abach teased her, "Parker's wise to your chicanery!"

"Which?"

"The playground."

"Yes?"

"He told me so."

She shrugged. "Hmmm."

"How'd you do it?"

"I just told Ruth aiding orphans was Parker's idea, which was true, by the way."

"And what'd you tell Parker?"

"That Ruth was afraid he wouldn't approve."

"Wasn't there a simpler way, a more direct approach?"

"Oh, I think it saved a year's deliberation. They support each other unreservedly, you see?"

"How's that?"

"A secret society called native Texans."

They rode five or six miles in silence. Laurel gazed at budding trees, conscious of the warmth inside the closed car as late afternoon sun flecked it now and then.

The doctor glanced at his watch. "Well, Zero should be cutting his ribbon down at Cannes about now. What do you think about that rest camp?"

"I think Cannes is the most expensive place on earth for a man on TDY."

"Why do you say that?"

"Because Zero spends two or three hundred dollars any week he's there."

"You're not pinched, Laurel."

"No. But twice, I've had to send cables to get funds transferred to our joint account at Baton Rouge."

"He doesn't gamble that much."

"I know it. He tells me he's had the same thing happen every time he gets down there. Some airman or two who arrived with ten dollars on them and they go crazy in those night spots."

"They pay him back?"

"He says he hasn't lost a dime, but of course what they pay him goes right in his pocket."

"If I didn't know you better, I'd wonder if you were a tightwad."

As they emerged from the lower perimeter of the great forest, Laurel noticed on the horizon far beyond Beaumonde's hill a cluster of white thunderheads. "It's going to storm," she said idly.

"You'll be up late tonight!" accused her friend.

"Maybe. Shutting windows or laying out drain pans under the leaks."

The two rode along a mile and a half in comfortable silence before Abach asked, "By the way, you found us a new patient yet?"

"No." She shook her head in emphasis. "I'm not trying. Both the Blery children will be having repeat rounds. You've got enough to do right now."

"What about you?"

She knew what he meant. Had she lost interest? No. Of course not, but she had seen much earlier in the game the wisdom of Abach's initial reaction. There was simply no limit when one started out to repair a population—village, town, or area. Every mole on a storekeeper's face or hands, every limping peasant, even the coughs which echoed through a classroom. There was no place to stop if one dived in headlong, and so it automatically became a limited proposition.

She said none of these things, though, nor much else as they approached the hill of Beaumonde. At the edge of town, Abach suggested they go on up the Hill and dine with Monsieur Pitran at the Écu.

That night Laurel continued to feel edgy because one storm followed another until midnight when a particularly violent wind lashed torn branches against the first-floor windows. Laurel heard the glass crash onto the salon floor. When she reached the room, Olande was already securing a wool blanket across the broken window.

Back in bed, she heard a heavy piece of metal fly against the roof and was disappointed but not very surprised the next morning to find a wet circle in the plaster ceiling not far from her chimney. When Olande appeared with coffee, Laurel said she must send for a man to repair the roof. The maid paled, "Madame, I do not wish to interfere, but by French law it is the landlord's duty to have the roof repaired."

"I know that," replied Laurel, "but I do not wish to wait until *next* spring."

"Monsieur Hachère. . . ."

"The repair will cost money."

"But, Madame, there is only one man in Beaumonde who knows the art to repair slate shingles on a roof."

"One is enough."

"Madame," wailed Olande. "The man is Cambot, the bad imbecile!"

Laurel gave her a penetrating look. The fear was not pretended. Calmly Laurel said, "I have seen Cambot often, Olande. I have bought chestnuts from him for Brick, as you know. And I am no longer afraid of germs in his clothes for I saw inside his garret when we were on that Christmas Eve tour and I can tell you every board of the floor is scrubbed."

Olande's eyes were downcast, her cheeks flushed. "Madame, I doubt that you have in America. . . ." Her voice choked off.

"We have most troubles in America, including leaky roofs."

Leaving an unconvinced Olande, Laurel determinedly went out of the house and headed downhill toward the railroad station where Cambot usually was, this time of morning.

3

Chris was asleep and Olande had departed on an errand when Cambot rang the gate bell around two that afternoon. By the time Laurel reached the door, she found him gesturing inaudibly toward an enormous and weathered ladder already reaching toward the roof. He pointed then to a box set on the walk, a crude-handled, grease-soaked rectangular box from which protruded a

T-square, chisels, and a half dozen shingles. Laurel smiled and nodded acknowledgment. Cambot bowed deeply from the waist. Involuntarily, she again nodded. Then, she guessed his need to go into the attic. She stepped to one side, holding the door, but he bowed again and refused to go before her.

Finally settled at her desk, she heard high overhead the scraping of his boots as he descended the stairs. She paused once in a while to listen to the rhythm of his delicate hammering and chiseling. Soon, from the kitchen, she heard Olande's unusual clanging and banging of utensils in predinner cooking. When Chris awoke, the maid set him down in the kitchen with carte blanche to pots and pans. Laurel knew Olande was nervous with the odd man working on the house and wandering periodically through it.

It was more than an hour after his entry that Laurel paused to have a cigarette. She listened acutely, hearing through the library floor sounds of Olande closing a dresser drawer in her bedroom, and Chris's fluffy, soprano gurgles. But something was silent. Laurel listened. She sped up two flights of stairs and peered quickly around the attic. Cambot was not there. Down the stairs she fled, down the hall and through the front door. The ladder still leaned against the eaves. She backed nearer the courtyard gate to peer at the roof but he was not there. Puzzled, she let her gaze descend the ladder a rung at a time, until her eye clung to the eighth from the bottom, which was a jagged pair of ends slanting obliquely to the ground.

Laurel bounded the few steps across the courtyard to a broad Pfitzer juniper, certain before she saw the bright tear in its limbs what she would find. Mercifully, Cambot was conscious. She wedged her back against the shrub foliage and bent over his supine form. Teeth against her lip, she peered at the opaque eyes, which seemed illumined only by a glaze of pain. He made an effort to speak, but the sound came in convulsive grunts like those of a winded child.

Surprised by her own voice, she spoke in the French tense automatically issued to children, "Thee must lie very still. The doctor will come." She glanced down then at her hand which, seemingly of its own accord, clasped his firmly. "Olande!" she yelled at the top of her voice, and in answer came the creak of the front gate. Laurel whirled. Abach's eyes darted to the broken rung of the ladder before, wordlessly, he turned back through the gate and got his kit from the car.

He telephoned the outcome from the French hospital. Cambot had, miraculously, no fractures—only bruises and a sprained hip. Also, the jag of the rung had opened his scapula to the tune of four stitches. It was a week later, however, before Abach told her the entire story.

"When I told him why Stigault, who's the head of the French hospital, and I wanted to look at his eye, he remained immobile. Afterwards, Stigault asked him how he'd like to have clear sight back in that eye. He nodded. I asked him whether he was afraid to let an American doctor operate and he pointed to me and shook his head. He wasn't afraid. Stigault and I agreed not to tell him I was getting Vernon to come up from Paris. Vernon's an eye man who needed four more operations when I left Am-Hop to get his Board."

"It's done, Abach? Already done?"

"Yep, Laurel. And Vernon says he can fix him a set of lenses which will do a lot for his other eye. He won't have to teeter anymore like a man walking the brink of Hell and already losing his balance. He'll walk and walk well."

"Thank God," she said. "By the way, Abach, how'd you happen along at the ideal moment?"

"I meant to tell you about that. I'd just left Stigault's office. He helped me out of a jam. You wouldn't believe such a thing could happen unless you'd been over here to see how things get snarled. There was a wreck the other night, American officer, barely scratched, but his date was killed. Apparently, he had a fear of getting tangled up with French authorities, so he told the gendarmes and Air Police and everybody that the woman was American. No papers on her. The French released the body on his word at the scene of the wreck. It was brought to our deep freeze to be sent later to QM morgue at Paris."

"So?"

"The stiff was still out at the Base. Turned out the woman was a prostitute—French—but on top of everything else she'd given this American officer an alias. So, through normal channels, none of us was getting anywhere. The Beaumonde police office reported politely back to everybody that no such person existed in the files of either Gregny or Paris. My exec had the idea of shipping her on to QM at Paris, but it seemed a little indecent. I went up to see Stigault and all he had to do was telephone his brother-in-law, the Chief of Police."

"But how come you stopped at my house?"

"I'd seen torn trees up and down the hill, and I just thought I'd drop in and ask what the storm did to your house. Of course, when I saw the ladder leaning against the roof, I had a pretty good idea."

"It's all so propitious, isn't it?" Her eyes were thoughtful. "I don't think I was sent to France for a certain time, but there's no doubt in my mind that you were, Sam."

"Damn Sam!" exploded Abach with frowning humor. "Nobody but the Air Force and Army ever punished me with that first name of mine—except you and Zero."

"You're a saint, anyway. Where you headed now?"

"This'll kill you. Parker got an invitation to attend the first Rotary luncheon Beaumonde's ever had."

"Rotary!" she shrieked.

"Yep! It's hit Beaumonde. You know, International."

"Are you one?"

"Well, yes. But Parker's one too. And the French were informed of that, but he badgered me into going because I speak French." He stood up to go. "Well, I'll be running along before the creamed chicken sogs up the patty shell."

"Oh, Abach!" she cried in mirth. "You don't think French Rotarians will have to put up with that standard male banquet fare, too?"

They parted laughing, and when Abach had gone, she walked upstairs and went onto the tiny balcony at the front of the house. From here she could watch the trolley emerge uphill from luxuriant trees, teeter across its bridge and disappear into more foliage. She gazed to the crown of Miss Victory amid the little park and saw, at the front of the olive wreath, a tangle of twigs and brush dangling gracefully. Her grip tightened on the wrought-iron railing as her gaze narrowed to identify the dull, mauve-scarlet of the mother cardinal who twitted at a mettlesome, crimson male descending to plant his feet on the head of the concrete dove held in the statue's hand.

For a moment Laurel felt at peace with the world. A heavy, sustaining peace which she somehow associated with the placidity of people in their sixties. Filled with the same lassitude—it was full spring in northern France—she stood again on the little balcony the last day of May, for she waited daily to see what the mother cardinal would do about the shortage of limbs when the baby birds had to learn to fly. That morning, however, Laurel studied the male bird with nettling preoccupation. The saucy thatch atop the scarlet head reminded her for all the world of Michel Berteaux's prissy self-confidence. Suddenly, she began to laugh aloud, thinking what had happened to Michel, but her laughter was quickly arrested by his arrival.

He brought his small Simca to a grueling halt on the sandy curb. He reached the front door without seeing her, his head down, eyes troubled, and no smile upon his mouth.

Laurel entered the salon to find him literally sunk into the couch, his béret slung aside like wadded paper. He glanced up, scarcely seeing her but saying, "I may have done a horrible mistake."

"What's the matter?"

"I've asked that girl to marry me."

Her heart smiled irrepressibly, but she kept a straight face, thinking of signs sixty and ninety days old. There was the letter Solange de Guilliamcourt had written Michel in February, asking him to recommend a guide service for her first (unchaperoned) fortnight of tourist Paris. Then came Véronique de Berteaux's sudden descent in mid-April upon the Compton house, her scribbling of the name Guilliamcourt in a small book after she detained Laurel long enough upstairs prior to departure to ask—to beg—the name of the girl which had come to her only through rumor.

"What did that girl say?" said Laurel lightly.

"She said, 'How about July first?'" His smile was rich and

distracted now. "Who but Solange would answer a wedding proposal with such a question?"

"She's very clever—very . . . well, elfin, Michel."

"Where's Zero? Still at Cannes?"

"No, he and Parker are up at Bruchstein this week. Really," she laughed, "I scarcely see him."

"Well," exclaimed Michel, rising to his feet, "you might at least register surprise or exclaim congratulations or do something befitting such an occasion!" He began to pace before the hearth.

She asked what his mother had said on hearing his news. Michel's eyes widened in declamation. "I *love* Solange! Why should I *punish* her?"

She throttled an impulse to heave the bundle of knitting at him. "Why should you punish Véronique? She's waited ten years for such a piece of news! Why shouldn't she enjoy it from the first?"

"My mother will abuse her. You wait and see!"

"Why?"

"Because she didn't find her."

Laurel's eyes were dark with anger. What right had he to act as if he were the first person on earth who had chosen his own mate? But as she glanced across the room, she felt unwelcome pity for him. He was still on the couch, both hands spread to cover his distraught face.

"Laurel," he moaned through his fingers. "I can't tell her! I can't! I'm afraid."

"Of what?"

"Her interference."

"All right, I can ease your pain. I told her a month ago. You know she came here with Philippe—drove down for the day? I'm sure her investigations came out. . . ."

He was on his feet, tiptoeing in rage. When his voice came, it was a hoarse rasp. "You bitch! You miserable, meddling fiend! How much did she pay you to spy on me? God damn you, Laurel!"

She could only blink as she heard his leather heels click rapidly toward the front door. Though the door had been open wide on his entry, Michel slammed it with vicious force.

She heard no more of him for a week, and did not bother to tell Zero of more than the proposal and alleged acceptance by Solange.

On June 7, Véronique's hasty note arrived: "Michel came to L'Alouette from your house last week—with glad tidings, Laurel. The date is not yet set for the wedding, but I predict it shall be a day or two around July first."

Laurel sent a telegram, briefly worded but assuring Michel's mother her joy was shared. Two days later came a second letter from the Marquise:

> My dear Laurel, Michel has confessed to me his naughtiness upon receiving your disclosure. Do not reproach yourself, Laurel. I came to you and you did what I asked. His reason is obscure now from the nectar of first happiness. He will come to understand your aid. The marriage contracts were completed two days ago in Paris and this coming week end we shall all go to Paris where Solange's father proposes to host a restaurant dinner for our meeting. I feel somehow you should be there, as I imagine you always are my own beloved daughter. At least, had she lived, she could not be more dear to my sometimes lonely heart, and bless you, my child, and both your children, and tall Zero. V.deB.

Zero was at home the June Sunday evening when Michel drove up to the Beaumonde house unannounced to park his car ahead of his future father's-in-law—a car full of Solange's relatives returning to Belgium from Paris.

Michel and Solange preceded the group into the courtyard, their heads almost touching as Michel spoke softly. From the salon window Laurel heard his words. He was explaining the Comptons' church affiliations; they belonged to the American version of the Church of England. Solange whispered back, "Then the Queen of England is the head of their Church?" Michel shook his head negatively, speaking of Sacraments, Baptism, Confirmation, Communion, Extreme Unction; of the Trinity and Hell and Heaven.

Laurel had no idea what might be conjured to serve eleven people but she could smile at Michel's determination to have his fiancée understand the Comptons were not ordinary pagans.

Solange, however, gave him a broad smile, exposing her faultless array of teeth. "Ah, oui?" she whispered in thin agreement, "but don't try to tell me they have the Bible!"

Zero was waiting to answer their knock, and already taking orders for drinks by the time Michel bent above Laurel's hand to plant a neat, somehow apologetic greeting. She was in the kitchen, beginning a cheese fondue when Michel caught her alone. "I owe you a thousand thanks for paving my way with my mother, Laurel. Really, I know it."

"I understand. Forget it."

Then he glanced back over his shoulder to be sure no one was approaching on silent steps. "Laurel," he said edgily, "don't bother cooking. I see you've no servant, and I've a wonderful idea, if you'll let me go through with it." He proposed in an unheralded show of generosity to provide the amount in francs that a Sunday evening supper for the large party would cost in dollars. "I'm dying to have my future father-in-law see the new Officers' Club, especially since it was decorated by Belgians."

The idea appealed to Laurel, who had dreaded table service essential to such a group. Solange's aunts were too aged to be initiated into the crudities of buffet dinner. "Go ask Zero," she answered, "and come back and tell me what he says."

In moments he was back to watch the delicious melted cheese and toasted squares being readied for chafing dish and tray. "He said, Fine! But Laurel, there's one thing you must do for me. Somehow." She said flatly that she was finished forever with the role of American meddler. "You'll agree with me about this," sighed Michel. "I don't know whether you've noticed that Solange wears that awful red lacquer on her toes. I can't say anything about it yet, but I wonder . . . could you somehow hint to her when you go upstairs?"

"No."

Nettled, he pocketed his hands and tried imagination. "You wouldn't mind offering her a pair of hose? I hate for American officers meeting my fiancée for the first time to see her bare feet through those sandals. I think it's a strike against you and Zero, too."

Laurel reflected silently that Zero had a fetish against dress shoes without stockings. Upstairs a bit later she struggled delicately to convey the offer of stockings without mentioning Michel, saying only that it was the custom during Sunday afternoon and evening in the Club.

Radiant Solange regarded her behind a bland smile and sighed, "Oh, merci, Madame Compton! But I'll wear stockings someday when I'm old—say, thirty."

Laurel thought of this again en route to Paris with Zero for an overnight stay the twentieth of June. She had no doubt that Michel was riding roughshod over proprieties governing a couple not yet married. Solange had no reason to dislike Laurel, she deduced, unless he had told her the proverbial "all"; and Michel would have waited until after their wedding—unless . . . unless . . . but what did it matter?

En route to the big announcement party to be given in the Jockey Club, Zero said to Laurel, "I guess we're luckier than we know—the only Americans to be invited out of five hundred couples."

Laurel laughed. "If Michel said five hundred, you'd better discount twenty percent."

"Laurel, what's the matter with that girl?"

"She's twenty. It will pass."

"Oh, Christ! That's no excuse for . . . what does she think a smile is? An excuse for a brain?"

"Michel loves her."

"Well, she hates your guts."

"I'm not marrying her," said Laurel drily.

"I don't like the way she eyes you when you're not looking."

"Oh, Zero—what does it matter?"

"God damn it, I don't like her."

"Well, she likes you. Of course, you never went for that ingénue type." Laurel yawned and went on, "She'll fill out nicely after a couple of babies."

"Yeah, and I wouldn't be surprised if Michel hasn't started the first one already."

"Don't be trite."

"Well, when you get right down to it, Laurel, what kind of a woman would marry him?"

"He's your friend, not mine."

"You're full of crap. In all the time I've put up with him, he's asked me about two subjects—hunting and war. Laurel, I've heard him search you for advice on everything from decorating his house to choosing his bride's trousseau to running his table for those hunts. And she saw that, too. He's probably got her craw so crammed full of your glories that she hates you for no other reason."

"Maybe so. I don't care. It's too late. We've only a year more to be exposed to them, after all."

"He apologized to me outside the door the other night before Solange's relatives got away."

"What for?"

"He said not to think anything about Solange's behavior toward you—because she's overawed by American women."

4

A golden sun intensified the blue of earth's dome on that July first. Not a single fleecy cloud cast its shadow on the road between Beaumonde and Belgium, making it harder than ever for Laurel to account for heaviness of heart which increased as each of the hundred and thirty miles sped by.

At the hour of the Comptons' arrival, the bridal party and members of both families were ensconced with photographers and so, having left cards with the Guilliamcourt butler, they drove on six miles to a resort hotel where Michel had reserved a floor for all of his invited guests who might wish to change clothes for the wedding.

Zero had conceded to Michel's request that he wear a summer

uniform with black tie and combat-awarded ribbons. (Zero drew the line when Michel said medals!)

Laurel disrobed of her black faille suit and carefully unwrapped the gown bought in Paris for this occasion. Of navy barathea, it had that stark simplicity of cut, that ease of line deliciously apart from high fashion. Her wide-brimmed hat was covered in pale green velvet and laced solidly on the underside of the brim with miniature lilies of the valley.

Zero let out a low, admiring whistle as she approached their rendezvous point on the mezzanine of the hotel. Bellboys, clerks, loiterers, and entering guests turned to stare after her as the couple left the lobby. Even the customarily frigid doorman called for, waited upon, and opened the door of their car without once lifting his eyes from Laurel's face.

Zero teased her during the short drive back to the Chapel edging the Guilliamcourt country estate. "You're mowing 'em down today, Madame Compton!"

She brushed an imaginary speck from the shoulder of her dress. "Makes you wonder, doesn't it, what kind of a world it would be if clothes had never got beyond a fig leaf?"

"Well, I'll say one thing—the way you look today will steal the *bride's* thunder!"

"You oughtn't to say that. It sounds like bad luck!"

"I'm not gonna take it back; no woman looks the way you do right now by accident."

She shrugged. "It's silly, but I did want to look well today—and now that I stop to think of it, why?"

"Where *was* Guy?"

Smarting about the cheeks with a sudden flush, Laurel stalled. "When?"

"At the big engagement party in the Jockey Club?"

"I've meant to ask you that. I've no idea where he's been or what he's done since that hunt in January."

"You're forgetting," said Zero calmly as he parked the car in a gravel area behind the small Church, "I told you he was at the Palace hunt those three days in Belgium—February." He cut the engine and took the keys out to place them atop the sun visor. "Laurel, maybe he got enough of Americans when I stood him up last January because of that alert. He wasn't very friendly to me in Belgium. I can't put a finger on it—but he was withdrawn. Michel said afterwards not to pay any attention; Guy was moody. But then, somewhere during the engagement shindig, I heard Michel cussing him to Philippe. Philippe said when Michel walked away that Guy hadn't even answered the invitation. Hadn't sent Michel any form of congratulations on his engagement. Oh, well—it's none of our business, but I have a feeling he won't show up today."

The pair sat in momentary silence, examining their separate thoughts before Zero made a gesture of impatience. "Well, it's twenty of twelve. Let's get inside and find our places."

The wedding march began when a small boy appeared in the doorway at back, sunlight picking up the gilt of his Prayer Book and a glint of gold in his thick hair. Rays of deflected light danced gaily on the ceiling a second before the boy escaped sunlight and moved into the shadowed aisle.

Next came Détrie, Solange's lovely, married sister, and in a moment, Michel, splendid in morning attire. Laurel swallowed with concealed effort. Her pulse raced. Beside Michel walked Guy, his eyes more hollow than they had been that May night in another century.

She turned quickly to stare at the Eternal Light on the foreign altar. Solange's father moved into Laurel's peripheral vision. He stared straight ahead, moving regally with his daughter's hand in the crook of his elbow. Seen gauzily through her fine veil, Solange had an ephemeral beauty.

The vows and nuptial Mass seemed interminable to Laurel. Then there came an hour and twenty minutes in the slow-moving line from château entrance to the second drawing room where the entire wedding party and two families received felicitations from four hundred guests.

Standing immediately before Zero, Laurel managed to swerve her gaze over Guy's face in the most inadequate of greetings. She had not one whole glimpse of his beloved face; she dared not—with Solange on Guy's left and Zero at her back.

Relieved to be done with the formality, Laurel welcomed the spasmodic winding of the reception line into the great courtyard and its dispersion beneath symmetrically planted oak trees where tables for eight or twelve or sixteen had been set above the luxuriant lawn.

A group of hunters began to cluster about Zero and Laurel, and on the surface she felt pleasantly diverted. She saw a servant approach Zero with a note in which Michel claimed Zero and Laurel were holding up start of the bridal luncheon in the château dining hall.

Instantly, Laurel protested. "Zero, we don't belong with their families today!"

"Christ, Laurel! You out of your head? We're guests! We do what they say!"

She felt a faint wave of nausea as she stood beside her husband in the archway of the gilt-encrusted dining room. Many of the French and Belgian faces beamed as brightly at the American pair as they had around Noël's or the Comptons' tables. Men were assaulting Zero now with ribald handshakes and hearty smiles, and the gay fellows began to form a ridiculously curved line, passing Laurel along with festive hand-kissing. This led her to the end of the great room, to a corner diagonally removed from Zero, Michel, and Solange. The hum of three languages sang around her as she was confronted by Guy. His head bent fleetly above her hand and when he raised up, he continued to hold her hand.

"We're marooned!" she said, glancing at the empty space on either side of them. Her eyes laughed, imploring him to smile.

He said in a low voice, "For a whole night of Hell, I believed the lie with which you tried to save me."

"Why didn't you show up at the engagement party?" she asked nervously.

"Laurel, I wouldn't be here today were it not Michel's wedding. I can't stand to see you across a room. Laurel, I must have you with me. My endurance is running out." The urgency in his eyes was unmistakable. She turned around to find Zero's back. Guy still held her hand. His eyes followed her gaze to her husband's head; Zero was encircled by a group of merry women.

"Guy," she pleaded, "I'm afraid people will. . . ."

"People? Look around this room, Laurel! How many of them

know you and I are here? Look at them! Laughing, flirting, subduing their impatience for the food and champagne. From this afternoon's champagne, there will be by tonight a dozen new. . . ."

Laurel interrupted, "Guy, this is scarcely the proper time to. . . ."

"When *is* the proper time? Laurel, I've waited alone six months for a letter or a telephone call or a visit from you. In the name of God, I can't work in the daytime. I can't sleep at night. I've walked over half of Paris, I swear by my life! How long—how long will you torture me with your silence?"

She said quietly, "It has not been always easy to remain silent, but it is possible to carry on life without you, however sad, I find. . . ."

"And I find only that we are both weak, you not to have come already and I not to have taken you and the children."

"All right, you force me to discuss what I have no right to. Guy, you're Catholic."

"Of course!" he said with visible surprise. "I shall always be, but I shall not apolo. . . ." Then the implication of her statement arrived, reflected in his inclined face, the slight elevation of his sorely troubled brow. "Few things in life are gained without sacrifice. I will not have to leave the Church, only to. . . ."

"I have never thought of myself as anybody's perpetual mortal sin."

"Then, Laurel, you understand my Church and you therefore realize how difficult has been such a decision?"

Laurel stared at him a moment. "Yes, Guy, I made that unforgiveable good-bye speech to you at Noël in a last effort to exonerate both of us. If I thought you could stop being a Catholic —ever. . . ."

"You're afraid, Laurel, and life is passing us by!"

"Let my hand go, Guy!"

"One word, Laurel. Yes or no?"

"No. Guy! No!"

His lips broke into a smile. "I cannot hear you, Laurel."

"No. No. No."

300

"*Laurel!*" shrilled Michel's voice above the crowd. "Tell Guy to quit whispering love words so we can begin lunch!"

Violently, Guy wheeled to face him. Alone, the bride and groom were already seated at the middle of the large oval table. Laurel's gaze darted swiftly over the still crowd. All eyes riveted to Guy. Then a waiter with an actor's sense of timing swept through the swinging door from the kitchen, balancing above his head a tray of glasses in which champagne already sparkled. The waiter swung in an arc, pausing barely long enough for Guy's hand to reach the tray.

Guy lifted a glass as other arms stretched tensely toward the gliding waiter and his tray. "I drink first to the bride. . . ." Guy's eyes flamed against Michel's like freshly red branding irons. "And to the groom! May he ever be—as bold!"

Guy raised his glass higher and riotous laughter ballooned in the room.

Still fixed to her spot, Laurel glanced from Michel to Solange, only to flinch at icy hatred in the girl's stare. At once, the bride fanned a wan smile across her pink-tinted lips, but Laurel had seen too much.

5

At eleven o'clock next morning, it was misting on the hill. A cloud extended as far down the peak as the roof top of 14 rue Père Marquette. Laurel sat in her library, studying the dismal weather. Both children played in the kitchen beneath the maid's feet; Brick was uncomfortable with a sudden cold. Zero, red-eyed, sheepish, and headachy, had left in a staff car an hour earlier to retrieve his station wagon, which was in Reims. He had passed out early in the evening on hundred-year-old brandy. Guy had driven Laurel and Zero's unconscious body back to Beaumonde.

All but a few miles back from Belgium, she had slept with her head involuntarily cradled against Guy's. This morning, she blushed amidst efforts to sort out reality and myth, for she remembered well enough the mortification she had felt at the sight of Guy supporting limp, virtually unconscious Zero from the car and up the stairs, but surely, she only imagined that the crown of her head still felt sensitive from caresses during sleep—and the whole of her left breast tingled—as if . . . but no!

She took a fourth sheet of paper and the wide-pointed pen and jet ink. "Guy," she wrote, "it was some kind of test, and now it is time to hand in the papers. . . ."

"Mama, it's raining."

She turned to the window where Brick stood. "Yes, Brick, but it didn't rain for Uncle Michel's wedding. That was the important thing."

"Mama, is rain French?"

"No, Brick. Rain is—it's universal."

"Mama, Philippe's not my uncle either, is he?"

"No, you know that."

"Then why must I call him Uncle?"

"It pleases adults to find children mannerly, respectful."

"Why?"

"Oh, it makes the world more agreeable. Between grownups, too. Philippe is about the age your uncle would have been. He loves you very much. It seems right, therefore, don't you agree?"

"Yes."

"By the way, he'll be arriving this afternoon for a few days' visit. Daddy invited him to come here from the wedding party in Belgium."

"But you like Uncle Guy so much more. Why can't he come here, too?"

"He's busy in Paris."

"I saw him last night. I woke up when he was carrying Daddy past my room." A flash of red mounted on Laurel's neck. She laid down her pen. The child ran to her, flinging his arms about her neck, his face buried from sight. "Last winter I was in the car with Daddy and Uncle Michel one day and—Michel —I mean, Uncle Michel—said funny things about. . . ."

Laurel's heart raced uncontrollably now. "About Uncle Guy and me?" Against her neck, he nodded. "Brick, grown people say things sometimes to surprise each other, the way you make faces for Chris."

He leaned back, staring at her with five-year-old candor. "Laurel, I came to the top of the stairs last night when Uncle Guy was leaving."

She steeled herself to face the situation frankly, whatever it cost. "And you heard me ask him to kiss me good-bye?" The child nodded, slightly relieved in his troubled eyes. "And you heard him say, 'Is that my answer?'" Brick nodded enthusiastically as if suddenly they had begun to play a question and answer game.

Laurel leaned back from him. "Why didn't you come on down the stairs? I'm sure Uncle Guy would have been terribly glad to see how much you've grown since January. You could have told him that none of your clothes fit."

"Does he love me too, Laurel?"

"What do you think?"

"Well," Brick thought it over. "He always treats me special. And he brings me books. And he reads to me and tells me stories. Laurel, what's the word for pois in English?"

"Peas. What Olande's shelling in the kitchen right now for tonight's dinner. Why don't you go and help her?"

Dry of eye, she watched the child skip from the room, and knew she had her answer:

"Guy, we must desist. That is my answer and I feel no real pity for either of us. Brick heard you come and go last night.

"It seems to me I have asked little of you except tolerance, but now I need your help. No letters. No flowers. No calls. And you must never come.

"Au paradis, mon étranger.

LDC."

Frantically, she scrawled his name and Paris address across the envelope, folded the page, got it into the envelope on the third try, and shouted for Olande to take it to the post office immediately.

When the servant was out of the house, Laurel lay with her head across her arms. But no tears came. She felt dry and strong—that cruel, purifying, and sterile strength of those forced to choose irrevocable right. So grieved, so absorbed in grief was Laurel that she did not hear her older son return to the library. First harbinger was a small hand upon her shoulder, his warm breath as he tried to peek at her hidden face. Without raising up, she turned a smile on him.

"Mama, I was afraid you were crying."

"No, Brick. I'm tired. I didn't have enough sleep."

"Oh."

He ambled to the window and Laurel watched him press his tiny nose against the pane. She sat up, staring through the glass at a windy shower falling from gray low-hanging clouds. Against the grayness, she saw silver rain trickling down the glass, and beheld somehow the image of Guy's face as it would look when he read her letter.

"Maman. . . ."

"Speak English to me, Brick."

"In a minute. Regarde, Maman—tears on the window. Maman, are tears French?"

"No." A stifled sob. She dared not cry before him.

"Then, Maman, what are they?"

"Like rain, Brick. Universal."

6

It was a good summer in northern France—very often hot. Peasants waded in the shallow winding creeks while barge families from Redan to Liège paused in midafternoon for swimming in the gray-green canal.

Almost every Friday afternoon Zero left with a new assortment of airmen to vacation at the Cannes rest camp, returning Sunday afternoon or evening with the previous sojourners. Determined to save his leave time for the coming hunt season, he declined to join Laurel and the children for a month's stay at Scheveningen in uppermost Holland. But Laurel had no active complaints against him. His delvings into her own funds had ceased. His travels and the household were supported by his salary, although Laurel had withdrawn a thousand dollars of her own money to give the children and accompanying Olande and her husband the vacation in Holland—a matter Zero was not interested in.

The first person heard from upon her return was Michel, who had spent two months' honeymoon on the Brittany coast. When Zero came home from Cannes, there was an amusing little farce in which Michel made great plans to entertain the Comptons as "our first guests." Zero insisted to Laurel that the invitation included dinner, but when the four had viewed colored slides taken on the honeymoon, Solange brought forth her specialty, a thin sherbet devised in her wedding-gift refrigerator.

Twice in the next fortnight, Michel dropped in with his bride at the convenient hour before dinnertime—and stayed. The next time the Comptons visited Noël, Michel got Laurel aside to implore that she somehow find a way to instill in his bride an interest in menu-planning and cooking. "A man can't live on shirred eggs and sherbet, Laurel, and let me tell you, that's what I've had since we returned to Noël! She doesn't like meat. She doesn't like salad. Laurel, she eats canned peanuts, eggs, and sherbet. And ice cubes. My God!"

She studied his petulant gloom, unable to restrain her amusement. But Michel was in no mood for jesting. "Laurel! Since the first evening in your house, I've dreamed of living in an atmosphere like that—carefree, easy-going warmth in which even a foreigner feels instantly welcome. Where there's always good food and good music and conversation. Laurel, you don't know what it meant to me to be able to bring my friends into your home whenever I liked, and you don't know what you've done for your country's reputation by your hospitality!"

She said with a straight face that he ought to hire regular domestic help instead of a weekly cleaning woman, that he ought to close off the second floor, but Michel wouldn't listen. At the end, he said simply, "Laurel, can't you help me?"

"Help you what?" she demanded flatly.

"Help us have the baby!"

Laurel managed to appear grim. "Most women are able to manage that without much help."

"But if Solange can't even cook, how can she have a baby?"

She wondered how she might have answered him had not Zero appeared over his shoulder at this moment. On the way home, she said to her husband that Solange was six or eight weeks pregnant.

"Laurel, what do you say we make a standing date with them to come and eat with us every Wednesday or Thursday?"

She held her calm. "Why do you say that?"

"Because I'm generally at home that time of the week, and because they're going to come anyway, and it might be better if we knew when to expect them."

"I have a better idea," said Laurel. "Let's start dropping in on them once or twice a week in time for dinner. That might wean them altogether."

"I don't want to do that, Laurel," he said sharply.

"Why?"

"You know God damned well night's the only time I'm really hungry—and I don't like shirred eggs or sherbet. Besides, we can't afford to make them angry."

"Why not?"

"Hunting season's only a few weeks off."

"Michel won't be having any parties this winter. Solange'll see to that."

"You're crazy. With his drawing room all fine and full of furniture now? Laurel, he'll have six hunts instead of four!"

She said nothing as Zero rambled on above the wheel of the night-piercing station wagon between Noël and Beaumonde, not even as he explained Michel's potential value. "After all, Laurel, my primary job is still Franco-American relations and Michel represents the number one Frenchman in this region. If a real crisis arrives, he's our last resort; he's definitely on our side. You never know who you'll need in this business."

Five or six miles went by in fogged silence, but Zero had his final word. "And besides, it's my last winter of French hunting."

Laurel's mind was sharply diverted from all this the next morning when Cambot arrived at 14 rue Père Marquette, unheralded and unbidden. After intricate efforts on both their parts, she finally understood his offer. It was the season to have chimneys cleaned, and he wished to oblige her. Surprised Laurel gave in with a shrug, and she was pleased to hear later in the day from Olande that the old fellow had been extremely prudent, having spread newspapers from hearth to door of each room as he worked. He did ten hearths and eight flues, including the kitchen.

Suddenly Laurel's final September in France was gone. The leaves had disappeared. Brick was back in school. The fog came cold, the wind piercing. Through October and November, Zero slept in his own house two to four nights a week, between regular week ends at Cannes and other passenger-carrying flights.

Laurel and Regina Edney went to the weekly Beaumonde market several times during these months. Laurel saw more and more of Ruth MacDonald to whom she confided more intimately than she had done to anyone since her marriage.

Ruth alone of all the women at Beaumonde knew the history of Laurel's long tie with Abach. She declared, "He's not only *your* friend, Laurel. There isn't a woman here who doesn't esteem his goodwill. He's a humanitarian. But of course, unless death somehow becomes fearless, doctors will always seem a little sacred."

Unfortunately, however, Ruth had asked an unexpected question. "Laurel, what's the matter with you and Zero?" And when Laurel stared at her, wide of eye and speechless, Ruth began to cry. This happened two weeks before Christmas.

7

Fontaine, the ubiquitous little postman, personally placed Guy de Brières' Christmas card in Madame Compton's hands on the morning of December twenty-ninth.

"My Christmas angel," read the note, which accompanied his lovely wood-block of the Vendôme, "what heaviness grips my heart in this glorious season to fear it could be the year of your return to America. Ever you are in my mind and heart, despite new and rather complicated involvements of which I cannot write except to say all that I pursue these days would be abandoned by your yes. In the meantime, I search each mail for my name in your beloved handwriting."

Nowhere was his name written or signed, but in the lower corner of the note, he had written in English: "Pray for peace." Laurel reread the note in privacy, wringing out drops of lonely comfort before she secreted it among paid French electric bills in a pigeonhole of the big desk.

She found herself next upstairs in her own room, fingering deeply into the knitting basket, but she did not take the suède-cloth bag of his emeralds up from the tufts of yarn. She sat with Guy's "Pray for peace" ringing over and over in her mind like the echo of a carillon.

The Base had ended its post-Christmas alert a day earlier than expected. Things were no better internationally, but certainly they seemed little worse. Paris papers daily bannered Algeria, but Guy was too old, and of course, the last in his family line—the last male. He could not possibly be called up for service. Laurel sighed, again and again, while dread intuition accompanied her through the day and into next morning, when she found at her door diminuitive Fontaine, whose permanent flush and dancing, beady eyes invariably brought to her mind an old, vulgar simile from Louisiana—"as chipper as a stud mouse."

Smiling that December thirtieth morning, she accepted from his hands two cards and a postcard gas bill before noticing the rolled calendar in his left hand. The sale—laughingly called— of such calendars brought Beaumonde firemen and postmen their annual tip.

"You're early!" she accused. "The New Year is two days off!"

Ever flustered when the lovely American deigned to talk with him, Fontaine quickly lowered his eyes and offered to come back in January if Madame preferred. "No," said Laurel with a shrug, "the price might go up. Come on in the kitchen while I see whether Olande has any house money in the cookie jug."

Fontaine reacted with a polite laugh, for there was of course no set price. The gift was entirely up to the generosity of the donor.

From the cookie jar, Laurel extracted a thousand-franc note and handed it to Fontaine. He handed her the calendar with an overdone bow of gratitude. When he raised up, Laurel was already in the act of lifting the old, nearly expired calendar.

"But, Madame!" protested Fontaine, "you discard two days! Can one afford such extravagance with the Year of Our Lord?"

Laurel replied, "Who will notice? Or have I guessed wrongly you are too discreet to tell?"

She lifted the old calendar away from its hook. What lay revealed froze both her eyes and Fontaine's. A dark-stained envelope dangled, spiked through one corner by the brass hook. Laurel blinked three or four times. Passy—Paris? November? And —God in Heaven! Guy's handwriting. The answer—the lost answer to her letter, which not once had she ever remembered to mention to him.

Laurel had the envelope in her hand; she tore the corner in her haste. Then she slammed it onto the tin-topped table because her hands could brace it there instead of merely shaking. Who? Zero? No. He would have confronted her immediately. Olande? Certainly not . . . a refugee from the mere idea of tampering with French mail—a grave offense.

She had not noticed the guarded look in Fontaine's eyes, for her mind raced too haphazardly over possibilities. No deliveries had been made into the kitchen; Olande brought into the house what groceries Laurel herself did not get from the Commissary. Abach had rummaged kitchen or pantry now and then, only to make himself a drink or, more usually, a pot of coffee.

There had been no stranger in the kitchen except Cambot. Cambot? Laurel whispered the name aloud. She saw as vividly as if it had been a day instead of a year the scene in Cambot's garret the previous Christmastide—the scrubbed boards—neat table—magnifying glass—and the French-English glossary. God! Oh, God! *Why?*

Now she caught the gape in Fontaine's lower lip, his sickening eyes, and the cowering tilt of his jaw. She saw it all at once as a person sees a room when returning to consciousness. She held the letter to her chest. "Cambot?" She repeated the name on a hunch. "How did he get this letter, Fontaine? How did he get my letter?"

Her voice had grown low, threatening. The Frenchman clasped one hand firmly with the other and waved them in an outward direction over and over as he spoke, like a convict pleading for mercy. "Cambot is mad, Madame! He is mad!"

"He is mad perhaps, but he is my friend. And I tell you now

before I read this letter, the man who wrote it has only to pick up a telephone and dial one number in Paris. . . ."

His hands flew beneath his chin, prayerlike. "I have a wife, Madame. And five children!"

"I make one offer," said Laurel, outwardly certain. "My discretion against the truth. The God's truth."

Fontaine took a step back, his normally flushed and sinewy face now harshly purple. "Madame, the honor of France rests with proper discharge of my duties. I am faithful to the mails. It is my sworn duty. I am known to be honest!"

"And I am known to be impatient," she muttered, feeling the role utterly. "Already, it has been pointed out to me that your children wear secondhand shoes."

"Madame," he simpered, "shoes for five cost a great deal."

"And that you have gossiped of letters received in this house from Normandy—gossiped to a housemaid on top of the hill." Eyeing him without mercy, she said abruptly, "I withdraw my offer."

She moved toward the door, as if headed for the telephone. Fontaine lost the last shreds of his composure. Wringing his hands, he managed to have a few tears escape as he fixed mute plea on her face. "No," she said, shaking her head. "Your silence is tantamount to confession. Get out!" She made a sweeping gesture with one hand. "Cambot will tell me!"

But Fontaine followed her into the hall. "Madame, it was an accident. I swear by Heaven!" Dolefully, he extended the mille-franc note toward her, as if parting with it grieved him far more than his unresolved dilemma. Laurel studied him, shocked that he was so greedy, so simple-minded. Did he presume for a moment that a thousand francs could compensate for the mishandling of a letter on which destiny may have hinged? She glanced now at the envelope pressed between her hands and felt a poignant desire to have the man out of her house so she could read what Guy had written.

"Fontaine, for God's sake! Get on your way!"

"Oh, Madame!" he called back, running down the hall, "Someday if God is kind, I shall find a way to make it up to you!" Laurel withdrew the marked, wrinkled, and worn sheets from the envelope, but she heard the postman's last rejoinder. "Merci! Merci beaucoup, sainted Madame Américaine!"

She did not hear the door slam, though; her eyes fell across Guy's salutation: "Laurel, my Christmas-eyed angel. . . ."

8

How blissfully uncomplex rang the intimate but reserved warmth in last year's letter! "My joy in hearing from you is at the measure of my surprise. Concern for your welfare is no new condition here but it removed customary boredom only to find my name written by your hand—and with so many pages, it is somewhat as if Heaven had smiled. . . ."

The letter went on to discuss the people of Beaumonde. Some of the biographical details were familiar to Laurel, but not the story of Cravet. She read:

"The present mayor will win again that election because he is exceptional. With old Monsieur Vervins, he shares one distinction: born, raised, a native of Beaumonde. His father and grandfather were in their times mayors, and it was his grandfather who organized and pursued the restoration of the Cathedral and ancient wall of the hilltop city. Laurel, I will tell you he is honest, fearless, and dedicated. Americans would have a hard time to discolor that reputation. He has known extraordinary suffering, for not only was his hotel taken apart, as you say, by the liberators, but one of them possessed his fifteen-year-old daughter who died the conventional number of months later in childbirth. This is no rumor. I was in the vicinity at the time. Do you suppose there is any way to change his disinclination toward Americans?

"About the MRP desirous of the job, I wonder how persons in Zero's position can have the proper intelligence when caught between warring factions of Frenchmen? Is it possible to believe the war bred a certain type of Frenchman who ran first on the bridges to meet the enemy, and now runs of old habit to meet Americans? No, Laurel, I am no Communist—God forbid! But I have seen too much what I have just said. According to your American history, I think there is nothing to compare except perhaps those renegades who allegedly sold ammunition (and whiskey?) to both pioneers and red Indians.

"As for French Communists, they are a peculiar lot. Most of them believe they are first Frenchmen, serving no country other than France. The tragedy is that if war broke out tomorrow, it would be too late when they learned otherwise. They do not realize what dictates they follow. Use caution. And remember not every French person loves you. If your car is by chance barricaded on some road or in some village, turn around and find some other way. Never, never tempt them, for combinations of wine and politics and poverty breed much the same evils, by whatever name they or their party is called."

Guy closed then with a warm, rather impersonal line, apologized for his wordiness, and signed one initial, G. Laurel sat for a long time at her desk, rereading the letter for some idea not perfectly recalled, and when she secreted it among other papers in the desk pigeonholes, only one of his disclosures remained uppermost in her mind.

Cravet, the Mayor of Beaumonde, who had been the most persistent of all thorns in the Franco-American side. At least three times a month, his name could be found below some nettling proclamation in the Beaumonde paper, most recent of which implored Beaumonde landlords not to refill vacated dwellings with American tenants: "Be faithful to your countrymen! Americans come and go but we are together until Eternity!"

When Chris was down for his nap, Laurel ambled into the kitchen where Olande was baking a cake. Laurel asked how long Cravet had been Mayor of Beaumonde. Was he Mayor at the time of Liberation?

"Oh, yes, Madame!" replied Olande with a grave face. "It is

a very famous and tragic story, for an American tank lieutenant who accepted the hospitality of the Cravet house—not the hotel—for three nights. . . . Madame, he forcibly abused the Cravets' daughter. It was the scandal of Beaumonde's Liberation, Madame. They had no money to send the girl away for a discreet time, and because they were of good family, they depended on compassion of people to spare her name, but it did not matter, Madame. She died in the birth. Oh, Madame! It was terrible. I do not know that it is true but I understand her father was drunk for a year after that, and I know for a fact that he does not drink wine to this day but water with his meals, for a friend of mine serves his table. He has a cook and a femme de ménage and a waiter, you see. . . ."

Laurel was about to turn out of the kitchen when Olande said, "Madame, it is strange that you speak of Cravet to me today, for I have just heard of his new tragedy."

"I beg your pardon?" Laurel was alert.

"His ten-year-old son lies gravely ill with poliomyelitis in the Beaumonde hospital—bulbar, the storekeeper called the disease. The French hospital directeur telephoned the Air Base hospital to have an iron lung with which to transport the child to Paris but. . . ."

Laurel's eyes were wide, her brain turning. "But the hospital at the Base has no iron lung."

Automatically, she moved to the library, sat down at her desk and reached for the telephone. Oh, if only Abach were where he belonged instead of in the States on two weeks' leave! With a lift of the telephone, he could have had somebody from American Hospital in Paris dispatch an iron lung by special car. Why had Parker fixed it up so he could go home and settle plans for whatever hospital or clinic he would enter the coming fall on his termination with the Air Force? Damn it! Just when he's needed. . . .

If only Zero didn't have his eye bandaged from a damned coal cinder. Zero could have walked into the hospital at Kirsten and talked the chief surgeon out of his only scalpel for such a cause, she was certain. But he couldn't fly for another eight or nine days. The eye man had been adamant.

Laurel got Zero on the telephone. It was ten minutes before two as she told him the barest facts. He said, "I'm coming home to work from there and find out what else you know about it."

At two minutes after two, he came through the front door, muttering about "the God damned Channel flying weather"—fog, mist, and a temperature on the ground of thirty-eight degrees. This meant, of course, icing in the upper air.

"Laurel," he said, "the first 104th pilot who hears about the deal will volunteer to go, and it gripes my soul I can't go myself, but I can't send some green-ass off in this soup. We've got to have a pilot who can get himself there and back next to blind." He bit his lip now, having taken her chair at the desk. "I know just the character, old Rip Turner. He's got a month more combat than I have—and what's more, built-in radar. He's the one who found the hole to come down last month when the gyro went out."

Rip Turner said Sure, what time should he fire his "cigar"? Zero retorted not until they found him a co-pilot, who did he want? "Well, Zero, you make it kinda hard. Ain't but one pilot around here 'sides you 'n' me and that's Jack MacDonald."

"Hell, ask him!" shouted Zero.

"Man, I'm buckin'. I gotta have that leaf turn silver the next round or else—"

"For Christ's sake, Rip! Don't banter like a woman while time's a-rottin'. Spit it out! What is it?"

"MacDonald's my Squadron C.O. You crazy? I can't tell him *you* chose *me* and now *I* choose *him*. Whatsa matter with ya, Zero?"

"I'll call him. Right now."

"He ain't got no phone out there at that shat-tow. Ruth won't let him have one, and this is one example why."

"I'll go get him. You stand by Base Ops and get the flight form fixed and go over to the BOQ and get a take-off waiver from Parker. Him personally. This stuff isn't gonna break before tomorrow."

The looseness of holiday work schedules was reflected in the homes. Zero arrived at the MacDonalds' house before three, only to learn that they were in Nouilly.

Laurel was moving in whatever direction occurred to her, meanwhile. On the bare chance of employing Abach's name with effect, she had telephoned the American Hospital to ask for Eggerton or Vernon, who had done the French operations in Beaumonde at Abach's behest, but Eggerton was in Weisbaden on leave, and Vernon had returned to the States.

She settled then for the nameless Officer of the Day, on duty at the great Hospital, but he gave her exactly the sort of courteous, hopeless, I-understand-but-there's-nothing-I-can-do-in-my-position commiseration she had dreaded.

At four o'clock, she sent Olande across the street to the store to learn whether the Cravet child yet lived, for had Olande returned with a negative report, Laurel believed there was yet time to telephone Base Operations direct and have the pilots intercepted.

By four, however, Louis Edney was climbing into the pilot's seat with Jack MacDonald beside him. Twice, the jet primer tractor fired its spark and a cloud of puffy black smoke was born to die in the still fog. Rip Turner stood with Zero Compton behind a shield a hundred yards away, and when the sleek black bird had turned its melting heat in a departing direction, had found its starting point on the North-South runway, Rip Turner began to swear—a feat he performed well enough when placid. Now, he was angry. "That bastard Edney! I wouldnta minded being outranked by some . . .' glory hog, but if there's anything in the world I got no use for, it's a God damned martyr."

For the next three-quarters of an hour, Turner and Compton slumped on the leather couches in the pilots' lounge on the second floor of Operations. The report came through that MacDonald and Edney had landed at 1653 at Kirsten—after three GCA approaches. The iron lung was being loaded.

Laurel did not see Zero, however, until a quarter before six, and from the scowl on his face she could guess how badly things had gone. The portable iron lung had been loaded and the plane primed for flight, he said, when the captain in charge of the Airdrome at Kirsten refused to give MacDonald and Edney a clearance unless the ceiling lifted to minimum five hundred feet and a mile visibility ahead. This was at fifteen minutes after five.

Zero accepted this news—outwardly. But instantly he did two things. On Parker's teletype, he sent a wire to the American Hospital in Paris—to its Commander: REGRET HOLIDAY INTRUSION BUT FEAR TO DELAY AT LOWER ECHELON. NEED PORTABLE IRON LUNG SNSP. MERCY MISSION. TRAIN LEAVES NORTH STATION FOR BEAUMONDE AT SIX P.M. CRITICAL BULBAR. I STAND BEHIND RETURN OF LUNG PERSONALLY. REGARDS. SAM F. ABACH.

Next, Zero telephoned Parker at his BOQ to ask that he personally telephone the Wing Commander of Kirsten Air Base and secure a take-off waiver.

"Zero," answered Parker gruffly, "I already did. But he and I had a fracas three years ago in the Pentagon. He wouldn't give me a drink a water in Hell!"

"Sir, how much does it mean to get that lung back here in time?"

"Well, Zero, I think we'd all like to see the kid have a chance to pull through."

"Full stops?"

"I don't know, Compton. I'd rather fly with you drunk than most pilots sober, but this jet business is a little risky with one eye!"

"I'm not gonna fly, Sir, but there's one way to get that lung back here quick if you give me a free hand."

"OK, have at it, man!"

Zero slammed the receiver in its cradle only long enough to break the connection before he telephoned for either MacDonald or Edney at Kirsten Base Operations. MacDonald, however, took issue with Zero. "When you and Parker've already got the Wing Commander wired in up here, you know damned well we can't make an illegal take-off without winding up before a flying evaluation board sooner or later. Zero, you're out of your head!"

Compton had been relieved at first to be speaking to MacDonald, because he knew which one had more flying guts, but, now, MacDonald surprised him. After a taut silence, Zero said in an even voice, "Listen, Jack! We got a mission here. To get that lung back here before the kid dies. Now, we both know Kirsten.

Either one of us could beat it up blindfolded and on the deck. Four miles off the runway, you need a minimum of three thousand—those foothills—and twelve miles out, you need five. Then you got five minutes to get your maximum eight thousand and you could come straight to Beaumonde on auto if you had to...."

"Thanks for the charting lesson, Zero, but I'm crazy about my hide."

"Christ, you gettin' a yellow streak down your spine?"

"How many drinks you had, Compton?"

"Not a God damn one, but I don't understand what's the matter with a pilot like you when you can see the tower from Base Operations and you ain't got the guts to lift your flaps. Jesus God! Suppose the Heinies were moving in with a two-ton-er? Would you ask some chicken Ops officer who flies forty-eight hours a year whether minimums were official? Christ, no! You'd get your ass in the air where it was safe. Now, listen, MacDonald! You listen to me! Parker's backing us all the way. Why sweat about boards? You count me a vote of one, and you get Edney's vote as soon as I hang up, and if that doesn't make two to one, I'll eat the sack of chicken feathers you can't seem to cough up!"

Zero slammed the telephone into its cradle and went home. There was no more he could do, for the staff car was standing by the landing strip, alongside the blue ambulance ready to haul an iron lung to the Beaumonde hilltop hospital. Two similar vehicles were marked to be at the Beaumonde railroad station.

When Zero entered his house, it was Laurel who spoke first. Stigault, head of Beaumonde's hospital, had called her a half-hour earlier to explain the Cravet child's plight, and to say that Cravet was willing to accept help from any quarter, even Americans. "Stigault's sick that Abach's away. He feels Abach could have done the miracle."

"Well, Laurel! Don't give up. I sent a telegram to AmHop in Abach's name, and if that works, there'll be a lung in the Beaumonde hospital by eight o'clock. Call Stigault and tell him to get ready. Don't tell him this—if MacDonald screws up his guts, there ought to be one here by six-thirty. Laurel, I'm pretty stewed with that MacDonald!"

Zero walked the first floor of his house, sipping bourbon and water steadily, rattling his silver dollar against his keys and coins inside one pocket, and staring from time to time into the fog which no longer held the purple of twilight. It was night.

Laurel knew his tension, and his agony. She was surprised, however, when the cuckoo sounded its single noise at seven-thirty, to have Zero say suddenly, "Christ, we forgot the Andersons' party!"

"Zero, we can't go to a party until—until. . . ."

"Laurel, I told you, MacDonald and Edney may not get here. Besides, they're big boys. They know how to take an alternate destination if they have to. If I were in their shoes, and I God damned well would have been except for this eye, I wouldn't expect them to stay home from a party to mother-hen my ETA. And, Laurel, could you whip me up some kind of a black patch to wear over this idiotic bandage. I feel like a partial boll of cotton the way I look."

She prolonged the ritual of dressing as far as possible, hoping against hope for a ring of the telephone, or Parker's arrival to announce the flyers' safe, successful return, and the completion of the mission. At ten minutes after eight she had just slipped a dress over her head when the telephone rang and Olande cried from the first floor, "Dr. Stigault, Madame! Come quickly!"

Stigault described Cravet's unabashed weeping as he climbed into the ambulance to accompany his stricken boy to Paris. Himself near tears, Stigault spoke in extravagant, emotional phrases —on and on—until Laurel could scarcely listen because of Zero's jaw-gritting impatience, his gestures for speeding the talk to conclusion so he could have a translation of what had been said. Nodding at Zero constantly through the second half of the conversation, Laurel hung up and sighed. In a mixture of English and French, she said as if to no one, "The entente with the mayor is finally cordiale."

Zero took a circle of loping strides about the small library, aglow with a smile. "Well, by God, it pays to try everything! There you are! I never dreamed that General at AmHop would really come through!" His smile darted to Laurel, her troubled eyes and compressed lips. "What's the matter with you?"

"Zero, I have an awful feeling about MacDonald and Edney. I'll put in the call to Kirsten. Maybe we can catch them and tell them need for urgency is past."

"Sure! If it'll make you feel easier. Besides, it's a fine idea!"

She grabbed the telephone and spoke as distinctly, as rapidly as possible. It was no easy feat to cross that particular border from a French civilian location. In about ten minutes, however, Zero Compton was on the line with Base Operations at Kirsten. MacDonald and Edney? No, Sir! They're not in the terminal. Not in the terminal, Hell! Page them! Look at the board and see whether they're inbound, RON or outbound. Not on the board, Sir! Well, Christ! Call the tower and see if they're waiting for take-off! Just a moment, Sir. . . .

Then, the whole connection was broken. Zero sputtered vilely but Laurel picked the telephone up to try again, and when Zero had the same technician from Kirsten back on the line, he was told emphatically that MacDonald and Edney had just taken off.

Laurel would remember the little things from the next hour. How handsome all the Americans looked, how busy their hands were with glasses, canapés, gestures, and cigarettes and lighters. How normal it all seemed. But then she saw Parker's grim face as he arrived and said nothing to anyone until he found Zero who, beholding all, got to Parker in four or five strides. Their heads together, they spoke a line or two apiece and, with a pallor never before seen, Zero turned to Laurel. When she could move, she followed them out of the room.

At the door, she said, "Did it . . . did it. . . ."

"Yes, Laurel, it burned," replied Parker.

"Trees. Those God damned trees at the end of the runway," said Zero.

Laurel slid under the steering wheel of the station wagon, into middle position as she had done hundreds of times. Zero got behind the wheel. Parker came around. They were moving, winding down the hill, past the park and 14 rue Père Marquette and Maxia's and the gas plant and on toward Nouilly.

"But Ruth?" croaked Laurel.

"Jack was thrown clear. He only has a broken neck," said Parker gravely. "Ruth's en route to Kirsten with my driver."

"Regina." The same voice, but this time no question. Laurel knew Louis Edney was dead.

"She wouldn't even see the Chaplain. She's waiting for you to get there."

Five or six miles passed in blackest silence, one face as rigid as the other. Laurel's voice came like a streak of lightning, "I hate every God damned airplane that ever sliced a cloud! I hate uniforms and rank and echelon and you, Zero, and you, Parker. You're a pair of greedy foul bastards! You *killed* Louis Edney. You did it, Zero, and Parker let you! And I'll tell. . . ."

"Laurel! Shut up! Or I'll take you straight to the hospital and have you put under sedation."

"Shut up, Compton! Let her talk . . . let her get it out of her system. . . ."

9

Regina heard Laurel's voice above the din in the small living room and shrieked from her bed, "Laurel, come here, and shut the door behind you!"

The blue eyes were puffed and circled, but Laurel saw the crying had passed. She went straight to the bed where she regarded the royal blue velvet hostess gown, the series of garnets, and Regina's hair arranged perfectly in a shining new braid. She had to say something. "Regina, I can't tell you how sorry I am."

"That's decent of you, Laurel. Decent."

"Regina!" she cried. "I loved Louis. I didn't mean to. . . ."

Regina frowned. "I say, Laurel! You look a fright! Are you well? Are you all right?"

Laurel's hands covered her face. "I loved Louis. . . ."

"If I'm not mistaken, old girl, that's my line. Now, Laurel! Look here! Stop moping and look at me! I pulled off a proper show for the blighters, but I can trust you to understand. A person with four children the age of mine has to be practical. I've been waiting for you to get here because there's no one else I can tell."

Laurel glanced up now at the glazed, almost feverish eyes, and wondered whether Regina had not taken some of the medicine she kept on hand to treat the local peasantry. But even as she listened, the nightmare grew taller, broader, and more bizarre.

Regina planned to go back to America for a proper length of time—say, six or eight or ten months—after which she would return to Beaumonde and Jean-Pierre.

"Jean-Pierre?" echoed Laurel, not believing her own voice. Jean-Pierre? There was only one whom Laurel knew in Beaumonde—old Monsieur Vervins!

A buzzing grated deep within her ears now, but she heard above the sound her one word, Why? "Because," said Regina flatly, "I'm beyond the age and weight of landing somebody rich, intelligent, congenial, *and* young."

Laurel stood up. "You're indecent!"

"I'm practical."

Laurel's hands flew to her hips. "You're outrageous!"

"You're naïve."

"But Louis. . . ."

"Louis was my first love. The love of my life. I've no regrets, Laurel. I gave him four sons, hot meals, and a warm bed. You ever see a more contented man? Stop and think! But he's gone, and I'm left with tomorrow."

"Oh, Regina!" wailed Laurel, feeling almost faint except for an undercurrent of indignation.

"Laurel, what do you think Heaven is like? I never really believed they had streets of gold like my mother used to tell me, but I sure hope one thing. With Louis Edney there, they'll have to bring in a good chef."

Regina stayed in her bed the next twenty-four hours. Zero, at Laurel's request, had delivered a note to Olande Soleil's mother, asking the woman to come and take charge of Laurel's house so Olande could be dispatched to Nouilly. Regina's maid would have sufficed, but Laurel had some need of her own servant through this day which she could not explain even to herself, for she had no thought of words such as "cheerful" or "sunny."

Olande, without asking, prepared their breakfasts, and without a question, began to receive and arrange offerings of American food which by noon filled two tables in the apartment—pies, cakes, jelled salads, desserts, scalloped potatoes, macaroni casseroles, a baked ham, a roast leg of lamb, and—Laurel counted —eight platters of meat loaves. When three wives from the Squadron arrived to take charge of the serving, Olande turned to the confused little Edney boys, returning two of them to the schoolyard to play while the smaller fellows napped.

The Chaplain came twice in the afternoon, and the legal officers with papers to be signed, and likewise, the American charged with transportation of the Edney household goods back to America. Regina declined the trying Memorial Service at the Base, stating emphatically there would be but one funeral—that at Arlington.

At six-ten on New Year's Eve, Rip Turner sat in the co-pilot's seat as Parker himself glided the C-47 into a leaden sky, bound for Orly Airport with Regina and the four sons of Louis Edney. Laurel wept beside the runway, in the car returning home, and in her bed that night.

It was her lot to return to the empty Nouilly apartment to supervise the packing and crating of all furniture, souvenirs, and those belongings which Regina could not cram into five suitcases. Every hour, on the hour, the silence of stunned Nouilly was shattered. The villagers had paid to have the Church bell rung twelve times, whenever the small hand of the clock pointed to Heaven. This was their tribute to Louis Edney, whom they referred to not as the American we loved, but as the only American who loved us.

Nine of the twelve hours, Laurel suffered the mourning peal. She stumbled into her own house before dinner that evening, rubbing her fingers against the imagined lint and leavings of Edney's uniforms, civilian clothes, even his pajamas, which she had not allowed the commercial packers to touch. Olande came running down the hall to meet her. As she took Laurel's coat, she whispered that Cravet and Stigault were in the salon with Monsieur. "Hurry, Madame! They don't speak English!"

Stigault, surprisingly, clutched Laurel's shoulders and kissed her on each cheek. Cravet did not wait for introductions, but bent deeply over her hand and then raised up red-faced and half sputtering and impetuously hugged her.

She stared from face to face, unseeing, listening to be certain whether the bell atop Beaumonde's Cathedral had just rung, or whether it was only a sound imagined in her ears. Slowly, she glanced down at her fingers which, of their own accord, rubbed stiffly together.

"Say something, Laurel! For God's sake!"

"Bonsoir, Messieurs!"

Dr. Stigault calmly took Laurel's right hand between both of his. "Madame Compton, are you all right?"

Laurel felt his middle finger against the pulse beneath her wrist. "His clothes, mon docteur, everything he left went into one single footlocker." Their eyes held, Stigault's heavy and compassionate, hers glazed. "And the bell—the bell of Nouilly. . . ."

Cravet backed—a step at a time—until the couch met the back of his legs and he dropped beside Zero, still staring at Laurel's face. But Stigault led her to a chair, and when she was seated, said in a low voice, "It is no day to drink toasts, but, Madame. . . ." He turned to Zero. "Comment est-ce qu' on dit—brandy?"

In late February, Cravet made his first proclamation of the new year: "Friends of Beaumonde, it is with humility that I declare my gratitude to the Americans and to God who has demonstrated by gradual restoral of my son His interest in the unity of our nations. Let us reflect today on the concern with a child's survival which caused two American flyers, fathers themselves, to give their lives in an effort to aid my son. Let our prayers reach to America where their widows and orphans now grieve, and let us give thanks for the brotherhood of man, and let us be kind, one to another. Marcel Cravet, Mayor of Beaumonde."

Laurel bought two extra copies of the paper. One clipping was addressed to Regina in care of Louis Edney's parents at Sullivan, Illinois. The other, she sent to Ruth MacDonald to Jack's home town, Spokane, Washington, where Ruth was newly settled in a suburban house.

Cravet's proclamation had been delayed until Jack MacDonald's outcome was final. A month after the crash, he had been flown from Kirsten Hospital to Walter Reed in Washington. Ruth's letter called it a blood clot. "I am grateful for what we had, Laurel, and able to see, whether it helps or not, that Jack would never have been happy had it turned out differently. Not to fly? Not to live without braces? The doctor told me he would have stood three inches shorter—and you know how he would have . . . well, Laurel. Every man has a limit to what he can take. . . ."

10

Laurel sat in the kitchen drinking coffee and contemplating the empty day ahead of her. The children were with Olande visiting her parents. Zero had gone to Cannes, taking his water skis and Laurel's icy greetings to Felix. Laurel was drearily gazing at the March weather when the telephone rang.

"Laurel? Thank God!"

"Michel?"

"Can you come, immediately? Something terrible has happened!"

"But you're—you're not in Paris?"

"No, we're at Noël. . . ."

"Solange?"

"Yes, and she won't let me call a doctor. She won't tell me what it is exactly. She just keeps calling your name. Laurel, it may just be one of those woman things, but for God's sake, come! And hurry!"

Less than a quarter-hour later, the station wagon creased the gravel of Noël's drive and came to a halt at the kitchen entrance. Laurel collided with the departing delicatessen owner from Redan who begged of her a thousand pardons. "Bonjour, Monsieur," she said with preoccupied haste and swept on, not noticing his leer as he backed away from the doorstep.

"Laurel? Is that you?" His voice came distant, as if from the third floor.

"Yes! Yes! Where are you? Where is she?" Laurel's knuckles were white on the curve of wrought-iron stair railing.

"Up here! Hurry!" She bounded up two steps at a time. Expressionless, Michel met her at the turn to the third floor and grasped her hand. "This way!" he indicated, turning up the next flight. As they hastened past the closed doors of third-floor rooms Laurel had never seen, she whispered, "I supposed you were both in Paris."

He said without slowing down, "Oh, I have to come once a week and see about things. Here!" He gave the door a push. She looked up at a vast skylight over the expanse of refinished parquet flooring. A pair of huge silk screens graced one end of the studio.

"What's the meaning of this?"

"Laurel!" he exclaimed. "Don't be an old lady! I've gone to all sorts of trouble for my surprise! The studio was only completed yesterday. Solange hasn't even seen it!"

"She's not here?"

"Why, of course not! She and my mother are perfect together —knitting and doing all those things women do at a time like this. Laurel, I'm going crazy in that apartment."

"You're a fiend!" Her eyes blazed.

"Don't be cruel! You know I never liked Paris except a few days at a time!"

She stared at him, incredulous now in her realization that he had fooled her completely.

"Laurel, aren't you even going to come in and see my studio?" He turned her toward the open door. She stiffened but he led her toward the Japanese-decorated screens. At that moment, her nostrils picked up an aroma. She heard the crackling of a log fire, and on the far side of the screens, she saw now a long chaise, resplendent in scarlet brocade. There was a low circular table in teak which bore two steaming cups of bouillabaisse ready to be eaten. A pair of gold-rimmed china plates lay to the side, and two wine goblets, and a platter of cold pheasant.

She turned to him, speechless. His voice chimed imploringly, "A loaf of bread, a jug of Fuissé. . . ."

Laurel laughed in spite of irritation. "And a mocha gâteau!"

"Give me your coat!" urged Michel. She looked at the iced Pouilly, golden pheasant, and the cake. What would it matter if she stayed for lunch? After all, she was going home in six more months. She sank to the chaise. In his hands, the cork parted from the wine bottle, and he seated himself beside her.

When she could eat no more, she drew away from the little table and eased into the firm end of the chaise. Michel disappeared long enough to set the table at the door, and when he returned, spoke enthusiastically of commencing her portrait.

Her hands flew to either side of the nape of her neck to brush back wet tendrils of downy hair. She felt overheated, almost drunk of the heat, but he saw what he wished in her pose. "You *are* Daphne—a goddess in purple. Laurel, take down your hair and take off your clothes. This is it! We'll start your portrait today. I've decided to do you in classic style."

She dropped her arms and straightened on the seat. "You tricked me into coming here, and my gluttony may have persuaded me to stay, but now it's time for me to go home."

"Why? We're not hurting anybody. Nobody knows. Besides, Zero wouldn't care. He's got Félicité."

She stood up, picked up her coat, and walked to the door. Michel followed. As they turned into the hall, she said the first thing that came to her mind. "This house is too cold for a baby."

He sidled toward her and put an arm around her waist. "A house is no colder than its mistress's heart. Laurel, you were Noël's mistress, the only real mistress she'd had in my time. I married a child."

They descended to the second floor, and to the first. She had not replied, and had no intention of replying. "Would you really leave me at this awful hour of the day? Laurel, what are we made for?"

"Michel, an invitation to bed from you is about as spontaneous as asking for a dance, isn't it?" Her eyes mocked him now.

"You're a fool!" he said.

She sensed deep inside a smoldering not destined to subside without trouble. In a too-calm voice, she said, "He'd kill you if he could see and hear you now!"

"Which one, Laurel? Guy or Abach?"

"God damn your soul!"

"Why, you bitch!" His eyes flamed in revulsion at her curse. "Why, you little bitch!"

"Guy'd *kill* you!" Her voice shook in the depths of rage. But Michel began to gloat, hands on his hips.

"Guy'll kill himself before he has time to kill any of us, and it's all your fault, too, Laurel. But how poetic! A modern tragedy! If it had been Abach, if you got a divorce, Abach could *marry* you."

"Guy's already asked me to marry him—a year ago—right in this house!" She bit her lips. It was the last thing on earth she had meant to tell Michel—of all people.

He laughed, insulting but somehow earnest. "He may have asked you something, but don't interpret it as a marriage proposal. Laurel, however I tease you, I've a certain affection for you, and I don't want to see you rub your own face in the dirt."

With both hands, she shoved him backwards. Her feet solidly braced, she watched him with a wrathful look. For an instant, she saw all the hatred, all the violent words, and all the humiliation which had come of her meetings with Michel.

In less than a quarter-hour, she brought her car to a sharp halt in front of the new Base Hospital, in the space marked "Reserved for Hospital Commander." The airman on duty followed her down the hall, saying, "Dr. Abach went to Brussels, Mam. Captain Simms is here. Would you like to see him?"

Laurel looked at the accommodating young man and said, "No, thank you, I'm going to Paris."

11

From the Esso station on the north side of Paris, Laurel telephoned Guy's office and then his apartment. Hardly surprised to have no answer at six o'clock on Saturday evening, she drove directly to his apartment house—past Le Bourget, Gaz de France, up Wagram, and beyond the Arc. Then, she changed her mind and wound her way back to the Champs and left the car in an empty space before Pan American's downtown office.

For a block or two, she walked along in fresh wind now spiked with pellets of rain which stung her cheeks. She stepped into the relative comfort of a taxi and murmured to the driver an address four doors removed from Guy's.

Before his apartment building, she faced a real obstacle. One needed either a key or an excellent reason to get through the locked street door. Desolate, thinking even of being picked up by the police for loitering, she opened her leather handbag and searched the bottom of it, as if a solution could be found there. She looked up into a stranger's admiring smile. He lifted his hat, bowed, and held the door open as he emerged, saying, "Ah, but is the world not turned by lost keys? Allow me, Mademoiselle?"

Laurel flashed him a grateful smile, entered, and stood still. The foyer was too small, in contrast to the stately air of the edifice outside. It was dank and ill-lighted and had an odor of disinfectant left over from mop water on granite. The narrow strips of carpeting, an unlovely brown like plug tobacco, seemed not dyed but merely weathered.

Her gaze darted to the stairs and the stained glass window on the landing. Going up, Laurel touched the dark oak paneling. Then she peered in afterthought over her shoulder to see that no one eyed her from the glass door of the keeper's office.

What would I have said? "I'm expected by the Count de Brières, but please tell me what floor?"

Now, an urge to abandon her quest swept Laurel. She could think of no way to locate his apartment without inquiry. At this moment, though, she espied the miniature, antique elevator waiting at the second floor. She stepped in and waited for the cylinder of the heavy swinging door to compress. *If it's meant to be, I'll find him!*

So saying to herself, she jabbed blindly at the worn buttons on the panel and when the motion of the shaky cage was arrested, she stepped out into a deserted hall and walked slowly along the third floor. *If only a telegraph messenger would arrive to deliver a bleu somewhere*—Laurel could have asked him and relied on discretion—for a hundred francs—*If only a cleaning woman would emerge from one of the glossy brown doors!*

No. It was impossible.

Slowly, leaden of step, she descended the endless, red-lighted flights of stairs. Glancing neither to right nor left, she crossed the depressing foyer and gripped the handle of the glass door to open it. Seeing the face opposite, she froze.

Philippe's eyes were no less incredulous than hers. He dashed into the foyer and planted a hand-kiss too swift to count. "Laurel, what are you doing here?"

"You'll never be a playwright if you use such trite opening lines!" she laughed sadly. "Philippe, where is Guy?"

"He left this afternoon. I'm using his apartment until Solange—until the baby comes." Still gripping her hand, he made no attempt to erase his worried frown. "Laurel, Guy's gone for another two weeks or so." She sighed heavily. "He hasn't allowed you to become involved in his intrigue?" he asked with strange urgency.

"I came to persuade him to arrest his plans—before it's too late," she said glibly.

Philippe pursed air through his lips, a hopeless gesture. "You may as well have come to return the tide. He's too deeply involved now, Laurel."

A numbed tingling shot to her fingertips. Cautiously, she searched Philippe's eyes. "What is he doing?"

"Laurel, I am not sure. He has told none of us, but it takes him out of France a week or two at a time. I have a strong suspicion, but nothing more than that, and I shall not tell you—in hope of being wrong."

Laurel withdrew her hand and secured her coat more closely about her neck, an attitude of imminent departure. Philippe suggested she come upstairs to the apartment. "I'll make us an omelet." He laughed shyly. "I know how."

She could not suppress a kind chuckle. "No, Philippe. I'm going back home. I was foolish to come."

"Then let me drive you? I've nothing to do all evening."

"No. I'll just make the North Station in time for the seven o'clock train," she lied. "Philippe, don't tell . . . anyone?"

Outside, she walked along feeling depressed. Guy was lost. Around her was a coral haze as moist and soft as the blended lips of lovers. Paris by night. The wind had stopped. Paris was dressed in her roof-top fog of pink tulle. On the Champs, Paris danced in millions of spherical mirrors—the discarded raindrops clinging to cars and store windows and chestnut carts and the plastic raincoats of promenaders.

She paused before a sleek array of sparkling automobiles inside a Champs window and studied their colors, thinking not of what she saw but of how soon she would lose Paris.

Suppose this is my last night in Paris? And I knew it? Where would I go? What one scene would I revisit? She whirled on one foot and spanned the sidewalk to the inner curb where three cabs waited with their meters idle.

Entering the first, Laurel gave the address of the restaurant where they had dined the first night she saw Paris.

"Dear Madame!" exclaimed the hump-shouldered proprietor. "You are *alone!*" Quickly, however, he retrenched, "But we have not had this honor in four months!"

"Oui, Frederich," she smiled, "much too long to go without peppers!" Her gaze roved the beloved room, registering disagreeably the cluttered change, the two dozen or more small tables crowded into space where there had been half as many, and the conglomeration of young faces somehow old of eye. They looked like a convention of third-year, government-supported university students, except their coats were a bit more frayed or ill-fitting. Yes, she hated to say even to herself that they looked like transient refugees.

"I am in no hurry for dinner, Frederich." Nowhere could she espy an empty table. "Perhaps there is a place I could have a small apéritif and listen to music until there is a space?"

He tossed his palms toward the ceiling in a wonderful apology. "It is no more a restaurant, Madame. It is but a mediocre boardinghouse, but you understand all that?"

The old man led her toward what appeared to be a gauze-draped wall spaced with pots of live palms. He parted the curtains on a square cubicle, offered her to pass into the booth, and hesitated long enough to strike a match to a globed candle. Laurel lit a cigarette and drew deeply.

An interim tranquility possessed her—changing wafts of aromatic dishes carried past to other tables; slow, warming sips from her clear goblet; ethereal tears of the Gypsy violin. More eager to remember than to forget, for the first time in months, she drank slowly, almost indifferently, having no idea that an hour had passed before she stared into the last burgundy-colored drop in her wine glass.

Then, into the edge of being there slipped a sound. A faintly heard voice. She turned and made out through the film of gauze a pair of blurred silhouettes at the entrance, the round hump of Frederich's shoulders and an extremely tall profile of a man who shook rain from his coat and then, put it in Frederich's hands. Pilots call it the point of no return, thought Laurel with paralyzing joy. *We* can't turn back! Philippe was wrong. . . .

As if all entanglements had melted, all grief vanished; as if Guy had come to waft her into that never-never land of love's enchantment, Laurel's heart raced. She leaned against the booth, her eyes closed.

Guy did not speak her name until she opened her eyes.

12

The gray at his temples was visibly whiter. His cheeks were hollowed with fatigue, and Laurel found a furrow in the classic brow, but still she drank in the marvel of his presence.

"What is it I see in your eyes, Laurel?" She did not avert her gaze as once she might have, but stared at him. His sigh was deep. "Are you well? You're so thin." Laurel tasted an ecstasy born of love, and suddenly, between them lay no tomorrow.

Tonight, however, returned very real in a simple, rather weary and undramatic clearing of the waiter's throat. From the opposite side of the curtains, a whiff of what he held reached the remote isle inside the booth. Guy drew back the curtain, saying, "I've had no time to eat these past twenty-four hours and so I gave Frederich our order at the door."

She stared at the plate set before her. "What is it, my angel?" asked Guy.

"Tomato, rice, paprika, salt, white pepper, basil, Gruyère, milk, and . . ." She sniffed again. ". . . probably Madeira. It's a bit curdled."

"No!" he shouted in mirth. "That strange look?"

"I was thinking what a tragedy it is—how I've always adored green peppers. And now, I shall never look at one without my heart breaking!"

Saying nothing, Guy took up his knife and fork, and Laurel, without conscious thought of doing so, began the motions of dining.

"Having accepted as quite final all that your letter said,

333

Laurel, I have played a game with myself to keep from writing or coming. . . ."

"A game?"

"Yes. But even so, last fall I was twice into the edge of Beaumonde before recovering my senses." His eyes were stricken as he watched her now. "A game, Laurel. I pretend you are already settled back in America, and you have forgotten me." His smile was ironic. "So you come alone to this place and Frederich telephones me! Sometimes, I ask myself if we are wrong to struggle against. . . ."

"What did Frederich say?"

"'The English woman is here—alone, Monsieur!'"

"The *English* woman?" cried Laurel. "But you came *anyway?*"

"I told him I knew no English woman, and he grew so impatient, he burst into an unmistakable description of you."

"Do you own this restaurant?"

"Non, merci! Why do you ask that?"

"Frederich has your telephone number, apparently."

"How shall I explain, Laurel? Since the war, I've dined here maybe every other month. But much has happened since I saw you. I have been out of France several times, theoretically on matters of trade exchange—goodwill, you say. Champagne, of all things. And for the same reason I make these trips, I now come to this place two or three times a week when I am in Paris."

"Guy?"

"He gazed at her a long time before going on. "Frederich and I are part of a team. Let us say we are engaged in a mutual project. I screen candidates."

"For what?" Her frown grew, but he proceeded in his explanation.

"He feeds them until they gain some position and lodging. Students, primarily, Laurel. Except in a few cases where pressure has grown too great on some individual."

"Too great?"

"Too great to trust wives or sweethearts or in-laws."

Her gaze had held on the agile, rapid movements of his mouth as he spoke. She could not ignore the change in his eyes. They glinted like ice. Twice, she swallowed in growing distress. But he's safe, she said to herself; after all, he has a French passport!

She was never to remember all they had said over the table, only the occasional picture of something new set before them—a delicate salad of scissor-cut raw spinach and shreds of raw beet—a smattering of Camembert—and shafts of freshly cut pineapple still crowned with spiked leaves.

"Guy, what would it take to dissuade you from this danger?"

"Laurel, my angel, do not place me in the position of a man at an auction."

"But you'd give it all up if—if. . . ."

He drew a deep, resigned breath and let it out slowly. "In such a case, I should have no alternative but to devote my whole life to caring for you and your children."

Laurel stared at him, envisioning for the first time some enchanted plane of being. Some year lacking numbered days. Some place where time is no mere falling and rebirth of foliage but an endless day of sun where no shadows grow tall. With a little gasp, she fell forward, face on her arms upon the table.

Guy stroked her crown tenderly. "What is wrong? Speak to me!"

Her fingers dug into her forearms. "If only I had the courage to leave him! If only—if only. . . ."

"Laurel, raise up!" Obediently, she regarded him. "Now say what you mean! You stay . . . you remain there from fear?"

"Not physical fear," she said quickly to dispel new turbulence in his eyes. "You don't understand! He's shrewd and ruthless. He's strongly imbued with a—a sense of possession. Guy, I'd never get through a divorce court and be able to keep my children. He'd buy witnesses if he had to—but don't you understand? He wouldn't have to now. I've played perfectly into his hands."

Guy wore no despair. On the contrary, he seemed encouraged. "Laurel, you don't make sense! My word has a semblance of veracity in French court."

"French court?" She eyed him desolately. "Guy, I came to France as a military dependent. Unless I commit a French crime, I might as well never have left America. Judicially, that is."

"What you imply then is that you can obtain freedom only by

returning to America?" She nodded, hopeless. "Laurel, suppose that when Zero leaves for Africa the first of May. . . ."

"Guy, that's classified—that date!"

His smile flashed in urbanity which shocked her. "Laurel, don't you believe by now there's no W.C. in France without an agent?" Then he said carefully, "What if, during that five or six weeks, Zero believes you have returned to Holland for a vacation with Olande and the children, or perhaps that you have seized an opportunity to make the Scandinavian tour?" Laurel stared, not fully en rapport. "There is my villa near Antibes where they should be perfectly safe. Of course, I should stay with them—until your return, Laurel—free. To the three people in all the world who best love you. Laurel! For life!"

Guy wavered before her eyes. The room blurred. Sound moved away. Laurel saw him through a heavy charcoal-colored mist brightened only by green and violet pinwheels which whirled like lusterless fireworks. "No, Guy."

"Is it final?" She gazed at him, unable to speak, pale from her spell of faintness. "Laurel, why?"

She heard then from her own lips the thought never before admitted in the darkest recess of her mind. If all else failed, Zero would kill Guy. Twice, she struggled to get on her feet and out of the booth. Expressionless but swift, Guy was beside her, and they were through the door of the restaurant, in the street, and riding.

For a long time, there was no sound between them except the hum of the motor and tires of the black Jaguar slapping methodically against wet pavement. Guy drove slowly, aimlessly. Near four o'clock, he raced a milk truck to a stop and when he had bought a litre, he teased Laurel heavily for trying to read by the bottle cap whether the milk was pasteurized. "Who cares, Laurel, if we die of a cow disease after these hours?"

"You're an idiot!" she scolded with grave affection.

"Yes, because you're mine and I can't have you." She handed him the barely touched bottle of milk and he set it on the street, slammed the door, and drove silently away. She rolled down the window on her side, welcoming moist, dank air on her face.

Somewhere, the chimes of a clock tolled. Guy drove on—on—and the clocks began to declare six.

Laurel said without looking at him, "My coach will turn into a pumpkin in twenty-four hours."

He braked the car amid the right lane of the broad boulevard and a car screeched past, swerving to avoid them. "How shall we pass finality?"

She reached up with both hands and cupped his chin. "Where you live."

A veil dropped between them. "Laurel, there are certainties in life which it is dangerous to ignore." Her hands fell back into her lap. "Since the night at Noël when I proposed to you, my concierge has had orders to surrender a key to a woman with red hair, green eyes, and a tilted smile. But now I have changed my mind. I cannot creep there with you like some boot boy out of the night. Laurel, I will not be consoled with a few hours of sensual pleasure from the most precious thing in the world to me!"

She turned from him so that he could not see her tears. "Words, Guy! Always words!"

"If you come, Laurel, it is forever."

"Forever!" she mocked through her sobbing. "While Zero runs off with my children and somebody rams you off the side of a cliff for gunrunning? Oh, Guy!"

She looked away and said, "My car is on the Champs, in front of Pan Am."

He put the car in gear and for several blocks of dawn-dusted silence, Laurel stared through half-closed lids at the windshield. When they reached her car, she got out and waved him on. She climbed in stiffly behind the wheel and closed her eyes for a minute.

When she opened them again, the boulevard was empty and the sun was just coming up in the East.

13

Two weeks later Laurel was back in Paris. Michel's fourth request for the Comptons had come in a telephone call to Zero's office. "We're going in to the city tomorrow afternoon, Laurel, but I didn't tell Michel because I don't think his mother ought to be bothered with a banquet for company. We'll stay at a hotel, and we'll take them out to dinner."

Véronique de Berteaux was relieved by their appearance. She said Michel had been on the verge of departing for Noël. "And I really think I'm too old, my dear children, to have this baby by myself! Michel belongs here—now of all times!"

What intrigued Laurel during the two hours they spent in the apartment was the unbalance of what Michel referred to constantly as "the situation." Solange, flushed of face, engorged with her creation, was not the axis around which the household rotated. It was Michel's serenity which those about him seemed bent upon preserving.

Toward Laurel, however, he exerted himself. A stranger would have assumed that she was his dearest woman friend, his ancient ally, the entrepreneurial godmother to the first child that had ever been born.

Véronique, to Laurel's disappointment, refused to go along for the dinner. "It's terribly kind of you and Zero, though, Laurel. Michel needs to be out and away from me." She detained Laurel momentarily from the others as they were preparing to leave and said discreetly, "My dear, how do you always know when to walk into my life? Michel had a simple errand at Noël which could have been done by telephone, but if you had not come, he would be there for the night!" Laurel smiled and refrained from reminding Véronique that the baby was not due for another ten days.

In the restaurant Solange squirmed often and heavily, seeking a position of ease. Twice, Laurel asked her in secrecy whether she wanted to leave, but the answer both times was a flushed, grim-lipped, "Non, merci!"

At a quarter before eleven, the four returned to the Berteaux apartment building. Michel reached across his wife, opened the door, and told her to go on up. "I'm going with Zero for a nightcap at his hotel bar. I'll be along in a moment."

Laurel could not see the girl's face, but she caught the extra fraction of a second Solange's hand gripped the door, and the slam as she shut it. Laurel bit her lips to keep from saying something to Michel; it would be no use. In her heart, she knew that this would only complicate an already impossible situation.

The men had drunk a good deal of wine during dinner, but to Laurel's certainty, only two or three glasses of wine and an Armagnac more than herself. Surely, since they were sober—she had never felt more clear-headed in her life—Michel would not remain long. However, the banter at the little club-shaped table went on and on, interminably, inconclusively, and they had drunk, Zero and Michel, three highballs each before twelve-thirty.

Disgusted, but hopeful of interrupting their preoccupation with trivialities, Laurel moved away to the bar. The bartender was amused when she asked for a cup of tea. She had espied a carton of tea bags. As he swung the stringed square around and around in the cup, she asked him abruptly, "Do you await the return of the King?" He eyed her in surprise, and did not answer. But a few moments later, he brought from behind his bar a scrapbook showing photographs of prizes he had won at a national bartenders' convention in Cannes the previous year.

Laurel looked and listened as he pointed out various French celebrities in the backgrounds. As he put the book away, he implored her with Gallic gestures to let him prepare her a sample of the cocktail with which he had won—gratis, Madame? When she shook her head and smiled, he shrugged and gave the standard palm-upward shrug. But he brought her another cup of tea, a fresh one, and as she sipped it, he lingered in front of her.

"The King, Madame? Ah, when my pockets are full of francs and there is no coal to be bought because of a strike, I long for the monarchy. I ache for it. But when I leave each summer on my two weeks' vacation in Italy—the Italian Riviera, Madame! Ah, then I thank God for the Republic! The King, Madame." He pursed his lips and stared down at the spotless chrome sink. "News of court life was very exciting. Such scandals!"

His gaze darted then behind her to the table where the two men sat with their heads together. "Madame," he said softly, "for an American you have almost no accent."

Laurel grinned. "How think you I am American?"

"By your husband." He nodded with a shallow motion.

"One is French."

"Not the one who keeps regarding your back. The tall one."

She listened acutely, hearing Michel say, "Give me the name of the man then who can be trusted to take your place. I accept him on your word. His place is ready when you go." Laurel dropped her head and stared into chilling tea. Michel and his sentimental falderol about nobody being able to take Zero's place either in the French hunting lines, or local society.

At six-thirty the next morning, she was awakened by the twist of the locked doorknob. Believing the hour early for an inquisitive hotel maid, and late for a detective's nightcheck, she got out of bed to test the lock and was about to move from the door when she saw a folded paper. It read, "Tenth Marquis arrived three A.M. Baby fine. Mother fine. Father—prognosis guarded."

Shouting the news, Laurel shook Zero. He rubbed his face and swept a hand to sleek his hair. Ceremoniously, he sat up and reached for his robe. And moments later, Laurel returned from the bathroom with a clean face and her hair combed, to find him sitting puffy-eyed but in great dignity on one of the chairs beyond the twin beds.

Dropping to a chair, she folded her robe neatly over her knees and reached for a cigarette. Zero stood up to light it, seeming half asleep. "Well, for Christ's sake! What do you propose we ought to do about the tenth Marquis *this* time of morning?"

"Well," she said, "if I were single and all by myself, I'd probably ring for a pot of coffee. And with that done, I'd try to decide what time to call the tenth Marquis's grandmother and apologize for delaying his father's participation in his welcome!"

The desk clerk apologized vociferously on the telephone. The "monsieur" had left the note around six A.M. with instructions that it be given them when they awoke. But a Spanish-speaking bellboy had misunderstood the clerk's instructions. "Only the cleaning crew is in the kitchen having petit déjeuner at this hour, Madame, but certainly, you shall have a pot of coffee! After all, a *baby* has been born!"

"Merci, Monsieur!" replied Laurel sweetly, "and congratulations!"

"Comment?"

"You read English very well!"

By eight A.M., headachy Zero owned a momentous revelation. The excitement of the baby's advent, of its being a boy, Zero's hangover—all had moved a bit to the side, exposing his sense of responsibility for Michel's absence in a crucial set of hours.

Five times he placed a call. Five times the line was busy. But at last, Laurel watched his face as it acquired a little beam. And she heard Véronique's excited voice, "Ah, Zero! A precious little boy! I have not gone to bed the night. I am halfway through the list of telephoning the news to my friends."

Zero eyed Laurel as he said gravely that they were both deeply embarrassed by Michel's tardiness. "Ah, no! Don't say that!" cried Véronique. "You saved my life! If you had not come, Michel would have been at Noël and I should have been obliged to have that baby alone!"

BOOK FOUR

1

Zero had been at Corliss four weeks and was due home the next day, when Laurel and Abach rode past the austere, modern four-story buildings at the main intersection of lower Beaumonde. She said, "You know, Abach, I'm going to get one of those new apartments for Francis and Olande. And time is growing short."

"What do you mean?"

"They'll have no place to live when we leave. Hachère is turning our house into business offices, so that destroys any hope of their remaining on as they are with some new American family. By the way, Hachère claims he's had six different American officers offer him a bonus and twelve months' rent in advance for the house."

"What's the matter? He had enough of Americans?"

Laurel chuckled. "I don't think it's that simple. They've got no place at their house on the hilltop to raise vegetables, and I think it's about killed them to have to *buy* potatoes and leeks. You know, Abach, these people don't mind spending a hundred dollars on a champagne brawl—the sky's the limit—but when it comes down to paying ten cents a pound for spuds they could've raised for nothing—that's a different color horse!"

"Americans are just as absurd at home. Look at people who'll pay thirty thousand dollars for a house—and take thirty years to do it—but they gripe like hell because it costs fifty dollars a month to keep the lights on, the fire going and the water running. It's all in the point of view, Laurel."

"Well, Olande deserves something. I think I'll buy a ten-year lease."

"In your position, that won't be much of a trick."

Assuming he referred to her personal income, she said, "No, it oughtn't to run over thirty or thirty-five a month. I hear that less than ten percent of those with priority are taking up residence in the apartments."

"Yes. But, Laurel, you realize what price Americans are paying?"

"What Americans?" she asked, more preoccupied with a vision of Olande's face upon hearing such a lease had been closed.

"The Americans who dickered to get in those apartments."

"It's their own fault, whatever it is," she sighed. "They still can't be bothered, the Americans who come over here, to make an effort to approach anything from a French point of view except girls and wine."

Abach replied with a grin, for the one side of Laurel completely predictable to him was her disdainful attitude toward Americans in France. As she eyed his profile, she thought once more of his frivolity at the splendid luncheon they had just attended. It was a farewell party for Dr. Stigault, who had been transferred from Beaumonde hospital to the great Sisters of Mercy in Paris as the new Directeur. There had been around the table Mayor and Madame Cravet, gentle old Vervins, and a number of other Beaumonde notables. Laurel had wondered whether Abach might not have exceeded his capacity at wine; his humor was more than sparkling, it was almost reckless.

As soon as they left, he proposed they drive to Brussels for the afternoon and "look around." Laurel consented for lack of a reason not to, but when she asked to drop by the house and tell Olande where she would be, Abach pulled his coup. "While you were getting ready, I told her we were going to Brussels for dinner."

"Oh!" she cried, "Aren't you the tricky one!"

Laurel studied the road and sprawling vegetation of the countryside—thriving fields of sugar beets, wheat, soybeans, all drinking late May sunshine. More to herself than Abach, she said,

"You know, I'm never myself this time of year. Wonder who I am?"

"I don't know, but try to get hungry. We're going to a country restaurant this side of Brussels where the specialty is green eel. Laurel, it's marvelous!" She eyed him, thinking this over, and afraid she would never be hungry again in her life, but by ten that evening, she had done justice to her Anguille aux Fines Herbes Bruxelles, and to a slice of ham in delectable Madeira sauce, an asparagus soufflé, and a plate of tiny radishes split to receive their dab of sweet cream butter.

Last came a dessert for which Laurel had no name—a fourth of fresh pineapple still wearing its thatch and thoroughly hollowed to nest a ball of sherbet inside mounds of pineapple cubes while a thick layer of beige tipped meringue glistened over the whole.

"Ananas en Surprise," murmured Abach.

"Olande would like that—she's a fiend for pineapple!"

"And chocolate and crème Chantilly just now?"

She glanced up in surprise. "Why do you say that?"

He shrugged, smiling. "The French craving-symbols." Laurel thought fleetly of how much more rapidly desserts melted from the kitchen of late, and how, sometimes, Olande forgot her mourning over the Compton children's shortening stay in France. "Three months, maybe two and a half, I'd say," sighed Abach.

"But it's the answer to my prayer!" cried Laurel, face serene, almost joyful.

"What is?"

"That God in His Infinite Mercy has seen fit to bless them with a child."

"What'd you expect Him to bless them with—a pony?"

"They're Catholic!"

He made a grimace. "You don't say!"

"But when she didn't become pregnant in a whole year, I figured she was meddling with fate."

He regarded her from crinkled eyes. "In what form?"

"Like those anti-ovarian pills you can buy in any French Pharmacy. You don't even have to have a prescription."

"I see!" Laurel was busy eating. She did not notice his frown. "How many is it safe to take in a thirty-day period, Laurel?"

"How would I know?"

"You've never bought any?"

"No, I've never bought any. I haven't even seen them. But Regina told me about them one day when we were in a pharmacy." She eyed her old friend in smiling impatience. "Now, Doc! Snap the kit and let's put all the diagnoses away!"

"Laurel, I wish I had a mirror in my pocket and a strong light. For a woman thirty-four years old, you're fabulous! God! When I think about it, you're more beautiful than you've ever been in your life."

Laurel was certain now that he was tight, for his words were far too personal. "What does it matter? Beauty is a cold asset when there's nothing left to fight for in life."

"Ah," he moaned, "you reek of chronic self-pity!"

"Shut up!"

"You could have had him."

"I know it."

"But not on your terms."

"I don't want to talk about it."

"All right. What do you want to talk about?"

"What year Brussels waiters serve coffee."

"I'm sure they'll get here before my plane takes off for the States."

Laurel eyed him in contemplation. "August first is incredibly near—a little over sixty days."

"And you and Zero take the *United States* out of Cherbourg August tenth. Laurel, something's coming to an end."

She thought now of his return to Baton Rouge. He would be free of the Air Force within ten days of his return, and flying home to take his place with Wallace and Brinkton in their obstetrical practice.

"Let's go, Abach. I don't want any coffee." She was on her feet without noticing the fall of his features. Scarcely had they hit the road back to Beaumonde before she began to pour her heart out to him—all that had happened with Guy the last time in Paris. Her plea. His refusal. Through it all, Abach said nothing.

His motive in taking Laurel to the restaurant had to be abandoned. He had believed the quiet warmth of those surroundings would give him courage to tell her he had sold the land adjacent to Paradis—his late father's place called The Willows.

He meant to tell her the truth, that the acreage was now being cleared for vats and experimental buildings and a great factory. An acetate company branching out from the East had been the only bidder willing to pay a price which would support his third of the new clinic. But Abach knew how such news would sadden her. She would scold him, perhaps weep, and say he had defiled the memory of both his father and his unremembered mother. In truth, he was relieved to be free of the tax obligation and the boring agricultural strings.

Before her gate Laurel alighted from the car. "Don't bother getting out. It's late, and you're tired." But he was already in front of her, gazing down at the familiar features dimly highlighted in solemnity by the street lamp before the apartment house across the street.

"Laurel. . . ."

"When you're ready to tell me what it was you celebrated tonight, I'd love to hear. Good night, Abach!" And she was gone, leaving an empty echo in the night, a chill upon the glory of a clinic not yet built.

2

The first week of June, Laurel went to the office of reparations payments and asked for the names of a half dozen French people whose apartments would be completed in early August, or even July, and who would be renting instead of occupying the apartments themselves. The clerk replied at once that he was forbidden to dispense such information.

Next day, dressed in French worker's garb, she loitered at the bar of Maxia's on the ground floor of the apartment buildings, sipping draught beer and listening. There were, however, but three customers during these early afternoon hours, and so Laurel wandered out of the place, pausing at three different shops. Regardless how casual her inquiry, how proper her approach, she gained absolutely no idea of where to obtain a potential lead.

Before Zero came home at five, she perused a mental file of French acquaintances who might aid her, but why bother them? After all, with the number of Americans moving into the reparations places monthly, Zero surely knew their source of supply. Suddenly, though, she thought of Monsieur Vervins, and decided not to approach Zero yet. After all, if Zero could secure an apartment at no less than the American price, Laurel could scarcely afford a *one*-year lease for a servant, much less five or ten.

On the last day of June, she drove to Vervins' farm, having despaired of running into him otherwise. He met her with disarming candor, insisting that she come first to the barns and see his new incubator just arrived from America. In this he had already bred one round of pheasants and two of partridges, he said, to free in his forest.

She declined his bid to lunch, or to enter the house. Hence, they lingered in his courtyard as the old fellow made a startling announcement. Regina Edney was arriving in England the next day. Laurel noted his almost obsequious joy. "Monsieur," she began. "You have been my friend. I take the liberty of warning you."

He shifted his weight from one foot to the other and let his gaze follow a darting goldfish from a circle of sunshine to the shadow of a lily pad. "It is my dream to marry her," he said.

"Monsieur!" cried Laurel. "She is only a year or so older than. . . ." But her words froze. It was too cruel.

"Than you, dear Madame?" He shook his head. "And she is marrying me for my money, Madame?"

Laurel averted her eyes to the lily pool, but still she saw his weathered hands—richly tanned and specked with all sizes of suèdelike brown moles. Slowly, they stretched out to her. She could not refuse.

"Madame! Madame! Do you not understand the courage with which she sacrifices her youth?" His hold on her hands grew. "I would rather die than hurt you, but permit me to say some of us are more careless of heart than you, my belle jeune dame!"

"Speak plainly, Monsieur!"

"Madame, if Eve had had no more courage than you, Adam would have become a monk and neither of us would be standing here now!" Laurel's heart protested, for Guy had never mentioned his name, nor he Guy's. "Ah, petite Américaine! How many women are given such a chance to make one man happy. . . ."

Ah, then he meant Zero?

"You had love's chance, Madame. I know. But where is that man today? Not only have you lost him but he is lost to France as well."

She made a quick, convulsive effort to withdraw her hands, longing to flee before hot tears fell, but old Vervins held on for one more line. "It is not I who am unkind, chère Madame. It is truth. And life. Ivory towers are well in books and stories, but the temperature of northern France ill affords them."

He dropped her hands and broke into laughter. "Forgive me, Madame! But to think you came here from fear I shall be duped by a woman!" His voice came strong, robust, virile. "Sweet Madame! Is there something else—something more wonderful to be duped by?"

Laurel's eyes glinted in the noon sun. Her shoulders squared. She stood as tall as possible. "Monsieur, I do not know, but if the world is really founded on mattresses, whether they be feather, horsehair, or foam rubber, I shall probably be the universal foreigner!"

Laurel waited only until Zero had his first drink in hand and was seated in the salon to begin her story of wanting to lease an apartment for Olande. Zero was displeased. "You've paid her the going wage, and we've given her lodging and utilities. No! I won't hear of it!" She only smiled.

He spoke again carefully. "Laurel, I can help you get a name, but it's a sore subject with me. There's been a deal going on for those apartments—a wholesale deal. Some French person gets the names of the apartment owners who live outside the Beaumonde area, and he sews up the apartments faster than they're finished."

"I don't see. . . ."

"Oh, Christ! Laurel, he gets contacts way ahead of time from the French owner and then he's ready when an American wants a place."

"So you suggest I'd have no luck? Is that it?"

"At the going price. Sure! But not . . . Laurel, you don't expect a place to be rented for thirty dollars a month when it'll bring in a hundred and twenty? You're pretty, but not that pretty! And certainly not for Olande!"

She thought in rapid calculation now: if the apartment was leased for thirty a month and subleased for a hundred and twenty, the difference was ninety dollars. Good God! "Zero," she said with controlled annoyance, "how many of the apartments are filled by Americans—roughly?"

"Altogether? Let's see! Starting with three out of the first ten last spring—a year ago—two months ago there were forty-two out of the ninety-six completed." He left the room to go mix himself a new drink. Stunned with the magnitude of the scheme, she saw neat figures leaping in her mind: Forty-two apartments at ninety dollars profit totaled $3,780. Ninety dollars a month. $3,780 a month. About $45,000 a year! And more apartments freed weekly!

Laurel ran to the kitchen. "Zero, what does the American get?"

He regarded her swiftly above the swirling smoke, a cigarette clenched between his teeth while he poured whiskey and then water into his glass. "I oughtn't to tell you, Laurel, but I know you'll keep it under your hat. It's all documented stuff. The native offered our man a third of the monthly net—a third of the rent, you see—but the American was apparently no fool. You see, he'd be clear out of the picture if he got sent back to the States or transferred to Germany or something—nobody stays here forever—no American—and the Frenchman would either be oriented enough not to bother with a new contact, or else the new contact could make his own deal. But at any rate, this American who started out demanded a thousand bucks a deal or no dice. And, Laurel, I don't blame him."

Her mind clicked silently: Forty-two apartments×$1,000. Suddenly, Zero's last sentence registered. She bit her lip and then screeched, "You don't *blame* him!"

"No! If he hadn't taken it up, somebody else would have. Laurel, that's money!"

"And you've let it go on—you in your position?" He nodded, gesturing her impatiently out of the kitchen. As she passed through the salon door and moved to the couch, she said, "I'm going to speak to Parker!"

He lifted a cool brow and looked down at a magazine cover. "He agrees with me entirely."

"On what?"

"On leaving it alone. Laurel, in the letter of the law, there's no crime. No infraction. It's perfectly legal for a French person to buy up leases and sublease them. I had it looked up. There's no rent ceiling on any house or apartment built *after* 1945. It all comes under the head of good business."

"But what about the American's infraction? Zero, don't tell me it's an officer?"

"Of course! But I've no intention identifying him for you 'til we're back in the States."

"Why isn't he transferred if he can't be court-martialed?" she cried heatedly.

"It doesn't matter much now. Laurel, in another three months, the apartments will be filled entirely. No new deals. After that, one American family will probably succeed another at rotation or transfer."

"But a year ago? Why wasn't he exposed then?"

"Parker thought about it, but as I pointed out to him, it wasn't an evil scheme from our point of view. God damn it, Laurel, we needed a break on decent housing! Sure, the guy picked up a ton of cash, but those apartments are new and roomy, steam heated, and right in the middle of town where an American wife has neighbors and a free bus to the Base when her car breaks down or the ice gets too bad. Laurel, if the system had been destroyed, we probably wouldn't have ten American families in there right now. I tell you, you can't get a better apartment in the States for a hundred and twenty dollars. Now, stop and think! Just exactly who *is* cheated?"

This aspect had not occurred to Laurel, and she deplored its veracity. Forty-two thousand dollars some American officer had made off his own countrymen in a foreign land. A God damned carpetbagger! Suddenly, the identity of the French opportunist became foremost in her mind. Hachère? No. He had no such daring scope. Martin? A peanut of a brain. He might sell a few obsolete tax stamps to intimate acquaintances, but never would he have the courage to embark on a long-range alliance involving money *and* Americans-at-large. Vervins? How ridiculous could one get! Then Risseau? Likely. The most likely up to now. But then Laurel saw the answer: Zero had said *he* once too often in the narration. Beyond any question, every finger pointed to extravagant, luxury-loving, officious Belle Tricot!

"Zero. . . ."

"Oh, Laurel! There's something I've been meaning to tell you. The last time I was in Cannes, I was invited out to the Moreaus' house for dinner."

Moreaus? Said by itself, the name at first landed on her ears as "morose." She stared at him blankly. "Laurel, her mother's one helluva fine cook!"

"Whose mother?"

"Felix's. Who do you think?"

She stared at him through round eyes. According to Guy, Félicité Moreau had lost her mother at birth! But Zero was watching her, and saying that she looked a little pale. "You've been doing too much, Laurel. You ought to slow down and start resting up for the trip."

Wordless, remembering finally to close her parted lips, she thought of something Michel had said back in winter—Zero has Félicité. *Zero has Félicité?* But that doesn't mean . . . Zero couldn't keep a woman. He hasn't got enough money! Besides, he's not the type to pay steadily for his . . . well, how would I know? Oh, God! It's all like a spider web made out of heavy rope and soaked in glue. . . ."

"By the way, here's something from your mother," said Zero as he drew a thin airmail envelope from his inner pocket. Came today." He tossed the opened envelope across from his chair and it landed on the carpet.

Laurel unfolded a newspaper clipping and saw a two-column photograph of a sprawling one-story structure only in the girder stage. "WORK BEGINS ON WILLOW II"—"Baton Rouge's Modern Maternity Clinic." Willow II? Hurriedly, she read: "The completion of Baton Rouge's most modern improvement in the field of obstetrics, a clinic and lying-in hospital, is scheduled for early spring of next year, said a spokesman for the head of the team of three doctors, Samuel F. Abach, well-known Louisiana obstetrician whose father will be remembered as a pioneer practitioner in the region, and who is at present completing a three-year contract with the military in North France. Also alumni of Tulane are Whittington Wallace and Raoul R. Brinkton, partners of Dr. Abach in the new venture, and who at present are. . . ."

She carefully set the clipping on the coffee table and said, "Abach's building a clinic."

"I read it."

"Well." She studied Zero steadily as if to postpone sealing together all the facts. "He didn't tell me."

"You mean he didn't ask you?" smiled Zero.

"Zero," she blurted. "Is it Abach?"

"Is who Abach?"

"He doesn't have a dime. Where would he get enough to secure that kind of loan?"

He regarded his magazine, sipping his drink. "Maybe he mortgaged that rich levee land you helped him reclaim?"

"Oh, Zero! Be serious! This clinic will cost a million dollars."

He arose and crossed to the coffee table in a few strides, picked up the clipping and read it fleetly through a quizzical frown, as if her implication had not occurred to him before. Laying down the picture, he said through an expression of enforced restraint, "Nobody is perfect, Laurel, but you're determined the people you love are little tin gods."

"Zero, is it Abach?" Her eyes pleaded for his quick No! but Zero only stared, not flexing a muscle or a brow.

"Why?"

"Because I could talk him out of it. I could persuade him to give the money back. Zero, you've *got* to tell me!"

He swallowed the last of his drink and turned his back. "I don't have to do a God damned thing except keep you from making a fool of yourself and messing in things that aren't your business. You leave Abach alone. Let him run his own life!"

3

Michel's first anniversary party scheduled for the night of July first was to Laurel just one in a series of farewells. She had been feted at luncheons, teas, banquets and even night bridge parties. She now kept a singular goal in mind: to maintain sanity and serenity a month and ten days—until France was again on the other side of the Ocean.

Solange greeted Zero ebulliently, "Oh, but you are handsome!"

"Zero!" shouted Michel. Neither host nor hostess spoke a word to Laurel before they ushered Zero away in the direction of the kitchen. So it went when neither Michel nor Solange had a favor or a question to ask her.

Laurel slipped quietly up the stairs, glad to find the baby alone and still awake in the nursery. Half his bedtime bottle was yet to be enjoyed, but he loosed one corner of his mouth from the nipple and smirked winsomely. Then, he began to suck the milk in a great hurry.

Philippe turned through the door and kissed Laurel's hand. He spoke gallantly of her loveliness, and pulled up a stool. The two leaned their folded arms on the crib rail and spoke quietly to each other as they regarded the feeding, sometimes yawning baby. They had stolen a quarter-hour before Michel burst in, jabbering that a nursery was an improper place for tryst. But he moved a chair between his brother and Laurel, and they sat like that, the three of them, bent over the baby's bed until car lights turned into the drive and flashed across the window.

Michel dashed up to the door and flung back, "I'll tell Solange the baby is well attended!"

When he had gone, Philippe stood up. "I must go! They'll have some job for me, Laurel."

She closed the shutters against the night, slipped a cover over the sleeping baby, and then went into the adjoining bathroom to rinse his bottle and leave it on a table. When Laurel reentered the nursery, there stood Guy, angled above the crib.

Outside the circle of sharp light cast by a wall lamp, she edged forward silently, slowly, hoping the baby would not be awakened if her presence startled Guy into sudden greeting. The second her foot crossed the perimeter of light, he swung about with the motion of a stalked animal, the muscles of his jaw flexing in tension. With the same swiftness, he dropped his guard. Laurel's outstretched hand went unnoticed as he crossed the space to crush her in his arms. She felt his breath in the hollow of her neck, and then he kissed her. . . .

"Laurel! Laurel!" Philippe's voice penetrated the paneled wood of the closed door. "It's time to go down. They're asking after you. . . ."

Guy's arms fell to his side. His head turned away. On fire one instant, now bereft and trembling, Laurel eased through the nursery door.

After what seemed to her an endless dinner, there was dancing which lasted until one-thirty. The Parisians were gone by two and the Americans by three o'clock. Zero got to his feet, saying to Solange that he wished to see the baby before saying good-bye. Pleased Solange, shoeless and wan, arose to take him upstairs to the nursery.

Laurel's gaze turned to Philippe as he pawed through one

empty package after another in search of a cigarette. She glanced at Guy, who studied a Rembrandt above the velvet Empire sofa on which he reclined.

Michel edged a chair quite close to Laurel's and spoke in a relaxed voice. "Laurel, we all suspected from the first you were a great deal more French than other Americans. You remember the Saturday you and Zero came to Paris to my mother's apartment, the night the baby was born?" She nodded, too tired to care. But Michel's vivacity penetrated even his fatigue. "The results of my investigation had been returned only that afternoon! Of course, I understood after discussing it with Zero why you'd kept it all a secret. But you shouldn't have been so modest, Laurel. Think of the time we'd have had in Paris!"

Her eyes darted to Guy, who pretended not to be listening, but she caught the faint tilt at the corners of his mouth. "Why, Michel?"

"Why?" he exploded. "Because your Villecroi bloodline is more distinguished than anything in Philippe's and my lines. Laurel, you rank us!"

She could not match his absorption. Her feet hurt. Even her legs were tired. And she longed to have a moment alone with Guy so she could unzip the lining of her white fox muff and restore his emeralds, which had been brought to Noël with no certainty whatever that he would be present.

"Ten years from now, Laurel," Michel continued, "you'll have forgotten Philippe exists because the only thing he's proven to you is that intellectuals survive among the gentility. Someday, Guy will fade in your memory. . . ."

From the corner of her eye, Laurel saw Guy's legs swing to the floor—like slow motion in a film. "But, Laurel!" said Michel, "You'll never forget me as long as you live. Guy has taken you through God knows what." He paused a moment and regarded his friend, then looked back at Laurel. "I don't know what he's shown you. I fear it's largely nothing, but you'll never look at a French word or book or picture or map or product without thinking how I took you through France!"

With the fur muff swinging on her arm as her hands knotted

together, she thought, I can give them to Guy in front of Philippe and no harm done. "Michel, it's late. Will you find Zero?"

"All right! But first, we'll say good-bye without those foreigners, your husband and my wife. American and Belgian!" His laugh was a clear gloat, a secret satisfaction known only to himself. "Philippe! Guy!" he called. "We've got to kiss Laurel. One kiss for France?"

Laurel suffered Michel's last kiss—a strange blend of desire and fraternity from his lips—because there was no way out. Philippe's was natural—a kind, tender brother underlining a poignant farewell.

Guy waited until the drawing room door closed behind Philippe and Michel to wrap his arms about her in a long, close embrace. She drew back quickly and performed her task, slipping the little draw-string pouch into Guy's coat pocket.

She buried her face against the rough texture of his jacket, seeing a blurred eddy of sienna, olive, and beige, and hearing the abrupt sound at the door, but neither Laurel nor Guy moved. His back to Zero, Guy said audibly to her, "Au revoir, Laurel! Au Paradis!"

"Not au revoir," came Zero's voice. "Adieu!"

Laurel stiffened. Guy let her go and turned to face Zero, no more than a couple of feet from him. She studied the profiled faces—one grinning, one bitterly amused. Zero's spread hand swung out and up, somehow imparting contempt, equality, forgiveness, and farewell. The wounded husband, late to learn, suffering of knowledge, deceived in trust, but proving his mettle in magnanimous good-bye.

Suddenly, her heart skipped a beat. Zero's hand was being declined. Guy eyed him unwaveringly now, no apology, no awkward compromise. Guy turned out of the room; his heels echoed briskly across the foyer.

Laurel put a weary hand in the bend of Zero's arm and led him from the salon, beginning what seemed a five-mile trek across the grand reception hall of Noël.

Good-bye to Noël?

Where was Michel? Where was Philippe?

Easy come, easy go . . . Vive the Air Force and those "inalienable," quick friendships that mushroomed wherever the moth of transiency lingered too long! And God damn the whole mess to Hell!

Passing beneath the high wrought-iron chandelier, she glanced up while attempting to steady Zero's slightly stumbling weave. Quick, unwanted tears stung her eyes as they focused on the black, bulb-dotted circle.

"Laur'l, by God, I oughta go punch him!"

She blinked, clung tighter to his arm, and tried to hasten their steps. "Zero," she said, fighting suffocation, "when we get back to Washington this time, let's skip the Chevy Chase bit and try one of those three-stories in Georgetown. . . ."

He halted just beneath the great archway of Noël's front doors: "Georgetown?" With some effort, his gaze focused down upon her. He straightened his shoulders to full height. "I had in mind a country place—maybe below Springfield or McLean. Laur'l, *not* Georgetown."

4

Laurel was grateful that Zero had spoken not at all of the evening at Noël, or of Guy, or even Michel. Whenever she glanced up from her kibitzing position about the gaming tables after another farewell dinner, she found her husband's eyes on her face. Previously in the company of the Hachères, Risseaus, and the rest of the French bridge-playing group, Zero had all but ignored her. His new attitude made her feel both guilty and wary.

She sneaked a look at the brass-faced clock over Vervins' Byzantine sideboard. It said fourteen minutes after eleven. Above the din of bridge and poker players' laughter and talk, her acute hearing picked up the sound of a jet plane almost over the house. Its swish in landing power sounded gentle compared to the thunder behind a take-off.

She walked unobtrusively to the front door and peered out into the night. Sure enough, a fluffy, silencing summer fog lay completely to the ground. The pilot had been making a blind landing. The telephone rang somewhere inside the house. A servant answered while Laurel returned to the crowd. She watched Zero as he was called to the telephone. When he returned, the look on his face caused her to freeze.

To Paul Hachère he said tersely, "Tell everyone to go home. A napalm has been discharged from one of our planes."

Paul frowned in confusion. "But no plane is allowed to fly directly over the city?"

"Yeah." Zero's shoulders sagged. "The pilot must have gotten off course. The ceiling's less than thirty feet over the hill. Hurry, Paul! Tell them!"

"A napalm?"

"Christ, yes! A gasoline bomb."

"Mother of God!" whistled the terrified Frenchman, who turned, his mouth quivering. "Go home, everybody! The top of the hill is on fire!" Laurel watched him turn three times in the middle of the floor before he could think what to do next.

Madame Risseau was already in the hall, grabbing for her mink stole, which clung to a hook. Dumbly, Laurel heard the silk lining rip. Paul whimpered as he tried to help his father get out of the door. Hachère Senior seemed ninety years old and almost idiotic in his sobbing hysteria.

Zero dragged Laurel out of the hall and along the drive. His grip held her even with him as he loped. Then she was staring through the windshield—staring and praying and wondering whether the first spark had landed in the yard at 14 rue Père Marquette. Thank God, a slate roof! Brick walls. Soon the hill came in view, two layers in the distance. A lower belt of black velvet speckled with winking street lights. And an upper tier, a vaporous, flat-bottomed cloud with a pale pink areola at left center. Above the tinted area of the cloud spewed tongues of flame. Laurel glanced sidewise at Zero. He drove with wild im-

361

patience, grinding the car to a halt in the street before the house, and when she hesitated a fraction of a second, he reached across her, opened the door, and pushed her out.

The next hour she spent listening to the firetrucks being mustered in from Marche, Redan, Marle and God knew where else. When the sirens continued to scream by the house past one o'clock, she made her decision. Believing the whole top of the hill afire now, she summoned Olande and Francis, instructing them quietly to take the still-sleeping children to Olande's village. "Yes, they will be frightened, Olande, but it is better now than to wait, for if the fog lifts, that will mean wind, and if the wind comes from the north. . . ."

Her knees trembled as she watched them depart from the front gate, Francis starting his motorcycle with still-sleeping Chris zipped inside the laborer's leather coat and only the small scarf-bound head visible. Brick, seated on the ledge at the back of Olande's bicycle, was wide awake and hugging the maid's waist desperately. Laurel called to Francis, "Whistle the dog! He wants to go with Brick!"

By three A.M. the fog was gone. The wind had shifted to the north. Neither by the breadth of pink glow nor the degree of smoke could Laurel gauge the fire, but the sound of fire engines no longer violated night's calm. A deathly quiet gripped the hill, pierced now and then by the screech of speeding tires or brakes, or the uphill grind of a heavy motor. On the couch Laurel slept intermittently until after six, when she heard the sound of the station wagon in front of the house.

She opened the glass pane of the front door and saw beyond the black grills of the gate not Zero but Abach, bareheaded and wearing wrinkled white pants and surgical blouse. Laurel tried to speak: Where's Zero? But she could only watch the doctor pause behind her gate, take off his glasses and rub his eyes with the back of his hand, and she knew he had come to tell her . . . come straight from. . . .

Laurel watched him put his glasses back on. Briskly, he swung open the gate. She opened the door as he ascended the three steps. "He's not burned, Laurel. He's all right." She backed inside the hall. "He got an old couple and their cat out without much trouble, but then somebody told him Cambot had gone back to the sixth floor to get his glasses."

"Cambot's all right?" she interrupted.

Abach nodded, and pressed on with his story. Nobody could contain Zero when he heard a human being was still on the sixth floor. He went up, and had scarcely had time to reach Cambot before the fire broke out on the ground floor. The Marche firetruck had a ladder tall enough to reach the third floor, and Zero got Cambot into the window and saw him begin to descend the ladder, but he couldn't take a chance to wait his turn. At the first-floor landing he jumped from the window. "I saw him, Laurel, poised in the window an instant before the other side of the building gave way. He jumped just like Superman—arms winging—knees flexed in mid-air," said the doctor, "and the weird part, just about the time he hit the cobblestones, the whole interior of the building collapsed as if it had been wired with dynamite."

Laurel said, "Thank God, you're all right!"

Abach frowned. "He's got a couple of sore feet, I can tell you, and a scalp laceration—four sutures but no concussion. Glass. I'm keeping him two or three days, though, for more X rays and a little sedation. His nerves are pretty shot, Laurel."

"How many French are. . . ."

"None, by the grace of God! The bomb hit the museum, a block from the Cathedral, and it sprayed fragmentary fire for quite a radius. The museum's gone, and three small houses, and that wreck of a tenement where Cambot lived. It caught fire from coiling electric lines, high voltage, which broke from a pole —apparently in the first blast."

"Who's the pilot?"

"A captain who reported in four days ago. Says his gyro must be about ten degrees off. He didn't know he was over the hill until he saw something he thought was a street light through the fog. He pulled up sharp and says his elbow must have caught the toggle. Anyway, it's a complete fluke, or else, he's making up the story. Zero knew him at Selfridge five years ago. And he told me while I was sewing him up he figures the investigation will prove the pilot was somewhere besides the ready room when the scramble was called. Maybe having a beer in the Club or a short snort at the BOQ. Anyway, Zero had the plane impounded in the hangar and he put it under armed guard so nobody can jam the gyro before he sees it or a board gets there. If Captain Herbert, the pilot, turns out to have had fuzzy vision from drinking—you know, those radium dials—well, I'm afraid Zero will have *his* gyro and a couple of other things before it's done. Of course, Laurel, Zero doesn't discount entirely the possibility of sabotage. . . ."

"Oh, God!" she sighed in exhaustion. "He could be lying in traction with an eye punched out and his pelvis shot away and what would he be thinking about? Whether he's gonna turn up a flying hot rodder and nail him to a board, or chase a Communist butterfly with a torn net!"

Abach took her hand and deposited it in his angled elbow, leading her to the kitchen. "The boys didn't wake up in the fire?"

At the sink, she began to make the coffee. "No, that is, I got them up. I sent Francis and Olande to take them to the Faures'."

"Well, good!" Abach sat down at the kitchen table and smoothed his thinning hair.

Laurel plugged in the coffee pot and sat down across from him. "I told Olande I'd come after them this morning."

"Never mind! Your circles aren't violet—they're purple! You get a morning's sleep and then go get them."

Suddenly, she covered her face with her hands and began to sob wretchedly, uncontrollably. Abach sat very still, watching. When she could speak, she turned to the window and kept her swollen, undried eyes on the marshaling yards where plumes of smoke and steam denoted arrival or departure of another day's train.

"Oh, Abach! I could . . . I don't know how I'll live out the rest of my life with him. Or why I can't care enough even to hate him. I don't want him hurt. I don't want him punished. He can't help the way he is. But God! You'd think as brave and fearless and all-conquering as he is, there'd be a sensitive side somewhere—a sense of propriety or a sense of rightness—he didn't have to tell me a thing like that. I don't care what you had to do to buy into your clinic—because I know humanity will be paid back—you'll deliver the poor people's babies on installment plans —and sometimes, for nothing—and you'll pay for plates when somebody can't afford X rays—but what was he trying to do by telling me?"

Abach stared at her. "Laurel! What are you saying?"

"You don't have to pretend any longer to me. Abach, I know about you and Belle Tricot and the American housing, and it's all right. If it had to be somebody, I'm glad—glad. . . ." But new sobbing overtook her and she failed to see the expression on Abach's face, or hear him mutter through clenched teeth, "The twenty-two carat bastard!"

He got up from his chair, not easily as was his nature but with a rigidity which pervaded his entire body. He went to the coffee pot and poured two mugs of coffee. Sitting back down, he pushed a cup across to Laurel, saying in a controlled voice, "You can't stay with him. Laurel, it's done."

Her hands dropped from her face in astonishment. Her mouth gaped. "I can and I must. For the sake of Brick and Chris."

"Laurel, it's worse than a parody. It's heresy. It's phrenetic. You'll wind up on alcohol or dope or. . . ."

"No, Abach. There's only one thing that could—that might. . . ."

"Guy?" Laurel nodded.

Abach bit into his lower lip, stirring his coffee and watching it pensively. "Laurel, you know Zero's been keeping that Moreau woman in a place at Cannes for over a year?"

"No one has told me. But yes, somehow I know it. But he's covered himself someway. I'd never be able to prove it in an American court without some tangible, irrevocable, unassailable— Abach! If Zero isn't hurt, why are you wearing those clothes?"

His laugh was no more than a snort, but the tension was broken. "The Cowan woman came in at four this morning—third stage. But we had a little respiratory trouble with the baby." Hand shielding his mouth, he gave release to a yawn.

"You'd better finish that coffee and go get some sleep. I'll get my coat . . ." She arose, as did Abach. ". . . and drive you back."

"No, Laurel! I'm going back to the Base in your wagon. I'll send it home by somebody later this afternoon."

"But why?"

"Because that way, I know you'll get some sleep if you can't leave the house."

"But who's this somebody you'll have bring it?"

"I would myself, but I forgot to tell you—I'm taking the four o'clock plane to the rest camp at Cannes."

"You?"

"Yes."

Yawning heavily, and admonishing Laurel to go to bed, he took leave. She returned to the kitchen long enough to detach the plug of the coffee pot, after which she went upstairs to take a very hot bath. Then, wrapped in her leopard robe, she unbound her chignon and fell face forward across the taffeta coverlet of her bed.

5

Laurel awoke restive one morning. But a fat lot I ought to complain! she scolded herself over her bedside coffee. Going home on the *United States*. Only eleven more days. . . .

Then, for the third time since Michel's departure for England, she dressed in riding clothes to go and exercise his horses. Downstairs, she said to Brick, "Why don't you come with me? There are two horses at Noël, you know?"

"Thank you, Laurel, but Olande promised to take Chris and me to the farce store on top of the hill and buy us presents—soon as Chris wakes up and eats. Laurel, may I wake him?" At his mother's nod, he bounded up the stairs.

She had started the car and was ready to drive away when Fontaine extended his delivery through the open window and in front of her face. Leaning back slightly, Laurel took the rolled newspapers, a flat-wrapped magazine about the size of *Reader's Digest* which she knew to be a monthly French cooking journal, plus two "occupant" envelopes and an official-looking letter addressed to Z. R. Compton, L.C., from Gaz de France at Cannes. Probably something to do with the rest camp, thought Laurel, as she laid the assortment in the seat beside her, but Fontaine hung on. Time and again as he spoke almost literally of nothing, his flashing eyes darted to the unopened mail, but they darted as well to the curve of Laurel's knee taut beneath the black riding breeches.

Unable to bear more, she apologized for her hurry, and in the heat of an unprecedented summer day—it felt more like Louisiana than France—she drove directly to Noël.

Leaving the car before Michel's garage, she reached back and took the flat-wrapped little magazine and, as an afterthought, the Gaz de France envelope. It was four or four-and-a-half miles to the secluded spring pool on the opposite side of Noël's forest. When they reached there, the fat gelding would need a rest. She might as well have something to read.

In another quarter-hour, she had left the stable, the greenhouse, the château, the vegetable-flower garden divided by a filament of lily pool, the grape arbors, and a square plot of Douglas fir saplings twelve to eighteen inches high imported from America a season earlier—Laurel's wedding gift to Solange and Michel.

The sorrel gelding lazed along, fighting his head and snorting. Repeatedly, Laurel swiped sweat from her upper lip and from the valley between mouth and chin. God! The heat was miserable. Who would have thought France. . . .

Laurel's knees bent lightly to the saddle as she leaned forward and gave the shining beast his head—full rein. His swiftness parted the sea of knee-high grass and left a rippling in his wake. The pins fell from her chignon and her hair leapt horizontally behind her head as the horse cleared a two-strand fence with a celerity fit for the wind. They were out of the merciless sun now, edging into the forest.

Laurel turned the horse with the slant of ten o'clock shadows and soon intercepted a two-laned path, one of many plaiding Noël's acreage at mile-and-a-quarter intervals. The horse had lost his frisky ambition now. Sweat streaks marred his velvet. His ears stood in the effortless position—straight up—and so she tied the four reins in one knot and dropped it above his mane. Then she reached back and withdrew the envelope, which was now wet on one side.

Inside, she found three long, narrow strips of paper. Electric bills. And in her first fleet perusal, she assumed once more some formless association with the American recreation camp, for certainly it required electricity, and electricity demanded payment. Suddenly, however, she realized Gaz de France wouldn't wait six months for payment. She studied the amounts—ten mille more or less for January-February, eight mille for March-April, and seven mille for May-June. Almost reluctantly, Laurel looked at the name in the upper lefthand corner—not the address, for it no longer mattered when one read the name: "Moreau, Félicité (Compton)." Then it said: "Certified Copy."

Laurel, being Laurel, had a singular reaction. She thought, "God damn! And my bill for May and June was twenty-six mille!" Then she examined possibilities. Had Félicité demanded typed copies and mailed them in hopes of exposing the fact which would almost certainly cause a final break between the Comptons? No, Félicité would have had no need to secure certified copies. She could have sent the originals for such a purpose. Then, it could have been Abach or Guy! Guy, decided Laurel, had waited until the last moment to step in!

She tied the horse in a little clearing where he could graze. Then, hunting her way through the heavy growth of currant bushes, their pale green berries rich with August promise, Laurel reached the pool. She peeled off her damp silk shirt and the rest of her clothes. She listened to the forest harmonies—pheasants, doves, partridge, frogs, crickets, and locusts—and then arched her body and followed her hands into the water.

Nine or ten feet below surface, her fingers closed on an egg-shaped stone slick with dark accumulation. When she climbed out on the opposite bank, dripping and tossing her head, she hurled the rock at a sign nailed to the laurel tree. Certainly Michel had stolen it from in front of the Officers' Club. It read: NO PARKING BY ORDER OF WING COMMANDER.

Lolling in the first coolness she had felt all day, she slapped at the wet ribbons which trickled down her legs, and when she was nearly dry, she walked a few steps to a leafy, mossy patch polka-dotted with sunlight and concealed from view by three heavily laden currant bushes.

Laurel lay down on her back, hair spread above her to dry. Her mind astoundingly blank and untroubled, she stared up at oak, sycamore, and laurel branches intermingled high above.

She was asleep when Guy found her.

6

The Cathedral chimes were striking four when Laurel cut the motor of the station wagon before her house. As she got out, she saw protruding from the front bumper of a blue staff car the official flag of the Air Base Commander.

From the open window of her salon, Parker called, "Hey, Laurel! Get in here!"

Yes, she lied, she knew Zero was being ordered back from Cannes that afternoon and would arrive near six-thirty. Yes, she knew what the Legion of Merit was. Yes, she could tell Zero he must attend an annual ball for wounded veterans of the Department of Gregny. Yes, Zero had full-dress uniform with epaulets. Yes. Yes. No, she wouldn't let the cat out of the bag. Yes, she understood fully.

"Christ, Laurel! You look a fright!"

"I took a fall, airing one of Michel's horses."

"My God! Are you all right?"

"Yes. Oh, yes. A hurdle. A bit high for a horse not accustomed to jumping."

"You're *sure* you're not hurt somewhere? You look a mess with that hair falling everywhere!"

Pale, her cheeks visibly drawn and with violet circles etched under her eyes, Laurel mustered a grin for the Colonel. She felt remorse that she was disappointing him by her vapid reaction to his announcements.

There was to be a ball in Zero's honor that night where the Governor of Gregny planned to surprise Zero with the Legion of Merit, France's distinguished award to foreign officers. And where Mayor Cravet expected to present a civilian medal for heroism in the fire, and a scroll signed by the grateful citizens of Beaumonde—Zero's effort on behalf of Franco-American relations, and a special citation from the head of Beaumonde's French hospital. . . . It's fabulous, thought Laurel dully. Two years ago I'd have shrieked with joy. Well, someday it will mean a great deal to Brick and Chris.

Zeno Richfield Compton, Lieutenant Colonel, United States Air Force, was every inch the dashing, colorful officer that night—all seventy-seven inches of him. The gilt lariat and silver insignia and wings flashed against the dark blue and black, and there were the variegated slashes of ribbon from which miniature casts of his medals dangled in compact rows.

There was, however, one surprise Parker had guarded even from Laurel. When the French presentations were done, the orchestra at the far end of the ballroom on the second floor of Beaumonde's Hotel de Ville blared unexpected fanfare. Parker stepped forward and faced Zero. Laurel glimpsed the small gold box in his hand and knew instantly what was about to take place: Zero's coveted promotion to full colonel.

Laurel's hands were steady as she received from Parker the silver eagles to be pinned on Zero's shoulders. Intent on her task, she avoided Zero's eyes, even after both eagles were in place. In keeping with custom, his lips passed hers in the brief congratulatory kiss. A delighted "Ah!" waved through the French.

Somewhere, a bottle of champagne spewed open. Zero's hand closed on her elbow and he guided her to the end of the room. Already, Laurel foresaw the next three-quarters of an hour to be spent in seesawing toasts back and forth.

Merci beaucoups, Madame America—*my* privilege!
Mais non, Monsieur France—I *enjoyed* it!
Merci, France!

Behind the Governor and his spinster sister, Laurel dropped her gloved hand on Zero's forearm and waited for the first step in what she thought of now as the puppet parade. What time would the damned thing end? Midnight? One? Two? And how many Americans would Zero bring home for omelet and serious bourbon? Until three or four or five or six or even seven?

"Laurel," said Zero, "it's the biggest night of my life. I feel humble—almost unworthy."

As if she were seeing him, really seeing him, for the first time all night, she let the impact of these words from Zero's lips penetrate her shell. Humble? Unworthy? Quickly, she said, "I'm glad."

He dropped his arms to his sides and went on, "God! If it were all to do over again, do you know the only thing I'd change?"

"Zero, what is it?"

"Laurel, I wouldn't have had this a surprise party. We needed a little time."

She laughed, half-tremulously, "Why, Zero! I don't see what could have been added if tonight had been planned six months ahead!"

"Oh, it isn't that!" He bit his lip. "But I'd like to have had time to get Michel here. Somehow, *he* deserves this, too!" Laurel took time to search his face, but Zero went on, "After all, he's the one who deserves recognition. How far would a couple of Americans have gone in this foreign country if he hadn't stuck with us? Look around," he said, "and show me one other couple who's seen France like us?"

She recoiled, catching her heel in the hem of her gown, but Abach's hands came beneath her elbows so that the fall, precipitously near, was suddenly no more than a ripple. The doctor said, "I'm taking Laurel outside for a bit of air. I don't like her color."

Abach tucked her hand in his arm and led her to the sprawling second-floor terrace which backed four tremendous, arched double doors leading from the ballroom. Neither of them spoke as Laurel walked to the grilled railing and peered down into the Square. High above the Square, the Cathedral carillon struck once. Ten-thirty.

"Laurel?"

Abach had lighted a cigarette. "You've seen Guy?" She nodded without glancing over her shoulder. "Today?" Another nod. "My God!"

"Oh, Abach!" But as badly as she needed to tell him of the long interlude in the forest with Guy, Laurel could not speak of it yet—perhaps never.

"Laurel, you can strike Chamberlain from my name. I'm through negotiating. But I apologize deeply, contritely. I didn't know what day Guy would come, or about this thing tonight for Zero, or—or anything, I guess." He sighed heavily.

"Don't apologize for anything. Zero would have done it anyway."

"Done what?"

"Said the night wasn't complete without Svengali."

"Oh, Laurel! That's not what I mean! I mean the gas bills and Félicité—"

Laurel turned to him, not disturbed but merely questioning. "Then you were the one?" He nodded his head. Laurel looked back into the street. "You were pretty determined to hand me over to Guy, weren't you? Why?"

At first he only shrugged, but then replied, "A piece of irrefutable evidence, you said. That was the ticket to Utopia."

"I had to have something to say—to postpone my moment of truth until I got out of France."

"You know what the truth is?"

Laurel breathed deeply. "I haven't known very long, just since four or five o'clock this afternoon. But I must have realized always, deep down, Guy could never marry any divorced woman. I just couldn't bear having him confirm it."

"What happened, Laurel?"

"Well, I said I'd go to Mexico and get one of those quick divorces. And Guy said, 'You'll be back before the leaves fall.' He began to talk about where he intended to put Brick in school. I asked where we were going to live. He said he knew the exact spot where he was going to build my house—between Versailles and La Mouche—a hill front. I laughed and asked him, Was he going to chisel it from granite or nail the boards with his own hammer? Oh, Abach! You should have seen his eyes, like a child's on Christmas morning. Nobody has ever seen Guy until they've seen him happy."

Laurel paused, drawing her breath deeply as if she expected Abach to help out, but he only waited. She laced her fingers together and studied them. "Then I said when I get back to France, let's not go flaunting. . . ."

Laurel found she couldn't go on in detail. She said quietly to Abach, "I realized in discussing the honeymoon that he had no intention of marrying me. He began to enumerate all the things he offered me unreservedly, love, protection, but not marriage. It was strange then, Abach, I couldn't cry. I felt some weird need to laugh so loudly it would scare the birds in the forest. I looked him straight in the eye and said with a smile, 'Well, I guess that about wraps it up.' Then I ran away without looking back."

"Well, bully for a proper and narrational ending!" murmured Abach. "Laurel, for God's sake, don't you ever just let yourself *feel* anything instead of seeing it all detached and making damned sure you live your characterization adequately?"

"Oh, Sam! For God's sake! Don't stick pins through me. Say I've been a simpering, ostrich-headed, middle-aged dreamer. Say. . . ."

"Laurel, while there's still time—let's quit trying to outsmart other people. I swear to you, what you and Guy had doesn't last. History defies it." He was silent a moment. "Laurel, let me take care of you the rest of our lives? There are many things we have to share—together."

"Sam, you've had too much champagne."

"Sam? God damn! Nobody has ever punished me with that first name except you and Zero!" Affectionately, she regarded him and said nothing. "'Sam, the champagne!'" groaned Abach to the stars. "Here I sell my old homestead, mortgage my soul, and hock my partners' scalpels to get a foothold which will sustain my belated bride! And what saith she? 'Sam, the champagne!'"

"Sam, what do you mean about selling your old homestead? You didn't sell The Willows?"

"I by-God did, my naïve little friend! Laurel, you didn't really believe. . . ."

"Then who?"

"I don't want to talk about other people. I want to talk about us. Time is running out. Our lives are half used up already. Maybe more. Zero's had his chance. Eleven years in orbit and your worlds never once touched. He'll get his star soon enough —with or without you. Laurel, listen to me! I love you—I love you with a ferocity that would send you scurrying back into that ballroom if you divined an atom of it. I can't remember a world in which I didn't love you. Sure, Zero loved you. You made him feel superior. Guy loved you because you made him feel complete. I love you because trees need rain and sun or they can't keep on giving shade."

"Oh, Abach! I—I don't think I could even . . . oh, Abach! What kind of a marriage would it be for you?"

"Laurel, listen! You'll accompany Zero back as planned. Tell him nothing until you reach the States. Then explain that you've waited until you're where sensation won't damage his career. In New Orleans, you'll open the Deschamps shotgun house and set up residence. Put Brick in school and file suit for divorce. When the loose ends are all tied in hard knots, I'll come and get you and we'll either go back and reopen Paradis or we'll build one of those push-button matchboxes—I don't care, whatever you want. . . ."

The strains of "La Vie en Rose" wafted out to the terrace, reminding both of them that they had to go in. Abach released her from a companionable embrace and said in rapid tones, "Now, Laurel, when the holocaust comes, don't haggle with him in court about settlement. Agree to whatever he wants in the way of property division, but make the agreement completely subject to his remarriage. He won't stay single six months. Old Lacey's daughter won't let him. You may as well have it straight—she's followed him ten years now from pillar to post. She left Maxwell a month before his school finished, intending to transfer to Paris but the nearest she could get was Weisbaden. . . ."

"Abach, you're wrong! I *know* her! Why, when Brick was a baby, she used to keep him lots of nights when we had to go out!"

"Yeah, I've heard. Well, Laurel, you can believe it or not—but she's been settled back in Georgetown about a month."

Laurel shook her head in gloomy wonderment. It was true that Zero was headed for Washington as Aide-de-Camp to three-star General Lacey. . . .

Swiftly, Abach secured her hand in the bend of his arm and turned toward the lights and music, but his gait was leisurely as they passed into the ballroom.